Tacy stared, dumbfoun mind still, a blank. Up in the oak tree a blackbird called loudly, and it seemed from another world. 'No,' she said. 'Not Martha. Martha wouldn't . . .' Martha couldn't have done the thing that she herself had turned away from, yet had been so near to doing . . .

Martha! Martha the plain, the girl who never went with boys. And Tom, Tom who could have his pick, who might have had her . . .

'He wanted you to know,' Nancy said, unhappily. 'I knew you'd be upset.'

Tacy tossed her head. 'I don't know why you should think that,' she retorted. 'I'm marrying, too.'

'You are?' There was disbelief in Nancy's voice.

'Of course, haven't you guessed? I'm marrying Francis. Francis!' she called, running to the door of the counting-house, seeing James and her father within, unheeding now, uncaring in the desperate attempt to hide her pain. 'Francis, come out. I've just told them our news, that we're getting married.'

During the Napoleonic wars a young wheelwright from the north of Scotland and a French weaver from the south converged on the centre of England, the silk weaving area of Warwickshire, married local girls, and became Joyce Bell's ancestors. Joyce Bell was born in Nuneaton, and as a child had two ambitions: to travel and to be a writer. After her marriage she went to live in South America for several years. On her return to England she started writing and has now had over 200 short stories and nine novels published. This is her third long saga set in her native Warwickshire, where she still lives. She has three children and one grandchild.

By the same author
The Girl From the Back Streets

SILK TOWN

—

Joyce Bell

ORION

An Orion paperback
First published in Great Britain by Orion in 1996
This paperback edition published in 1996 by Orion Books Ltd,
Orion House, 5 Upper St Martin's Lane,
London WC2H 9EA

Copyright © 1996 by Joyce Bell

A CIP catalogue record for this book
is available from the British Library.

ISBN: 0 75280 405 7

Typeset at The Spartan Press Ltd,
Lymington, Hants
Printed and bound in Great Britain by
Clays Ltd, St Ives plc

Though the main characters in this novel are entirely imaginary, most of the events took place as described, and are taken from a local diary in Nuneaton Library. The report mentioned is the 'Report from the Assistant Hand-Loom Weavers Commissioners', and was published in 1840.

PART ONE

The manipulation and management of a complicated silk handloom required a degree of skill, delicacy of handling, patience and ingenuity on the part of the weaver, the result was that the old handloom weavers, especially those engaged in the higher branches of this interesting employment were, for the most part, men of character and high ideals. They loved nature, poetry, philosophy and science, a fact proved not only by the many literary societies and scientific clubs that flourished, but by the honourable rolls of weavers who have distinguished themselves in various departments of art, science and invention.

THE SILK INDUSTRY OF THE UK
by F. Warner (Dranes, 1921)

Chapter one

The scarlet and black mail-coach raced north-westwards along the Watling Street, four horses at the gallop. It thundered past rural post-offices, the guard grabbing the mail-bag as it passed, rumbled into towns with blasts of the horn, and jolted between toll gates held at the ready. The mail-coach had to get through, its passengers were of secondary importance.

The passengers tried to believe that wasn't so. They planted their feet firmly in the dirty straw, they held onto the side straps as they were jerked and shaken. The man sitting next to the young girl was obviously a seasoned traveller. His hands rested on the silver-topped walking cane held between his knees, his tall hat sat straight on his greying hair. The girl herself, blue eyes sparkling, seemed to be finding the whole journey exciting.

'Is this your first visit to London?' The lady opposite wearing a blue bonnet and holding a wicker basket on her lap, had been gossiping ever since they boarded the coach in the yard of the Swan with Two Necks in Lad's Lane, when her husband had immediately fallen asleep.

'Indeed no,' the girl replied. 'I have always travelled with my father on business.'

'Really? And may I make so bold as to ask what business that would be?' asked Blue Bonnet.

'My father is Samuel Barratt of Chilverton, a master weaver,' replied the girl. 'And I'm Tacy.'

'Indeed?' Blue Bonnet gave a little sniff. Master weaver, eh? One of these Great Masters. He'd have a penny or two to spare, no doubt. 'What do you weave, cloth?' she finished.

'Silk,' the girl replied proudly. 'Silk ribbons.'

'Ah.' Blue Bonnet unbent a little. 'I have the most beautiful ribbons on my best gown. Three inches wide, with a pretty pattern of leaves in gold.' For ribbons were essential for ladies in the year of Our Lord, 1813. They trimmed their bonnets, tied up their hair, their dresses, their slippers. They were used for sashes, frills and favours. Small children were enveloped in ribbon, as were the cushions they sat upon, the curtains at the windows. Ribbons were everywhere, plain, striped, checked, watered, shot, shaded and figured. 'And, of course, the purl-edged ones,' Blue Bonnet ended. 'All the rage now, purl-edged ribbons.'

'We do know,' Tacy said mischievously, and Blue Bonnet sniffed again. Saucy madam. Looked as if she'd be a flighty piece, given her head. But no doubt her father held her in check; could be stern, she'd wager, even if he did have a twinkle in his eye. 'Are you affianced?' she asked.

Tacy Barratt gave a quick look at her father from beneath her lashes. 'No,' she said, and Blue Bonnet raised her eyebrows. Didn't sound too sure. Bit of a secret there, she guessed. Yet the girl was, what? Sixteen, seventeen, hair not up yet, escaping from her bonnet in a merry ripple of red-gold curls. A vivacious face with dimpled cheeks . . . perhaps a trifle petulant round the mouth, used to getting her own way . . .

Samuel Barratt gave Blue Bonnet a steady look that clearly told her what he thought of chattering women, and for a little while she was silent.

Tacy stared at the blossoming countryside around them, lush with wild flowers: buttercups and cow-parsley, daisies and bluebells. The whole world had

4

sprung into bloom, could it only be May? Surely summer itself was here. She thought of Tom. Tom, whose black eyes could dance with merriment one minute and flash with rage the next. No, she was not affianced yet, but soon she would be. Tom loved her, he'd said so, and she loved him with every breath in her body. Her father would have no objections . . . would he? . . . for even though he was only an ordinary weaver, weavers were earning good money now . . . Of course, they said Tom was wild, like all the Jacques, but they were excellent workers, and if they liked to spend their money in the Weavers' Arms and at the races, well, why not?

It would soon be the May Fair, and this was the loveliest time ever, Maytime. For a week before the fair fiddlers went from house to house playing music, some-times till three in the morning, then at the doors of houses in the afternoons, collecting money in the even-ings. Papa would let her go with her friends, he always let her run around with the weavers. Then she could slip away with Tom, as she had a week ago, and he'd kiss her again, and maybe . . . She trembled at her thoughts.

Of course, it would depend on Grandmamma. Grand-mamma, who had brought up the motherless Tacy, had said sternly last year that the fair was no place for a young lady.

'But I've always been,' she'd pouted.

'In the afternoons, yes. But you were a child then. You are growing up, Tacy.'

Yes, she was growing up. She knew that when Tom touched her, when he'd lifted her skirt. . . . Even now she blushed as she remembered the feelings he'd awakened; trembling on the brink of womanhood, the world seemed new to her, she delighted in every-thing.

She loved the trip to London, the warehouse at the docks, the tea clippers, the tall ships bringing spices from the East – and, of course, silk from China and Bombay. There were so many wonderful things in the world she feared she'd never have time to see them all.

They jolted into the Midlands, as dusk brought deep shadows to the road edges. 'We'll soon be home,' Tacy said.

Blue Bonnet sniffed again. 'I wish I was. I can never get away from London fast enough. Why, for all we know Boney might have landed.'

Tacy's mouth twitched. 'We didn't see any sign of him. Anyway, Papa says that won't happen now.'

The woman looked unconvinced as she studied Tacy's blue pelisse and the peep of the yellow muslin dress beneath. Fashionable colours. At least she was decently clad. Some of these women in London ran about near naked in their semi-transparent frocks and no corsets beneath, though they did say the so called Classical styles were on the way out. Good thing too, showing ladies' bodies like they did. It was indecent.

Now the road was the ancient border between counties. They turned left into Warwickshire and the passengers perked up. There was a blast of the horn, the horses were pulled back to a slower speed, then the iron-shod wheels thundered into the yard of the Red Lion. And as it did so Tacy saw the young man wavering on the edge of the carriageway, saw him slip sideways as the coach veered to the left, saw him miss the great hooves by a hair's breadth, to fall against the side of the coach and be thrown back to the road.

'Whoa!' shouted the driver, and the steaming horses were still, lights shone out from the inn in the gathering gloom. And now all was hurry and bustle, the passengers were alighting, demanding their luggage, but Tacy was out first. 'Did you see that man fall?' she called to the guard.

But the guard could not leave the coach. 'He were drunk,' shouted the driver. 'He's all right.' There was not a moment to be lost, much less wasted on drunks. They had to change the horses.

'Papa,' Tacy called, but she did not wait, she was running across the road to where the young man lay in the shadows of the trees. She reached him, touched his arm. 'Are you hurt?' she asked.

He stirred. 'No. No, I'm not hurt.'

From his accent he wasn't a local man, and as he sat up Samuel Barratt joined them.

'Well now,' he said. 'The driver thought you were drunk.'

'I'm not drunk. But I did have a glass of ale on an empty stomach, and I suppose it went to my head. I came out to see where the coach was headed.'

'Way up north now, to Liverpool, that's the mail-coach. Where are you bound?'

'Coventry or thereabouts.'

'Well, you'll not get a coach for Coventry tonight, and not from here. Are you staying at the inn?'

'It's full.'

'Then if you'd like to come home with us I can gladly give you a bed for the night, and set you on your way tomorrow.'

'That's very kind of you.'

'We live here, in Chilverton, just a few miles from Coventry. My coachman has brought the chaise, so shall we get aboard?'

As the young man staggered to his feet and was helped by Samuel into the chaise, Tacy studied him by the lights shining from the inn. Tall, with thin white face, grey eyes that were somehow troubled. His high boots were

7

shabby, though his jacket was new, and his hair was very short even by today's standard. Then the lights were gone, and she could see only the blur of his face. She wasn't unduly curious, her mind registered it, no more. Another of Papa's lame ducks. As the chaise left the unpaved lane and entered the cobbled streets of the town, passing timber-framed houses with thatched roofs, Tacy looked round eagerly. Through the Market Square, where there were a number of people about, mostly men, with here and there one or two women standing talking, and inside the Weaver's Arms there was light and merriment. And then they were into the High Street to halt before the end house in a row of imposing dwellings, each standing in its own grounds.

'The Red House,' announced Tacy. 'We're home.'

The Red House was, like its owner, solid and substantial. It had been built by Samuel's father, one of the first of the Great Masters, and the only one in Chilverton. The Barratts, although wealthy now, still kept to their Non-conformist tradition, which meant they seldom mixed with the social lions of the town, the lawyer, banker and physician. Dissenters were regarded as being not quite gentlemen, and most men, once they'd made their money, changed their allegiance and bought a pew in church. Samuel refused to do this. He, like his father, imported the raw silk, had it thrown and dyed in Coventry or Macclesfield, then distributed it through the undertakers, or middlemen, to the weavers. The Barratts were very highly regarded in Chilverton, but Samuel never forbade Tacy to mix with the weavers.

Tacy was the apple of his eye. Married late in life, his wife had given birth to several children who died in infancy. Then his only son, James, was born and, two years later, Tacy. She was the image of her mother and, in Samuel's eyes, could do no wrong. To him she was still a child, a beloved gift, fruit of his love, the legacy left by his dear Elenor who had died giving birth to her. She was brought up by Samuel's mother, who balanced his over-fondness with her own unbending strictures. Grandmamma had her rooms in the Red House and nowadays often kept to them, emerging only for meals. Nevertheless, she was still a force to be reckoned with.

If the young man was a little awed by the Red House he didn't show it as he entered the wide hall with its fine staircase. Sarah Jane, the middle-aged housekeeper, came to greet them.

'Welcome back, Mr Barratt, Tacy,' she said. 'Supper is ready and waiting.'

'Good,' Samuel replied heartily. 'This young man will be staying with us tonight. Perhaps you will show him to a suitable room. James not in?'

'You can wash your hands in the kitchen, titivate afterwards.' Sarah Jane was obviously regarded as one of the family and the modern fad for cleanliness hadn't quite reached her. 'James said he'll be back later. And Mrs Barratt has had her meal.'

They gathered in the dining-room, its white-panelled walls contrasting with the oak sideboard, table and chairs, and Samuel said, 'We will eat first and talk afterwards. Good food is to be savoured, not gobbled down as a pastime to talking. Sarah Jane has spent a long time in the preparation of it.'

'But allow me at least to introduce myself,' the young man began. 'I am Francis Barratt.'

Tacy gave a little squeal. 'Why, so are we Barratts. Are we related?'

'Well, it isn't really my name,' Francis began, but Samuel waved his hand.

'Enough, Sarah Jane brings in the soup, and it smells

good.' He bowed his head and said grace, as she placed the steaming bowls on the table, and a spicy aroma of chicken stock mixed with thyme and rosemary filled the air.

They were all hungry, and the soup was eaten almost in silence, as was the saddle of mutton and cold chicken which followed. Samuel said, 'We drink no ale in this house, Sarah Jane makes a fine cordial which quenches the thirst.'

'That will suit me well,' Francis nodded.

'I have seen too much drunkenness,' Samuel went on. 'Seen the harm it can do.'

'So have I,' Francis agreed.

Tacy raised her eyebrows at this, but no more was said, as Sarah Jane brought in a big cheese and cold pie. And when they'd eaten their fill Samuel said grace again and they went to their rooms before moving into the parlour with its autumn colourings on the walls, its curtains of buff chintz, and its elegant chairs. A tall piano with green silk pleats on its ornamental front stood in one corner; there was a tiny window seat looking into the walled garden, and upright flower stands of basketwork on either side. Samuel seated himself and bade Francis to sit too.

Tacy had changed into a perfectly plain white dress, with a high waist and full skirt, but made of silk, and edged with blue patterned ribbons. Francis gave her an admiring look as she sat down, which she took as her right. She was used to admiration. Francis had changed his boots for buckled shoes, but he wore the same jacket, and Tacy recalled he had brought with him just one small bag. Now her curiosity was roused, but she had to wait for her father to begin.

'Well now.' Samuel sat back contentedly, a man who, however far he travels, always likes to be home. 'You were telling us your name.'

'Yes,' Francis hesitated. 'My real name is Baroux.'

'French,' stated Samuel.

'My father was French, we thought it better – '

'Yes, indeed, the French are not exactly popular at the moment,' Samuel said, drily.

'But I understood that the people round here are of French descent,' Francis said.

'Huguenots fleeing from religious persecution, yes. But all that happened a hundred years ago, and Napoleon has turned up since then. We are fighting French Papists. And there has always been a great deal of rivalry between the silk weavers of both nations.' He paused. 'You said you were going to Coventry. You have friends there perhaps?'

Again Francis hesitated. 'No friends. I want to look for work.'

'You do not have work in – ?'

'Plymouth. I come from Plymouth. Yes, indeed, I did have work. My father died when I was five. My mother was the daughter of a clergyman, she had been a governess, and she obtained a teaching post, which meant she was able to take me with her, and indeed to educate me. I was taught accounts and figures and worked for a time in a counting-house – ' he broke off, and they waited.

'Then,' he resumed bitterly, 'I was press-ganged. I was forced to the sea, taken on a frigate at Plymouth, and never saw land again for six long years.'

'You never went ashore?' That was Tacy.

'We were never allowed ashore, they thought we might escape – as we would have. They used to bring boatloads of women aboard when we were in port – ' he broke off. 'Begging your pardon, Miss Barratt.'

'It's a heinous custom, the press-gang,' Samuel said, heavily. 'Men treated like slaves. Wilberforce presses for freedom of slaves, yet we have this – '

'We were treated worse than slaves,' Francis said, and his mouth was a thin line of bitterness. 'Flogged, beaten . . . When I was discharged I determined to put as much distance between me and the sea as I could – '

'So you didn't like the sea?' The door had opened and a tall young man entered, wearing the same fashionable pantaloons and a plain jacket showing a fancy waistcoat beneath. He was not unlike Tacy though his hair was darker, his face more forceful. 'So you didn't like the sea, whoever you are,' he repeated.

'James.' Samuel was frowning. 'This is no way to greet a guest. You must forgive my son's high spirits,' he said to Francis. 'Pray continue.'

'There's no more to be said.' Francis seemed a little sullen. 'I am here now, I look for work.'

'Were you at Trafalgar?' James was determined not to let the matter drop. 'No, that was eight – nine years ago. So you wouldn't see much fighting.'

'Trafalgar wasn't the end of sea battles,' Francis returned. 'The French are still building ships of the line, and our fleets have to blockade their naval arsenals. Frigates have to keep the seas clear, protect the shores – '

'And surely a work to be proud of, not run away from,' said James.

'I don't see you fighting,' Francis returned, a little acidly.

James flushed. 'I am in the militia,' he said. 'And would have volunteered for the front if Father were not so against it.'

'I am against all wars.' Samuel was stern. 'My mother's family were Quakers.'

'We are championing the cause of liberty,' said James.

'Liberty for princes and sovereign states, not the liberty of peoples,' said Samuel.

'My father is all but a Radical,' James told Francis. 'A rebel heart beats under that quiet exterior.'

'We live in an age of debauchery,' Samuel countered. 'But what can you expect when the Prince of Wales himself spends his whole time in the pursuit of pleasure, when he married a German princess yet they say he was already married – '

'So plans to divorce poor Princess Caroline,' put in Tacy.

'I believe the nobles were the same in France,' Samuel went on. 'So who can blame the people for rebelling? Yes, at the start I was with them, before the Terror.'

'My father the Radical,' repeated James, sitting now, swinging one leg over a chair.

'I want no part in politics,' Francis put in. 'Nor in war. All I want is a quiet life.'

Tacy stared at him. She had noted his looks of admiration, had thought him a handsome young buck. Now she was not so sure. She was used to men arguing, stating their beliefs strongly; beliefs in war and fighting and honour. Oh, it was all right for her father to have his odd ideas, he was an old man. But a young man should be bold and courageous. Francis was diminished somewhat in her eyes.

And it was obvious to Francis that the father and son did not get on, for Samuel rose to his feet now and said, 'I think I will retire.'

'But Father, I have urgent business to discuss,' protested James.

'We will discuss business in the morning,' Samuel told him, 'Goodnight to you all.'

In his room Francis Barratt looked at the simple trellis-pattern wallpaper and matching curtains, at the bed-covers of blue and white. What did James, sleeping in such comfort, know of the rigours of life at sea?

He undressed slowly and got into bed, but he did not sleep. He had not told Samuel the complete truth – but it was a truth that was so new to him that he still had hardly taken it in. He had not learned the story of his birth until he finally left the sea.

The sea. He shuddered as he remembered the long hours of toil. Not a particularly robust child, he had led a sheltered life with his mother at the little private school, had never known the hardships of labour in the fields or on the sea, where the merchant seamen, who were also press-ganged, at least knew what to expect. He himself had always had a poor head for heights, yet he'd been forced to climb the rigging. He remembered the first time, the man standing below forcing him on while he clung terrified to the ropes, seeing the bows plunging deep into the swell, hearing the wind rising, shrieking through the rigging, bending topmasts and t'gallants, and himself vomiting . . . seeing another lad fall with a sickening thud, to be smashed to pieces on the deck. And he unable to move.

He was flogged for that and forced up again. And the fear of another flogging vied with the fear of the height and won – he reached the top. But every time he repeated the climb there was the same sickening dread, it never left him.

He had seen action. Days when the decks became tacky with blood, and the wounded were carried below to the surgeon's dim platform where the sound of saw grating through bone mingled with the cries and groans of the mutilated men. On the decks those fortunate enough to have been killed instantly were bundled into the sea.

Yet the men welcomed action. It was a way of forgetting the lash and the bosun's rattan cane; being crowded together in dangerous conditions aloft; half-stifled below in heavy weather when the ports were closed and the stinks nearly choked you.

After two years Francis had been ill with a fever and vague shooting pains all over his body. He had not complained, many men were ill; scurvy was still a scourge, many suffered from strains and ruptures caused by heaving the great heavy casks of water and provisions, cannon and carriages, or from fevers from the wet hammocks and bedding, the poor diet. But when he'd fallen from the rigging on to his head and was unconscious for hours he was confined to bed for a day and left to the ministrations of the drunken surgeon. The next morning he had been too ill to work, but the surgeon pronounced him fit to take his turn at scrubbing the decks. He hadn't any real friends who might help him – he didn't know why – or why, when the bosun asked why the work hadn't been done, he told him it had been Jimmy Watts' turn for duty. Jimmy Watts, a thin, undersized lad with little to say, had been flogged – and died. And then another seaman came to him. 'You're a liar,' he'd spat out, 'and a sneak-thief.'

Suddenly a red mist swam before his eyes and he'd grabbed the man by the throat until others separated them. Afterwards no-one spoke to him at all, they spat as he walked by.

He was filled with horror. What was happening to him? What had he done? He, nice Francis Barratt. Now he seemed to be two people, the once nice boy and the man with a black shadow on his brain that frightened him lest it might envelop him again.

He had longed to get home, to his mother who would dispel all his fears. His mother, who had been everything to him, who he missed more than he could say.

And he came home to find her dead!

Her few belongings were left with a neighbour, together with a letter.

And now his world was turned upside down indeed. For the letter told him that her husband, Jean-Pierre Baroux, was not his father; his real father lived in Chilverton, a place he'd never heard of, where she had been a governess, where, when pregnant, she'd been forced to leave . . .

He had to get away from Plymouth, and Chilverton was as good a place as any. In the middle of the country, it was as far from the sea as he could get. He did not realise it was himself he was running away from.

But maybe he'd find his mother's family. His dear, dear mother who had been so cruelly wronged by his true father. *Father.* He cringed at the very word and he would never forgive him. Unless . . . Perhaps there had been a reason for his seemingly callous behaviour. Perhaps he was sorry for what he had done. Francis had his name, and if he could learn that he was a good man, it would take the black shadow of fear away from him. If he knew there were no bad character traits that he, Francis, might have inherited.

But the thought of this parentage was so new to him that he had hesitated in telling Samual Barratt, especially when he saw the type of man *he* was, honourable, upright. Would he disapprove of a bastard? More so than the son of a Frenchman? He didn't know, so he said nothing. He hadn't lied, he told himself, guiltily. Not really. But he liked people to think well of him, as they had when he was with his mother.

So he'd start this new life somewhere around here. Yes, he'd like to stay here. For already he was very attracted to the young Miss Barratt, though he knew this was hopeless, why should she look at him, a nobody? But if she could only begin to care for him, he could perhaps regain his self-respect, forget all the guilt . . .

Tacy's room was covered similarly with trellis-patterned paper, but traces of femininity abounded. The curtain edges were adorned with wide bands of shining silk, little bows of ribbon at top and bottom; there were pretty trinkets on the dressing table, and on one wall a small portrait of the mother she'd never known.

Tacy did not miss her mother. It was her father whom she loved, who was all in all to her. Papa, who had lifted her on to the front of his saddle when she was little more than a baby and rode through the town with all the people smiling at the pretty child. Papa, who later let her sit with him in the chaise, and later still accompany him to London. As she grew into an even prettier girl she knew she only had to ask and he would grant her every wish. But she had few unreasonable demands – as yet. She was happy; she loved the Red House, loved Chilverton, the weavers, the clacking looms, the shining silk. And as she grew into a strong-willed young lady it was Grandmamma who frowned and feared for her should the world not always accede to her wishes. James would snort and say pride goes before a fall. And Tacy laughed. Self-willed and self-absorbed, her thoughts now were not of the war, or of Francis, but of Tom.

She had hoped he'd be lingering around when she returned, but then – how would he know exactly when that would be? She'd told him Monday, true, and he knew the times of the mail-coach, but Monday was always a holiday for the weavers.

She remembered, as she had every night when she lay in bed since it happened, when he'd kissed her. They'd been walking quietly through the fields at the back of the cottages – was it only a week ago? – when he'd stopped and pulled her down on the sweet smelling grass. He drew her to him and pressed his lips to hers . . . not in a gentle way, either, when would Tom ever be gentle? But a long hard kiss that set her heart pounding as he breathed, 'I want you, Tacy. I love you.'

They'd lain back together, and she'd seen the sun glinting through the grasses, heard children shouting in the distance, as he began to stroke her leg, underneath her skirt, touching her . . .

Surprised, startled as a young fawn, she'd stiffened momentarily, and then he'd said, disappointingly, 'You're not used to this sort of thing, are you, Tacy?' And she'd wanted to say, 'No, but go on, teach me . . .'

He hadn't . . . she wondered why. After all, they were going to be married, if he loved her as he said . . .

Now she lay at nights, aroused, wanting him . . . wanting him to teach her how to love . . .

Breakfast was early and eaten, as always, in silence. James was there, obviously impatient, but Samuel would not be hurried. Only when the meal was over and grace said did he lead the way into the parlour, beckoning Francis to follow. He led the way to a glass door which opened into the garden. 'Maybe you would like to look around,' he suggested courteously. 'It is another beautiful morning.'

Francis drew a breath. 'And a beautiful garden too,' he commented. The early spring flowers of daffodils and primroses were in little banks around a grassy centre. At the side were rose bushes, a lilac tree beginning to flower, an early clematis wound itself over one wall, and at the very bottom, a huge oak, from which a blackbird called.

Francis understood the gesture had been to stop him from being bored rather than prevent him hearing the conversation, but he could not help but overhear through the open door, though most of it meant little to him.

Samuel had seated himself in his favourite chair. 'Now,' he said to James. 'What is all this?'

'It's George Healey,' James replied. 'He's started up on his own.'

Samuel was surprised. 'George Healey? But he is my undertaker.'

'Not now he isn't.'

'You mean he left without giving notice?'

'He just called in, all pleased with himself and his new venture.'

'But he has a few looms of his own, which he runs with some journeymen. You mean he's getting more?'

'No, Father, that's not what I mean. He is starting a much bigger venture. We have so many orders, business is booming, what with the French out of competition and the big purl time – '

'And so many weavers in the Army,' said Samuel.

'Exactly. So George is starting a system of half-pay apprentices. The learner is taken to work the loom; gives George half his earnings for teaching him, the other half being for himself or his parents, as they are mostly young lads.'

Samuel asked, 'But has he the capital to start a business?'

James was pacing round the room, angrily. 'I understand the London merchants are financing him. And he'll pay the weavers less, of course. Our weavers are earning more than a pound a week, as you know. Why, in Coventry, they're so well off the weavers advertised in the local paper for fifty watchmakers to come round on a Saturday night and shell peas for them – '

Samuel said, 'Calm down, James. I agree this is distressing. But it is a problem of the war. When our weavers come home we shall go back to things as they were.'

James stopped pacing. 'Shall we?'

'Of course. George Healey pays less, so who will work for that?'

'Father, don't you see? Once Healey starts with cheap labour he won't stop. Having more weavers around will only make matters worse.'

'We have agreements, James.'

'The days of gentlemanly business and gentlemanly agreements are over, Father. If Healey and other little masters come creeping in, they won't go away. They won't fight fair, as you do. Healey is a shifty individual if ever there was one, he always was. Father, I tried to tell you he wasn't to be trusted but you wouldn't believe me. You think everyone is the same as you, and they're not. Don't you see what they're starting? You pay the weavers full price, you always did. He won't.'

'There is a list of prices, James.'

'Never written down.'

'There was no need to write it down.'

'Exactly. You are a gentleman. You pay for work at full price whether there is much or little. But the little masters won't. They pay half price to children. The work might not be as good, but why should they care? They sell in the market quickly, they make their money quickly, they will undercut you.'

There was a sudden silence, and the blackbird called loudly, the scent of sweet growing things wafted in through the open door.

'The old manufacturers will never stoop to this,' Samuel said.

'Then, Father, they will go under.'

'All this is nonsense, James.' But Samuel looked perturbed. He stood up, began to walk across the room.

The sunlight slanted through the window, reflecting his shadow in the looking-glass.

'Father, there's a new world coming. Lots of things are changing. Why, over in Nottingham and Leicestershire they're bringing in power looms and men are breaking them because they're afraid this new industrialisation will mean they'll lose their jobs – '

'We can't have power driven looms for silk, it's far too delicate and sensitive. No, I'll hear no more of this, James.' He reached the door.

James, frustrated, beat his clenched fist into his open palm. 'Oh, Tacy, can't you make him see?'

'No, James, because Papa will never change into a cheapjack. And I don't blame him. I think you're wrong, too.'

At the door Samuel smiled at this approbation from his favourite child. He asked, 'Who is doing the undertaking now, James?'

'I am. Who else?'

'And the accounts?'

'We need another man in the counting-house, I can't do both.'

Samuel pondered, then walked back to the garden door. 'Francis,' he called.

The young man moved towards him and Samuel studied him for a moment. 'It seems as if providence sent you here,' he said. 'We need a man in the counting-house. Can you furnish me with a reference from your old employer?'

'Gladly. I will give you their name and address.'

'Good. But we needn't wait. You can begin immediately.' And, as Francis looked startled, 'I have no undertaker, you see.'

'Undertaker?'

Samuel smiled. 'I forgot – we all know about weaving

here. The undertaker is the middleman. He gets the silk from me, prepares it, gives it out to the weavers, fetches the woven ribbons back, paying the weaver two-thirds of the money he receives. He runs some looms of his own as well. But you will need to know a little about the weaving. Get Tacy to take you down to the Patch, show you around. And now – ' he sighed, heavily, 'good morning to you all.'

Chapter two

Chilverton was a small market town, and like most of Regency England, it was vulgar, noisy and uninhibited. It laughed and it cried, it lost its temper, it shouted, but it was never dull. Prize fights were held regularly, there were parades and processions at every opportunity, with oxen roasted in the town centre and the people regaled with roast beef, plum pudding and ale, followed by dancing in the streets. There were fairs and statutes, visiting theatrical players, performing animals and cockfights. There was the Town Crier, blacksmiths round the lanes, pedlars with bulging packs – and a brand new canal, bringing a whole new means of transport to the town, which formerly had nothing but packhorses and carriers' carts unable to navigate the miry roads in winter. Now the canal carried coal around the country, ribbons to London, and passengers up and down on packet boats. For the thoughtful, there was a library, and a Mechanics' Institute in the making to teach reading, writing, arithmetic and music.

Francis knew little about small towns, but as they walked he could see it through Tacy's eyes. There was a colliery on the outskirts, but the main employment was silk ribbon weaving, spread from Coventry, where it had been started by the Huguenot refugees who fled from France in the seventeenth century and left a legacy of anglicised names and thin dark faces in the area, together with their methods of working, such as the undertaking system. Ribbon weaving was a domestic industry, there was hardly a house in the whole of the town that did not have its loom. The weaver worked on the loom, and was helped by the whole family; they were not separated into children and adults, but worked together, winding the silk, filling the shuttles, picking up and preparing the warps.

They could choose their own hours. Sunday was always a holiday when most of them went to chapel, Monday was a holiday too – 'Saint Monday', and sometimes there was a Saint Tuesday as well, depending on whether they wanted to go to Warwick races or not. By the end of the week they were working late to get the work finished for Saturday, but that is how they liked it. They were not ruled by the clock; time was their servant, not their master. Now, with the French rivals out of the running, orders were plentiful and money just as plentiful. The ribbon weavers of the Coventry area had always been more highly paid than the broad looms of Macclesfield and Spitalfields, so the ribbon weavers might be excused for thinking themselves the aristocrats of an aristocratic trade.

All this Tacy explained to Francis as they walked along the High Street, with its imposing houses, similar to her father's. The shops were in the Market Square at the bottom end of the street, and a few ladies were walking towards Miss Bradley's Millinery, while a horseman rode to Mr Jepson the saddlers. But Tacy and Francis walked in the opposite direction, towards the Patch, where most of the weavers' houses were situated. *Where Tom Lives*, Tacy's heart was singing.

Aloud she said, 'I hope you'll like living here, Francis.'

'I'm sure I shall,' he answered. 'But tell me, what's this big purl time your father was talking about?'

'Oh, purl-edged ribbons are all the rage now, we cannot make enough. They're woven with horsehair edging to the warp, then it's withdrawn from the woven ribbon, leaving scallops on one or both sides.' And, at his look of puzzlement, 'I'll show you when we get to the looms.'

They walked on, but at the end of the High Street she stopped so suddenly that Francis went on a step before he turned. 'Look!' Tacy hissed. 'George Healey. He's moving into that house – '

Francis looked. At the gate was a cart holding furniture, and walking towards the door was a large man with florid face and with him a thin woman with sharp features and frizzy red hair.

'That's the half-pay man?' Francis queried, interested. 'Moving house?'

'Yes, but why is he coming here if he plans to start another loom-shop? There won't be room.'

She took a few steps towards George and he, seeing her, called. 'Well, if it isn't little Mistress Pretty-face staring at us.'

Tacy flushed at his tone. 'I just wondered what you were doing,' she said.

'We're moving in. We don't have to ask your permission,' snapped the red-haired woman.

'Hush, Louie,' George admonished in a bantering tone. 'Though it doesn't matter now what we say, does it? She won't go running home to Papa with talk, and if she does it won't hurt us.'

'Why, I never – ' Tacy began.

'Now I can do my own work, see?' George interrupted. 'No more, Yes, Mr Barratt, No, Mr Barratt, did I go to chapel on Sunday, Mr Barratt? No more listening to his mealy-mouthed talk. Or James' suspicions. *Have you put the correct weight of silk in the warp, George? Have you been working on your own account here?* Yes, Miss Pretty-face, I've done all that, and I've been working on my own account for years, with your silk. Now go and tell Papa that.'

'And don't ask us what we're doing here, we have other plans,' called Louie.

'You're a thief, George Healey,' Tacy cried. 'James said you were.'

George laughed, and Tacy moved away. She could hardly credit what she'd heard. Brought up by her father to believe in men's goodness, how could it be that suddenly the world was changing? Some of this she tried to explain to Francis, but he replied, 'There are bad people, but I suppose your father would say you have to return evil with good.'

'That's all very well,' she said hotly. 'I'm afraid I'm not so saint-like as Papa. Really – ' they had resumed their walk. 'I never liked George Healey, but I didn't realise he was so horrible. And his wife is worse.'

'Why did your father choose him to be undertaker, Miss Barratt?' asked Francis.

'Because he's a good worker and a good businessman – or so we thought. Obviously he was deceiving Papa. Or maybe he wasn't so bad at first, I don't know. He came here as a journeyman weaver from Derby or somewhere, we don't really know much about him, but he worked hard. They do say he's got worse since he married that Louie Glover, as she was.'

'She doesn't seem the most charming of ladies,' said Francis.

'Charming! I should say not. She belongs to one of the worst families in Chilverton. Why, her sister Lottie is the town's harlot. Yes, it's true. I do know what I am talking about, I assure you. She keeps a house of ill-repute.'

'Villains and harlots,' said Francis, and his voice held a peculiar note that Tacy did not notice.

'You get them everywhere, I suppose, and don't call

me Miss Barratt, everyone calls me Tacy.'

'An unusual name,' Francis commented.

'It's an old Quaker name. It means silence. No, don't laugh, I know it doesn't suit me, but there we are, I'm stuck with it now. Anyway, let's forget the Healeys and visit some nice people.'

The trees of the High Street gave way to the plainer end of the town, where they turned right past the Weavers' Arms on the corner, then a number of thatched cottages, towards two newer rows of small terraced houses. There had once been a green here – or so the weavers said. To the better end of the town it was known as the Patch, but now all that remained was a small area just big enough for old Mrs Gardner to let her pig root, it being nearer to her front door than the Common, and for the boys to play football. But, cottage or house, every one had a large window downstairs to let in maximum light, and from some came the clack clack of the loom, though not many. It was obvious that others were still on holiday; women were talking in the doorways; outside, old people sat in the sunshine. A group of tiny girls in faded sunbonnets and frocks that, while far from being their best, were still bedecked with ribbons, were clasping hands in a ring and singing:

> Ring a ring o' roses, a pocket full of posies
> Atishoo, atishoo, all fall down.

and, laughing, they fell on to the dusty roadway.

Older children were making their way to the fields at the back of the houses and Tacy remembered something her friend Martha had said when they were children. *The cottages huddle together on the edge of the wilderness.* Martha never said very much but sometimes she'd come out with these odd little sayings. For there was no wilderness, unless you counted the Common, which was wild enough in its way, but the fields and meadows were green and flower-filled where the children sat and made daisy chains and asked each other if they liked butter when a buttercup was held under the chin. Farmer Black's fat cattle grazed down by the stream and gazed with curious eyes at the weavers who picked elderberries for wine or who, like Martha's father, searched for rare flowers to talk about at the Mutual Improvement Society.

Tacy led Francis to the end row of cottages and he could see that she was full of suppressed excitement. She was a girl of moods, he decided and wondered if, on the way back, he would dare put his arm around her. He guessed she was spoilt and wilful, but she was the loveliest thing he had ever seen; she reminded him, in her colouring, of his mother. If only he could bury himself in her she would take away all those bad memories, and the worries about the father he still had to find.

They had stopped at the end house of a block of four. At the side was a piece of land, and here an extra room had been built, covering the entry, so that Tacy and Francis had to enter through a small passage. From the kitchen came sounds of talk and laughter, and as they reached the back door, two girls and their escorts spilled out. The girls were obviously sisters, both with black hair and eyes, and were dressed very fine, with silk shawls over their pretty dresses, and they said hallo to Tacy as they passed.

A third girl stood in the doorway, a younger replica of the sisters; she too called hallo to Tacy. 'Come in, do,' she invited, and led them into the kitchen. This was a small, untidy room, though its furniture was good and the table laid with a damask tablecloth. The dresser along one wall held fine cups and plates, with rougher earthenware on the shelf below.

'Sit down, Tacy, tell me all about London. But who's your friend?'

'He's Francis Barratt, going to work for my father in the counting house. Francis, this is Nancy Jacques.' Tom's sister. Nancy gave Francis a flirtatious look. 'A relation?' she asked.

'No, just coincidence,' Tacy replied, looking round. Where was Tom? 'I've brought him to see the looms.'

'Well, you know where they are.' Nancy pointed.

Tacy retraced her steps and now Francis could see that the side extension held several looms – all silent. There were no people inside.

'This is a Dutch engine-room,' Tacy explained to Francis.

He stepped towards the nearest loom. 'I don't see any engine.'

'No, it's hand operated, but it can weave up to six ribbons at a time. Plain ribbons mostly; fancy ribbons are woven on the single hand-loom.'

Francis went to inspect the looms, and Nancy drew Tacy back into the kitchen. 'Now tell us all about it,' she pressed. 'Did you see those London ladies in their almost naked dresses? They say they damp them to make them cling.'

'No, of course not. You know Papa would never let me go to a ball.'

'I'm sure *my* father wouldn't mind. And here I'm stuck in Chilverton and can't see anything. You *should* go, we have to study fashion.'

'Mr Fotheringay tells us about fashions.'

'Did you see him yesterday? What was he wearing?'

Tacy smiled at the question. When, as a child of ten she had first seen Mr Fotheringay he had on a morning coat of purple, with puffed sleeves, a waistcoat of canary, and knee breeches of green. He wore a wig, and his face had two bright spots of red on his cheeks that she did not know was rouge. 'Why is that man dressed so funny?' she had asked Papa when they were out of hearing.

'He's a Bond Street lounger,' Papa replied shortly, and before she could ask what a Bond Street lounger was, went on, 'But he has good connections at Court and keeps me informed of coming fashions.'

This was necessary for the ribbon trade for the Court set the trends in fashion. When Princess Amelia died in 1810 – said to be the favourite of the King's many offspring – deep mourning was ordered for six weeks. No fancy ribbons were sold, for black ribbon was the only acceptable trim to bonnets and dress, and when mourning was extended for another six weeks, several manufacturers in Coventry were bankrupted.

'Yes, I saw Mr Fotheringay,' Tacy told Nancy. 'He wears stays, I am sure. And he had on a pair of cossacks – that's trousers drawn in at the ankles with bows. Bows, Nancy! So they look like a petticoat. And his coat was padded at the top, like a lady's bosoms.'

Nancy burst into a peal of laughter.

'People in London do dress comical,' Tacy went on. 'I saw a lady in trousers.'

'No, I cannot believe that.'

'It's true. She wore a velvet pelisse and trousers underneath.'

'La, if ladies are going to wear trousers what about our ribbons? Those London ladies are very fast, I reckon. Perhaps she was one of the ladies of joy. Perhaps Mr Fotheringay will wear the ribbons.' Nancy gave a hoot of laughter. 'Anyway, I'm surprised that your Papa deals with him.'

'Yes.' But then Papa didn't approve of much of the world he dealt with. He said the Prince Regent held a rackety court, with bucks and buffoons, scholars and fugitives from debtors' prisons.

'Did you see Prinny?' asked Nancy. 'They say he dresses well, though he's so fat. And his poor wife – '

'Poor nothing,' said Tacy, testily. 'I did see her once driving through London, and she looked most peculiar. She wore a frizzed wig, and her face was painted. They say she never washes and talks coarsely, that's why the Prince cannot bear her company.'

'Well, it's a pity he had to marry her when he was already in love with Mrs Fitzherbert, and married to her some say.'

'But she couldn't be queen, she's a *Roman Catholic*,' said Tacy, shocked.

'Oh, I know, but the people sympathise with Princess Caroline,' Nancy argued.

Tacy frowned. Why was Nancy talking about London when she knew she wanted to hear about Tom. Was she doing it to tease? She had to know. 'Tom not in?' she asked as casually as she could.

'He's gone to see your father.'

Now Tacy's heart gave a wild leap of joy and the ready colour came to her cheeks. Had he gone to ask permission to court his daughter? But she must pretend not to know. 'Why?' she asked.

'Why? He's angry about this half-pay scheme George Healey is starting,' Nancy replied.

Tacy was taken aback. 'But is it that important?' she asked.

'Tom thinks so. He's in a tearing rage.'

So he hadn't even waited to see her. Tacy was distressed, but too proud to show it. She tossed her head. 'Come, Francis,' she called. 'We'll go,' and she led him out into the sunshine. 'Sorry you didn't see much there,' she apologised. 'Mrs Walters lives in the next house;

she's a widow, so she took over the weaving when her husband died. She's got a lot of children, Enoch is the oldest, then Matt, who's in the Army, and all these –' she waved her hand vaguely at the children spilling out into the yard.

'We'll go to Uncle Abel's, that's the one at the end,' she continued, knowing she was talking too much, she always did when she was upset or nervous. 'He's not really my uncle, his mother and my grandmother – on my mother's side – were sisters. But I always call him uncle. He's one of our very best workers, he's bound to be in today.'

Francis gave her a curious look, but he followed her to the brick cottage, with its wooden bench outside holding a bowl of water for washing.

This kitchen was neat and well cared for. The chairs and table were obviously handcrafted and beautifully made. A fat Toby jug squatted on the mantelpiece, flanked by candlesticks. On the shelves were cups and plates and the family Bible, while the rag rugs on the quarried floor looked warm and cosy.

But the kitchen was empty, so Tacy led the way into the front room. Here the loom almost filled the space, though Abel Pickard sat close to the enlarged window. On the other side of the room a girl sat at a small machine, not unlike a spinning wheel, to fill the pirns for the shuttles. The window was kept tight shut to keep the moisture in the silk, and the fire was never lit in case the chimney smoked and damaged the delicate ribbons, while soot would ruin them completely.

'Hallo, Uncle Abel, Martha.' Tacy introduced Francis, and though Abel nodded a cheery greeting, Martha hardly spoke.

Uncle Abel's had always been Tacy's second home. She spent a lot of time there, except when there was the smallpox outbreak which had carried off Aunt Susan and two of her children. Martha was left and she kept house for her father, and helped him with the weaving. Abel was an industrious, intelligent man, a respected chapelgoer, and there was a strong bond between father and daughter.

Martha – Tacy's other friend. A plain girl, with thick straight black hair and large brown eyes. Her muslin dress was plain too, with no trimmings except for a bow of white ribbon at the neck. Martha never talked about lads the way Tacy and Nancy did. Tacy felt it was because she was plain, she knew she wouldn't stand a chance – or maybe she was just not interested. Whatever the reason, it gave Tacy a feeling of superiority, the superiority of an attractive girl to a plain one.

Abel said, 'Martha, why don't you get some refreshments for Tacy and the young fellow. I shall stop in a minute when I've finished this piece.'

'When I've wound this pirn,' Martha answered, not moving.

'Francis is to work in the counting-house,' Tacy explained, to cover the awkward pause. 'So I'm bringing him round to get some idea of weaving. Uncle Abel always has the most difficult work,' she went on, turning to Francis. 'Dutch engine-looms can weave six at a time, but the most complicated patterns have to be on the single hand as I told you.'

'I see.' Francis gazed with respect at Abel's movements, his hands and feet moving to pass the shuttles and work the treadles.

'It's a pretty pattern,' he acknowledged.

'Aye. This is how it's done, see?' Francis leaned forward as Abel explained. First treadle to drop four threads under the warp, second treadle to lift one thread over, with the next row in a different sequence, necessary for the weaving of satin, and the ribbon fell from the loom in a cascade of blue and silver.

'So you're going to take on James' work?' Abel asked Francis.

'That's right,' Francis agreed.

Abel stood up and moved to the back of the machine. On the heavier looms, where the richer satins and sarsenets were made, a weaver of ordinary strength could not continue indefinitely passing the shuttle. To rest his muscles he was obliged to take a turn at 'picking up', smoothing and cleaning the silk as it passed from the warp. He said, 'James told me about it. I don't like what I've heard.'

'And neither do I.' At the voice in the doorway Tacy swung round, and a deep blush flooded her cheeks.

The young man who stood there was dressed for walking. His hat was tilted rakishly on his black curls, his cravat tied in a loose bow; his shoulders were broad, his hips narrow in the grey pantaloons. His black eyes that could change so rapidly from rage to mirth were flashing now as he said angrily, 'We've got to stop it, Abel. This man's going to ruin the trade and all of us with it.'

Abel left the loom. 'I hear you've been to see Mr Barratt.'

'I have.' And now Tacy saw several other men behind him, crowding into the small kitchen. 'And we got no help from him, either.'

'No help? What did you want him to do?'

'Why, he could stop it. He knows all the important men, here and in London. He could talk to them, prevent Healey getting money.'

'I don't think Papa would do that,' Tacy put in.

And now Tom turned to her, and there was no soft look in his eyes, only anger. 'What do you know about it?' he asked.

Tacy was shocked at his tone. Oh, she'd seen him in tempers before, many times, but he'd never spoken to her in this way. She opened her mouth to retort, but Abel put in, peaceably, 'No, no, that's not the way, Tom. We can't interfere with a man getting money.'

'Why not?' Tom asked. 'George Healey's using underhand methods, why shouldn't we? Else we'll all be working on half pay.'

'That's not the way,' Abel repeated. 'Anyway, Mr Barratt can't stop the London money men from financing him.'

'But he knows all the silkmen who deliver the silk. A few words from him in the right quarter would soon stop George Healey from getting any work.'

'We've never done things that way,' Abel protested. 'Certainly not Mr Barratt.'

'Then what is the way, tell me that?'

'Why, we'll get all the weavers together, and pick a spokesman to talk to Healey. That's the way we've always worked, Tom, not rushing off half cocked – '

'And you think he'll listen? George Healey's as crooked as they come. Often, when he gave the work out he'd weigh the silk, tip the scales so it was overweight. Then he'd weigh the finished ribbons – they'd be less, so he'd charge us for wastage.'

'We can speak to the lads who are working for him – '

'Donkey 'em round the town, you mean. They ain't weavers, Abel, they don't belong in our Guild, we shan't do nothin' wi' them.'

'All right, calm down, Tom. I grant you it's serious, but I still say we should get all the weavers together. Let's arrange a meeting. And you – ' He turned to the men in the kitchen. 'You pass the word around that we'll hold a meeting tomorrow night. Here.'

'All right.' The men nodded and slowly walked out of the kitchen.

And Martha said to Tom, 'Come, sit down, and I'll make us a cup of tea.' And Tacy stared as she took his arm and led him to a chair, marvelling at her gentleness, knowing that she herself would meet Tom's rage with temper of her own. A temper that rose at the sight. How dare Martha appropriate Tom in this way when she knew he belonged to her, Tacy.

She said, 'I think you're making a fuss about nothing, Tom. My father says that when the men come back from the war it will all blow over.'

'And I told your father he's wrong,' Tom retorted.

'You – told him? How dare you?' Tacy was really angry now, at Tom, for ignoring her, at Martha; at the whole business she hardly understood.

'I dare a lot,' Tom replied, and again Martha held his arm while she handed him a cup of steaming tea. She did not offer Tacy any and this inflamed her all the more.

'Come, Francis,' she said, and put her own hand on *his* arm. 'I think we'd better go,' and she pulled him out through the door into the sunshine.

'Let's go home,' she said abruptly once they were in the road, and they began the walk back, Tacy marching in front, head held high.

'I find the weaving most interesting,' Francis said, trying to keep up. 'I have never seen a loom before, at least, not a silk ribbon weaver's. Strange how you see all those fancy patterns and never think how they are made.'

Tacy did not answer.

'What is it, Tacy? Has all this talk about half-pay apprentices upset you?'

'Why should that worry me? I don't run the weaving, Papa does, and James to follow.'

He said no more and they walked to the Red House

where they parted, Francis going to the warehouse to look for Mr Barratt, Tacy to the parlour. Her father would be in the counting-house, she knew, and she wanted to ask about Tom, but decided to wait. There was something even more important to ask about than this silly squabble. She would wait till the evening.

Supper was eaten in silence, as always, and then they went into the parlour. Tacy had put on her blue dress, one she knew to be a favourite of her father's, and her hair was tied with blue ribbon. Samuel sat in his usual chair, with Grandmamma opposite, her embroidery in her hand. Tacy took the little red velvet footstool and perched at her father's feet. 'Papa,' she began. 'It's the Fair on Saturday.'

'I know it.' Was Samuel still angry? His voice was stern. She said, 'I can go, as usual, cannot I, Papa?' trying to keep her voice casual.

'Better not,' Samuel said.

'But, Papa . . . why not?'

'I think it better you do not go this year.'

'But I always go. Papa, you can't mean it.' Tacy's voice trembled, with shock, with disbelief.

'You are too old to go running around Fairs, I've told you before.' This was Grandmamma.

'I'm not, I'm not. Everybody goes. Oh, Papa, it's so unfair. And this year I wanted so specially to go – '

'Oh, and why is this year so special?' asked Grandmamma.

'I don't want you to go.' That was Samuel, firmly.

Now Tacy jumped to her feet and faced her father angrily. 'It's because you had that silly argument with Tom Jacques, isn't it, Papa? You know I am friends with – Nancy . . .'

'Don't talk about things you know nothing of,' said Samuel.

'Well, it wasn't important, Papa. Tom was just worried about this new system – '

'That's as may be, but I don't take kindly to a young lad telling me how to run my business,' said Samuel.

'I'm sure he didn't mean that, Papa.'

'Young hothead,' grunted Samuel. 'He was very rude, and rudeness I cannot countenance.'

'I think the men will talk it over and perhaps come to you to tell you – '

'I shall not see Tom Jacques,' said Samuel. 'And no more on the subject, if you please.'

Tacy knew her father, knew how far she could go. Knew that when he spoke in that certain tone he meant every word. A soft breeze blew in and she walked to the open window, fighting her tears. Couldn't Papa see that this silly feud would ruin her life?

She walked into the garden. She knew Tom and she knew Papa, both stubborn men in their own way. But surely this quarrel would soon blow over, it was so senseless, all about nothing. And Papa must be right, he always was.

She sat on the oak bench, carved lovingly by the local carpenter. She wished Francis would join her, but he had gone to his room. She wondered why, had he gone off in a mood?

As she brooded, James joined her. 'Well, well,' he teased. 'Cinderella cannot go to the ball.'

'Shut up,' she said.

'Trying to make her a young lady, when she'll never be anything but a hoyden.'

'Pig,' she said, without expression.

'Shall I bring you a fairing?' he asked, tweaking her hair.

'James,' she asked, 'was it a bad quarrel between Tom and Papa?'

'Yes,' he answered. 'You know Tom Jacques, what a temper he has.'

'And he shouldn't tell Papa what to do.'

'Not when it comes to some of the things he suggested, no. But he's right in another way, George Healey should be stopped.'

He moved away and she pondered his words. Yet even now she could not think it was more than a storm in a teacup. Certainly not more important than the Fair. She studied the flowers. The daffodils would soon be over, then gillyflowers and pansies would take their place, later still the roses . . . If she couldn't go to the Fair she wouldn't see Tom . . . She'd just have to sit here listening to the fiddlers – oh, it was monstrous.

And it turned out just as she thought. She sat at home; she heard the music, the noise, the shouts. She half hoped Tom would get a message to her, perhaps by Nancy – but no-one came. It was the first year she'd missed the Fair since she was a toddler.

But Tom would no doubt win a doll for her on the coconut shy. She brightened at the thought. And once the merrymaking was over, things would be back to normal again.

But she had to know . . .

She ran down to the Patch on Tuesday morning as the Fair was packing up. Men were loading wooden frames of booths onto waggons, the horses were ready to start. They began to pull out, leaving an air of desolation over the Common, with remains of the merrymaking lying everywhere: snippets of ribbon in the sawdust, discarded sweetmeats, a broken doll.

At the Jacques' cottage, Nancy met her at the door, tying her bonnet strings, wearing her best gown, pale green flowered sarsenet with a full skirt. 'Tacy,' she said.

'I'm just going out.'

'Oh.' Tacy was disappointed. 'Where are you going?'

'Fred Pettit asked me. He fancies me.' She laughed self-consciously.

'Does he? I didn't know.'

'Well, he was at the Fair.'

'Oh, Nancy, Papa wouldn't let me come,' Tacy said.

'Whyever not? Because of Tom?'

'No no.' Tacy tried to laugh deprecatingly. 'He said I was getting to be a young lady now. Isn't it silly?'

This was the wrong thing to say, for Nancy reared up like a young filly. 'Is it?' she asked. 'You mean we aren't ladies if we go to the Fair?'

Too late Tacy remembered that Nancy had a touch of the Jacques temper too. 'No no, Nancy, you know he didn't mean that. But come,' she coaxed. 'Tell me about it. What happened with Fred Pettit?'

'Well, we went to the Fair together, Tom, Martha and me,' Nancy said, mollified. 'Fred joined us. We went a walk later.'

Tacy stared. A walk, Nancy and Fred? So what about Tom and Martha? Had it been anyone else she might have been jealous, but Martha was so plain – no, she couldn't be jealous of Martha. Tom would stay with her no doubt out of kindness, out of friendship, and because she, Tacy, wasn't there. But she must know. 'Where is Tom?' she asked.

'Tom?' echoed Nancy vaguely. 'Oh, he's out somewhere. It is Tuesday, you know, he never works Tuesday, and the day after the Fair as well . . .'

'No, of course.'

'Here's Fred.' And Nancy gave a giggle. 'Isn't he the most handsome fellow you ever did see? I'll be off, Tacy.'

She ran to join her swain leaving Tacy to walk disconsolately home.

★

A soft dusk fell over Chilverton. The looms were silent now. From the main street came the slow clip-clop of a horse which seemed to know he was on his last lap before resting for the night. Beyond the Patch the trees were dark masses, and barn owls began their nightly hunting; sweet country smells did their best to smother the ranker smell from the open ditch near the road. Candles flickered in windows, and in Abel's cottage men and women were gathering for the meeting. Tom was there; Mrs Walters – who everyone knew had her eye on Abel – and her married son, Enoch; more weavers and journeymen, crowding the kitchen so some had to stand in the front room and others in the doorway. Martha was putting on her bonnet.

'What, going out, Martha?' asked Tom.

'It's the social club meeting,' Martha replied. For, just as the men had their own meetings, so did the women, though they all joined together to run the benefit club for sickness and unemployment.

Martha pushed her way into the front room, then up the narrow twisting staircase to fetch her shawl from her bedroom. There were two bedrooms in the cottage, but one was simply the enlarged landing and here Abel slept. Martha took out her shawl from the wooden chest under the window. It was of flowered silk, so fine that she did not wear it very often, but the colours of orange and yellow shone vividly over her grey gown.

When she came downstairs the meeting was well under way, and no-one seemed to notice her.

'I don't rightly understand it,' Enoch Walters was saying. 'What it means – '

'It'll mean half pay for all of us,' Tom told him. 'Else we'll all be out of work.'

'An' that'll mean parish relief and soup kitchens,' Bob

Pettit put in. 'You don't want that, Enoch Walters, wi' all your little 'uns, three, ain't it?'

'An' another one comin',' said Enoch, gloomily.

'By God, Enoch, you look a slow fellow, but you're a bit over hasty in bed, ain't you?' Tom's eyes were merry again.

'Be thankful you ain't married, Tom Jacques,' Enoch muttered, sulkily.

'Married? Not me. Court all and marry none, that's my motto.'

'Ah, you'll think different when some wench gives you the glad eye,' Enoch told him.

Martha slipped out, and walked slowly towards the Weavers' Arms, where the women met. Inside the smaller room she joined her friends, some of whom were drinking ale, though Martha did not drink. They could see over the small partition into the taproom, with its sawdusted floor and wooden tables where men sat smoking long pipes.

'You're quiet, Martha,' Betsey Allsop said after some minutes. 'Summat on your mind?'

'No,' Martha shook her head. 'Just thinking.'

'Thinking about this half-pay business,' Emma Goddard nodded. 'It's goin' to ruin us, I reckon.'

They talked on, but Martha said little, and as soon as she decently could, she left and began the walk home.

It was quite dark now, there were no street lamps in the Patch, though one had been erected in the Market Square. So when someone said, 'Hello, Martha,' she jumped.

'Oh, it's you, Mr Redmond,' she said as the tall man materialised beside her. 'Are you going to the meeting?'

'I was, if I'm not too late. I had to see old Mrs Benson, she's poorly.'

'Oh, I'm sorry. Is there anything I can do?'

'No no, she has two daughters nearby. But I fear she's not long for this world.'

John Redmond was the chapel minister. Thirtyish, unmarried, he was unlike the locals in his colouring, being fair, with steely blue eyes. Like them he was thin, but his thinness was of the type seen in those who, in childhood, never had enough to eat. He always strode purposefully along as if he were ready to right all wrongs. He lodged in a shoddy room in the Patch, and was dearly loved by his flock. An impassioned orator, as so many chapel preachers were, his words were often greeted by rounds of applause and cries of assent. And in the larger gatherings, when people would come from miles around to hear him – walking all the way – there would be waving handkerchiefs and raised umbrellas while their owners jumped up and down in excitement.

The meeting was not over, and as they entered the lighted kitchen, Mr Redmond said, 'That's a pretty shawl, Martha.'

'Ah,' agreed Abel. 'She should wear her glad rags more often.'

'Mr Redmond,' Tom greeted him. 'What do you think of the way things are going, eh?'

'I fear for the future,' said Mr Redmond.

'Sit here, do,' said Enoch Walters, relinquishing his chair. 'And tell me what you mean, Minister. What do you fear?'

'Why,' replied Mr Redmond, looking round the weavers. 'You have all been making beautifully crafted work, and never worked at a mad speed because you were paid at full price whether there was much work or little. Now this old constitution of trade is breaking up, falling into anarchy. These new little masters acknowledge none of the ancient bonds; now competition will be extended in full force to the *price* of labour as

43

well as the extent of employment. Because they put money first, before honour.'

The weavers were silent, knowing it was true.

The last two weeks of May were still warm with balmy breezes. Children ran over the fields picking bluebells — those who weren't required to help with the weaving — and even those who were had the long weekend and Monday and Tuesday. But June began wet and windy and the children stayed at home.

Tacy had not visited either Nancy or Martha's house again. In the past she had run down when the fancy took her, now she was uncertain. At seventeen, in the throes of first love, afraid to show her feelings, she had never actually told either of the girls about her love for Tom. When Nancy teased her she had tossed her head and said she cared for nobody; if he asked her to walk with him she still laughed when she came back, pretending it was all a game, never admitting to anything deeper. She was Tacy, attractive Tacy, all the boys liked her, and Tom was just another string to her bow.

Now she was hoist on her own petard.

But that was it, she told herself, Martha didn't know how she felt, how Tom felt. Not that it mattered, not that Tom would bother about Martha, the plain, but still . . . she'd go down and explain how things were.

She ran down to the Pickards' house as the June sun was trying to break through the clouds. It was quite chilly, so she threw a light shawl over her spotted cambric dress. It was Thursday, the looms were busy, there was no sound but the clack-clack from each house.

Abel was weaving a tartan, and Tacy entered hesitantly. But Abel welcomed her as always, and if Martha seemed quiet, well, she always was, wasn't she? But she rose and went to the kitchen when Abel suggested tea, and Tacy wondered if her uncle had reprimanded her the last time she was here.

Tacy followed her into the kitchen, where she was hanging the kettle on a hook over the open fire. While she put out the earthenware cups, brown and green, Tacy said, 'I haven't seen Tom lately – not to speak to.'

'Haven't you?' Martha kept her eyes lowered.

'Have you?' Tacy persisted.

'He's been here,' Martha replied. 'There have been meetings.'

'Did – did he ask about me at all?'

Martha put a jug of milk on the table. 'No,' she said.

Tacy turned to the window, looking at the first shoots of the peas and beans in the back garden, the potatoes that would last the Pickards through next winter, carefully stored under the beds upstairs. 'I am in love with him,' she said, baldly.

Martha clattered the cups. 'A lot of girls are,' she answered.

'But – ' Tacy wanted to say: *he belongs to me*. Didn't Martha understand? She swallowed and went on, 'I just wondered if – why – he's turned away from me.'

And Martha said, 'You must ask him that yourself, Tacy.'

Tacy was silent. This wasn't going at all well . . . Yet what had she expected? She looked at Martha and thought: she isn't at all concerned about me.

She had never tried to analyse Martha before; she had just been there, plain Martha who said little, just tagged along. Now she had a strange thought, Martha didn't like her. And was surprised. She, Tacy Barratt, had always been so popular . . . hadn't she? . . . She said, 'I thought you'd sympathise.'

'Why should I?' Martha asked. 'You've always had everything you wanted, haven't you, Tacy?'

The clack-clack of the loom stopped and Abel came into the kitchen. Martha handed him tea and an oatcake. And then young Billy Walters ran to the door, stumbling over the too long trousers inherited from his next oldest brother. 'Mester Pickard,' he piped. 'Me ma wants to know if there's a meeting tonight.'

'Yes, there is,' Abel told him, and said to Tacy, 'We have formed a committee and I have been picked as spokesman. We shall go to see Mr Barratt again tomorrow evening.'

Tacy said nothing, but she resolved to be there.

Martha chose a large piece of oatcake for Billy, and Tacy forced herself to chat normally. But she felt, perhaps for the first time, an outsider, and as soon as she could she made her farewells and returned home.

She did not say anything to her father about the coming meeting, but waited until she saw the deputation approaching, then stepped into the yard and stood behind her father. She saw Abel come forward with several other men, including Tom. Samuel halted. 'I shall not see Tom Jacques,' he said.

'Tom, wait outside,' ordered Abel, and Samuel led him into the office.

Tacy followed Tom, standing now outside the gate. 'Tom,' she ventured.

He looked at her, but there was no friendliness in his gaze. 'You'd better go in,' he muttered. 'You aren't allowed to mix with me.'

'Oh, don't be silly, Tom, of course I can talk to you. Why, it's nothing.'

'It *is* something,' he said, eyes flashing. 'Not to be allowed in the house. It *is* something when I am right. Go. Leave me.' And he turned his back.

She returned to the house. She did not wait to see Abel nor to hear what they had said. Her world had been

46

turned upside down, and for what? A silly argument about prices that didn't even affect them. She could not help but side with her father, Papa was always right. She knew he and James would be talking about the matter endlessly, she closed her ears. Lost, she turned more and more to Francis and he, not unnaturally, thought she was beginning to like him as she spent her days now, not with the weavers, but in the counting-house.

The warehouse ran alongside the house, jutting out in front, and Tacy had always loved to visit it. Its walls were lined with shelves filled with raw materials, designs and drafts, and packets of ribbons waiting to be delivered to London. Delivery by pack-horse had been slow, and often dangerous if highwaymen appeared, so both Samuel and James had welcomed the new canal. Formerly goods had often been lost in transit, and Samuel wondered now if George Healey had had something to do with losses, blaming them on the carrier.

Samuel was in the warehouse when Tacy walked in on the Wednesday. She passed the large pair of scales for weighing the silk, the baskets of shining bobbins and warps, down to the mahogany counter leading to the counting-house with its tall desk and safe for the account books.

Francis had mastered the books, but he wanted to know more about the weaving. He had been surprised to learn that some of the terms were so different; some were French. He knew that you wove with warp and weft but here weft was called tram or shute, and passing the shuttle was shooting down. Most puzzling of all were the measurements and he asked Tacy, 'What does the cost of a ribbon 8dy mean?'

'Oh, ribbons are not measured in inches, but in pence, and written dy,' she explained. 'An eightpenny ribbon is one inch wide.'

47

'I see,' said Francis, his brow clearing. 'So the cost of weaving a piece thirty-six yards in 2dy is ten shillings, deducting the expenses of filling in the loom, hire and loom standing – '

'That's the undertaker's work,' interrupted Samuel.

'But, Father, I haven't had time to do the books and give out and collect the work,' expostulated James, busy sorting out a bundle of silk for a waiting weaver.

'I can do it all,' Francis said, hastily. 'If only I knew what it all meant.'

'You must take him to the loom again,' Samuel decreed to Tacy. 'He'll understand the measurements better if he has it explained on the spot.'

So Tacy was forced to return to the Patch. And she could hardly visit the area and not go to see Nancy and Martha. Perhaps it was as well, she could keep up the pretence that nothing was wrong.

She talked to Nancy, but when she went to the looms, it was never Tom's, but his father's, and she stayed close to Francis the whole time. And Tom would look at her in a serious, almost sullen manner. Yet, deep in his eyes, something of the old look remained, that which made you know you were a woman, as if he could see right through your frock and petticoats – your chemise even – that made older women say 'Oh, he's cheeky, that one.' But he did not laugh and joke as before, he said little. So, again she turned to Francis.

And, as they walked back through the clack-clack of the looms – it was Friday, the busiest day, when even the children and old people were indoors helping – Francis said, hesitantly, 'I wish we could go out together one evening.'

Tacy brought herself back to the present. 'Well, we can,' she answered. 'Do you mean go for a walk?'

'Would your father allow it?'

She shrugged. 'He need not know.'

Francis hesitated. 'I would not want to do anything to displease your father.'

'Oh,' she said, impatiently. 'Don't be so stick in the mud. I've often been out walking – ' and he wondered jealously who with, but said nothing, he hadn't the right.

'Is there no other pleasure here?' he asked. 'Assemblies, theatres?'

'La, Francis, Papa wouldn't let me go to a theatre, at least not to the bands of players who come here occasionally. The men are always drunk and the women – ' she shrugged expressively. 'And no, there aren't many Assemblies we can attend, either. Papa does not mix with people very much, or rather they don't mix with him. It's his religion, you see.'

'Oh well.' Francis touched her hand. 'I do like you, Tacy.'

And it was balm just to hear that someone liked her, for she suspected he meant *love*.

She dimpled. 'Do you, Francis? Then we shall go for a walk one day, when we come back from inspecting the weaving, what's wrong with that?' And I hope I see Tom Jacques, she thought.

'Do you like me, Tacy?' he pursued.

'Of course I do,' she answered, lightly.

But Francis did not notice the light-hearted tone. He had had little experience of flirting, he thought she was serious.

He thought how much he needed someone like Tacy to love him, to believe in him, now more than ever. For he had slipped out one Sunday evening when the family were at chapel – for no pressure was put on him to accompany them – and had gone to the village of Meddlestone, only to be told that the Vicar, his mother's father, was dead, the family scattered. Yes, there had been a number of daughters, yes, they did go as governesses, one named Florence? They thought so, but it was all a long time ago.

Francis had been bitterly disappointed. He had hoped so much to find someone to remind him of his dearly loved mother.

He wondered more than ever what his father was like . . .

When breakfast was over now in the mornings, business was discussed, all the family joining in, including Grandmamma. Francis had at first been a little in awe of this lady; although in her seventies her faculties were unimpaired. Tall, she was straight as a ramrod, walked with a stick, but walked like a soldier. And she knew as much about the business as anyone present.

But she was kind. There was the morning she stopped Francis as they were about to leave. 'You look tired,' she observed. 'Aren't you sleeping?'

'Not too well.' And then, lest she think he was complaining about his room, 'I have nightmares.'

'About the sea?' she asked, shrewdly.

'Well – yes.' *About the lad who died because of me. And my rage* . . . But this he could not tell anyone. Maybe she guessed something for she patted his arm. 'It's all in the past now,' she said. 'Look to the future. You seem to be settling in here well.'

'Yes.' He sighed. 'It's quiet here. That's all I ask, a quiet life.'

Grandmamma smiled ruefully. 'I'm not sure if you're going to get that. Up till you came it was quiet, but now it's changing.'

'I seem to be a Jonah,' he said, remembering the ship.

'No, it would have happened anyway. We have a happy little society here, Francis, an enlightened society.

The weavers have money, they are independent – too independent for some.'

'Some?' he queried.

'Those in power do not like the working classes to be independent. Or to question, or *think*. Weavers at their looms can do a lot of thinking. They're too Radical, Francis.'

And the very next day the simmering trouble erupted. So another business meeting was held, but after supper this time, on James' instigation.

'Father,' he began. 'The men want a list of prices to be written down.'

Samuel was plainly taken aback. 'It's never been done. Don't they trust us any longer?'

'They don't trust George Healey,' James said. 'They were gathered in the street yesterday. They are opposed to his half-pay scheme, and they're worried the same thing will happen to them.'

'It will not,' Samuel said. 'I give them my word.'

'But you cannot make that promise,' James argued. 'We don't know what will happen in the future.'

'I will never pay my men less than the proper rate,' Samuel avowed.

'And I think you may have to,' James enjoined. 'Word is going round that George Healey is bringing in more people, and is going to build houses for them.'

'But where will he get the money?' asked Grand-mamma. 'The London bankers won't finance this, surely.'

'I have heard that Sir William is behind them. Our local bigwig.'

'But I thought the gentry didn't agree with trade,' said Francis.

'Oh, the gentry like to say they're above trade, but they're all into it,' James snorted. 'Canals, coal pits –

Sir William owns this pit, it's on his land. And he owns most of the shares in the canal. Always ready to make money, the gentry.'

'Aristocrats are beginning to fear the industrialists getting too much wealth and power,' said Samuel. 'Many of these men are Quakers and Methodists – '

'And the Establishment prevents Nonconformists from going to Oxford or Cambridge,' put in James, bitterly.

'So we have built our own schools and colleges, and very good they are,' his father returned, with equanamity. 'We're going to build a university in London that will be far in advance of either Oxford or Cambridge, they have grown very lax over the years. Ours will be very modern, with science subjects. But the aristocrats pretend to look down on industry because they want to keep the power in their own hands.' Samuel frowned, and little Emma, who helped Sarah Jane, came in to light the candles in the silver candlesticks on the mantelpiece and the new Argand lamp on the polished round table. 'We must get men into Parliament who will vote for Nonconformists being allowed to enter the professions,' he ended.

'How can we when Nonconformists are not supposed to be admitted to Parliament?' asked James. 'And the House of Lords would block it.'

Samuel smiled. 'And you wonder why I am a Radical, James. Because I know the fight we've had. And now it seems we'll have to fight Sir William.'

Francis asked through dry lips, 'Sir William who?'

'Why, Sir William Fargate,' answered James. 'He is a scoundrel. His wife left him and has since died, his son's left home, he lives alone and takes any woman he can pick up. In trading matters he is our enemy – '

But Francis could bear to hear no more and escaped to

his room as soon as he could. There, shivering with shock, he took out his mother's letter. With trembling hands he lit the candle and began to read.

My dear son,

I doubt if you will ever see this letter, I fear you are dead, as are so many who were press-ganged in such a cruel fashion. But in case you are alive, I feel you should know the truth. Jean-Pierre is not your father. I will tell you the whole sorry tale.

I am the daughter of a clergyman who had too little income and too many children. The boys had to be educated, the girls too, after a fashion. At the age of eighteen I was sent out as governess to a member of the gentry in Chilverton.

He seemed a charming man – to me, who had met so few men. His wife was dead, and I knew nothing about him, I spoke to no-one; the servants felt I was above them in station, and I fear I felt this too, so I heard no gossip. I fell in love with this man, and I expected, when I allowed him liberties, that we would be married.

Foolish girl that I was, foolish as the silliest young serving maid – sillier, perhaps, for I had higher expectations. When I was with child I told him innocently, and he turned me out cruelly.

I was distraught, I think I went a little mad. I dared not go home, so I ran to London . . . there by chance I bumped into Jean-Pierre, the man you know as your father. He had been a prisoner of war, one of the first, and had escaped from the hulks. He rescued me from God alone knows what fate. We married for our mutual convenience, he for protection, myself for a husband. We went to Plymouth because Jean hoped to get back to France eventually . . . alas, he was re-captured, not dead, as I told you.

The rest you know. Left alone, I was able to start teaching. At least I was a respectable married woman now, and I was able to give you a good start in life.

Forgive me if this hurts you, Francis. The man who wronged me is still alive, no doubt. His name is Sir William Fargate . . .

Francis shivered as though with an ague. He wished his mother had not told him. At least the Frenchman was a decent sort . . .

Now he knew from where he inherited his bad streak. From his father. From the rottenest man in the district. It must be kept secret at all costs.

He was thankful he had not told the Barratts. They must never, never know . . .

Nancy seldom came to the Red House. There was no reason why she should not, Tacy felt that it was simply that the weavers were happy in their own end of town — she had to join them, rather than vice versa. So when the back gate opened and she saw Nancy enter the garden she ran out in pleased surprise. 'Nancy, come in do . . .' She paused at the look on her friend's face. 'What is it? What's wrong?'

'It's about Tom,' Nancy said. 'I thought I ought to come and tell you.'

In the seconds she waited, thoughts shot through Tacy's mind; Tom was ill, he'd had an accident, a runaway horse had knocked him down, he'd been hurt . . .

Nancy said heavily, 'He's getting married.'

Now the thoughts were running wild. She wasn't hearing aright, she couldn't be . . . 'Married?' she echoed stupidly. 'Who to . . .?'

'To Martha.'

She was joking, she had to be. 'Martha?' she gasped. 'Martha? But he's never . . . *Martha! . . .*'

Nancy said unhappily, 'They've got to get married.'

Tacy stared, dumbfounded, all thoughts gone, her mind still, a blank. Up in the oak tree a blackbird called loudly, and it seemed from another world. 'No,' she said. 'Not Martha. Martha wouldn't . . .' Martha couldn't have done the thing that she herself had turned away from, yet had been so near to doing . . . It was a joke.

'It's true,' Nancy said.

'But when did he go out with Martha?' Yet Tacy was remembering Martha's strangeness, her evasiveness, Nancy's too . . .

'It happened at the Fair.'

And now anger came, helping her to survive this shock. 'I suppose Tom was drunk,' she accused.

'Perhaps,' Nancy said. 'But it happened even so. And now Martha's having a baby.'

Martha! Martha the plain, the girl who never went with boys. And Tom, Tom who could have his pick, who might have had her, Tacy . . . He *could* have had her. Then *she* might be having a baby. Tom would be having two babies at the same time, what a joke that would be. The whole town would be laughing.

'He doesn't have to marry her,' she said, and was surprised at the coldness in her voice. 'There are plenty of bastards running around, no one would point a finger at him.'

'Oh yes they would, when it's Martha,' Nancy corrected her. 'When it's Abel Pickard's daughter, who's a good-living girl, you know that, Tacy.'

'And since when did Tom care about what people say?' flashed Tacy.

'He wanted you to know,' Nancy said, unhappily. 'I knew you'd be upset.'

Tacy tossed her head. 'I don't know why you should think that,' she retorted. 'I'm marrying, too.'

'You are?' There was disbelief in Nancy's voice.

'Of course, haven't you guessed? I'm marrying Francis. Francis!' she called, running to the door of the counting-house, seeing James and her father within, unheeding now, uncaring in the desperate attempt to hide her pain. 'Francis, come out. I've just told them our news, that we're getting married.'

Chapter three

Samuel said heavily, 'She is too young to marry.'

The lamplight gave a soft glow to the parlour; outside, the night sky was midnight blue. The longest day had come and gone, the nights would soon be drawing in. Grandmamma wondered how many more winters she would see as she replied, 'She is seventeen, Samuel.'

'She is a child.' He sat, stern and unbending in his favourite chair, but his mother sensed the pain beneath the stiffness, and was sorry for him.

'No, Samuel, she is not a child,' she said, more gently. 'You have treated her so for far too long, I did warn you. Allowing her to run wild with the weavers, what did you expect?'

'What have the weavers got to do with it?' Samuel asked, blinking.

'The weavers are an independent lot where morals are concerned. They treat the marriage bond too lightly. Most of them have to get married, to use their own expression.'

'Yes, and we know why. Because they are not allowed by law to celebrate marriage in their chapels, only in a church. So they try to dispense with the church, as they have in worship.'

'I know all that, Samuel. But do you wish it for Tacy?'

Samuel moved restlessly, rubbing his fingers along the polished table, a habit of his when troubled, as if he somehow gained comfort from the movement. 'A fellow we met such a short time ago,' he mused, wondering at the strange workings of fate. He had invited the young man to stay with them, trusting him, as he always trusted people – too easily, James told him – now he found that he had been courting his daughter . . .

'I confess I wonder at her reason for rushing into this with young Francis,' Grandmamma echoed his thoughts. 'She's hardly known him five minutes, although I did notice that he seems fond of her. But I would have thought an older woman would suit him better.'

'Older? What do you mean by that?'

'He's been hurt, he needs someone old enough to understand; old enough to let him lean on her. Someone experienced in the ways of the world.'

'I would not hear of such a marriage,' Samuel said.

'She seems set on him.'

'As you say,' Samual continued as though she had not spoken. 'We hardly know him, or anything about him. He's not the man I'd have chosen for my son-in-law.'

'Then who would you have chosen, Samuel?'

Silence. The climbing rose tapped upon the window, an owl hooted. 'Who?' Grandmamma pressed.

'When she was older a suitable match could have been found.'

'Such as? How many men are there in the town that you'd consider suitable? The lawyer's son? The banker's? They are church, Samuel, and their wives would have to be church also. Would you prefer that?'

'You know I wouldn't,' said Samuel, irritably.

'So who is left but the weavers?'

Samuel moved heavily, and his mother stood up, went to him, put her hand on his arm, though they were not a demonstrative family. 'I understand how you feel,' she said, and she did. Samuel still saw Tacy as his beloved child; thoughts of marriage were pushed away into the distant future. She said, gently, 'Yet you wouldn't want her to be an old maid, would you, Samuel, never to know the joys of motherhood?'

'Of course not,' he replied testily.

'I'll have a word with her,' Grandmamma said. 'Find out how forward she has been – with the weavers.' The last was in an undertone, and Samuel did not hear. 'And when you speak to Francis, Samuel, mention that Tacy is not your heir,' she added, more loudly.

Samuel did not answer, and Grandmamma went out, closing the door quietly behind her. Even so, a draught was caused, and the lamp flickered, sending shadows round the room. Samuel felt his hopes flicker with it. I've been remiss, he thought, I should have found suitable young men for her to meet. Men like myself, from Coventry or Birmingham, the Cadburys have a son, Mamma knows them . . . Quakers, like all Dissenters, forced into trade because the professions were closed to them. That's what angers James, he couldn't attend the town Grammar school because his parents had to be church; he didn't have the freedom to go to Oxford or Cambridge for the same reason. Strange how James, the forthright, yet might have given way on that if I'd allowed it. You had to be strong to go against the herd . . .

Samuel felt a pain in his chest; he was troubled with indigestion at times like these, though he said nothing, just bought an elixir from the apothecary. But the times were growing more frequent. He thought of Elenor and sighed for the days that were gone.

'Now, miss,' said Grandmamma, the next morning. 'What's all this about you wanting to get married?'

Tacy tugged at the bedcover. She always made her own bed, it had been part of Grandmamma's upbringing, to help Sarah Jane and little Emma as much as possible. Maids were not over plentiful in Chilverton, girls preferring the good pay and freedom of the weaving. So Tacy made her bed and said sulkily, 'I do.'

'Why?' The question came like a pistol shot.

'Because I am in love.'

'Love!' snorted Grandmamma. 'I thought you were in love with Tom Jacques.'

The colour spread over Tacy's face, as she stammered, 'How did you know that?'

'There's not much goes on in Chilverton that I don't know,' said Grandmamma, who had noted Tacy's telltale blushes when Tom Jacques' name was mentioned and drawn her own conclusions. She waited.

A flurry of rain beat against the window panes as Tacy smoothed the bedcover and compressed her lips. 'Tom Jacques is going to marry Martha,' she said.

'Ah.' Grandmamma paused. 'And did he kiss *you*?'

Again the blush. 'Yes.'

'And more than that?'

Tacy remembered the touching and her colour flared again, and again Grandmamma drew her own conclusions. 'He loved me,' she said, defensively. 'He told me he loved me.'

'Yes, men are apt to say that,' said Grandmamma. 'You are – ' she paused, delicately, 'all right?'

'Of course I'm all right,' replied Tacy, puzzled as to just what Grandmamma meant.

Grandmamma pursed her lips and wondered. 'And are you going to be happy with this young fellow you're in love with now?'

'Yes, of course. Francis loves me. He's very pleasant.'

And wounded, thought Grandmamma. She said no more, but went to the kitchen to supervise Sarah Jane prepare the meal. Dinner was eaten at four o'clock, after which the men usually went back to their work, though they stopped for a break and a cold collation at twelve. Samuel was helping James pack the ribbons for despatch to London, but when the lunch break was over, Grand-mamma called him into the small room leading off the hall, from which another door led to the counting-house and warehouse, and was used as a study or office. 'The girl should be married,' she said, without preamble.

'*Should* be – ?'

'Yes,' testily. 'Heavens, Samuel, she's old enough, she's ready for marriage. Leave her running wild and she'll be getting into the same sort of trouble as Martha Pickard.'

'Oh no, not Tacy,' said Samuel.

Men, thought Grandmamma. How little they know. She knew she couldn't tell Samuel that she believed Tacy had been making love with Tom Jacques and that, just in case there was a baby, she should be married. She knew that, had she voiced her suspicions, he would have insisted she stay with them, no matter what. And Tacy would have been the one to suffer, and the child. Laughed at for being spurned by Tom Jacques, spurned for Martha Pickard. Men's principles could be too high. Women had to be devious at times; they learned in a hard school.

'Yes, Tacy,' she replied. 'She's already fancied herself in love with Tom Jacques – '

'Tom Jacques?' Samuel bridled. 'That I would never countenance – ' And Grandmamma wondered if he had suspected Tacy's infatuation; if that was why he was so angry with Tom.

'Then?' she asked.

'It's all so hurried – '

'Not necessarily, Samuel. She can be betrothed for a year or so.' *While we see.* Grandmamma moved towards the door, she knew Samuel had work to do. She was a little uneasy about Francis, he was quiet, yes . . . too quiet . . . ? She shrugged off her misgivings. No doubt it would be as good a match as any; she did not believe too much in love as a basis for marriage. Nor did she have much sympathy for Tacy, whom she thought spoilt and wilful. James had always been her favourite. It was James who mattered, after all, he who would inherit the business, not Tacy.

'I'll talk to them,' said Samuel.

'And don't forget to remind Francis that Tacy will not have money of her own,' warned Grandmamma. 'Just in case he has ambitions in that field.'

She went upstairs to her own room, sighing. These family problems tired her these days.

Tacy's eyes had followed every movement of her father since she made the announcement yesterday. She said little, avoiding being alone with Francis, while she awaited the summons that she knew would soon come. She did not wish to displease her father, but she was determined to marry Francis. From thinking, a few weeks ago, that Martha did not know about her feelings for Tom, her thoughts, after the declaration, swung in the opposite direction; now she felt the whole town must know she loved him and was laughing because he had to marry Martha. At all costs she must prove that she was not in love with Tom; marrying Francis would stop all rumours. Further than that she did not think.

The summons came the minute dinner was over, but it was Francis Samuel called to the office, not Tacy. And once in the small room he did not sit, nor ask Francis to do so, but said, 'You decided on marriage without the courtesy of telling me.'

Francis was embarrassed, as he had been since Tacy's

declaration. He could hardly say he hadn't asked Tacy to marry him and risk upsetting her when he did want to marry her. But he appeared to have been acting behind Samuel's back, and this he objected to.

He said, trying to find a way to explain, 'Sir, I do love Tacy, and would dearly like to marry her in the future. But I did not dare ask, I felt I was not good enough.'

'Why not?' snapped Samuel. 'Are your parents so low born?'

'Indeed, no,' replied Francis. 'I told you my mother was a governess.'

'Yes, from hereabouts. Then what is her name? Who was she?'

'Her name was Florence Brooks. Her father was the Vicar of Meddlestone, a small living. But she was forced to leave home – '

'I see,' said Samuel, as he paused. 'Left home to marry, you mean? Because her father did not approve?'

'Something like that.'

Samuel grunted, thinking he understood. The girl had become besotted with some Frenchman and her father had objected. 'You have never been in touch with her family?' he asked.

'I tried to find them, but the Vicar is dead.'

Samuel grunted again. He did not dislike Francis. 'How old are you?'

'Twenty-one.'

'And your religion? You have not been to church or chapel since you came here.'

'I was brought up church like my mother,' said Francis. 'But I fear that when in the Navy I let it all go. But I'm willing to attend chapel with Tacy.'

It was still raining, the wind was rising, and they could hear above it the clip-clop of a horse and rumble of a heavy cart. Samuel waited till the noise died away.

Francis, thinking he was about to be turned down, put in, 'I will try to make her a good husband.'

Samuel, remembering Grandmamma's warning, and wishing to make sure he was not marrying her for her money, said, 'She will have no money. You will have to support her.'

'I have nothing, you know that, except for my earnings,' Francis said. 'But I can save and work hard. It is all I ask.'

'And where do you plan to live?'

'I don't know,' replied Francis, unhappily. 'I admit I had not planned on marrying just yet.'

This speech sent the young man higher in Samuel's estimation. He said, 'Leave me now. I'll have to think it over.'

Francis went straight to his room where he walked to the window and watched the rain streaming down, flooding the ditch in the middle of the road. He felt that his life was at a turning point. If Samuel agreed, he and Tacy would be married, his dreams would come true. It was a dream that Tacy should love him – Tacy was a good girl, like his mother had been, the dearest mother a boy could wish for.

He thought over his early life, being taught by his mother, staying in home with her in the evenings, never going out with other boys, never wanting anything else.

Not until . . . Now he allowed himself to remember the thing he preferred to forget, the night he'd overheard men laughing about the street down by the quay where *those women* lived. And he'd gone down one night, impelled by a curiosity he could not control, even though he despised himself for being interested in *those women*. But the men had been explicit – 'an' she had no clo'es on'. He tried to eliminate the thoughts, but they would keep coming till he had to go down just to see . . . he would never go with *those women*, of course, they were bad women, he only wanted to stay with his mother.

He had crept quietly down to the little street near the quay. A girl was standing outside one of the mean huddle of houses wearing a skimpy frock that you could see right through, see the swell of her breasts as the material clung to it, see the outline of her legs right to the top, and he'd caught his breath, leaning forward . . .

And then the hand on his arm. 'In the name of the King!' The Press-gang.

He blamed himself bitterly when he woke on the ship. He had been bad, his mother would tell him so. And he was being punished . . .

Yet when the harlots came on board and one took him he felt a strange thrill, and didn't object the next time . . .

But now he *could* forget. All of it. Now he had Tacy, who loved him, who was a good woman. Tacy would make his shattered life whole again. He could even forget that bad man, his father . . .

Francis had to wait two days for Samuel's verdict. He waited while Samuel talked to Tacy and guessed how she would insist on marrying him because she loved him. Then Samuel made his decision known.

'The marriage will have to wait,' he pronounced. 'We hardly know you. You can be betrothed in the meantime while I make enquiries and we'll think more about it. But if the marriage takes place then you can live here with us until you find a house of your own.'

Tacy was overjoyed, Grandmamma smiled frostily. Only James raised a dissenting voice. 'There's trouble coming,' he said. 'What use will Francis be, who knows nothing of silk?'

'You prefer Tom Jacques?' asked Grandmamma, acidly.

'I would. He has the right ideas about silk.'

Grandmamma wondered what Abel Pickard thought about it.

Martha Pickard had been born to the clack-clack of the loom, she grew up with silk. In the evenings, when his work was done, Abel would take her on his knee and tell her the old legends of how a Chinese princess married a prince of Khotan and took silkworm eggs with her, hidden in her headdress. 'That's where silk originated, China,' Abel explained. 'They were weaving silk there thousands of years ago. But they kept the secret of it, and disclosure meant death. Till this princess spread it.'

Martha attended a small Dame school and learned to read from the old Bible, but she learned history from Abel's book on silk. 'The old trade route from China to the West went from Kashgar, merchants from all over Asia would meet at Kashgar bazaar,' she read. 'Caravans came there from the east, the road south is the oldest trade route, older than all history. On this road, across mountains and deserts, the people of the Tigris and Euphrates, Mediterranean countries and the Nile, were in contact with the people living around the Yellow River long before our written history had begun. The route was given the name we now know it. The Silk Road.'

And Martha learned geography from the chart of the old Silk Road, and she'd murmur the names to herself. Peking, Rome, Lyon, London . . . and Chilverton. She'd see the lonely road, the camel caravans travelling over deserts and mountains with their precious loads to end here, in her father's cottage, to be made into things of beauty. She was entranced, drunk with its magic. And even when Abel explained that East Indiamen with billowing sails brought silk now from the ports; to her the Silk Road always meant lonely camel caravans in the desert, Chinese princesses and a trade as old as time.

Martha seldom talked about her innermost thoughts and dreams, and Tacy made the common mistake that because a person is quiet she has little feeling. Martha was quiet because she preferred to be; she did not waste time in idle chat or girlish giggles about lads, but she noticed them all the same. Anyone looking into her eyes would have seen a turbulence that spoke of passion. Tom Jacques looked, was intrigued, and looked again.

Martha had been in love with Tom Jacques as long as she could remember. She knew he was wild, he and his brothers were known for their carousing at the Weavers' Arms, while his father was said to work better drunk than sober. Tom had many girls, but he was also a silkman. Like her father, he had the delicacy of touch necessary for the weaving of silk, he understood the magic and the memories of the Silk Road as she did. Loving him was as natural as breathing. She knew he'd been hanging around Tacy, and was jealous.

When she went to the Fair with Nancy she had no idea what would happen. She wore her sprigged muslin, her best bonnet with the blue ribbons, and her new shoes, for when her dad had a good week she had it good too. A woman weaver received seventy-five per cent of the male's earnings, and though she was not a weaver, Abel paid her this rate for doing the picking up, weaving the pirns, and taking a turn at the loom.

In the fairground there was the smell of damp grass and sawdust, and another, deeper smell, of animals, which added the extra dimension to the Fair, that of strangeness tinged with fear, of another world encroaching on their small town and its homely ways. Past a small roundabout, driven by a donkey, a jugglers' booth, a stall holding odds and ends, toffee-apples, gingerbread, coloured ribbons . . .

The barrel-organ was playing 'Oh dear what can the matter be, Johnny's so long at the Fair'. And behind them a voice began to sing, 'He promised to buy me a bunch of blue ribbons, to tie up my bonny brown hair' . . . Tom.

'Would you like a fairing?' he'd asked. He'd tossed the woman a coin, unfastened one of the bunches of ribbons and gave it to her. And she'd pinned the fairing to her frock, and he'd stayed with them. And before long Fred Pettit joined them, too, talking to Nancy.

More revellers poured in: girls with ribbons and flowers in their hair, boys with sprigs of May blossom in their buttonholes. They laughed, sang and shouted. Someone tried to climb a greasy pole and failed. The barrel-organ puffed out its melody.

So they walked and laughed and sang. And when it grew darker Tom pulled Martha away from Nancy and Fred towards the trees at the side.

She knew full well what he was doing and what he wanted. The sky was darkening. Naphtha flares were lit around the booths, making the Fair a many-splendoured thing. And he kissed her and drew her down to the ground. And the stars came out as he made love to her and she responded till the stars whirled around in glory and fulfilment.

She didn't mind that she was having a baby, she would marry Tom and that was what she wanted. Her only worry was what her father would say, or rather feel. He wouldn't be angry, that was not his way, but he would be pained. And he was.

'I hadn't thought my only daughter would get married this way,' he said.

'I'm sorry, Father, but it's always been Tom for me.'

'But has it been you for Tom?' asked Abel. 'And I would have thought better of him if he'd come and told me himself.'

'He is coming round, Father, tonight.'

The whole town was gossiping about Tom's forthcoming marriage. Who'd have thought it? they asked. Martha Pickard, her so quiet and plain. A good girl, an' all. Well, Tom Jacques was doing the decent thing. And here everyone thought he was after young Tacy Barratt, it was well known she'd been making eyes at him and he'd been seen walking with her over the fields. You'd have thought he'd have gone for her, wouldn't you, he was ambitious, that one. But o' course, Samuel Barratt had upset him over that half-pay business. And Tom didn't like it. They were like that, those Jacques. Wild and given to roguery when they were in the mood for it – didn't one on 'em go off to Americy after he'd been caught poaching or summat? – yet should somethin' upset them they'd make a stand and you couldn't move 'em. And young Tom was the same. He was ambitious, but he was proud. He wouldn't crawl.

Tom didn't tell anyone just how he felt. He knew that Martha was a decent girl, but he had been surprised at her passion, surprised and pleased.

'You're a fool to be ruled by what's in your trousers,' his father told him, while more girls than Tacy wept at the news.

But he faced Abel with equanimity. He was doing his duty, he couldn't do more. And Abel was a careful man with money.

'Where will you live?' Abel asked practically. Then, as Tom hesitated, 'Best thing is for you to live here. You could go to your home and work your loom, then come back. We have two bedrooms.'

So the marriages were decided.

Martha was getting married on the first Saturday in

August. Tacy and Francis had invitations to the wedding, and this caused quite a furore. First Tacy said she would not go, then, realising everyone would suspect the reason, decided that she would not attend the church, but go to the wedding breakfast and for this she would need a new frock. And for a new frock she must go to someone good, in Coventry or even Birmingham.

Grandmamma said no. How could she travel for fittings every other day, and what was wrong with Mrs Bradley of Chilverton? Tacy pouted, stormed a little, Grandmamma was firm, and in the end even Samuel lost patience and said it was Mrs Bradley or no one.

So Tacy went to Mrs Bradley's establishment in the Market Square and refused to say what the dress would be like. She hinted at blue with white trimmings, and warned that it would be expensive. Grandmamma snorted that Samuel indulged her far too much, and James said she was a spoilt brat.

But Tacy told no one of the nights of weeping when she sat by her open window and breathed in the scent of the roses; the gay yellow tea-roses, the pink moss-roses, Old Blush from China, and the red damask that had been cultivated by the Romans of the Imperial Caesars. Uncle Abel had taught her about roses and she'd always thought she'd carry a bouquet of the finest ones at her wedding to Tom. Now Martha would be carrying them, and the perfume nearly broke her heart.

It had been a good summer on the whole and August was no exception. The wedding was to be at twelve o'clock, and half an hour beforehand Tacy went to her room to begin dressing. At one o'clock she was still there, the family ate lunch without her and retired to the parlour to wait. At half past one Grandmamma tapped on her door, and James shouted, 'Are you still alive?'

'I'm coming,' she called.

They went back to the parlour and sat. James impatiently, Grandmamma drumming her fingers on the chair. Samuel returned to the office. The bedroom door opened, they heard footsteps on the stairs, then she was framed in the doorway and they all gasped.

Her dress was all white, silk, with a high waist and low neck. The hat was big brimmed, with a wide blue ribbon tying under the chin, bending it into a bonnet shape. She looked like a bride.

Grandmamma said, 'That's a mite dressy for a weaver's wedding, Tacy.'

Tacy tossed her head defiantly.

'Trying to outshine the bride?' asked James. He turned to Francis. 'Well, don't just stand there, tell her what you think of it.'

'I – well, it's her choice,' said Francis.

'Pah!' snorted James.

Tacy held out her hand imperiously, her cheeks dangerously red. Francis put her hand on his arm and they walked to the door.

They drove to the Pickards' house, where already sounds of merriment could be heard. The chaise was left, and Tacy, followed by Francis, went to the wide-open back door.

The kitchen was crowded, people stood outside in the yard, and as Tacy walked round there was a sudden hush. Everyone looked up, and a little ripple went round the room. She stopped in the doorway, face flushing, then Martha stepped forward. 'Come in, Tacy,' she said, and Tacy tossed her head and entered.

Martha wore pale grey, loose fitting, and camouflaged with many ribbons, though it was still obvious that she was pregnant. It was a serviceable dress, one to be worn on many occasions, and Martha, as always, looked plain and dowdy. The house was decorated for the wedding, and on the table was the spread, bread and cold meats, pork and chicken, presided over by Mrs Walters. There was no ale, for Abel was against drink but, with the flexibility of the weaving dissenters, he allowed home-made wine, far more potent than ale, and many would be tipsy before the night was out.

Tom was talking to a group of men, and he was as handsome as ever. He stared at Tacy and nodded, and though he did not leave the men, his eyes swivelled towards her again and again.

She felt a glass pushed into her hand and, self-conscious now of her finery and all the staring eyes, she drained it and asked for another. 'It's elderberry wine,' Mrs Walters warned her. 'Bin' in the cellar for a year, strong as can be.'

Tacy started the second glass and felt her face grow hot. She felt embarrassed and lonely among all these people she knew so well; they began singing and she wanted to escape but didn't know how. She looked for Francis, he too was standing alone beside a group of weavers near the front room, he would be no help. She saw Mr Redmond, the minister, sitting next to Abel, and thought he looked sad. Perhaps he too was lonely. Her own heartache made her more perceptive of others, previously she would never have noticed. The minister nodded to her gravely, and she nodded too, then turned away from his penetrating eyes. But the wine was beginning to work, her courage had returned; she no longer wanted to leave.

Bob Pettit was playing his fiddle. When someone asked, 'Who'll sing solo?' she said, 'I will.'

And they stood her on a chair and she sang, 'Drink to me Only with Thine Eyes' and everyone went quiet. And she called, 'Drink, drink, all of you – ' and then

Francis was beside her, lifting her down, saying, 'Hush now, Tacy. Shall we go?'

'No, of course we won't go,' she cried, loudly. 'We're here to enjoy ourselves. It's a wedding – ' she gave a hiccup. It didn't matter, she wasn't the only one getting tipsy . . . She lost Francis again and didn't mind.

It was getting dark now and Abel lit candles. She suddenly felt weary. The noise made her head ache, she felt faintly sick and desperately wanted a breath of fresh air. She managed to get to her feet and walked outside, through the crowded doorway, into the cool of the garden where the old apple tree stood, and she rested her hand on its friendly trunk.

Then she saw another figure standing before her. Tom.

'T–Tom,' she said. 'I – I didn't know you were here.'

'I was waiting for you,' he answered.

Her head was spinning, the wine had loosened her tongue, she knew she shouldn't speak, but she knew too that he was here before her, Tom, her love . . .

'Why?' she asked. 'Why did you marry her?'

'You know why.'

'Couldn't you have waited for me? I thought you loved me.'

He looked at her in the gathering dusk, her hair tumbling around her face, flushed, disordered, but lovely. 'I do,' he said.

He put out one hand, caught her arm, then he was clasping her to him, his lips were on hers.

'Who's this?' someone said near. 'Who's here?'

And she turned, picking up her skirts, running back to the house. She was gasping. 'Francis,' she called. 'We must go. Where is my bonnet?'

People were staring at her, her hair, her dishevelled appearance. Seeing Tom in the background.

And then she fled.

In October the Allied armies defeated Napoleon at
Leipzig. 'It's all over now, thank God,' said Samuel.

And indeed it did seem so. As Christmas approached
the weavers began to trickle home. Faces Tacy had not
seen for years; Matt Walters, Jim Bailey, Harry Pettit, all
back to find their work practices changed, for these men
did not own their own looms as Abel and the Jacques did,
they were not 'first-hands', they were journeymen
weavers, working on George Healey's looms – or they
had been. Now they were not wanted, and they trooped
up to see Samuel.

He was in the warehouse with James when the men
tramped into the yard. 'Hey, Mester,' called Harry
Pettit, the spokesman. 'What the hell is happening?'

Samuel and James and Francis all went into the yard.
Tacy came out of the house to listen, throwing a shawl
round her shoulders.

'Where's our undertaker? We've bin to see George
Healey and he tells us he don't do it no more.'

'That's right, he works on his own account now, and
not for me,' replied Samuel.

'But we worked for him, in his loom-shop. They was
his looms . . . What do we do now?'

'What did he tell you?' asked Samuel.

'Why, he tells us he's on'y tekking half-pay apprentices, whatever they may be.'

'He'll have to stop it now,' said Samuel.

'Did he tell you he'd stop it?' James asked the men.

'No. He told us we could work for him at the same
price. What's he mean? We ain't apprentices, we served
our seven years, we had full rates before the war. What's
goin' on, Mester? We go to fight for King and Country
and come back to all this.'

A few spots of rain began to fall, and there was a low mutter from the men. Samuel held up his hand. 'Don't worry, you'll be all right,' he told them. 'I'm your employer, as always, and I am responsible for you. James is your undertaker now.'

'But where's our looms?'

'I'll have to buy more,' said Samuel.

'An' where'll you put 'em?'

'Where indeed?' muttered James.

'Hush, James,' said Samuel. 'I am responsible for these men, and I shall see they are all right.' He faced the men. 'Give me time to find premises and I promise you you'll have work as always.'

The crowd dispersed, their faces clearing. 'Aye,' said one. 'Mester Barratt allis sees us right, he were allis a good mester.'

Samuel stood in the yard, deep in thought, the rain falling in little droplets on his uncovered head. 'Come inside, Father,' James said, and they walked back to the warehouse.

Inside, James stopped. 'We can't do it,' he stated.

'We must do it.'

'Father, it will cost enough buying looms without buying more premises.'

'I can rent a place.'

'But all the time George Healey is undercutting us.'

Samuel brushed the rain from his shoulders. 'He'll have to stop.'

James turned impatiently. 'How? And supposing the work doesn't keep up? Suppose they bring in steam power . . .'

'The weavers would never stand for that. James, you look for trouble. We have more orders than we can carry out, we need more looms.'

'But will George Healey expand too? And him under-cutting us?'

'I think,' Samuel said, 'we had better go and see George Healey.'

They set off the next morning. The rain had turned to sleet, there was a bitter wind blowing. Smoke curled up from chimneys, candles flickered inside the houses. 'The dull dark days before Christmas,' said Samuel.

They walked past George Healey's new house. 'At least he's not brought looms here,' James commented.

Down to the edge of the Patch, where the loomshop stood, a long, squat building with several windows and double doors at one end. They could hear the clack–clack of the looms as they reached the door, and James pushed it open. 'Can't wait outside,' he muttered.

The looms filled the room, the nearest only feet away from them, and a pallid, undersized youth of about sixteen was throwing the shuttle. 'Hey!' James called. 'Where's your master?'

'Don't know,' said the boy.

Samuel took a step forward. 'You're not local boys are you?' he asked.

The youth didn't look up. 'Nay,' he said.

'Then where do you live?'

'We sleep here, on the floor.'

'Good God!' exploded James. 'It must be freezing now – '

'Well, if they don't like it, they know what they can do,' said a voice, and they swung round. George Healey stood behind them. 'And what are you doing here, may I ask?'

'We have come,' said Samuel, taking off his silk hat, 'to ask how long you are going to keep on with this half-pay business.'

'That's none of your affair,' retorted George Healey, his eyes glittering in the gloom. 'But since you ask, that's the new system. I buy the silk, I don't need no undertaker, I put my weavers to work, then I sell the ribbons.'

'Your weavers,' scoffed James. 'They're not weavers.'

'They're learning,' said George Healey. 'And if they don't, there's plenty more where they came from. Paupers.'

'Their eyesight won't last long in this poor light,' James said. 'What's happened to the candles? And if they sleep here all through the winter they'll be dead by spring.'

'Have you no thought for your own weavers who've been in the Army?' asked Samuel. 'They are honest men, they have rights as men.'

'They've had it their way too long. Now they take what I offer.'

'But they've served their time. Seven years. You can't ask them to work for half pay.'

'I don't ask them to do anything. They take it or leave it.'

'While you make a fortune,' snapped James.

'Well, I ain't a Quaker, only letting hisself have five per cent profit. I work for money.'

'Nothing like this has ever been done before,' said Samuel.

'Then it's time it started, and it's started now. And it'll continue, you mark my words. This way I make the money, and if you've got any sense you'll do the same, or be put out of business.'

'I have never put money first,' said Samuel. 'We all worked together.'

'No, but you've had plenty of money, ain't you?' sneered George. 'You was all right.'

'I will never see my workmen lose their rightful payments.'

'Then you'll see 'em starve.'

'Come, Father,' said James. 'We're wasting our time here. The man's a cheapjack as Tacy said.'

They walked home almost in silence. In the hall, they took off hats and overcoats and little Emma came to ask if they needed refreshments, or a warm drink, but they waved her away.

In the parlour James said, 'It's no use, Father, we'll have to change.'

'Never.'

'Then – '

'You called the man a cheapjack. And you want me to be the same?'

'Yes, because if the world is run by cheapjacks then we have to join or go under. I can see that, Father, George Healey can see it. How long will it be before dozens of other little masters join in with their pauper apprentices?'

'I will never join them.'

It was their most bitter argument, and it continued all evening after work. Tacy sided with her father, Grandmamma did too, but Francis, when he and Tacy were saying goodnight in the hall, voiced his doubts.

'What if work doesn't keep up, Tacy? Your father will have to spend an awful lot of money. And I heard a whisper that ladies were getting tired of the purl ribbons.'

Tacy laughed. 'Oh, Francis. Are you taking an interest in fashion now? Papa knows best. Come, kiss me goodnight.'

Tacy wanted to get married. Not merely to show the town that she didn't care for Tom Jacques, but to show herself, and to stop herself from running down to Tom begging him to take her in his arms again.

But Samuel refused to hurry, he had to know just who

this young Francis was. He visited Plymouth and spoke to the businessman who had employed him, and was told that he was a good, conscientious worker, and his mother had been an educated, genteel lady. As Francis had said there was no trace of the family of the former Vicar of Meddlestone, so Samuel had to be content. He agreed that the marriage could take place in the spring. 'Early spring,' said Tacy, and March was decided.

Tacy said she didn't want any bridesmaids, but was overruled. 'One of your friends, of course,' said Grand-mamma. 'Martha cannot be so now, but Nancy . . .'

So Tacy went to see Nancy in the evening when she knew Tom would be at the Pickards', she had heard all about their living arrangements. The Jacques' kitchen was full, so Tacy took Nancy outside into the garden.

'Bridesmaid, yes, of course,' said Nancy. 'You're going to marry him then?'

'You know I am.'

'But you don't love him.' It was a statement. Tacy almost confided in Nancy then, telling her how lost she felt, how desolate, but Nancy had her own confidences to impart. 'I'm getting married as well.'

'Nancy. You are? When?'

'In three months. We're leaving Chilverton. Going to Coventry on the watchmaking, Fred's uncle's there. Fred says hand-loom weaving's finished.'

'Course it's not finished, Nancy. You do talk silly.'

'That's what Fred says,' Nancy repeated, obstinately.

'I shall miss you, Nancy,' Tacy said, desolately. She seemed to be losing all her friends, Nancy, Martha, Tom . . . She wanted to talk about Tom again, she wanted to talk about him all the time, but better not. Not to Nancy. Nancy was too knowing. She could think of no excuse to talk about him, so she went home.

But that night, as she stood with Francis in the garden,

he kissed her, and it was not the same as Tom's kissing. Frustrated, not understanding why, she pressed her body to his, only to have him draw away. 'No, Tacy!' he said.

He was surprised and a little shocked. He had had no dealings with nice girls. 'We must wait till we are married,' he said, primly.

'Why?' Tacy asked, sulkily. 'No one else does. Look at Martha.'

'But you can't want to be made with child?' he asked, shocked again, and she did not say she would welcome it, to show Tom Jacques how little she cared for him.

But Francis was not to be swayed. He knew that Samuel was disapproving, and was determined not to blot his copybook in any way. Moreover, there was the little matter of his parenthood, and his guilty secret. He wondered if he should marry at all. He had bad blood. Maybe it would be passed on to his sons. In the meantime he attended chapel as he had promised Samuel, and was surprised at the pleasant atmosphere and the rousing hymns. If Methodism was born in song, as was said, then Chilverton's Independent chapel on the hill carried on the tradition; with no prayer books as yet, the congregation sang.

Religion had meant little to Francis. The church he'd attended as a boy had been grey and dreary, with an elderly, scholarly vicar who mumbled learned sermons way above the heads of his flock. Now he tried to find solace for his troubles in the little chapel, but when they sang 'Guide me oh Thou great Jehovah' rousingly, he felt outside the communal exhilaration, and even the quieter 'O worship the Lord in the beauty of holiness' didn't move him. He wished it would.

Grandmamma kept a sharp eye on the couple; walks over the fields were not allowed, there was nothing but the sheltering tree in the garden, for which Francis was thankful. Tacy was *good*, she must stay that way.

Tacy was lonely. Samuel went to London on business, but this time did not take her. She no longer ran to the weavers to see Nancy and Martha, so was at a loose end. She wished she were a weaver too. Grandmamma had already taught her the rudiments of housekeeping, now she tried to teach her erring granddaughter sewing and embroidery. But Tacy, the wilful, disliked embroidery.

'It is a lady's occupation,' said Grandmamma severely.

'But I don't want to be a lady,' said Tacy disconsolately.

'Then what do you want, miss?'

'I want to be married.' And she spent more time in the counting-house, with Francis.

Martha's baby – a boy – was born on the last day of February. Tacy said she couldn't visit, she was too busy preparing for her wedding. But Grandmamma gave her an old-fashioned look, so Tacy shrugged and amended that she supposed she'd have to go.

She entered the Pickards' kitchen. Abel stood by the door, pleased and proud, but there was no sign of Tom, for which she was thankful.

'Come upstairs,' invited Abel, and she followed him up the narrow winding stairs into the front bedroom where Martha lay on the big bed, and in her arms, the baby.

He was the image of Tom, his tiny face was Tom's in miniature, and Tacy knew a sudden, overpowering envy which she tried to hide. 'What are you going to call him?' she asked coolly.

'Martin Abel,' answered Martha. 'After his two grandfathers.'

Tacy looked at Martha. She was still plain, but somehow you didn't notice the plainness when you knew her well. Or perhaps it was the look on her face that changed her. A look of serenity, of tranquil fulfilment, pronouncing that motherhood was all that Martha desired. Tacy stared at the baby that had effected this look, that had been the cause of Tom having to marry Martha, and was racked that the baby wasn't hers and Tom's. It should have been. This baby was the reason for Tom's marriage, and now she felt only dislike for the child, a feeling that was to stay with her for many years.

'It's my wedding next week,' she said.

'I know.' Martha's gaze was direct. 'And I shan't be able to come.' *You knew*, her eyes said. *You arranged it this way*. And Tacy tossed her head and murmured that she'd have to go. She was glad to go . . .

She was having another dress made by Mrs Bradley, though Grandmamma noted she took less interest in this one than the one she'd had made for Martha's wedding. She had said she wanted a lavish celebration, so Samuel invited a number of his friends from Coventry and Birmingham, as well as many of the weavers.

It was a fine early spring day. She entered church on the arm of her father. She looked round bemused at the people, seemed almost in a daze. She had to be prompted to make the responses, and almost stumbled as she turned to go.

Then finally, the triumphant walk down the aisle, out into the blazing sunshine. Outside stood a crowd of weavers, nodding, smiling, wishing her well. She walked on, arm in arm with Francis towards the waiting carriage. And – down by the lychgate, Tom stood alone. And now his eyes were sullen, watching her step into the carriage, and he didn't move as she drove away.

The house was full of guests, and Tacy moved through them all in a dream, hardly seeing most of them. And when they had gone she and Francis moved to the bedroom overlooking the garden.

There was no such thing as a dressing-room, and she felt Francis' eyes on her as she undressed. Then, instead of looking at him, she went to the window. A waning moon was streaked with clouds and she watched it dully, wishing Francis had simply taken her quickly.

'Tacy,' he said, and she climbed into bed. 'Are you shy?' he asked, kissing her, and she wanted to turn away from the encircling arms, to run away, never come back . . .

He was gentle with her. He seemed almost awed, for she was hardly aroused. She made no move to return his embraces and he accepted this without comment.

But long after he slept she lay awake, thinking. So this was what it was all about. For the rest of her life she would be Mrs Francis Barratt. And she loved Tom.

Now she realised what she had done.

Chapter four

In April, 1814, the Allied armies entered Paris, and Napoleon abdicated. King Louis XVIII returned from exile.

There were rejoicings everywhere, and Chilverton planned to celebrate Peace with a grand procession of the different Friendly Societies carrying their flags and streamers and wearing their cockades and sashes. One lady would be dressed as Britannia, seated in a gig drawn by two grey horses, with four of the Yeomanry following. The people would be given roast beef, plum pudding and ale, and there'd be dancing in the streets.

Tacy listened eagerly to the talk of the celebrations, remembering processions of the past when she, Nancy and Martha, had joined in the fun. No more. As a married woman she could no longer run down to the weavers, yet she had no house to manage, Grandmamma and Sarah Jane saw to that. Marriage to Francis was little different from their betrothal, they slept in the same bed, that was all. For if she, in a moment of petulance, decided she did not want his love-making, he simply turned away, seeming grateful for any crumbs that were thrown from her table – or bed.

And when, after breakfast one morning in May, Samuel said, 'It seems the Czar of Russia will be coming to London, that will mean more processions and balls. It will be good for trade,' she wished she could be there. So, when James went to the warehouse, she followed him.

'James,' she began. 'These London processions. The

royal family will be part of them, won't they?'

James shrugged. 'How do I know? The old king won't be there, he's locked away, poor old man. Mad as a hatter.'

'But the royal dukes?'

'I tell you I don't know. Why?'

'Well, a year ago, Nancy Jacques found one of those pamphlets belonging to her brother; lampoons, don't they call them?'

'Scurrilous satires,' supplied James.

'Yes. Published about the royal family. It said that the Duke of Kent was detested for his brutality in the Navy, and the Duke of York was disgraced when they found out his mistress had made a profit out of selling military commissions. And the Duke of Cumberland – ' she broke off.

'Yes?' asked James, impatiently.

Tacy remembered how she and Nancy had giggled over the lampoon. Now they'd read that the Duke of Cumberland was an incestuous pervert, and though they knew what incest was, they could not understand the rest of it.

'Come on,' said James. 'I don't have all day.'

'Oh, it's nothing.' No, she could not ask him, and oddly, it never occurred to her to ask Francis. But the thought of seeing those royal reprobates was exciting, and she longed to go.

The following morning, as, breakfast over, they stood in the hall, the men ready for their work, Samuel announced that he would be going to London shortly. Tacy opened the door of the parlour and hesitated. The room was clean and bright, with the early morning look of freshness and the sweet smell of beeswax polish from the round table. The sun did not reach the parlour until the afternoon, and little Emma had already lit the fire.

Tacy thought of London and said cajolingly, 'Let me come with you, Papa. I always used to.'

'But you are married now, Tacy,' Samuel pointed out, and Tacy sighed. What in heaven's name did that matter?

'London stinks to high heaven in summer,' put in James.

Tacy said cunningly, 'Why cannot Francis and I go instead of you? I know all about your retailers and agents, and Francis needs to learn about them.' And, she thought, we might see some of the processions, that she knew her father would not want to see.

James guessed her plan. 'You want to see Prinny,' he teased.

'I hope not,' Samuel said. 'The man's behaviour has scandalised the whole world.'

'And so many lampoons written about him,' James went on, looking innocently at Tacy. 'Charles Lamb called him the Prince of Whales, Leigh Hunt's been put in jail for his writings – '

'People feel sorry for his wife, Princess Caroline,' Tacy put in hurriedly, before James could say more. 'We do here in Chilverton.'

'I don't know why,' James said. 'They say she dresses dowdily, and washes so little that the Prince finds her presence distasteful.'

'James!' warned Samuel.

'Well, soap isn't cheap and anyway, they say the old Duke of Norfolk's servants could wash him only when he was drunk,' said Tacy. She would have liked to add that she'd heard that the Prince too was drunk on his wedding night, though the marriage was consummated, for nine months later the Princess Charlotte was born, but she knew her father would not approve. So she ended, 'The Prince wants to divorce her.'

'Well, he has Lady Jersey and Mrs Fitzherbert,' said

James. 'And Caroline has her own establishment where she holds rowdy parties, and they say she has a son by another man –'

'That will do, James,' Samuel said.

'Yes, be quiet, James,' Tacy put in. 'Or Papa won't let me go to London, and I do so want to.'

Samuel thought about it. And because he was busy, ordering more looms and looking for a place to house them, he agreed. They could go in his place, and if he realised that Tacy chose to go when the Czar would be there he said nothing.

Tacy prepared for the day with care. She had recently had a new dress made by Mrs Bradley, of striped silk in blue with a matching pelisse of white muslin lined with blue. She wished she dare leave off her petticoat as some ladies did in London, but she knew Samuel, and no doubt Francis too, would disapprove. Tom wouldn't object she was sure. But then Francis had none of Tom's liveliness or gaity, he seldom laughed, and she loved laughter. Perhaps she'd be able to cheer him up on the trip, impart some of her own sense of fun . . .

They caught the early morning coach which would get them in London before nightfall, Tacy looking elegant, Francis smart enough in the new dark blue frock coat he'd bought for their wedding. In London they took a cab to the quiet respectable guest-house where Samuel always stayed, and Tacy's heart lifted as she saw the crowds thronging the streets; the route to St James's Palace was filled with coaches and carts; wooden stands had been erected on street corners.

'I wonder how the people will greet the Prince,' she mused. 'I've never even seen him.'

They entered the square lobby of the guest-house with its potted plants and handsome time-piece, to be greeted by Mrs Robinson, the owner, and shown to their somewhat plain room by one of the little maids. They ate in the dining-room, then went to bed. 'We have a busy day tomorrow,' said Tacy. 'And I do want to get a glimpse of the Prince – and the Czar maybe.'

But as they went down to breakfast she stopped, amazed, at the sight of the figure standing in the lobby.

'Tom!' she gasped. 'What are you doing here?'

'I came on business, same as you –' and, as Francis joined them, added, 'To see the new Jacquard looms at Spitalfields.'

'But how did you know we were here?'

'You always stayed here with your father, you told me. I'm staying at an inn not far away. I thought I'd come to see you.'

Tacy looked at him, saw the old devil-may-care glint in his eyes and said hurriedly, 'Francis, I've forgotten my gloves. Would you mind fetching them for me?'

When he'd run up the stairs she hissed, 'Tom Jacques! You have no business in London or anywhere but Chilverton. What are you playing at?'

'I came for a holiday,' he said innocently. 'I came down yesterday on a fly-boat, on the canal.'

'Fly-boats are not supposed to take passengers.'

'Oh dear.' He grinned again. 'The men on the boat had got hold of some tickets and I relieved them of three – we had a little game of cards.' And then as Francis' step was heard, he resumed his innocent look. 'I have three tickets for the Haymarket tonight to see the opera,' he said as Francis returned. 'I wondered if you would like to join me? The Prince and the Czar will be there.'

'The opera?' She knew Tom had no interest in the Czar. He was too much of a Radical for that. And the theatre . . . ?

She had never been to a theatre. Not many respectable people did go to the London theatre, or even walk about after dark. Yet now the new gas lamps were replacing the old oil ones it was said the City of Sin would be safer. But theatres were still considered disreputable, and the usual programmes were just a mishmash of bits of plays, farce and vocalists, while operatic evenings consisted of extracts from various operas. Distinguished courtesans occupied front line boxes at Covent Garden and the streets themselves were full of prostitutes. Tacy knew none of this, she only knew her father would not have approved, and this gave it added spice.

'We'd love to go,' she said. 'Wouldn't we, Francis?'

Francis nodded, a little coldly, but Tacy did not notice. She was too flurried. But now Tom was on his best behaviour. He asked Francis how he was keeping, was he well? Was he settling down at Chilverton? He, Tom, always enjoyed seeing anything to do with the weaving, naturally.

So then what more natural than they should ask Tom to accompany them on their business. First to the new East India Docks, which replaced the old ramshackle wharfs, where Tacy checked the imports of silk with the warehouseman and gave orders for the skeined silk to be transported to Chilverton.

'Why don't you tell us about the Jacquards at Spitalfields?' asked Tacy sweetly, as they stood near the warehouse on the dockside. And Tom launched into a detailed description that made her open her eyes wide. He *had* seen them. She gritted her teeth and he smiled again.

On then to Mr Jarvis the wholesaler, in his office overlooking the river. Mr Jarvis was a neat, quiet man in his forties, unlike Mr Fotheringay in every respect from his dark frock-coat and spotless neck-cloth to his businesslike manner of speech. Mr Jarvis never wasted words. But unfortunately, this time he made a *faux pas* when Tacy said, 'This is my husband, Francis.'

He exclaimed, 'Ah, I see you are a silkman,' to Tom, who was studying samples on a table. Tacy hastily put matters right, but Francis did not smile.

'We have sold out of purl ribbons and sarsenets,' Mr Jarvis told Tacy. 'So if you could send more of these? A few fine gauzes, I think, and tartans.'

'I have brought samples of our newest shades,' Tacy said, spreading before him ribbons in delicate colours. Primrose with a lilac edge, green with purple, rose and brown, some speckles, others frosted or diced. Mr Jarvis liked them and placed orders, to Tacy's delight.

'These celebrations are good for trade,' nodded Mr Jarvis, and, well pleased, she bade him goodbye.

It was still only midday, so Tom took them to the Brown Bear in the Haymarket, where they ate chops and kidneys. Francis said little, and Tacy did not know whether he was in one of his sullen moods or just being quiet. When Tom suggested he showed them round the town she agreed readily, thinking it might retrieve the situation. She could, she knew, have sent Tom packing but, wilfully, she decided against. If Francis was in a pet, then too bad. And she did want to see the opera.

So – 'Yes!' she cried, eagerly. 'When I came with Papa, we had to sit in the stuffy guest-house when business was over.' Really, there was some advantage in being a married woman, she thought, much more freedom.

So they hired a hackney coach and explored. How much of London Tom knew and how much of their journey was just chance and left to the cabby she couldn't guess. But they drove away from the grand buildings of Georgian England, and the streets of uniform three storeyed houses and straight roadways with neat white pillars by the door, and swerved into narrow back streets where little old women sat selling apples and ragged children swarmed in winding lanes and courts. The cab-drivers raced each other, shouting and swearing, and it was all part of the fun, until they were forced into an alley-way so narrow the coach could not continue, for lying in the cobbled road were men, women and children, huddled in front of dirty tenements and cellars.

The driver halted and jumped down. 'We'll have to go back,' he muttered.

'But what are these people doing?' Tacy asked.

'Drunk,' said the driver, succinctly. 'Too much gin.' And now Tacy could see there were scores of gin shops interspersed with the wretched tenements.

'And the children?' she asked uneasily.

'Ho, they lives on the streets,' explained the driver. 'Parents turn 'em out ter fend for themselves.'

'They live on the streets?' Tacy gasped, horrified.

'Ha, they'll die soon enough,' said the driver. 'Come up now, Darkie, back now, back.'

'Wait a minute,' Tacy cried and, taking all the coins she had in her reticule, she threw them to the children who grabbed and fought for them – at least those with the energy to do so, others just lay supine.

The coach was back on the main roadway now, and into the City, where bakers in white aprons shouted, 'Hot loaves!' and milk-maids with pails suspended from yokes on their shoulders were watched by slaveys in mob caps leaning out of windows. And everywhere the crowds were shouting for Princess Caroline.

'Oh dear, that will humiliate the Prince,' commented Tacy.

'He hates her because she is so ugly,' Tom said.

Francis said little, and when they went to an inn for a meal he was still quiet. He was resentful. He should be the one showing Tacy around London, not this impudent creature; *he* should be impressing her with his knowledge so that she would gaze at him in admiration. He was her husband. He wasn't jealous of Tom, hadn't he been to his wedding? But he did object to being made to feel inadequate. He knew he would never excel in silk, neither the weaving nor the buying and selling they'd seen today. He hadn't the interest, and he wondered, for the first time, where his future lay.

Up to now all he'd wanted was Tacy. Tacy to still his fears, erase the black shadow that still enveloped him. He knew Samuel had told him that Tacy would have no money, and he rightly suspected that was to warn him off if he had designs on that score. Yet, it was unthinkable that Samuel would leave his daughter penniless, so perhaps in the future he would be able to buy a business of his own, some sort of accountancy work would suit him fine. But that was way ahead in the distant future.

Tacy was enjoying herself too much to notice his silence. Or if she noticed she dismissed it as one of Francis' moods. And moods irritated Tacy.

Crowds lined the roads on the way to the Haymarket, and surrounded the theatre, so that they had to fight their way in, but successfully got up to the gallery, where Tacy looked round in wonder. The theatre was filled to capacity. Women in white satin and diamonds and men in uniforms sat in the boxes. When the Prince Regent and the Czar came in the house rose and sang the National Anthem.

The opera began and again, Tacy was spellbound at the glitter and the brilliance. And then – she was aware that Tom, on her left, was holding her hand. She drew in a breath, but did not take her hand away.

Came the interval and she sat with flushed face, trying to talk to both Francis and Tom, hardly knowing what she said. She knew Tom had come just to be with her . . . Her eyes sparkled, she loved a spice of danger.

Just as the second act was about to begin there was a stir in the house. The box opposite the Regent was empty, but now, noisily entering, was the rejected princess, shapeless and spangled, wearing black velvet; on her head an elaborately curled black wig, her face daubed with white lead and rouge. In the silence she curtsied to the Czar, who rose to his feet and bowed, compelling the Regent to do the same. Everyone cheered.

The lights dimmed and again Tom held Tacy's hand, and the rest of the evening passed in a blur of glitter and diamonds and song – and the nearness of Tom.

Samuel had bought six more looms and installed them in an old warehouse at the back of Mr Jepson the saddlers in the Market Square. It was farther for the weavers to walk but they were pleased to have work again. Though both Samuel and James frowned as Francis gave them the figures for the month. 'Too much expenditure,' said James.

And then they discovered where George Healey was building his houses.

'At the back of his own home in the High Street!' gasped James. 'In the garden of the place he just bought.'

'Impossible,' said Samuel. 'How many houses can he get in there?'

As the summer wore on, heat burned from the cobblestones and the weavers strewed their floors with lavender from their gardens to hide the smells from the gutters and cesspools, they saw how many. A dozen tiny cots, built round his one yard, with one privy and one pump for all.

'And he's bringing in more weavers,' said James. 'More people from outside for his half-pay schemes, ''cos our men won't take it. Father, we must act.'

They were in the parlour, the door was open, letting the fragrance of the roses fill the room. Tacy thought her father looked tired. 'I cannot stop him, James,' he said.

'No, because you're not a member of the Vestry, you're not church. If you had been you could have talked with those in authority to stop this man.'

Samuel said nothing.

'He will ruin us, Father. He can bring in as many people as he likes. Married people with children. He won't allow them to rent one of his cottages unless they work for him.'

'What would you have us do?'

'Burn his cottages down.' And this cry was echoed by the weavers whom Tacy saw gathering outside.

'Burn his cottages. Break his looms the way the Luddites are doing,' shouted Tom Jacques.

Now the Red House was full of James' anger. It exploded every time he heard of George Healey's latest doings, every time he brought in another family to his tiny cottages. 'They'll bring disease,' he raged. 'One privy, one pump, it's madness, it shouldn't be allowed.'

Samuel saw it all with a heavy heart. But he would not act. George Healey was undercutting him now and he was forced to drop the price of his ribbons, though he did not reduce the payment to the weavers.

Tacy was, for the first time, worried, confused. Spoiled and petted as she had been, yet it was all within her father's strict and honourable way of life. She knew him – none better – knew him to be a good, kind employer known for his honest dealing.

Yet now that wasn't enough. These men were bringing in new ways that her father didn't understand. Greedy ways. Tom Jacques had been right all along.

Christmas came and went, and Tacy heard that Martha was expecting another baby. She wished she were having a baby too, it would perhaps fill this gap that had been left when Tom deserted her, keep her worried brain from puzzling over the changed town.

And then on a bitter day in February they heard the voice of the Town Crier. 'Oyez, Oyez. Take heed. Napoleon has slipped out of harbour and at the head of a thousand men he set sail for France . . .'

On 1 March, as the first daffodil shoots were showing in the gardens he landed in Antibes and marched to Paris.

On 3 March they sat in the parlour. Tacy was tremulous with news. She was, at last, with child. She wanted James to leave so that she could tell her father that he would soon have a grandchild. A little boy like Martha and Tom had, with black eyes and dark hair . . . Papa would be so pleased, it would take that worried look from his face. Grandmamma would be happy about it too . . .

James said, 'Father, we will have to bear the brunt of this campaign, and there is not much time. Russia and Austria are not up to strength —'

'Neither are we,' replied Samuel. 'So many men are home.'

'Exactly,' said James. 'Wellington recommends the immediate transport of an army to the Netherlands to form bases for a march on Paris. Many of his best troops are gone to America from the Peninsula. He needs men.'

Samuel lifted his head. 'Why are you telling me this?'

'I have enlisted,' said James. 'I shall take a commission with the Greys.'

Samuel stood up heavily, and Grandmamma said, 'Oh no.'

'Men are needed,' James went on. 'I want to go. I don't see any point in staying, you and I don't agree on anything. I can't see any future for me here.'

'James,' protested Grandmamma. 'You must not talk like that.'

'Why not? It is true.'

Tacy slipped out of the room. Her news would have to wait. She wished James were not going, even though he teased and tormented her she was fond of him. And she wished he and Papa didn't have to part in such an unfriendly manner. Really, James needn't have said what he did. Perhaps he'd retract it before he left.

But James retracted nothing, and in two days he was gone. The house seemed strangely quiet without him. Samuel had more work to do, and when not busy was absent-minded, unusual for him. He listened for the Crier to bring news of the campaign and even when Tacy told him of the coming grandchild he seemed unmoved.

But it caused the first quarrel between Tacy and Francis. She had said, 'Papa, soon you will be a grand-father,' and had sat at the velvet stool at his feet as she had when a little girl. And he'd patted her head and said, 'That is good.'

'A son,' she said. 'You'd like that, Papa.'

'It is excellent news,' Grandmamma beamed. 'We will ask Sarah Jane to bake a special cake tomorrow.' She stood up, went to the bell-pull. 'Sarah Jane, hear our news,' she told her. 'There is to be a new generation of Barratts.'

And then little Emma was brought in and there were more congratulations and exclamations of pleasure. Only Francis was quiet.

And in the bedroom, as she began to undress, Francis said, and his voice was cold, 'You didn't tell me you were with child.'

'No. I didn't think.'

'You should have told me before your father.'

Surprised, Tacy looked at Francis. He had made no move to undress, but stood by the bed, his face white with suppressed anger. 'I am your husband,' he said, and his lips were trembling. 'I should come first.'

'Yes, of course, Francis.' Tacy pulled her cambric nightdress over her head and slipped into bed. 'Come on, you silly, no need to get in a pet.'

But he still stood there. 'You were wrong,' he stated.

'Yes, I was wrong, I admit it. But I wanted to cheer Papa up, he looks so sad these days, and . . . old. Come now, Francis.'

Still he did not come to bed. He walked to the window and opened the casement, and the sound of rain came through the darkness, swishing down from the skies. The candle flickered and went out.

Tacy thought contritely, I should have told him. But he's so quiet, I never notice him. And sometimes he goes into a sulk and sits alone in the bedroom and I don't know why. But I must try to be nicer to him, it will be easier with the baby, and when James is home, we'll all be happy together. I shan't think any more about Tom, I haven't seen him since we went to London – at least not to speak to . . . They say Princess Caroline is gone to Europe, scandalising everyone, went to a ball as Venus, naked above the waist . . .

She drifted off to sleep.

The campaign was brief. On 19 June the Battle of Waterloo was fought. The Town Crier shouted in the street: 'Hear ye! The Duke of Wellington has won!'

'Thank God,' said Samuel, feelingly.

News filtered through. Napoleon was sent to St Helena; this time he was vanquished.

Tacy settled down to await the birth of her child.

As July brought heat and thunderstorms, Samuel sat in the counting-house. Tacy was sewing – at last, said Grandmamma – when she heard the clop-clop of a horseman in the road. Heard the front knocker bang as though someone was in a hurry, went to see.

She was too late. Samuel was already in the hall, a paper in his hand. He turned as she entered.

For a time he didn't speak. His face was grey. Tacy said, 'Papa?' Then, alarmed, 'Papa, what is it?'

And her father said, 'James is dead. Killed in action at Waterloo.'

Dead. The word reverberated round the room, and now Tacy's brain only seemed to accept patches of what was happening. Her father standing still. Grandmamma – she hadn't see her come in – going to Papa. Then Sarah Jane, throwing her apron over her head and wailing.

Tacy went to her room, looked over the garden with its full-blown roses, their fragrance drifting in through the open window, the syringa tree loaded with blossom.

Here she could be alone with her grief.

The family mourned. Mr Redmond came to pray with them and Samuel thanked him, but Tacy turned away.

How could God allow James to be killed? James, so young, so handsome. She worried about Grandmamma. She had loved James, he had been her favourite, how could she bear this?

In the event it was not Grandmamma who died, but Samuel, the sturdy, who had a heart attack and was dead before they could summon a doctor.

Samuel had been well liked, indeed it would be hard to find one person who disliked him. Even George Healey was among the crowds of friends and neighbours who came to pay their last respects, while Samuel lay in state in the parlour. The whole house was soon filled with wreaths, and the family were touched to see how many remembered. The poorest weaver managed to send a few flowers, bearing words that were revealing in their simplicity. 'To a good man. A good master.' Some of the smaller bunches held messages that were poorly written, some had to be written by others and marked with the cross of the sender who could not write himself, some had words laboriously spelled out by children who learned their letters at the Sunday school. 'To Mester Barratt who gave us a fowl. With love.'

The funeral was held at the church, by law, burials were not allowed at the chapel, and the list of mourners was impressive. Grandmamma, Tacy and Francis were in the first coach, drawn by black-plumed horses, then Abel Pickard and other relatives, all the dignitaries of the town; members of the weaving fraternity including such important people as the Birds from Coventry; representatives of the weavers themselves, Tom Jacques among them. No one worked on that day, those who did not crowd round the church stood in silence in the street as the cortège passed by. No one moved, even the children were silent. Tacy, in her black bonnet and black crepe dress under her black cloak, was filled with wonder. It was as though they were mourning what Samuel had stood for; it was almost as though they were mourning the passing of an age.

The funeral over, Tacy stood with Grandmamma and Francis in the parlour, with the mourners who had been invited back. She did not weep, she had not wept the whole time. She was still in a state of shock, yet underneath, so deep as to be barely recognised as yet, was anger. She felt she had lost everything – no, not quite, there was still the little life within her. And when the mourners left and she escaped to her room (she always thought of it as her room, as though Francis didn't count) she addressed God. Dear God, don't take this last thing from me. Or I swear I'll never love anything again as long as I live or be kind to anyone, ever.

She slept little that night, and when Francis tried to put his arm around her she shook him off. But she was up as usual in the morning, and after breakfast she sat with Grandmamma on the two easy chairs in the parlour. Samuel's chair stood conspicuously empty. She said, shaking her head as if to clear it, 'I didn't know Papa was not well.'

'He'd been working too hard since James went away.' Was there a hint of reproach in Grandmamma's voice? 'All the undertaking on top of everything. And I think he worried about James far more than we realised.'

'Well, it's over now,' said Tacy.

'What's over?' asked Grandmamma. 'Life goes on.'

Tacy shrugged impatiently. 'There won't be a business without Papa and James. We'll have to sell it.'

Grandmamma touched her lips with a fine handkerchief and could not hide her horror. 'Sell it?' she asked. 'Sell the business?'

'Well, what else can we do?'

Grandmamma stood up, her figure still erect. 'Do? What weavers always do when the man dies. The wife or daughter carries on.'

'Oh no, Grandmamma,' said Tacy. 'We have no-one now. Francis doesn't know enough.'

'But you do.'

'I cannot do it all.' I haven't the interest, she might have added.

Grandmamma said no more to her. She sent Francis to the counting-house. 'We won't need anyone in the warehouse today, the weavers will stay away out of respect, and anyway it is Tuesday. But I'll be on hand if anyone needs me.'

Sulkily, Tacy went to her room, feeling guilty. 'I have to think of the child,' she excused herself. Oh, if only this hadn't happened, if only Papa were here . . . She tried to marshal her thoughts, to think clearly and could not. She did not go down to dinner, and Sarah Jane brought up a tray which she refused.

And that night she lost her baby.

She woke to such pain she cried out. Francis, alarmed, called Grandmamma and was despatched for the physician. He bustled in, Dr Warren, large and full of his own importance . . . Sarah Jane was administering to the girl, now writhing in agony.

'It's nearly seven months,' Sarah Jane told the doctor. 'Too soon to live, I expect.'

Grandmamma was holding her hand as the pains came. Tacy sobbed, 'Don't let me lose it. Don't let me . . .'

But as dawn broke grey and chill the baby was born dead – a perfectly formed little boy.

Tacy lay in bed refusing to see anyone. Mr Redmond called, so did Abel and Martha. Tacy said no to them all. They sent their sympathy, they sent flowers, she ignored them. She ordered Francis to another room, and when little Emma brought her meals she pecked at them then turned her face to the wall. And she hated the world.

Dr Warren gave her boxes of pills, and said testily there was nothing more he could do, she had to make an effort. Grandmamma talked to her and could not rouse her, and now Grandmamma began to lose some of her sprightliness. Mr Redmond talked. Tacy did not even answer. In the warehouse the weavers came for their pay and Francis gave them what money was in the house. But when they asked for more work he did not know what to give them. George Healey stood in the background, waiting.

And then Tom Jacques called at the Red House.

'Let me in,' he ordered as Sarah Jane answered the door. 'I want to see Tacy.'

'No – it isn't seemly –' protested Sarah Jane, but he pushed past her and ran upstairs, while Grandmamma stood in the hall and did nothing to stop him. He knocked at Tacy's door and went straight in.

Tacy did not move. Tom said, 'Get up.'

She turned then, amazed. 'Tom Jacques!'

'The same.' He stood at the foot of the bed.

'What do you want?' But she sat up.

'Get up,' he repeated tersely. 'It's Saturday, the weavers need their work. Francis is standing dithering about, he don't know the difference between sarsanets and fine gauze, nor who does what best.'

'I don't care,' she said, sullenly.

'But I do.'

'Then you give the work out.'

'I have. But I cannot do the ordering, nor get the money that is needed to pay them from the bank. Only you can do that till the affairs are settled.'

'I'll do it later. Don't you realise?' she added, anger replacing her lethargy. 'I'm ill. I'm unhappy.'

'So are the weavers unhappy with no money to buy food. Think about them instead of yourself.'

'I'll think about nobody,' she muttered. 'Not again.' *I made a vow.* 'I'm not getting up.'

He stepped a little closer. 'You will,' he told her. 'When you see the visitor you are having in a minute.' He turned to go. 'You know where I am if you want me.' And he ran down the stairs, out of the house.

Dazed, Tacy sat back. But now she heard a commotion downstairs, a banging on the door, voices in the hall, loud voices. She was affronted. Did they not know that this was a house of mourning, that straw had been placed in the roadway to silence the iron-shod wheels, because she had been ill? She pulled on a wrapper and walked down the stairs.

George Healey and his wife stood in the hall. George in a cutaway coat in blue, Louie dressed in a Wellington hat with tall soldier-like high crown, edged with a feather, beneath which her frizzed red hair stuck out stiffly. She wore a green pelisse and an orange dress beneath. Even allowing for the day's fondness for colour, this was excessive. And in a house of mourning!

'What do you want?' Tacy asked in astonishment.

'Go back, Tacy,' Grandmamma said. 'Go back to bed.'

'Why,' George Healey said, ignoring Grandmamma. 'I've come to help you. I know how you're placed, things haven't been going too well for you, have they, in the weaving? And who but me can help?'

'*You* – help me?'

'Of course. I will run the business for you. I will do more, I will take it off your hands.'

Louie had moved forward, she was looking round the hall, peeping into the parlour. 'I like this,' she said.

Grandmamma stepped forward, but she said nothing. Tacy stared at Louie, then swung back to George. 'Just what are you saying?' she asked.

'Well, you want to sell, don't you?'

'Do we?' Her voice was ice-cold.

'That's what I heard. And it makes sense. Your father wasn't doing too well lately, the work's falling off and he pays out too much. Better you get rid of the business now before you go bankrupt like that man in Coventry who's run off to Americy.'

Tacy didn't speak. Grandmamma's hand tightened on her stick. In the silence they could hear a pieman shouting in the street, his singsong voice, 'A-ll hot, a-ll hot,' echoing round the room, then fading slowly. A horse clopped by.

Louie had moved into the parlour now. 'Yes, I like

this,' she said. 'Of course, I'd want to make changes, this is old-fashioned stuff. But we'd be all right here, George.'

Tacy had followed her, and the sight of Louie Healey touching her mother's possessions woke Tacy from her torpor. The Healeys at the Red House? The *Healeys*!

And now she was as angry as James had been, as Tom had been. Tom, who'd been right all along, and her father wrong. Papa, who had merely tried to do the honourable thing, who could not see evil when it stared him in the face. Her rage mounted. Louie Healey with her mother's precious china that had been imported from the Far East in an East Indiaman by Samuel's father to give to his son and his bride as a wedding present. A bowl made in Chelsea, one of the first English porcelain wares to be made. Little cameos. George Healey sitting in her father's chair that none of the family had touched since he died! George Healey, who had started all the trouble, who had been the cause of her losing Tom!

'You — take over my father's business?' she cried, and her voice was a whiplash. 'You — who helped to kill him? I wouldn't let you into this house. Not ever!'

'Oh come now,' George blustered. 'Don't be so high and mighty. We are your friends. How can you manage alone? With an old woman and a man who knows nothing of silk —'

Tacy held up her head. 'I can manage,' she said. 'I shall run the business and succeed. Now get out of this house, George Healey, and don't ever come in again.'

And she went back upstairs and started to dress.

Chapter five

The sky was grey over Chilverton. 'Sky's full of snow,' people said. 'It's too cold for snow and it won't be warmer till we get some,' riposted the jokers among them, as they did every year. Not only was the sky grey, their hopes were grey too. The big purl time had ended abruptly in the middle of 1815, just when all the young men came back from the wars. Trade was slack generally and French ribbons were being smuggled in.

Martha Jacques bundled two-year-old Martin into his little coat, cut down from one of Abel's, and put on her own well-worn cloak, which showed she was pregnant again. Seven months old William was asleep in his cradle, and she called to her father, 'Will you listen for Will, Father? I'm going to the mill and the market.'

'I'll listen,' said Abel.

Tom was working, but she knew better than to leave the children with him. Tom was a good enough father when he was in the mood, but too often he was not. Tom hadn't changed. He still liked his evenings at the Weavers' Arms, even if money was short, even if Abel frowned. And he still had an eye for a pretty girl, though if he ever went so far as to take one for a walk, Martha had not heard of it. Nor would she have minded too much. The only person she would have objected to was Tacy, and that didn't seem likely now.

She put on her bonnet, and this contrasted with her shabby cloak, for the brim was covered with bright yellow ribbon. Martha liked trimming hats, and sat many an evening sorting and matching ribbons, some for her own bonnets, some for any other who could afford a copper or two to spare. She took Martin's hand, and together they walked into the town. The mill always sold 'leavings', poor quality flour at a cheap rate. Before the war ended few would bother to buy it; now there was a crowd round the mill every day.

Martha stood in the crowd, waiting till the miller could serve her, shivering a little in the biting cold. An iron-shod cart rumbled past through the muddy roads, sending sprays of dirty water over them, two horsemen added their own splashes. Martha packed the flour in her bag, then walked to the market, where a woman stood before her unsold cheeses, shouting for customers to buy. Martha looked for candles, which were expensive. Yet they had to have them for their work. And her father still had work – Tom, too, for that matter. They were both good workers, now weaving fancy satins, and there was always a demand for these. But this work strained the eyes in the dull dark days of winter.

There was a clatter, and a pony chaise drove by. Martha looked up and saw Tacy. She didn't speak. You didn't speak to Tacy these days. She was a termagent, driving herself, driving everyone who worked for her, her mouth a thin line, her pretty hair drawn back in an unbecoming, unfashionable bun. Tacy Barratt intended to keep Barratts solvent in spite of the half-pay apprentice competition from George Healey.

She had taken the reins after her father and brother had died, to everyone's surprise. Little Tacy Barratt, the spoilt, the pretty miss, was going to run the business. George Healey laughed and sat back, waiting for her to fail.

No-one took heed of the fact that the business now legally belonged to Francis, the outsider, but Tacy's husband. Tacy remembered James' words and knew he was right. Francis was not a silkman, he could not manage something he knew so little about. If Francis felt any resentment he kept it to himself. He had hardly realised what was happening. He showed her the books, and she was appalled to discover how little money they had. The business had been running at a loss for weeks. And when Mr Moss, the manager from the bank in Coventry, had called to see her she was further shocked by his news.

'I didn't call earlier, out of delicacy,' he explained. 'Your sad loss, your illness . . . But I have to tell you that things are in a bad way. It seems your father has been paying out too much, buying more looms to keep men employed – '

'Bad? How bad?' she had asked through dry lips.

'Very bad,' he repeated. 'If you carry on in this way you will be bankrupt. In fact, I would advise you to sell now while you have a going concern.'

She thought of the Healeys taking over the Red House, putting the weavers on half-pay. She had thrown back her head. 'No,' she'd replied. 'I won't sell. I'll make it pay.'

He left, and she was afraid. For all her life money had been there without question, now suddenly it was going, and she was alarmed. She recalled her own expenditures, the gowns for Martha's wedding, her own; she had to have a big show . . . Then there was James and his Army commission to be paid for . . . Paying the weavers more than he was getting for the ribbons he sold . . . Oh poor Papa. And now she was alone with the consequences, quite alone, there was no-one to turn to. Grandmamma was ailing since she had caught that chill at Samuel's funeral and it would not seem to leave her. She tried to carry on as normal, but some days she was unable to leave her bed, and Sarah Jane looked grim.

Tacy would have liked to turn to Francis, but she learned that he was useless as a prop. He could reckon up figures, but when it came to discussing the weaving she had to explain every tiny detail, and he merely stared blankly, saying little. She had to carry on alone.

The first thing she did was to drive to the Patch and call a meeting of the weavers. 'Right,' she said, as they gathered before her. 'From now on there will be no undertaker at Barratts.'

'Like at George Healey's?' asked Luke Lakin. They hadn't yet learned to be deferential to Tacy.

'In competition with George Healey,' retorted Tacy. 'Unless you all want to be on the Parish.'

Her tone was sharp and there was an uneasy mutter. 'So who collects the work?' asked Bill Pettit.

'No-one. You fetch the hanks of silk from the warehouse,' she replied. 'You see to the winding yourselves, you weave it, and then on Saturday you bring the finished ribbons back to me at the warehouse when you will be paid.'

'And do we get more for having to fetch and carry?' asked Joe Bates, who fancied himself as a wit.

'You'll be lucky if you don't get less,' Tacy replied.

The weavers muttered among themselves, but there had been no trouble – so far. Tacy gave out the work as she'd said; she went to London to meet the silkmen and the buyers, and if she were tired she did not show it. She drove everyone relentlessly, including herself.

If there had been Grandmamma to hold her back it might have helped, but in the first cold spell of winter she developed pneumonia, which proved fatal. The illness did not last long. Her temperature soared, her breathing was painful to watch. Tacy and Sarah Jane nursed her day and night, but in three days she was dead. Tacy bore this further blow without showing any strain on the surface, she tightened her lips some more and pushed away any feelings of sorrow. Some day she would think about it all, when she had time. Some day she would pine and mourn, but not yet . . .

Sarah Jane carried on with the housekeeping in Grandmamma's place, and told her when Emma, the little maid, decided to leave. 'She's going to clean for Mrs Jennings, the Chief Constable's wife,' said Sarah Jane. 'Says she's overworked here.'

Tacy shrugged. 'Aren't we all? I'll get someone else. A workhouse child. She'll have to work or be sent back.'

'Why not have two, share the work?' Francis tentatively suggested.

'Because I can't afford two,' Tacy retorted.

So Susie came from the workhouse. Thirteen years old, she was pale and undernourished, but once fed, she did not become a little drab, she showed signs of rebellion and of answering back.

Tacy's love life was minimal. Occasionally Francis timidly asked her for her favours, and she agreed. Not out of love for it or him, but because, deeply ingrained, was the thought that this was a wife's duty. But she made it clear that she was being generous.

'Don't you want children?' Francis asked once.

'No.' *Not again!*

'But – you'll need a son to carry on the business.'

'We'll think about that when the time comes. At the moment it's all we can do to carry on ourselves. I don't have time to have a baby.'

So Francis meekly gave in, and this only made Tacy more irritated. If only he were more like Tom . . .

Francis never told her that he was grateful for her love – such as it was, for he still believed she'd married him for love. He didn't tell her of the darkness he felt was in him, which he tried to overcome. If he had told her it was doubtful if she'd have understood.

She was hard these days, and once or twice stopped to wonder at herself. Where was the light-hearted girl who'd had the world at her feet? But she realised that world had only been possible as long as Papa had been there to sustain it with his money. Now he was gone, and the world was threatened by George Healey and his vixen of a wife. He would have no mercy, and Tacy knew she had to fight the same way. If she ever felt like giving up, the thought of George Healey in her father's chair gave her new heart, and she carried on.

She felt sometimes as if she were encased in a suit of armour, nothing was allowed to touch her. Whether the armour would ever be taken off she did not know.

She no longer went to chapel, but to church, where the important people were, including Sir William Fargate. As Francis had been brought up church it made little difference to him, but the weavers grumbled, and Uncle Abel frowned, while some muttered that her father would turn in his grave if he knew.

She saw little of the weavers now except about work, but she said good evening to the lawyer and the doctor on Sundays. Sir William, in his family pew, was always the first to leave, and no one dared leave before him. If Tacy was surprised at the hierarchy in the church, where the important people sat at the front and the labourers and servants at the back, she said nothing.

The lawyer and the doctor might say good evening but their ladies had not, at first, been so forthcoming. Tacy could almost hear their whispers. 'That's the Barratt girl.' 'Yes, but her father was a most respected man, Samuel Barratt. Chapel.' And then a frosty nod.

She was more hesitant about attending the social gatherings, for she had not yet been invited to their houses. Chilverton society was very clannish, and between them, the lawyer, the banker, the doctor, the Chief Constable, ruled the town. Sir William orbited above them; no-one quite dare ask him to dine.

And, of course, there was the Reverend Mr Hewitt, the curate, whose grievance in life was that he *was* the curate. For the vicar had three livings, and resided in a county town where he could hunt and fish to his heart's content, leaving Mr Hewitt to do his work for a miserable stipend of less than fifty pounds per annum. And Mr Hewitt had connections; he too would have liked to hunt and fish and potter about aimlessly in the day and drink port in the evenings. Instead, he scurried hither and thither, harried his parishioners, especially the weavers, who had a name for being Dissenters and Radicals and Mr Hewitt hated both. Brought up a youngest son of seven in a manor house, he was not used to town ways. In the country maids curtsied to him and men touched their forelocks – not here.

So he eyed Mrs Barratt's conversion to church with suspicion. He did not believe for a moment that she wanted to change her faith, no, she was one of those Radical Dissenters who had organisations in London and Birmingham and believed in democracy, which was almost socialism; Jacobins, ready to start rebellion anywhere. Her very work proclaimed it, working as if she were a servant girl, and she not even a widow. Most improper. 'We cannot have her stirring up trouble among my parishioners,' he cautioned his pale, yielding wife. So, not having been in the town long enough to have known Samuel Barratt, he set his face against Tacy, and his flock followed.

Tacy had no idea she was regarded as a Radical socialist. She was running the business because her husband just was not capable. She suspected that many wives were forced into the same position, though not, perhaps, quite so openly. She fumed inwardly at hidebound conventionalism, and waited.

In October, when the distress of the town was increasing, the poor rates doubled, and French money – formerly taken – was refused; it was decided by the town's elite that a Ball should be held to help the poor of the town. Tacy saw this as her chance to meet them socially. She and Francis would attend. Her father had never in his life been to a dance, nor had she; Samuel had simply sent substantial donations to any good cause. 'This time we will go,' she said to Francis.

'But Tacy, you are still in mourning – for your father, your grandmother, for James,' protested Francis, shocked.

'Francis, I am not going for pleasure, it is business. These people can help me.'

'I don't see how.' Francis, unusually, seemed in an argumentative mood. 'They don't sell ribbons or do much about them except hold balls for the poor which *they* enjoy.'

'They're the important people,' Tacy said impatiently. 'They decide who's going to do what in the town.'

Like George Healey being helped by Sir William. He was the big fish in the little pond of Chilverton, and it was he she was angling for. If she could persuade him to help *her* and not George Healey . . .

'What are you going to wear?' asked Sarah Jane. 'Your white wedding gown? The white gown you wore at Martha's wedding? I'd be ashamed, Tacy Barratt. Going to a *ball*. What would your Grandmamma have said?'

'It's for charity,' Tacy said, shortly. Sarah Jane was the only person who dared say much to Tacy these days. She seemed, with age, to be getting more critical. *And more cantankerous*, Tacy added to herself. For years she had looked the same, fading hair, indeterminate age. Now her hair was white, not a pretty white, but discoloured by a yellowish tinge. Her feet were swollen, and she padded about in old shapeless slippers. Tacy knew the house did not have the spotless brightness it had had under Grandmamma, knew that the pert Susie gave Sarah Jane a lot of cheek before she'd do anything, but she herself just did not have the time to see to everything.

'I'll get my gown dyed,' she told Sarah Jane now. 'Grey, I think.' And Sarah Jane went away, muttering.

On the night of the ball she dressed with care, thinking it was a long time since she had tried to look elegant. Her gown was a little old-fashioned, for the end of the wars brought a change in the shape of women's dresses. The waist rose even higher, the skirt came straight down from the waist to just above the ankles. The bottom was much wider and much more decorated with elaborate sleeves. She frowned at her apparel and wondered if she dare buy an overdress of pink satin which was so fashionable now. But better not, not to meet the stiff ladies of the town, and not while in mourning. So she compromised by fetching yards and yards of Abel's silver and blue ribbon – for which she paid handsomely – and trimmed the edges of her dress. Then, half satisfied, she and Francis drove to the Assembly Hall.

They were forced to go in the chaise, Tacy wishing she still had the carriage. She knew everyone would agree with Francis that she should not be here, but she cared little for what people said these days, something in her *wanted* to rebel, to hit out at the world. So she held her head high as they entered the long room, lit by myriad candles in chandeliers and banked with chrysanthemums and michaelmas daisies and a few late roses, and with four musicians at the far end.

There was a small crowd of people gathered, the

church crowd. No one nodded or smiled as they walked to seats at the side. Tacy's face burned, but she tried to appear unconcerned.

The music began and she studied the ladies' gowns. Some were fairly plain, but one or two were in high fashion; low cut, with puffed sleeves and sweeping long skirts with ruffles and ribbons. Tacy was glad she had trimmed her own, she thought she would pass. But waists were small again, she'd have to get new corsets – when she had time.

'I cannot dance, can you?' she whispered to Francis as couples lined up before them.

'A little,' he replied. 'This is a quadrille, the steps are quite easy. Come, I'll show you.' Together they went on the floor. And still no-one spoke or nodded to them.

Oh, Tacy thought angrily. If only I could *show* them . . . stupid lot of nincompoops. If only something would happen . . .

And something did. A man appeared in the doorway. He did not look round, but everyone stared at him. All the respectable people, in their respectable clothes, their coloured clothes, as was the fashion, wore nothing like this.

He had on a blue silk coat with covered buttons, white marcella waistcoat, and black florentine silk knee-breeches, with white silk stockings. He was not a young man, his face was florid, and he looked neither to right nor left as he strode forward.

'Why,' Tacy giggled. 'He looks almost like one of these new Dandies they talk about. Except he isn't painted, and I don't imagine he's wearing stays. You can tell he's a man.'

'Who is he?' asked Francis.

'Why, Sir William, of course,' she answered.

She felt Francis stiffen beside her, but took no heed,

she was wondering how she could attract Sir William's attention. If only she could! It would serve two purposes. To show these stuffed dolts that she was as good as they, and to get his help. The Reverend Mr Hewitt had been perfectly correct in thinking Tacy came to church for an ulterior motive, though it was not to incite his flock to rebellion, but to insinuate herself into their good books and get to know Sir William, the big fish.

Sir William walked over to Mr Broadbent, the banker, a man reputed to be worth a fortune, and then he danced with Mrs Broadbent, a large lady with a red face and floral gown who somehow appeared to be wearing too much of everything, though Tacy thought her coloured turban was out of fashion, and wondered why Sir William could not notice *her*.

Her chance came in the interval when the dancers were invited to the supper room to partake of a cold buffet. Francis went to one table and Tacy went to the other, where Sir William was taking a glass of punch from the bowl. She stood behind him so that when he turned he bumped into her. With a little squeal she jumped backwards but somehow one or two drops of the punch spilled on to her dress.

'I do beg your pardon,' said Sir William. 'Please allow me —' and he scooped up a serviette.

'It was my fault,' Tacy said. 'I was too curious, looking to see what was on offer. No, please, there is no damage done, I assure you. This is but an old dress.' She waved her fan vigorously and smiled.

'I don't think we've met,' said Sir William. 'Here, Broadbent, introduce us, do.'

Mr Broadbent turned, but Tacy put in, quickly, 'I am Tacy Barratt, and my husband is over there.'

So then, of course, Sir William took her back to Francis, who hardly said a word. But Tacy was vivacious, and when Sir William said, 'The music is starting again, one of these new waltzes. I wonder, Mr Barratt, if I may have the pleasure of a dance with your wife?'

Francis nodded, surlily, and Tacy, frowning prettily, said, 'I would indeed love to try, but I do not waltz, Sir William.'

'Then I shall have the pleasure of teaching you,' he smiled, and he whirled her on to the floor.

He was a good dancer, and it was not too difficult to follow him. And when the dance ended he said, 'You must have married out of the schoolroom, Mrs Barratt, that is why I have never seen you. Did you not have a coming-out?'

'I did marry out of the schoolroom,' she answered. 'But my father did not allow me to dance. We own a silk business,' she ended.

'Samuel Barratt,' Sir William nodded. 'And your husband a Barratt too – is that coincidence, or did he take your name?'

She laughed prettily. 'Coincidence, but a lucky one, for I could not allow the business to be called anything but Barratts, not ever.'

She wanted to ask him if he were interested in silk, but the waltz had ended and he took her back to Francis.

He did dance with her once more, however, and she knew that he found her attractive. She went home well pleased, and took no heed of Francis' sulky manner. And when Sir William saw her in church the next Sunday he bowed and said good morning, and all the ladies smiled too.

Stupid lot of snobs, thought Tacy. But she now had entrée to their houses, though there were no more dances as yet.

Mrs Warren was the first to ask her to an evening soirée. Mrs Warren, the doctor's wife, was tall, with masses of dark hair, well dressed, obviously much younger than her husband, and quite a pleasant person, Tacy discovered. The Warrens lived at the far end of the High Street, so Tacy and Francis were able to walk there. The house was a little larger than their own, and the drawing-room was well-proportioned, with a fire screen of embroidered silk and cherrywood armchairs, while Egyptian ornaments gave tone to the room. They had the new sash windows, and beneath them were set out a number of little card tables.

'Do you play whist?' Julia Warren asked Tacy tentatively, knowing that Dissenters were against gambling.

Tacy said, 'Well, I never have, but my husband will teach me.'

'Don't let us lead you into bad ways,' came the sneering voice of the Reverend Mr Hewitt from behind her.

'Oh no, you won't do that.' Tacy disliked Mr Hewitt because she sensed he disliked her. 'I shall go to the Devil in my own way.'

She had to sit at the side while the others took it in turns to play, chatting with Mrs Broadbent, large as ever, Mrs Peabody, the lawyer's wife, smaller, with jutting bosoms, and behind, Mrs Hewitt, who never seemed to say a word to anyone except to echo her husband. And Tacy was bored. She thought how much there was to do at home, in the business, instead of sitting chatting to a lot of empty-headed women whose main topics of conversation were the new hairstyles and the doings of Princess Caroline in Europe. She hoped Sir William would come, but he did not. No doubt he would think Chilverton society – however highly they rated themselves – beneath him. But she waited . . .

Now it was December and the sky was full of snow.

Tacy had been to the canal wharf to fetch the bundles of silk from the boat, hoping the winter would not be too bad and the canal not freeze over or the boats would be unable to run. Back at the Red House she turned the pony over to the lad, Jobey, and asked him to carry the bundles into the warehouse. Now they had no carriage there was no coachman, nor gardener, just Jobey to do all the heavy work around the place, a gangling untidy youth who slept above the stables and was sullen and careless – but cheap.

As Jobey left she saw a figure approaching through the yard, and she halted. It was Tom Jacques.

'Tom!' she said, surprised. It was the first time she'd seen him alone since he'd been to her bedroom. He came to fetch his work and to bring the finished ribbons back, but then he was just one of a crowd, and he'd said no more than Good morning and Thank you. 'You don't want more work?' she asked now.

'No, I just wanted a word with you.'

'Oh, right. Come in.'

Together they went into the warehouse, with its shelves piled with hanks and bobbins, its windows letting in a certain amount of light, but not much. A lantern glowed on the counter, and she sat on one side on the high stool, while he stood on the other. She felt nothing.

'I came,' he said, 'because I heard you were going to take two shillings off a gross of twelvepenny satins.'

'I am, and reduce sarsenets too.'

'That's too much.'

She sighed wearily. 'You know how things are. Too many weavers, people not buying so many ribbons. George Healey undercutting all the time.'

'And so we all have to suffer.'

'I'm suffering too.'

He raised his eyebrows and she said in a low voice, 'Tom – when my father died – I found that there was little money. Oh, he wasn't bankrupt as George Healey said but – it was bad . . .'

And she recalled again the shock she'd felt when the bank manager had told her just how things were; even now she had nightmares about going bankrupt. When Grandmamma died and she was quite alone, and she'd turned to Francis and found there was nothing there to lean on or advise . . .

She said, 'Keep it to yourself, Tom, I don't want George Healey to know.'

He moved restlessly. 'I told you how it would be,' he said.

'Yes, I know. And what would you do if you were in charge?'

'I told you that too. Get rid of George Healey.'

'How?'

'Burn his looms, burn his cottages like the Luddites are doing.'

'And all that would do is send me to jail as they're jailing the Luddites. No, I'll get rid of him, Tom, but not that way.'

A sudden gust of cold wind blew the door open, the lantern flickered. 'What way then?' Tom asked.

She knew he wouldn't approve of her plan to inveigle Sir William. Tom was proud. She had been – once. Now she seemed to be plotting first with one, then another.

She sighed, and the lantern flickered again. Tom walked down the warehouse and closed the door; returned and stood before her. 'So how are you these days, Tacy?' he asked.

The change of tack confused her; she stared into his face and the old look was there in his eyes. 'I'm all right,' she said.

'You don't look it.'

'Oh thank you, Tom. You mean I look a fright.'

'No, I mean you look as if your husband don't fuss you enough, don't cuddle and kiss you as he ought.'

'Tom Jacques!'

'I'd have cuddled you if you'd married me.'

She caught her breath. Her heart was pounding as it had not for a long time. 'And whose fault is that?' she said, low.

'Well, you know how it was. Your father refused to let me near. If I'd have known . . .' he broke off.

She was still. The warehouse was a long room and the one small light left deep shadows in the far corners. It seemed to Tacy as if she and Tom were alone in the world.

'And what about Martha?' she asked.

'Martha's a good girl,' he stated, and she was annoyed that he should say so. She turned to go.

He said, 'How much do you know about the new Jacquard looms?'

She halted. 'A little. I don't know much.'

'It's a great new invention. It could lead to all sorts of new ways.'

'So how does it work?' she asked, interested as always in aspects of weaving.

'There are big cards,' he explained. 'They have holes punched in, matching the design you use. Each hole lifts a needle in the harness over the loom, and so a thread of silk. They take a long time to fit up.'

'It sounds a bit complicated.'

'Yes, but it makes the work easier. It weaves more intricate designs and you can do more at a time.'

He picked up a length of satin ribbon and held it up, seeing it shimmer in the unsteady light. 'This is beauti-ful,' he said, reverently. 'Silk is beautiful. I could never do any other work.'

There was a silence, then she asked, 'So you want to buy a Jacquard?'

'I haven't the money. That's why I don't want you to drop the prices any more.'

'How much are they?'

'Twenty pounds or so.'

She gave him a hard look. 'You want me to lend you the money?'

'I didn't say that. I don't beg money from you or anyone. And you don't seem too well placed to lend anything anyway. Besides, I'd have to alter the building. A Jacquard is too big for an ordinary room, you have to knock out the ceiling.'

Now she looked down at the counter. The light was fading, the afternoon was gloomy, the wind seemed to have died as soon as it was born. She made some rapid calculations. 'I'll lend you the money for the loom,' she offered. 'You'll have to pay for the alterations yourself, you and your brothers can see to it. It will pay me, help me to get better ribbons.' *And I can give you something that Martha cannot . . . Money!*

He leaned over the counter and touched her hand. 'Thank you, Tacy,' he said.

She drew back, shivering at his touch. The lamp shone bravely in the gathering gloom.

'Why don't you come down to the Patch again?' he asked. 'We still have the social gatherings at the chapel, we sing and, yes, laugh, even though we're poor.' He leaned forward persuasively. 'You don't want to go to that old church, with the curate huffing and puffing and Lawyer Peabody opening his mouth like a big fat fish, and Mrs Peabody singing "Drink to me only with thine eyes".'

'She doesn't sing that in church,' said Tacy. But she was smiling.

'Remember that night when we were kids, and we stood outside their house, and she was in the drawing-room, singing. "Drink to me o-o-only – "' His voice took on a shrill falsetto, and again she smiled at the memory.

'I remember,' she said. Her smile turned to a sigh. 'Things are different now,' she added.

'But what do you do in the evenings?' he asked. 'Sit alone in that big house?'

'With my husband,' she corrected. 'And don't say any more, Tom. I must go.'

He shrugged his shoulders in a comical, helpless gesture and moved to the door. She watched him silently.

No, she couldn't go back to the Patch. She couldn't take life as it came, as Tom did. Tom laughed at everything, then when displeased got into a rage. Then it was all over and he was laughing again. Tom would not plan for the future.

He had lost money, yes, but she had lost her father, her brother, her grandmother, her baby, and a little of her had died with each. No, she couldn't be like Tom.

But she wished she could.

She went into the Red House thoughtfully. Should she let Francis kiss and cuddle her more than she did? Was the armour cracking a little? Or was it just that she did not want Tom to think that she was neglected? It would be good to work together on these new Jacquard looms, she and Tom . . .

When supper was over she did not go back to the office as she usually did, but sat before the fire in the parlour. Francis looked his surprise when she began talking of her plans for the future, of new looms, new designs. And when they retired for the night she undressed slowly, waiting for Francis to join her.

He kissed her and he cuddled her, and they made love. It didn't satisfy her.

But that night Damaris was conceived.

Tacy did not want the baby. Her temporary softness disappeared, though she was not sure if there might be a permanent crack in the armour. But she wanted no more of Francis and told him she would prefer to manage without the encumbrance of a child. Her hope was that it would be a boy.

She worked with Tom, overseeing the new loom. It was to go in the extension of the Jacques' house, which meant knocking out and raising the one-storey roof, a job Tom, his father and brothers did themselves. All the weavers crowded round in admiration, asking where he'd found the money. Only Martha said nothing.

Christmas passed quietly, and in the New Year Tacy was back at work, giving out the silk and paying when the finished ribbons were brought in on Saturdays. The weavers had made it an occasion, they dressed in their best to walk to the Red House, black top hats, Sunday suits. They stood in line, and Tacy sat at the warehouse counter with her big box of money. Now Tom was always last in the queue, and when she had paid him would stand and talk to her, mostly about work, and she was glad she had someone with whom she could discuss matters. Tom could be a tower of strength in this way.

'Tacy,' he said one cold morning when frost covered the cobbles and men had to lead the horses in case they fell on the slippery surfaces. 'You know we get the Jacquard cards from Coventry, where they are prepared from the designs. Well, this new order we have, it is for twelvepenny ribbons with rose and green colourings. I don't care for this design, I remember Abel used to weave a much better one with big roses and green leaves, do you remember?'

'Yes, it was very popular. You want to use that? We'd have to get it put on the cards.'

'I thought it would be better. But Abel no longer has the design, and we don't remember the details. Do you have it somewhere?'

'Father would have had it, I expect. I'll look tonight.'

'Right.' He turned to go and she asked.

'How are you, Tom?' Wanting to keep him talking.

'I'm fine. And you?'

'I shall be better when I've put George Healey out of business.'

He grinned. 'Well, you know what to do. It will come to that in time, you mark my words!'

'Tom, don't –' but he was already walking away.

Tacy was tired. Saturdays were always taxing, and her pregnancy was making itself felt. She took the money box and the account book to Francis in the office then began to search for the missing design.

It was not in the office, so she went to her own room. Could she have put it in with some papers? Where . . . ? She searched through her chest of drawers, but found nothing. Yet they never threw away any designs.

She went to her father's room. It had not been touched since his death . . . She gazed at the four-poster bed, a familiar lump coming to her throat, then she quickly looked through the bureau in the corner. Nothing.

She stood, puzzled. Where else was there? It wouldn't have been put in Francis' drawers by mistake, would it? She moved back to their room, pulled open the top drawer of his chest, ruffled through the papers. Right at the bottom a thick unmarked envelope caught her eye, and she took it out, curious. It was unsealed and she opened it and read: 'My dear son . . . Jean-Pierre is not your father . . .'

She looked up, startled. What was this? A letter to Francis . . . *Your loving mother* . . . Jean-Pierre is not your father.

Why hadn't Francis told her this? Why had he deceived her? And who was his father? She read on: 'Forgive me if this hurts you, Francis. The man who wronged me is still alive. His name is Sir William Fargate.'

Amazed, Tacy stared ahead. Sir William Fargate . . . and Francis had never told her. Never breathed a word. Let her think he was the son of a Frenchman . . . why . . . ?

She was running to the door, letter in hand . . . down the massive staircase, almost colliding with Francis as he came in from the office. 'Francis!' she cried. 'What is this?'

'What is what?'

'This letter from your mother.'

'Why – ' he jumped forward, snatched it from her. 'You've been through my private papers!' he accused.

'I was looking for a design. But I didn't know you had any secrets. And now I find this. Is it true? That you are the son of Sir William?'

'I don't know. I prefer to think I'm not. It's not a thing I'm proud of.'

'For goodness sake, why? Don't you see what this might mean?'

His face was white, his lips trembling as they had once before when he was angry she remembered. 'I want to forget it,' he said.

'Oh, Francis, don't be so stupid. Don't you see? He might be able to help us, if you make yourself known to him. After all, they say he's behind George Healey.'

Francis was shaking. 'Do you think I'd go begging that man for help?' he cried.

'Why not? He owes you something.'

Francis was tearing his mother's letter to shreds. 'No,' he said, violently. 'No, I don't believe it. He's not my father.'

'But your mother said he was. You can't deny it.'

'I will deny it,' he shouted. 'You must never tell him or anyone, never, never, never.' He took hold of her shoulder and shook it because his arm was shaking so.

'Francis!' she cried, and he loosed her and ran upstairs to the bedroom. Mystified, she followed him and he clung to her like a child.

'Tacy,' he said. 'You don't know what is within me.' And then he was making love to her in a way he never had before, almost violently, so that she was shaken.

She said no more about the letter. But she thought he was making a fuss over nothing. Really, Francis was odd at times.

Chapter six

On 2 May 1816, Princess Charlotte married Prince Leopold of Saxe-Coburg. England rejoiced, none more so than the weavers of Chilverton, who were kept busy with orders for fancy ribbons.

The Princess, only child of the Prince Regent, was reputed to be a little wild and forward – indeed some said she swore and wore drawers, a modern innovation, and had kicked up her legs so that they showed. But she was the darling of the people, and it seemed she was marrying for love, unlike her father, and they looked forward to the time when she would be Queen and they'd be rid of the present family for good.

Tacy was overjoyed at the way things had turned out. Her own child was due at the end of August, and the fact that the weavers had been busy in the last months of the winter was good news. It helped her too; she was not so driven, and was pleased now that she had lent Tom the money for the Jacquard.

She had made preparations for the time she might be incapacitated, and had asked Tom if he would take over the giving out of work, should she be off Saturday. 'I don't expect I will,' she ended.

But with the usual perversity of babies, it was on a hot Saturday in mid-August when she felt the first discomfort. As it was little more than cramps, she said nothing, hoping she'd get through the morning. After all, they did say one's first labour could take an unconscious long time. Yet had ever the weavers been so slow, she wondered, standing talking in groups of two or three before coming to the counter. She had to check the ribbons, pay the money, then move to the stacks of silk to draw down hanks for the next week's work. And it was while doing this that another, sharper pain struck her, forcing her to cling to the wooden shelves till it passed.

She turned back, but now Tom had pushed his way through the weavers. 'I'll check, you pay out,' he ordered. 'And I'll give out the work. Can you manage that?'

'Yes, thank you, Tom.'

'Right. Come on, you lot, get a move on. I want my dinner. Joe Bates, one piece sarsanet, eightpenny.' And he quickly checked over the thirty-six yards in one piece, and weighed it. Tacy paid Joe and said, 'Give him the same, eightpenny sarsanet,' and Tom pulled out the hanks of shining silk.

The heat consumed them. The warehouse was usually cool, but not today. Tacy was wearing a loose muslin dress, with a light shawl round her shoulders to try to camouflage her condition; this only added to her discomfort. But together they were soon finished and as the warehouse emptied, he asked, 'Are you all right?'

'Yes. Thank you, Tom.'

'Come on, then, let's get you inside. I'll see to the packing and get it down to the canal. Who takes it, that half-soaked streak, Jobey?' And, as she nodded, 'But where's your husband in all this?'

'He had to go to London.'

'*Today?*'

'Yes. We didn't – it's early, two three weeks. And he had this appointment.' He stared, and she added, 'I'm giving up the importing, Tom. I shall deal with a silk broker from now on.'

'Oh Tacy. Why?'

'Because I cannot do it all,' she cried, pettishly. 'My father had James on the accounts and George Healey as undertaker. I have just Francis. I can't afford anyone else – ' as he made to speak.

'No, but it's a pity. All to be done in bits and pieces instead of seeing the whole thing through – ' He broke off as another pain caught her and he took her arm and led her into the house. 'Sarah Jane!' he called. 'Come quick!'

Sarah Jane shuffled in.

'Do you want me to fetch anyone?' Tom asked.

'No,' Sarah Jane said. 'You can go. This is no place for you.'

'He's helped me a lot,' Tacy admonished her. 'And yes, you can call at the doctor's, Tom. Tell him my pains started this morning.' And to Sarah Jane's clucking, she was led to the bedroom.

She had engaged Dr Warren, though convinced in her own mind that a midwife would have sufficed – that was all the weavers had. But, eager to cement her friendship with the church people, she had enlisted Dr Warren's appearance.

And wished she hadn't, he didn't seem to be much help. The baby was a long time coming, the hot day merged into an equally stifling night as she lay, tossing and moaning, with no breath of air stirring.

Dr Warren, large and self-opinionated, who liked to sleep in his bed at nights, went home, saying he would call again in the morning before he went to church.

'In the morning?' screeched Tacy. 'Won't it be here before then?'

'You should have had Mrs Walters.' Now it was Sarah Jane's turn to admonish when he'd gone. 'She's better than any old doctor.'

'She should be, all the kids she's had,' muttered Tacy.

'Do you want me to send for her?'

'No.' Tacy knew the doctor would be mortally off-ended if she was delivered by an amateur midwife, so she endured the pain and discomfort and the grumblings of Sarah Jane.

'We've managed before,' said she. 'I delivered you, you know that? And your poor mamma, such a delicate lady, so gentle. Your papa worshipped her. And you look like her, that's why he was so set on you. But you ain't the same in your ways, though. I don't know who you tek after, I really don't.'

Tacy gritted her teeth and studied the wallpaper by the light of the flickering candles. Samuel had had the wallpaper changed when she was married, the trellis pattern had gone, now there were roses twining round archways . . . More expense . . . Yet – she had wanted it done, she recalled. The casements were wide open, letting in the noises of the night, owls hooting, the neighing of a horse, and though there was no breath of air the candle-light wavered and the roses on the wallpaper with it. Tacy watched them dully and longed for morning.

The doctor arrived again when he'd breakfasted, and by now Tacy was barely conscious. Sarah Jane adminis-tered to her, letting her cling to her with each pain, wiping her wringing wet face. 'It won't come,' she told the doctor.

'Out of my way,' ordered the doctor, brusquely. And, in a hurry now to get to church, he put his hand inside Tacy, grabbed hold of the child and pulled. As it emerged he fell backwards on to the carpet, the child screaming above him. And now Tacy did lose con-sciousness.

When she came round Sarah Jane was still wiping her brow. 'There, there,' she soothed. 'You're all right now.'

Tacy didn't feel all right. She felt as if her insides had been ripped apart, as indeed they had, stitched together by the doctor with no sterilisation.

'Don't you want to know what 'tis?' asked Sarah Jane. 'It's a little girl.'

'Where is she?' asked Tacy.

'Oh, doctor took it.'

'Took it? Why? It's dead, isn't it?' Tacy struggled to sit up.

'No no, lie down. He said you won't have no milk, so he's going to find a wet-nurse.'

Tacy frowned. For though a wet-nurse suited her well, for she still had to take trips to London, had to move around the weavers, yet this overbearing behaviour of the doctor annoyed her. He might have waited to find out . . . 'Who could he find at such short notice?' she asked.

'Martha,' replied Sarah Jane.

'*Martha?*'

'Well, she had a baby a bit ago, and she can do it,' said Sarah Jane.

Martha. Yes, she'd had another boy, Amos. That made three. Tacy sighed.

She hadn't realised how weak she would feel. Nor how lucky she was to survive the doctor's bungling treatment. But she sat up as Sarah Jane returned with some broth. 'I don't know how I'll manage now,' she grumbled. 'I ain't as young as I used to be, and that Susie's hopped it.'

'Where's she gone?' Tacy paused in the act of putting a spoonful of broth in her mouth.

'She's bin hanging after one of them young colliers from Borley Common,' Sarah Jane told her. 'Wanted to get married, and now I reckon she's done it. Says she's in the family way.'

'We'll have to get someone else,' said Tacy.

'Who?' Sarah Jane demanded. 'You know weavers won't go in service. Even if they ain't got no work, they won't tek this.'

'I'll have to get another girl from the workhouse.'

Sarah Jane grunted. 'Much good they are. But I can't do it all myself. Pity none of your old friends 'ud come up and help out, but there you are, you think you're too grand for them now. An' the church lot won't come and scrub floors, not they. You'll have to get help.'

Tacy sank back onto her pillows. Get more help, give the work out to the weavers, pay them, fight George Healey . . . Get more help, where was Francis . . . ? Had he talked to the silk broker? Would the silk be the same . . . ?

The candle guttered and went out. The roses on the wallpaper faded into the darkness.

Martha moved round the table slicing the cabbage and dropping the pieces into the bubbling pot on the open fire. The meat was roasting in the Dutch oven, a contraption that suspended the roast on a hook from a revolving wheel, with a curved metal sheet, burnished bright, in front of it to speed up the process. She had half hoped Tom and his brothers would build her a real oven at the side of the fire, they were good at that sort of thing, but although Tom had promised, so far nothing had materialised. There had always been something else to see to, the Jacquard loom to be installed, getting it set up . . .

She hadn't seen Tom since yesterday afternoon when he brought his pay – he always did this – and told her that Tacy's baby had started. But she never did see much of him at weekends, he worked late Thursdays and Fridays – often all night – so he would stay at his mother's, for with all the girls married, there was room enough. But he was always home for Sunday dinner.

The baby in the cradle began to cry and she said, 'Rock the cradle, William,' and the toddler stood up obediently.

Martha finished her cooking, threw the bowl of dirty water outside, then picked up the still whimpering baby and, grabbing a faded sunbonnet, took him into the garden where she sat on a chair, nursing him, William playing at her feet. Three-year-old Martin was at chapel with his granddad. As the house was at the end she could see into the road. Groups of people – those who were not at chapel – were talking, women standing in doorways, wiping their brows, saying 'Ain't it hot?' Then she saw a familiar figure walking towards her gate, saw her come to the garden. 'Nancy!' she cried.

'Hallo. Yes, I'm over for the weekend. Caught the new coach from Coventry to Tamworth.'

'But you'd have to walk from the Watling Street?' Martha asked. 'In this heat. And how's Fred and the watchmaking?'

'Oh, very good, he's doing fine.' Nancy looked smart in her striped sarsenet dress, high necked, and with a beehive bonnet of plaited straw. She leaned over the baby. 'So this is the new one. Lawks. Martha, you want to tell our Tom to sleep at Mam's all the time.'

Martha smoothed the baby's head. 'I love babies,' she said.

'Just as well. And he's another little Jacques, I see. Like Martin. Tom couldn't deny him if he tried. But William – he's different, ain't he?' And she studied the fair hair and serious face of the second child.

'Yes, I think he takes after my father.' Martha held the baby over her shoulder and patted his back. 'He's like him in his ways too.'

'You mean he won't be a hell-raiser like the Jacques.' Nancy grinned. 'I hear Tacy's having hers now. Don't envy her in this heat.'

'Yes, Tom said yesterday.'

'He went up again this morning.' Nancy saw Martha stiffen slightly. So she didn't know! 'I think they need help, Tacy's badly and Francis is away, there's only that old woman.'

'Yes.' Martha stood up and went back to the hot kitchen, laid the baby in the cradle and took up a bowl of loganberries picked from the garden, emptied them into another pot and suspended it from a pothook over the fire, moving the first cauldron out of the way. Nancy followed her but, hearing a commotion in the road, went to investigate, Martha following. And saw, to her surprise, a carriage rumbling over the cobbles.

It pulled up outside her own cottage and from it alighted Tom, and Dr Warren holding a baby. Martha stepped back into the kitchen and the doctor pushed his way in without waiting for invitation. 'You're Martha Pickard?' he asked.

'Yes.' Martha, true to her dissenting principles, neither curtseyed nor called him sir.

'Here.' The doctor held out the baby, and Martha, having little choice, took it. 'It needs a wet-nurse,' he ended. 'I understand you can see to it. No doubt you will be paid.'

'Whose child is it?' Martha asked, though she knew before he told her. Tacy's.

The doctor left without another word and entered his carriage now surrounded by numerous gaping children, and stared at by women from doorways. Inside, Martha turned to Tom.

'You told him,' she accused.

'Well, Martha, he wanted someone and I didn't like to

think of it going to some grubby drab who does it for the money.'

'Why can't Tacy see to her own?'

'The doctor wouldn't allow her. If you'd been there, Martha – nobody but that old woman croffling about and Tacy in labour all night, and the doctor pulling the baby out of her so that he fell backwards wi' it on the floor.' He turned to his sister, who was watching eagerly. 'They need help at the Red House,' he told her. 'Young Susie's gone off – you go up and lend a hand, Nancy.'

'I don't know if I'd be welcome,' Nancy objected. But Tom gave her one of his angry looks and she went. And now Mrs Walters was in the doorway, fussing in to ask if she needed help, and Abel and little Martin walking along the road.

Martha sent Mrs Walters packing, then stood in the middle of the kitchen. She was angry. She'd thought, when she married Tom, that he would forget Tacy – and that Tacy would forget him. After all, Tacy had Francis . . . Tacy always had everything . . . while plain Martha stayed in the background. But it seemed that their lives were to be forever entwined. She knew Tom helped Tacy in the warehouse and excused this, it was, after all, his work. But this . . . this was different. Why should she have to do anything for Tacy . . . ?

Abel was in the doorway, looking his astonishment. 'What's going on?' he asked.

Tom was staring at her, waiting. For the first time she glanced down at the sleeping child. And one look at the tiny, crumpled little face and she was lost. 'I'll do it,' she said.

After dinner, when Tacy had pecked at the meal Sarah Jane provided and lay back, still exhausted, she opened her eyes to see her old friend beside her. 'Nancy!' she exclaimed.

'Tom asked me to come,' she said, a little ungraciously.

And Tacy whispered, 'Thank you, Nancy.'

'Was it bad?' Nancy asked, curiosity getting the better of animosity. 'And what are you going to name her?'

'Damaris Jane, after Grandmamma,' replied Tacy.

Nancy helped out on the Sunday and Monday. Then Francis returned, and Nancy said she'd really have to get back to Coventry. She had been shocked to see Tacy's wan, white face; she could see she was in pain, but now she looked a little better. So she thought it was time to inform her about the weavers.

'Abel's not well,' she said.

'Uncle Abel? Why, what's the matter with him?'

'He's got a cough, and he looks poorly.'

'I didn't know,' Tacy murmured.

'Well, you never come down now, do you?' Nancy asked, tartly, but Tacy shook her head.

'I don't have time,' she answered.

'You've got time to go to the church meetings and the balls,' Nancy said, and Tacy didn't tell her that she had hardly been in a condition to go to balls lately, and hadn't been invited to any more soirées, no doubt for the same reason. But she knew she'd have to visit Martha. Not merely to see her own baby, but to see Uncle Abel. She felt only a faint curiosity about her baby. The child was well, she was living, and although she was annoyed that Martha had the nursing of it, yet if it had to be . . .

But first things first. She must get help in the house. She got up after a week, but was surprised how weak she felt. 'Francis,' she said. 'You must get a girl from the workhouse.' And Francis went obediently, and returned with Bess.

She was a tall, handsome girl with fair hair and an

ample figure. Not exactly a workhouse brat, Tacy thought.

'Have you been in the house long?' she asked.

'I just went in to have a baby.'

'Oh. And where is the child?'

'Dunno. They took it off me.'

'When was that?'

'Three months ago.'

'Pity we hadn't known. You could have nursed my baby.' Better than Martha having it, Tacy thought, resentfully. 'Well, Bess, you look quite strong. You're not local?'

'I'm from Teddleton.'

The village past Borley Common. 'Well, there's a lot of work to do, Sarah Jane is getting old. And then there'll be my baby to look after — she's at a weaver's cottage now.'

Bess looked sulky, but she worked willingly enough. And Tacy received a visit from Mr Redmond.

She was sitting in the warehouse, checking over the stock. For though Tom had given out the work and she trusted him implicitly, she had to know what silk was there for further weaving. She was still weak, and had to rest on her high chair every quarter hour or so, when she tried to puzzle out if she had done the right thing in changing to the silk broker. It would save her time, but he would not give more than three months' credit. She wished she could have gone to London herself instead of trusting to Francis, who was so unknowing about silk.

There had been a thunderstorm in the night, and it had cooled the air somewhat. But the sun was shining again, sending beams of light through the narrow windows, slanting down to the floor between the piles of silk. And through the beams walked Mr Redmond, and greeted Tacy.

Tacy sat back. 'If you've come to ask why I go to church you're wasting your time,' she told him ungraciously.

'I haven't,' he said, mildly. 'If you are happier going to church, then do so, by all means.'

'I'm not happy,' Tacy said, angrily. 'How can I be happy when I've lost so much?'

'You have your husband, and your baby.'

Do I? Martha has my baby. She has Tom . . .

'You haven't been to see her yet? That's really why I came.'

'Oh?'

'Have you decided about the christening? Chosen the godparents?'

'No.' Tacy thought rapidly. She couldn't ask the church people, with her chapel association.

'I thought you might ask Martha.'

Martha?

'She is helping with the child,' he said, reasonably.

'That wasn't my doing. Anyway, I offered remuneration, but she refused.'

'Yes, I expect she did. Martha loves children. Think about it, Tacy. I know you are having to carry many burdens, but I'd hate to see you get bitter.'

'You expect me to turn the other cheek? My father did that, Mr Redmond, and where did it get him? To his grave. While George Healey gets on in the world.' Her eyes filled with angry tears.

'The wicked flourish like the green bay tree,' quoted Mr Redmond. 'It was ever thus.' A shaft of sunlight illumined his face. 'I'm against the present troubles just as you are. But there is a right way and a wrong way. I have been thinking, and I have a suggestion. That all the weavers join together –'

'We can't do that, can't hold meetings, thanks to the Combination laws –'

'I was thinking of a petition to Parliament,' Mr Redmond said.

'A petition?' Tacy asked, surprised.

'Yes. French ribbons are still banned, and so many are smuggled in as you know. Now there is talk about freely trading with the French again. We have to discuss this. So you see, it would help if you came down to see Martha again, let the weavers see that you support them.'

'Support them?' she cried, angrily. 'What do they think I am doing? Why am I slaving away with all this work? If George Healey had his way I'd have sold out to him, and where would they be then? And I only go to church to get people to help us.'

'Well,' Mr Redmond said after a pause. 'I'm not sure I agree with your methods, Tacy, and I know the weavers don't understand – '

'They think I'm just out for myself.'

'Well – '

'All right,' she conceded, wearily. 'I'll come. I have to see my baby anyway.'

'And if you could use your influence to stop the more lawless elements wanting to harm George Healey – '

'If you mean Tom Jacques, then hadn't you better ask Martha? She's his wife.'

Mr Redmond turned to go. Tacy said, 'I'll ask Martha to be godmother. And I might ask Tom to be godfather.'

Mr Redmond said, gravely, 'Thank you, Tacy.'

She watched him walk away, his shabby black coat, his trousers tucked into worn hessian boots, the hat in his hand green with age. Mr Redmond was not paid by the establishment as the church clergy were, but by the subscriptions of his flock. And when they had little money, the minister suffered too.

She wondered if he knew how she felt about Tom, and if he would have been so eager to draw her back into the weavers' community if he had known. Or would he have thought it all worthwhile?

The heat had returned the following day when Francis drove her to Martha's in the chaise. It was Wednesday, and a few looms were working, but not many. Children were running in the fields, the boys kicking an inflated pig's bladder, or climbing trees, the girls squatting round in circles. A few others, Martin among them, played in the street. Abel was sitting on a chair outside his front door and Tacy was shocked at his emaciated appearance.

'Uncle, how are you?' she cried, and as she alighted Martin ran to stroke the pony, who shook his head and snuffled.

'Middlin',' Abel replied, but Mrs Walters, who was never far from Abel if she could help it, called from her front doorway, 'He's poorly, Tacy, poorly.'

'Have you seen the doctor?' she asked, and he nodded, for the weavers had their own benefit club, which paid out in cases of sickness. 'What did he say?'

'Told me to eat plenty, and get fresh air,' said Abel, and Tacy was pleased that she had brought with her a box of tea and a cheese from the market. She hadn't known what to offer, but knowing how much they liked tea she had decided they would not be offended by that, it would make a change from the herb tea they drank when money was short. The cheese she had put in at the last moment.

'Is there anything I can do?' she asked, but Abel shook his head. And she wondered why she hadn't noticed he looked poorly when he brought his work back. Because I'm always in such a hurry, she answered her own question.

'I'll be better when the weather cools off,' Abel said. 'This heat mithers you.'

Tacy and Francis went round the back into the little

kitchen where the heat was ferocious, for Martha had to have a fire for cooking, though she'd let it go out now. The two babies lay in the wooden cradle, both crying, and were being rocked by William. Martha was washing baby clothes in a bowl on the bench outside the back door. There was no sign of Tom.

Martha came indoors, wiping her hands on her apron, and was given the cheese and the tea. She led them to the cradle, and Tacy stared down at the child, her child. She seemed to bear no resemblance to herself, her tuft of hair was dark, indeed she looked more like Martha than Tacy. Martha picked up the child and placed it in Tacy's arms. She smelled a little of sour milk, but looked healthy enough.

'I do thank you for taking care of her,' Tacy said. 'Is it too much for you?'

'I manage,' said Martha.

'And Uncle Abel – can he work?'

'A little. I help out.'

Tacy asked Martha if she would be godmother, and she agreed. And Abel, who came in, seemed pleased.

Yet Tacy felt uncomfortable; she didn't want to stay too long. Now Francis was holding the baby, and was smiling. Abel sat down in his chair, and Mrs Walters fussed in, followed by several of her innumerable children. The kitchen was overcrowded.

But none of the other weavers came, so Tacy led Francis back to the chaise.

'Uncle looks poorly,' she said as they drove back. 'I hope it isn't the consumption. They say it runs in families but I don't think Uncle's parents had it, so maybe it's not that.'

Francis wished she hadn't talked about inherited illness. He had looked at the baby and thought her charming, he would love this child. But he had fearfully searched the little face for any likeness to Sir William, the man he thought was responsible for his own dark shadow.

'You want me to be godfather?' Tom asked Tacy, his eyes laughing. 'I'm not a very religious person.'

'That won't matter.' Tacy did not tell him it was the *father* part of it that interested her, that made her feel closer to him, to imagine that Damaris was *theirs,* and not Martha's.

But he agreed, and the christening was duly carried out by the Reverend Mr Hewitt. And some time later, Mr Redmond told Tacy that he was preparing the petition, and would she like to come to Abel's . . .

The hot summer had merged into a warm autumn, and even now the weather was quite mild as she walked to the Patch. There were quite a few weavers gathered inside Abel's kitchen, overflowing into the yard. Matt and Enoch Walters, Jim Bailey, Bob and Harry Pettit, Luke Lakin . . . 'I couldn't ask all the weavers – ' Mr Redmond began.

'No, else you'd be put in jail,' Tom said. 'They're tightening up the law on meetings since someone tried to shoot the Regent.'

'If they did,' put in Harry Pettit.

'They did,' Tacy said. 'I was in London and I was told it was true. There were all sorts of demonstrations in London, someone saw a cap of liberty in Spa Fields, and tricolour flags.'

'The Government fears revolution,' said Mr Redmond, soberly. 'But there is so much unemployment in the country – and so much repression. But I am a little worried about this talk of trading with France, letting in their ribbons – '

'Letting in ribbons – to rival ours?' asked Tom hotly.

'What was the war for anyway? Beats me why, as soon as we've done fighting, and getting killed, then they straightway start trading wi' the enemy and put us out of work. Who won the war then?'

Mr Redmond said, 'All wars are futile. But I have the petition here, asking the Government to look into the plight of the ribbon weavers before they take such steps. Now, if you will all sign, then I will take it round the other weavers, and then place it in the Town Hall for more signatures. Those who cannot write can just make their mark.'

'They won't tek any notice,' Tom said. 'It's action we need, not petitions. Action against George Healey.'

But he signed the petition.

Before she left Tacy heard one item of disquieting news. It came from the Pettit brothers, always first to know what was going on. 'George Healey's going to build more houses,' said the tall, curly haired Bob.

Tacy turned quickly. 'More? But how can he? There's no more room in his back.'

'No, but there's room in other people's,' said Bob. 'Mr Broadbent's yard, they say.'

'Who says?' Tacy asked.

'Why, you know Healey's mekking his loom-shop bigger?' Now the plumper, brown-haired Harry, spoke. Tacy nodded. 'Well, we was talking to the builders on it – men he's brought in from outside, mark you, not Chilverton men – they told me. It's their next job.'

Tacy was appalled. 'It shouldn't be allowed,' she said, hotly.

'Can't you do anything?' Luke Lakin asked.

'What can I do?'

'You go to church. Talk to 'em about it. Tell Mr Broadbent he's likely to have 'em burnt down if he ain't careful –'

'Luke!' cautioned Mr Redmond, but Tacy was turning to go. And she worried about it all the way home.

'This is monstrous,' she said to Francis after supper as they sat for once in the parlour. Francis said nothing, and Tacy, as always, felt impatient with him. He'd been more than usually taciturn ever since the quarrel about Tacy finding his mother's letter with its disclosure about his father. Tacy couldn't see what the fuss was about. Couldn't he see that Sir William might help them if he knew? And goodness knows, she needed help desperately.

Who could she talk to about it? She still attended church, but her pregnancy had kept her away from any other functions, or so she assumed. She imagined it was not done to mix in polite society when pregnant, although it was all right for the weavers to work till the last minute, as she had done. But it left her out of touch, and not knowing how to get back in. Whom could she approach?

She went through them all. Mrs Peabody . . . Mrs Jennings, Mrs Warren . . . Of all the ladies Mrs Warren was the most pleasant. And she had invited Tacy and Francis once to her house. Yes, she would see Mrs Warren. She must think . . .

In January baby Damaris was weaned and brought home by Bess, who cared for her willingly, perhaps putting her in place of her own lost baby. And Tacy thought of a plan.

In the second week in February when the weather was turning colder, and the first snow of the winter had fallen, Tacy stood in her upstairs window watching the road. And when she saw Dr Warren leave the house on horseback she ran down, put on her overshoes and a warm cloak, and walked down to the Warrens' house. She could see no sign of life outside the Broadbents', though Bess had told her that there had been a pile of wood delivered last week.

She knocked at the Warrens' door, and a little maid answered. Tacy asked for the doctor. When told he was out, she stood, hesitating.

Mrs Warren came into the hall. 'Who is it, Mary? Oh, Mrs Barratt.'

'I came to see the doctor.' Tacy kept up the pretence.

'I'm afraid he had to see a patient. Would you like to come in and wait? Is it urgent?'

'Oh no.' Tacy hesitated again, then stepped into the hall, whispering, 'You see – it is a delicate matter, I do not know if I dare talk to him at all.'

'Would it help if I were there?'

'Oh . . . yes . . . if you would be so kind . . .'

'Come into the drawing-room, and we'll wait together.'

They sat, and over a dish of tea, Tacy, eyes lowered, talked of the worry about whether she could have another child after her difficult confinement, and Julia, who had no children, sympathised.

The talk passed to other matters, Tacy praying that the doctor would not return until her mission was accomplished. She asked if Mrs Warren had heard about Mr Broadbent's cottages.

'Indeed we have.' Julia frowned. 'I don't agree with it myself, we shall have them almost at our back doors.'

'Cannot we stop him?' Tacy asked.

'We-ell, of course, it's difficult. Sir William is behind Mr Broadbent, I mean, he finances the bank in part, as I suppose you know. So I'm not sure what we could do.'

Tacy tried not to grit her teeth. Sir William, always Sir William. 'I suppose not,' she sighed. 'Though – there are meetings from time to time aren't there? I know little of such matters, of course.'

'My husband attends the Vestry meetings,' said Mrs Warren. 'Then there is the committee formed to help the poor –' Tacy pricked up her ears, 'I am on that one, as my husband does not have the time –'

'You are? Then ladies are allowed?'

'Well, as I said, I go in my husband's place. But – would you like to help? I am sure that, as you have a business, you could be admitted. That is, if your husband would not wish –'

'He is a stranger to Chilverton, and does not have the same concerns,' Tacy told her. 'In fact,' she ended truthfully, 'the running of the business is left entirely to me. And I would love to do all I can to help the suffering of the poor.'

When the doctor returned, Julia put Tacy's problem to him. He told her not to worry, she could have a dozen children if she wished. Then Julia mentioned the committee, and Tacy left, thinking she wanted no more children, certainly not a dozen. But she did not particularly value his opinion, she remembered he had told Mrs Wynn in the Patch that she'd never have a child and she had four . . .

But she had gained her ends, she was on the committee. Julia was a nice person, she thought. How easy it was to fool nice people.

The first meeting was held on a blustery day in March in a small room over Mr Broadbent's chambers. Tacy walked to the Market Square, stopping to look critically at Mrs Bradley's new bonnets, was she using enough ribbon for trimming? Satisfied, she passed the druggist's with its array of coloured bottles and its big jar marked leeches; past Mr Jepson's the saddler from whence came the smell of new leather, and Mr Carr's horse tied outside while the owner haggled within, and finally to the bank, the side door open, leading to a wooden staircase.

She entered a little tentatively, having been careful to put on her warm grey mantle over her grey and blue gown, with a hat trimmed with her favourite silver and blue ribbon. It was her finest outfit, though she intended it to look quite casual. The others were already there, Mr Jennings, Mr Broadbent, Mr Hewitt, Mr Peabody, Mrs Warren and, of course, Sir William.

Mrs Warren introduced her as their new member and she was asked to sit down. Talk began, but no one seemed in a hurry to discuss Mr Broadbent's houses, or indeed the poor. The gentlemen exchanged views on politics, the doings of Lord Liverpool, the Prince Regent, Cobbett's *Political Register*, the 'twopenny trash' as Mr Peabody called it, saying it should be banned, as Tom Paine's *Rights of Man* had been. 'They might get into the wrong hands,' finished Mr Peabody, darkly.

'There's been trouble in the north, I believe,' said Mr Jennings. 'Had to call in the troops.'

'I think we should do something to help the poor in our town,' said Mrs Warren, bravely.

'But there aren't too many poor here,' said Mr Broadbent.

'And if there are it is entirely their own fault,' said Mr Hewitt, peevishly. 'When doing a full week the weavers earned nearly as much as I do. Then the minute they have a little short time they're complaining, instead of saving their money as we do.'

Mr Peabody said 'Hear, hear' but Tacy said, sweetly, 'The cases are not quite the same, Mr Hewitt. You have your money every week of the year, plus a house. The weavers do save, they have benefit clubs and so on, but when they have short time week after week, then their savings dwindle, and if they cannot pay the rent, they can be turned into the street.' She was getting angry. How little they know, she thought.

Julia Warren said, peaceably, 'Shall we think of some way of alleviating their distress?'

'What distress?' asked Mr Peabody. 'All they need to do is work harder.'

Now Tacy lost her temper, although she had promised herself she would not, that she would be all sweetness and light. 'How can they have work when George Healey brings in outsiders all the time to work more cheaply?' she asked hotly. 'So then our weavers come on the Parish,' and she shot them a look of triumph. Think about that, she thought. You won't be so keen to pay extra rates, will you?

Their faces were blank, only Sir William gave her an amused glance. But they decided to hold another ball at the end of March to help the poor, and again Tacy told Francis they must attend.

The Assembly Hall was decorated with new spring flowers, and as Sir William entered, Tacy wished with all her heart she could introduce Francis as his son. But he came over to ask her for a dance, and bade her save the supper dance for him too. And now many of the other men also wanted to dance with Tacy, and she urged Francis to ask the ladies. 'We must socialise,' she told him.

The supper dance was announced and Tacy went with Sir William. It was a buffet, as before, and when he had filled two plates, he led her into an ante-room. 'Now we can talk,' he said.

They started with the usual trivia, how pleasant the ball, how it would help the poor weavers . . .

'But,' Tacy said, wide-eyed, 'what is the use of helping the poor, when George Healey insists on his half-pay schemes, putting them out of work?'

'It's the way of the world,' said Sir William. 'The way of the world.'

They had finished their suppers. Sir William took the plates and put them on a side table, then sat closer to Tacy.

She decided to be bold. 'You're such an important man,' she whispered. 'Why do you bother with the likes of George Healey?'

He put his arm around her. 'He's a good businessman, that's why.'

'And I'm a good businesswoman.'

'Are you? You've got damn fine eyes.' And he bent his head and tried to kiss her. Tacy endured it, then broke away.

'I just need – ' she began, but he leaned towards her again.

'Don't worry your pretty little head about business,' he said, thickly. 'There are better things to think about . . . eh?' and again, his lips sought hers.

Tacy stood up. She knew she would not get anywhere with him in this amorous mood. 'The music is beginning,' she said. 'Let us dance.'

But I'll get you yet, she vowed, as they went back to the ballroom.

As a cold spring led into a chilly summer it became known that the Princess Charlotte was expecting a child. Tacy was overjoyed. This could only mean more fancy ribbons, and indeed, Mr Jarvis sent a number of extra orders.

Tacy thought long and hard about the coming birth, said to be expected at the end of October or thereabouts. Supposing the child were a boy, what celebrations there would be. Princess Charlotte was the heir to the throne, her son would be next in line . . . if it were a son.

There was a fifty-fifty chance. Girl or boy, there would be great rejoicing in the land, there'd be balls and ladies would need many new dresses. But if it were a boy, and she had a plentiful supply of extra ribbons made for a boy, she might make a fortune . . . She went to see Tom and Abel.

'It's taking a chance,' Abel demurred.

'But how much we'd gain if it were a boy.'

'What had you in mind?' he asked.

'I thought a new design, could you get something done on the Jacquard, Tom?'

'I could. But we get the designs from Coventry, you know that. If we had more looms we could design our own cards –'

'Yes, yes, but now?'

'It would cost.'

'We'll do it,' she decided. 'Get a design, Tom. Something on blue ribbon, something original, bells, babies . . .'

Tom was sketching. 'How about this?' he asked.

This was a wide ribbon in blue with pictures of a baby in white. A gold crown at the side, and the word Prince in between.

'That's it,' said Tacy.

'I'm not sure if the Jacquard could take this,' demurred Tom. 'Better on a hand-loom.'

'I can do it,' said Abel.

'It'll cost,' repeated Tom.

'Do it,' Tacy said. 'We'll have yards of blue with the baby from you, Abel – and you Tom, can do the one with bells and crowns. And – don't let anyone else see the design. Can you trust the Coventry men?'

Tom shrugged. 'As much as you can trust anyone.'

'Do it, and if it's a boy we'll make a fortune. If it's a girl we can keep them for next time, she's bound to have a boy some time. We'll be able to get more Jacquards, Tom.'

Tom nodded, and Abel returned to his loom, and began to cough.

Spirits lifted in the summer, for in August the price of bread was reduced and was sold in the streets in barrows. 'Things are looking up,' said Tacy. Things seemed better all round. Abel's cough improved, baby Damaris celebrated her first birthday by taking two steps unaided, even Sarah Jane stopped grumbling.

In November came the blow. So sudden and so horrific they could hardly believe the Crier. Little groups of people huddled in the rain, listening to the shocking news.

Princess Charlotte and her baby were both dead.

The weavers were genuinely sorry, even though it would put them out of work. The Princess had been well liked, and on the day of the funeral all shops were shut, and both church and chapel held services in the evening, people dressed in black.

Black! After the funeral the Prince Regent went to Brighton where he was to spend three months in deep mourning. Tacy faced ruin.

She sat looking at the accounts.

How could this have happened? Never in her wildest dreams had she imagined anything so bad. She would have lost money if the baby had been a girl, but to have no baby, and no Princess . . . Oh, babies did die, and women in childbirth too . . . But what had the doctor been doing? Was it neglect? It must have been. The country agreed, and though the Prince and Prince Leopold both cleared Sir Richard Croft from blame, he was so reviled that he committed suicide. And to think the Duke of Clarence had ten bastards . . .

Now she was in debt. The imports had to be paid for, the broker would not wait. Mr Jarvis's orders were not usually paid until the retailers paid him, and she always allowed him credit. Now there would be no sales.

She had to get money.

She knew her bank in Coventry would not allow her any more credit – she was already overdrawn. Who else? Mr Broadbent in Chilverton . . . ?

What had Julia Warren said? Sir William finances Mr Broadbent. It was her only hope.

Three months without sales! She said to Francis, 'I'm going to see Mr Broadbent. He can lend us money.'

She went to the office in the Market Square, next door to Mr Peabody. Next to them was the Fleur de Lys where the gentlemen went to order a midday repast, or drink a little and smoke a pipe. Trembling, she pushed the thick oak door and entered.

Brown panelled walls, a brown counter, where the clerk came to her, and she asked to see Mr Broadbent.

She waited, then was taken into a comfortable room, suitable for a man of comfortable means; a well-set, middle-aged man in fine cloth frock-coat and silk cravat. Tacy thought fleetingly that she wouldn't be able to protest about his building houses now.

He rose to greet her, listened as she asked for a loan. Then he asked for full details of the business and how she came to lose money. She told him, unwillingly, of the Charlotte fiasco.

'Then your judgment was at fault,' he pronounced weightily.

'These things happen in the weaving,' said Tacy, shortly.

'And your husband agrees?' asked Mr Broadbent. 'Now you are married the business belongs to him.'

In theory, Tacy thought, angrily, though I do all the

work. Aloud she said, 'Yes, of course.'

'I shall need his signature,' said Mr Broadbent.

'That's no problem, Francis will do as I ask.' But it irked her to have to *ask* Francis when *she* ran the business.

'Then – if you will grant me a few days,' he said, non-committally. 'I will let you know. If you could call again on Friday.'

She thanked him, too depressed even to assume pretty manners. She knew why he had to wait. He had to consult his superior – Sir William.

On Friday she heard his reply. They would be granted the loan, at a fixed per cent.

It seemed reasonable. She had borrowed money, she would pay it back. A straightforward business deal.

Perhaps Sir William liked her enough to be kind. But she did not tell Francis that Sir William controlled the bank . . .

Francis said nothing when he signed for the loan, any more than he had when Tacy started running the business after her father died. But resentment was building up inside him. He did not recognise the feeling, but he had felt it once before, on the ship when he'd been forced to work at things he hated. It was the resentment of an inadequate man which in time would lead to an explosion.

Chapter seven

In 1819 there was trouble all over the country. Weavers and spinners in Lancashire had been on strike, as had the keelmen on Tyneside. In Chilverton, three footpads robbed Mr Broadbent of money, a watch and snuff box, and were hanged on the gallows at Warwick. A youth was found guilty by the magistrates of robbing a garden and fined five pounds for trespass; if he defaulted he would be publicly whipped. A sect of Ranters preached in the streets and were fined fifteen pounds for not having a licence. They chose to go to jail. Mr Philimores' Company of Comedians held their theatre at the Fleur de Lys.

Bess went to see the Comedians and enjoyed herself hugely. She would dearly have liked to see the public hanging too, but Tacy said she must stay with Damaris.

Tacy herself kept a low profile these days. She had attended no more balls nor committee meetings since her visit to Mr Broadbent's bank; she did not want to see Sir William. After the death of the Princess she had no option but to leave the weavers without work until more orders came in, and she regretted heartily her haste in making the extra ribbons for the new baby which would never be used – or at least not until a Prince was born. And as the Prince Regent refused to live with his wife again this event seemed unlikely.

The mourning period passed and orders trickled in again, and Tacy was able to start repayments of the loan. But she had to reduce prices to the weavers below the List of 1816, which caused some complaints. And when Queen Charlotte – George III's wife – died in November the Court was thrust into mourning again. The Crier requested shops and warehouses to close for the day, but few did so, unlike for the funeral of the Princess. The weavers had no love for the Queen, and they were getting tired of Royal funerals.

There was a good deal of restlessness in the town, and Tacy wondered if it was time to start going to the Committee meetings again. She spent her evenings now sitting in the parlour, sometimes with Bess and little Damaris. Francis might come in for ten minutes or so, but he said little, and soon went back to his counting-house, and if she tried to talk to him he barely answered. Since the baby's birth he had not moved back into her bedroom and he never attempted to make love to her now and she wondered drearily if this was all her life was going to be.

Of her child she saw little, except for the odd hour Bess brought her into the parlour. Damaris was a placid little girl, though with a will of her own, something Tacy was not to realise for many years, for, as Bess might have told her, she did not stamp or scream, but simply went her own way regardless.

Bess, once her workhouse ill-treatment had worn off, had blossomed into a buxom young woman, full-breasted and with long hair, supposedly brought back in a chignon, but too often loose and flowing round her face. She was strong, and even Sarah Jane could find no fault with her work. She was up at the crack of dawn, she scrubbed out the kitchen and hall, mopped the parlour and the dining-room, lit the fires, and had the kettle boiling for breakfast before Sarah Jane shuffled in. Then she looked after Damaris, usually taking her out in the afternoons, often down to the Patch.

No-one ever queried where she went, and if she found one or two young weavers waiting to walk over the fields, she and Damaris would accompany them. And more than once, Bess and a swain disappeared behind a hedge, leaving Damaris alone to make daisy-chains, or to pick blackberries in season. On one such occasion Damaris marched off to Martha's on her own, leaving Bess to follow.

Another time, Bess wanted to go one way, Damaris did not, and without a word the child turned towards Martha's. Bess chased her, smacked her, then picked her up and carried her. Once on her feet, Damaris did no more than turn and walk back. Bess, laughing, caught up with her. 'You're a caution,' she said. 'Come on then. Your way.'

Damaris loved her Aunt Martha. She would sit in the little kitchen which always seemed to be full, both with her own boys and other people's, but Martha never turned anyone away. Quiet fair-haired William, just four now, was always protective towards Damaris, though Martin, the eldest at six, and learning to read and write at Sunday school, would tease her unmercifully. Mossy, another black-eyed little rogue, always 'into things', was her own age, and the latest baby, Josiah, called Joey, also resembling Tom, seemed to have his mother's placid temperament. At least he lay quietly in his cradle for most of the time.

Aunt Martha had a soft, ample lap, always willing to hold some fretful child and soothe away their troubles, Damaris included. Her voice was soft too, unlike Tacy's, which could be sharp at times. Sometimes in the evenings – if Damaris were lucky enough to be there at that time – she would trim bonnets with ribbons, and was so good at it that her friends would ask her to trim theirs too and in return would pay her, or give gifts of pork from a newly killed pig, or little clothes for the boys.

'See,' she would say to Damaris, watching intently. 'How you can make changes in bonnets. Put a wide black ribbon around and it is ready for a funeral. Change it to a pretty rainbow one and you're ready for a ball. Then – and she draped a red ribbon over the yellow straw, 'Now you see poppies in the cornfield.' And Damaris *could*.

But in the daytime Martha had to take over from Uncle Abel more and more these days. Then Damaris and Martin and William would be her helpers, taking the pirns from the machine to the loom, carrying the bobbins. And Uncle Abel would tell them about the wild flowers in the fields, and how to distinguish the different birds. And he'd sit a lot in his own garden, among the marigolds and the pansies and the hollyhocks, but Uncle Tom had to help him dig the vegetables.

She liked to go to Uncle Tom's house too, and he showed her his great new Jacquard loom, and the first time she had gazed in wonder at the brown cards with holes hanging right up to where the ceiling should be, and when Uncle Tom said those cards made the pretty patterns, she asked, 'Is it black magic?' for Martin had been teasing her with tales of black magic until Uncle Abel threatened to smack him. Uncle Tom said, 'Not quite, but I'll show you how it's done when you're bigger.' And she would sit, fascinated, watching the brown cards drop slowly down, while Uncle Tom's fingers manipulated the shuttle so fast that it seemed to move on its own. And his fingers would caress the silk as if he loved it, and Damaris learned to love it too. She knew right from the start that the Barratts' weaving business would come to her, and she had no inclination, ever, of doing anything else.

On Sundays Damaris went to chapel with Bess, for her mother did not always go to church in the mornings, and the evening service was late for a young child. Damaris preferred chapel, for Martin and William were there, and of course Aunt Martha and Uncle Abel. And she joined in the rousing hymns with gusto. To Damaris, Aunt Martha's was her first home, the Red House came second.

If Tacy had no time for her daughter, it gave Damaris more freedom, which suited her, and left Tacy to get on with her work. So everyone was satisfied. Her father did not loom very largely in her small life, he smiled and petted her when he saw her, but that was not very often. When he sat in the parlour he was, if Mamma was there, quiet and subdued as if he were thinking about something else.

But now, as June brought welcome warm breezes and the fields were starred with daisies and buttercups and dandelions for the weavers to make wine, Tacy felt she must get to another committee meeting. For although they did not always meet to discuss ways of helping the poor – most of them considered this unnecessary – there were gatherings held every month in the same little room for talk. After all, these were troubled times, with riots all over the country, and they only had to remember France and the revolution . . . Wilberforce had been right to pass the Combination Laws to stop people meeting to improve conditions or wages, or to go on strike, and to send them to jail if they did any of these things. So Tacy put on a pretty blue gown – she was out of mourning now – with her hat with wide ribbon tying beneath the chin, and set out, passing Mr Broadbent's yard with its crowd of little cottages huddled inside, and on to the Market Square.

She entered the committee room somewhat hesitantly, but was greeted warmly by Julia Warren. 'We haven't seen you for such a long time,' she said. 'But I know how busy you are.'

Sir William came in, he greeted her too, but said no more, and Tacy wondered what she had expected. That he'd ask why she dare borrow money? That he'd try to kiss her? He was followed by Mr Jennings, the High Constable, a man heartily disliked by the people for his hectoring manner. He was a tall thin man with a red face and a habit of clearing his throat with a loud H'rmm. Mr Peabody, Mr Broadbent and Mr Hewitt made up the rest of the committee.

The first talk did not interest Tacy, and, as the afternoon wore on, she began to think she had worried unduly, that it was her imagination that something was going on in the town, until Mr Peabody spoke.

'I believe there has been trouble locally,' he said, taking out his gold snuff box. 'Meetings have been held in the Patch.'

'Meetings?' asked Mr Jennings. 'Outdoor meetings?'

'I think the weavers are in great distress,' murmured Mrs Warren.

'They are, and have been for a long time, as we all know,' Tacy said, shortly. 'I expect if they have nothing to do, they just stand and talk together.'

'Oh, it's more than that, I heard,' said Mr Peabody, tapping his snuff box. 'I think they're out for trouble — some of them, that is.'

'And which ones would they be?' asked Mr Jennings.

'I heard the name Tom Jacques mentioned,' Mr Peabody told him. 'I hope they're not going to begin all this Union nonsense, as the weavers in Lancashire did.'

'Combinations are against the law,' said the High Constable.

'Exactly,' agreed Mr Peabody.

'H'rmm. I'll have to keep my eyes open,' said Mr Jennings. 'Take the ringleaders before the magistrates, eh? H'rmm.'

Tacy left, trying not to appear in too much of a hurry. Julia Warren asked her when she was coming to the Assembly Rooms again, and she smiled and said, 'Soon, of course.' Then she went home.

They were awaiting her arrival for dinner, which was now taken about five o'clock. Francis was sitting in the parlour while Damaris was playing with Bess in the garden. Tacy wanted to ask Bess if she'd heard anything about meetings in the Patch, but preferred not to talk about it before Francis.

Tacy did not go to Martha's house very often, she did not want to see Tom's wife and family, it only brought home to her what she had lost. Tom still helped in the warehouse and she was able to talk to him about the work, and could pretend that they would go home together. For after six years of marriage she felt more alienated from Francis than ever. They would discuss work and the accounts amicably enough and that was all. Francis seldom sat in the parlour now but would disappear, presumably to his own room, and she knew he'd always had these moody spells. But if he did remain in the parlour when she was not working herself little would be said, so, when Damaris had gone to bed, Tacy had started the habit of reading, and was currently working her way through Miss Austen's novels. But if she should look up she would find Francis' eyes on her with a sort of watchful look, though when she met his eyes he immediately turned away. But she was uneasy.

So she tried to forget with Tom. He stayed every Saturday when she'd given all the work out, and they'd discuss matters. And she'd see him bending down to pick up a bundle of silk, see how the black hair curled into the nape of his neck, and she would stare at the nape, so boyish and somehow defenceless and want to kiss it, and take him in her arms . . . then she'd give herself a little shake and remind herself that he was not a boy but a man, father of four children. Yet he was only twenty-six, and she twenty-three . . . But it was his being the father of the four children she could not forget. Martha's children, that kept on being born almost every year, while she and Francis . . . So she kept away from the Jacques' house, hating to see the signs of domesticity, to see the boys, especially Martin, whom she saw as the cause of it all.

So when would they be having their meeting? How could she find out? Tom had said nothing on Saturday, but then, she had been in a reflective mood herself, having only come back from London the previous day. Since taking on the loan from Mr Broadbent, she tried in all ways to cut down on any needless expenditure, and she confined her visits to London to one a month. Mr Jarvis was no problem, he could send his orders by post, and though she liked to see the broker occasionally, her main reason for the journey was Mr Fotheringay. Mr Jarvis would send her orders for what was needed now, but Mr Fotheringay would tell her of what was coming, what the ladies talked about, and he was invariably right. But Mr Fotheringay being, as he implied, on the fringes of the *ton*, could not do anything so vulgar as accept money for information, no, they had to keep up a pretence that all was talk between friends, and it hadn't been easy at first to find a way of recompensing him without insulting him. When her father was alive they could meet in Mr Fotheringay's chambers, close to Mayfair where the fashionable society lived. But after his death they could not meet in a bachelor's apartment – or so he said – and another way had to be found. Mr Fotheringay would not take her to a vulgar inn – though Tacy would not have minded – so in the end they settled on Vauxhall Gardens, or Ranelagh, up the river and up the social scale, and they had season tickets for both, costing one guinea each, for which Tacy paid, together with meals and any other incidental expenses. Tacy wondered sometimes if it was worth keeping Mr Fotheringay on, and this was one of the things she discussed with Tom, but he thought she should.

Tom knew she had borrowed money after the death of the Princess Charlotte, but she did not tell him any other details of her finances. She had started repaying the loan, but it was hard going, and sometimes she felt – especially after going to London – absolutely *wrung*, tired of having to count every penny, grudging the trip to London with its coach fares, her absence from the warehouse. She left Francis in charge, for someone had to be there to give out work to any weaver who required more, and when coming back she always had to check that Francis had not made any mistakes and given fine gauze to Joe Bates who could only manage sarsanets. Then the rush to get the ribbons packed and down to the canal, the preparing for the next week . . . no, she had had no time to talk to Tom. Yet he had said nothing about any meetings, no doubt he knew she would disapprove. But she had to warn them, and did not want to tell Tom himself; knowing him he would take no notice. No, she had to be there to tell them all, warn them of the dangers.

There was only one person she could ask, who might know – Bess. So, after supper was over, she went to the kitchen.

She liked the kitchen, it was always warm and friendly. Copper pans gleamed in the firelight and Sarah Jane sat in the old wooden rocking chair beside the new hob grate her father had installed, which was built right into the chimney breast with extended cast iron hobs over a door for the oven. Several hams hung on hooks from the oak beams, while Damaris and Bess sat at the scrubbed white table, Damaris eating a piece of oatcake – she always ate in the kitchen with Bess.

Tacy greeted her daughter, who smiled, but went on eating. 'I wondered,' she said to Bess, 'if you had heard of any meeting in the Patch.'

Bess hesitated, and it was Damaris who said, 'Yes, it's tonight.'

Tacy looked at her in surprise. 'You were down there then?' she asked Bess.

'Well, we call in Abel's from time to time,' Bess replied.

'Oh.' Tacy was nonplussed. She wasn't sure if she wanted her child to visit Martha's very often. 'I know you take her for walks,' she said to Bess. 'But –'

'What's the harm?' asked Sarah Jane. 'The child needs others to play with, can't sit here all day with a lot of old folks.'

Tacy supposed she was right. Anyway, she hadn't time to think about it now. She nodded, and left, and prepared to go to Abel's.

She could hear no sound from any looms as she approached. Children were playing in the road, a sure sign that no work was being done. Still, it was Tuesday, but she felt apprehensive all the same. What was going on? She looked for the weavers.

They were together in Abel's kitchen. Tom, his brothers, Mr Redmond, the Pettits, Joe Bates, Luke Lakin, Jim Bailey and his brother, the Walters ... several more crowded in the front room. Martha was not there, nor the children, obviously she had taken them upstairs. She entered, and a silence fell.

Then Tom said, 'Well, look who's here.'

'Have I no right to be here?' she asked, a little angrily.

'You're a gaffer,' muttered someone from the back, and she waited for Tom to say it was all right, but he didn't.

She said, 'I've come to warn you.'

'Warn us what the rich folks are saying?' muttered Joe Bates, always a rebel.

'Yes,' she cried. 'You must all go home. Mr Jennings is watching you.'

'What?' Tom was laughing.

'You've been having meetings!' she accused.

Silence. Each man looked away or at his neighbour. No one spoke.

'Oh come on,' Tacy said, impatiently. 'I'm on your side, that's why I'm here.'

'All right, so we have to discuss matters, and there isn't room here for everyone,' said Tom.

'What exactly did Mr Jennings say?' asked Mr Redmond, quietly.

'He said he'd be keeping an eye on Tom,' Tacy told him. 'And if he finds you combining to try to improve your conditions, to start a Union, or to go on strike, he'll have you before the magistrates, and then you'll get three months' hard labour.'

'Well, we are thinking of starting a union,' said Tom defiantly. 'So we must have meetings. We've got to improve our working conditions and the only way to do that is to stop George Healey –'

'You mustn't!' Tacy cried.

'Mustn't what? Meet outside? Start a union?'

There was a buzz of talk, and Mark, Tom's brother, said, 'He's right. We do have to talk together.'

Now the talk grew heated, and Tacy stood in the doorway, looking towards Abel to calm them down. But Abel sat white and still, too poorly to remonstrate. The talk grew louder, one man jumped on the table.

Then Mr Redmond stood up. 'Quiet,' he called, 'if you please.'

The muttering died down.

'We will meet together,' said Mr Redmond. 'We'll meet in the chapel.'

Silence. A gust of wind rattled the windowpanes.

'In chapel?' asked Bob Pettit.

'Of course,' said Tom. 'No constable can drive us out of there. We'll have a meeting in chapel. Room for all and to spare.'

There was mounting excitement. Tacy was caught up in it, and said, 'Oh yes.'

But Tom said, 'I don't know if this is for you, Tacy. You're on the other side, and you're church.' She wasn't sure if he were joking or not, but she followed them to the chapel, where Mr Redmond stood before them.

'Friends,' he said. 'We are here to join together to fight for freedom. We have been fighting for freedom for a long time, freedom to worship – for which some of us had to take a perilous journey over the sea to America. Now we are having laws made to take away our freedom to ask for enough pay to live on, to combine. Weavers in Lancashire are forming a union and we will too. Here in our chapel we will again fight for freedom.'

And there were resounding cheers.

In July there was trouble in Birmingham, and a month later 80,000 people assembled in St Peter's Fields in Manchester to hear the Radical orator, Henry Hunt, address a meeting. The local JPs ordered the yeomanry to disperse the crowd with their sabres and a dozen people, some of them women, were killed and 400 injured. The 'massacre of Peterloo' appalled the country, though the Prince Regent sent the JPs a message of thanks and congratulation, and the Duke of Wellington strongly supported their action. Henry Hunt was sentenced to two and a half years' imprisonment for his speech at the meeting, and the government placed further restrictions on political agitation.

All this seemed to inflame the weavers. The chapel meetings continued, but Tacy heard no more of what was going on until Tom and Bob Pettit called to see her. She was, as always, in the warehouse, and as they entered she turned in surprise. 'Why, hello,' she began. 'I was just counting the silk for next week's orders.'

'It's not about orders,' Tom said. 'We are here as spokesmen for the whole of the weavers. We have our meetings in chapel, and we want our prices adjusted.'

Tacy put down the hanks she was holding and moved to the counter. 'You mean?' she asked.

'We mean we cannot go on like this, prices being reduced all the time. We want to return to the old price list of 1816.'

Tacy stood still. 'I can't do that,' she told them.

'If you don't,' Tom said, 'we shall go on strike.'

The sunlight gleamed through the windows of the warehouse, showing up a thin covering of dust on the counter. Tacy automatically swept it away as she asked, wearily, 'How can I pay you more when George Healey pays so much less?'

'We're going to see him as well, don't you worry,' Tom said. 'It's time for a reckoning with George Healey.'

'Tom.' She was hurt now that he was taking this line with her, when he knew she'd been doing her best, when she thought they were comrades. 'You know I can't pay more. I haven't had the orders.'

'And you know we can't live on the money we get now. What are we supposed to do? Emigrate? Or die of starvation, like Abel?'

'Hush, Tom,' murmured Bob Pettit, but Tom was in a rage, his black eyes flashing.

Tacy faced him. 'What about Abel?' she asked. 'Why isn't he here? He's not such a hothead as you are.'

'Abel's dying,' said Tom. 'As you'd know if you ever came down to see.'

'And whose fault is it I don't come?' she flashed. 'Who told me I wasn't wanted at the meetings in chapel?'

'Because you're a boss,' Tom retorted.

Tacy was hardly listening as he ranted on. Was Abel dying? And was it because he hadn't enough money? But he'd always saved in the past . . . yes, but now there was Martha, and her children . . . yet Tom worked too . . .

Bob said, 'I'm sorry, Tacy, that it's come to this. But we are in trouble.'

She walked to the end of the counter, looked over the piles of silk. There had not been many new orders from Mr Jarvis, and Mr Fotheringay had not been very encouraging. The death of the Queen hadn't helped matters, coming so soon after the Princess, ladies didn't seem to have the heart for festivities. She had had to reduce prices again, and hadn't realised how angry Tom had been about it. This, no doubt, was the cause of his recent coolness towards her. Yet . . . what could she do? She was so tired of the eternal pinching and scraping, of trying to make ends meet when too often they wouldn't. But she couldn't afford a strike, nor to alienate Tom.

She said, abruptly, 'I'll pay by the List.'

'Good,' said Tom. 'Come, Bob.'

But Bob hung behind. 'He's worried about Abel,' he told Tacy. 'He don't mean half he says.'

'You don't have to explain Tom to me,' she answered, and wondered drearily how she would manage.

That evening she heard the Crier in the street, and she went out to listen. 'Take heed. There will be a meeting of journeymen and weavers in the Patch tomorrow morning at nine o'clock. Take heed . . .'

'Oh no there won't,' shouted George Healey. 'I'll stop that. Where is the constable?'

The Crier had moved to the Market Square, and Mr Broadbent came out of his office, portly and business-like. Then Mr Jennings appeared, and Mr Broadbent and Mr Healey formally requested that the meeting be abandoned.

'At least wait till we hear from Coventry, see what they are doing,' said Mr Broadbent.

Tacy turned back to the Red House, and Francis was with her. 'If you drop prices any more you'll have difficulty in meeting the loan repayments to Mr Broadbent,' he warned.

'What can I do?' she asked. 'Francis, go down to the Patch, see what's going on.'

Francis went, and returned to say the weavers were all in chapel, at a meeting. 'There was a lot of shouting,' he said. 'I think Mr Redmond was trying to calm them down, but they wouldn't have it.'

'And Tom?' But she knew the answer. Without Abel's steadying influence there would be no holding Tom. Mr Redmond might try, though she wasn't sure how far he disagreed with Tom – if at all.

She went to bed wearily, and was up early in the morning. Already the sun was shining, it promised to be a hot day. A day for pleasant relaxing, not for wrestling with intractable weavers. She pulled on her dark blue muslin dress which she wore for warehouse work, hurried through breakfast and went into the warehouse.

No one came in, but it was Thursday, usually a day when the weavers were busy finishing their work. Yet, was it her imagination or was there a strange hush over the town? She pulled on a sunbonnet, and went to the road. Nothing moved.

But in the distance she could hear – what? A faint

stirring, a rumbling noise from the Patch. She hesitated. Go out in this shabby old gown? But she felt a flutter of apprehension, almost of fear. She started walking.

And knew her fears were well founded. Groups of weavers stood around in the Patch, and as she neared them she grabbed the nearest person, a woman. 'What is it?' she asked.

'They're on strike,' the woman said, flatly.

'We're stoppin' work till the regulation price accordin' to the List of 1816 is maintained,' someone was shouting, she could not see who it was.

Now they were marching, over a hundred, men and women, towards George Healey's loom-shop. He met them at the door.

'No!' he yelled. 'If my hands leave they shall not enter again.'

His weavers stood in the doorway, white-faced, George Healey before them.

Tom shouted, 'Let's donkey him. He always pays under price.'

'Get away!' yelled George Healey, and now his wife joined him, arms flailing as if she would fight them herself. 'I'll send for the yeomanry,' she cried.

'Send for the Cavalry,' shouted George Healey. And now the High Constable appeared, followed by Mr Broadbent and Mr Peabody.

'I'll send for Captain Ludford Ansley of the Cavalry,' fussed Mr Peabody, importantly. 'I told you how it was.'

Mr Jennings stepped forward. 'No need for the Cavalry,' he said, marshalling his constables in readiness. 'We can manage.'

Then Joe Bates came down the road leading the donkey that belonged to old Betsey Bates, his great-aunt, who lived in a shack on the Common and rented the beast out for a shilling plus sixpence with a little cart.

He trundled the donkey towards Healey's and Tom grasped the nearest of his workers, he was lifted on to the donkey's back, face to tail, and to boos and catcalls was driven through the streets.

'Get George Healey,' a weaver shouted. 'He's the one.'

Tacy saw Martha in the crowd, little Joey in her arms, the others clinging to her skirts. Mr Redmond was beside her. Bess was there, holding Damaris. Tacy called, 'Tom! Leave it now.'

Too late! Tom stepped towards George Healey, grabbed at him, Healey lifted his clenched fist, Tom dodged it and grasped his coat tails, the constables pulled him back, led him away. He was taken to prison.

Now there was scuffling and fighting between the constables and the weavers driving the donkey. The man on its back was rescued, Joe Bates and Bob Pettit were taken to jail. Tacy pushed her way towards Mr Redmond. 'What will it mean?' she asked, in agitation.

'They'll have to appear at the Assizes,' Mr Redmond replied, soberly. 'It could mean transportation.'

'Oh no!' whispered Martha.

Tacy wheeled round, and in a moment she was back at the Red House. Round the back, to the stables. 'Jobey!' she called. 'Jobey! Quick! I want the chaise.'

There was no answer. No sign of Jobey.

'Oh drat the fellow.' Tacy was half-crying in frustration. 'I must go . . . it will take too long to get the chaise myself.' What to do? Ride horseback? But she didn't have time to change into her riding outfit.

She looked down at her old blue gown. Hardly the dress to go calling, but the skirt was wide, she could ride without a saddle . . . astride. It would be much quicker, over the fields. She led the horse out into the yard, hoisted up her skirts, stood on the mounting-step and was on the horse and away.

Thank heavens Papa cannot see me, she thought.

There was a back lane running behind the houses, so she did not have to go through the High Street. She skirted the Patch, though she guessed most of the weavers were still in the Market Square, and on to the Common.

Brownie was a small, quiet horse more used to ambling around with the chaise than riding free, Tacy wondered if he even knew what galloping was. But as they left the Common – deserted now – and went on to open fields Brownie sniffed the fresh morning air and began to enjoy himself. Part of Tacy, the part that was not worried sick about Tom, enjoyed it too, bowling along over the green green grass, passing some harvesters in Farmer Wilton's meadow, where the great waggons were tended by men in smocks and women in sunbonnets who all stopped to wave as she passed. She wished she had the leisure to ride more often, to relax in a pleasant manner, instead of always being harried and rushed with no time to spare for pleasure.

It was hot, yet the breeze kept her cool enough. She tucked her dress between her legs endeavouring to cover at least a part of her limbs as they entered the last lap, the road to Fargate Manor. Up the long drive, past the neat lawns, the flower beds, and into a small coppice of trees, where she called, 'Whoa,' to Brownie, slid off his back and tethered him to one of the trees. She walked to the door and rang the bell.

'I want to see Sir William,' she said imperiously to the maid, lest she think her a serving wench and send her to the back door. And please let him be in, she prayed. Please . . .

'Who shall I say is calling?' asked the maid.

'Mrs Barratt. It is a matter of urgency.'

She was admitted into the hall with its thick rugs and

wide staircase leading to the upper rooms. She paced up and down as she waited. What to say . . . ? She had to save Tom, she couldn't bear it if he were sent to prison, or transported to another land. She faced the fact squarely. She loved Tom. She would sacrifice anything for him.

By the time Sir William appeared she was composed enough, knowing what she would tell him. She took off her sunbonnet and wished she looked better. She glanced down at her gown and saw to her horror that, where she had tucked it in over the horse's back there were two brown lines from the horse's sweat, and she held the sunbonnet in front of her to hide the marks. Her hair had come loose from its tight band, she could feel it dropping over her forehead and didn't realise that Sir William, descending the staircase, saw only a mass of wayward curls, and the figure of a girl showing up clearly through the tight muslin dress.

'Well, Mrs Barratt,' said Sir William, leading her into the drawing-room. 'You come to see me?'

'Yes. I have something to ask of you.'

'Then pray be seated.'

She sat on a couch with rolled end and claw feet, he sat opposite and waited.

'Sir William,' she said at last. 'I always seem to be asking for your assistance.' He bowed his head, but did not help her.

She looked round the room. Another time she would have liked to study the Chippendale furniture, the paintings on the walls, now she was too full of anxiety. Her gaze returned to him, quietly dressed now in his dark green frock-coat over a yellow waistcoat, and the usual pantaloons, tight on his portly figure. She drew a breath. 'Sir William,' she said. 'I shall tell you a secret.'

'Oh?' He did not move.

'I am married to your son.'

He laughed, showing several discoloured teeth. 'What nonsense is this? My son Lewis is far away.'

'No, this is another son, one you did not know you had. Did you not know Florence Brooks?'

'I did.' He didn't seem perturbed, she noted. What had she expected?

'She was his mother. She left your employ. Francis is your son.'

'And he didn't see fit to tell me?' He seemed faintly amused.

'No. He is proud. He prefers not to presume.'

'But you do presume.' Was he laughing at her? She'd hoped he'd be disconcerted, that she'd have the advantage. Or that he'd look on Francis as family.

She moved her sunbonnet, then remembered its purpose and put it back. From somewhere came the barking of a dog. She said, 'I have a favour to ask of you, Sir William.'

'Carry on.'

'The disturbance today. Several of the men are in prison.'

'And rightly so.'

'Then you have heard?' And, as he nodded. 'One of them – he is one of my best workers. Tom Jacques.'

'And?' He looked faintly bored now.

'You are a magistrate, Sir William. He has been taken to prison. Can you not get him out?'

'No no. He has to come before the Bench tomorrow. That is the law.'

The law! Who cared for the law? 'But you will be on the Bench, will you not? You can release him then?'

Now he stood up and walked to the great window overlooking the flowerbeds, the well-tended lawns. He stared out, then turned. 'I might,' he said, and moved towards her. 'But what do I get in return, hey? I think this is not the first favour I have granted you.'

'No.' She got to her feet, the sunbonnet dangling from her hand, uncaring now of the soiled dress. 'I am deeply grateful. I – '

His arm was around her now. 'So what do you give me in return? Eh? A kiss?'

'Yes. Yes, a kiss.'

She felt his lips pressing hers in a kiss so unlike those Francis gave her, even on that strange night when he was so upset, that she flinched. It was as though he were insulting her in some way, a way she hadn't known, hadn't realised that kisses could be insulting.

She pulled herself away, drew herself to her full height. She was still Tacy Barratt.

He was watching her. 'You're not ready for that,' he stated. 'How old are you, Tacy?'

He'd called her Tacy. As if she were some little light o'love. 'Twenty-three,' she said.

'So old? One day,' he said, softly, 'I shall have the pleasure of teaching you all you do not know.'

She said, 'W–will you release Tom?'

'I will. And when shall I see you?'

She turned towards the door. 'Oh, I'll see you sometime,' she said, carelessly.

'No, I want a definite meeting. How about tomorrow?'

'Yes. All right. Tomorrow.'

She was at the door now, through the hall. He followed her. 'What time?' he asked. 'Eight o'clock?'

'Eight o'clock,' she repeated.

He opened the great door. 'You will come here,' he said. 'Tomorrow at eight.'

'Yes. Goodbye, Sir William. And thank you.'

She ran to the horse, patiently waiting, uncaring now whether Sir William saw her or not. She climbed onto a low branch of the tree, mounted, and thankfully rode away.

She had no intention of seeing him tomorrow, or any other day. He could wait, as the boys she'd used to know always waited for her favours. Now she had to get back to see what was happening.

But Tom was safe, that was all that mattered.

Chapter eight

Martha, like all the weavers, could not afford to do too much housework because it roughened the hands and this would spoil the silk. So she left the heavy tasks for Saturday or Monday, when the men dug the gardens for the same reason. Winters were always bad, when hands grew red and chapped, and chilblains sprouted on fingers kept cold with no fire. Then Martha would get out the cream she'd made in the summer, a mix of elderblossom, warm buttermilk and white honey. But this year she hadn't had time to make any cream; she had the children, she worked on the loom, and Abel's illness had grown steadily worse. And now, as the year drew to its troubled close, she feared that her father's life was ebbing with it.

The door opened, letting in an icy blast of air. Mr Redmond came in carrying a bucket of coal. He placed more on the fire, then turned to Martha as the clock struck nine.

'There's no need for you to stay the night,' she told him. 'I can manage. You stayed the night before last.'

'And you sat up with him last night,' Mr Redmond replied. 'You must get your rest, Martha. You have the children to see to, weaving to finish, all the washing.' For every night Abel's bed was wringing wet with sweat.

'Mrs Walters has been in this afternoon,' Martha told him. 'She washed the sheets and his nightshirt.' And had said, listening to his interminable coughing, 'You hate to say these things, but it'll be a mercy when he's gone.'

And she'd wiped her eyes on her apron. Mrs Walters' tears were always near the surface.

Mr Redmond fetched a bucket of water from the pump, poured some into the pot on the fire, then they sat at the table to eat the pie Martha had made, lit by the flickering candle. Abel coughed repeatedly, they could hear the sound all through the meal, and twice Martha went up to the landing bedroom to see him. The second time she brought back his plate with the food untouched.

'He can't eat,' she said. 'I'll make some tea, he likes that. Wait, Mr Redmond, and I'll give you a cup before you go to sit with him.'

'If you have enough to spare,' Mr Redmond said.

'Yes. Tacy sent me a box, which is kind of her for she is struggling herself.' Martha sighed. 'I sometimes wonder where it will all end.'

'At least Tom wasn't sent to jail,' Mr Redmond remarked, as, the meal ended, they sat one each side of the fire. 'Poor Joe Bates and Bob Pettit have six months, and Bob's the quietest of the Pettits . . . Is Tom out again?'

'He's working. It's Friday.'

'Oh yes. Will he be in later?'

'Maybe. When he works late he usually stops at his mother's all night.'

Mr Redmond looked into the fire, then again at Martha. We sit here like a married couple, he thought, and wondered what Martha was thinking. Did she ever think of the times they sat together talking about work, about life in general? Did she remember how many times she used to sit thus with her father, but seldom with Tom? Who knew what Martha thought? She listened to everyone's troubles, sympathising, always ready to stretch out a helping hand; of her own she said nothing. He recalled when he first saw Martha, saw her plain face;

now he thought the face beautiful, a mirror of the goodness within.

'I would have thought,' he said, heavily, 'that at a time like this Tom would have finished his work earlier in the week.'

'Well, he does take the boys to his mother's. She's been looking after them.'

There was a little silence, they could hear the wind howling. Mr Redmond said, 'I'm sorry – I have no right.'

'You do have the right. You are our minister.'

'No!' He turned round so suddenly that she was startled. 'No, Martha. I don't speak as a minister, I speak as a man.'

She said nothing, but stood up, poured water from the pot into the bowl on the table and began to wash the plates.

'I tell you so that you will understand *why* I criticise . . . ' Then, softly. 'Did you not know how I feel for you?'

She said, honestly, 'I wondered . . . But you mustn't. You know that. I am married to Tom.'

'Who cares for no-one but himself.'

Martha sighed. 'But I know that, I've always known it. We grew up together. And it's not as simple as that, Mr Redmond. Tom is a rebel, yes, but he works for the weavers. He thinks of them, of changing the world. He doesn't have time for his family.'

'But your father worked for the weavers. So do I.'

They both thought of Abel lying coughing his life away. How many times had he given food to those with little in the house, given away the money he'd worked so hard to save? To end up little better than a pauper himself. That would never happen to Tom.

Mr Redmond said, 'I'll go up to Abel.'

He went up the narrow stairs and Martha finished washing the plates, then threw the water outside into the garden. She saw a line of rime covering the plants, the trees, and closed the door quickly. She could hear her father coughing monotonously, the sound that went on night and day; Abel coughing his lungs away.

She began to rake out the fire. Then something made her pause and she banked it up with slack. Who knew what the night might bring?

Outside, a flurry of sleet beat against the windows. An owl hooted mournfully. Mr Redmond wore his topcoat yet shivered, for the bedroom was icy. But Abel burned with fever, and Mr Redmond wiped his brow gently, bathing his face from the bowl of water beside the bed. He was so emaciated that he was little more than a skeleton, bones covered by a thin layer of flesh, no more.

'Try to sleep, Abel,' Mr Redmond said.

'Nay.' Abel gave a grimace that should have been a smile. 'I'll be sleeping soon enough.' He began to cough.

Again Mr Redmond tended him. He wanted to say, 'Lie still, don't talk,' but did not. If the man wanted to talk in his last hours, did it really matter?

'Would you like me to say a prayer, Abel?' he asked.

'Aye,' Abel said. 'The twenty-third psalm.'

'The Lord is my Shepherd, I shall not want,' murmured Mr Redmond, his strong voice low. 'Yea, though I walk through the valley of the shadow of death, I will fear no evil, for Thou art with me . . .'

Abel said, 'You're a good man, Mr Redmond.' Breath. 'How long you bin here?'

'Oh . . . about seven years.'

'Pity you weren't here sooner.' Again he had a bout of coughing. Again Mr Redmond tended him, wiped his brow. 'Martha . . . a good girl, you know . . . deserved somethin' better.'

Mr Redmond did not answer, and Abel seemed to fall into a doze. He roused, said, 'Keep on eye on Martha when I'm gone, will you, Mr Redmond?'

'I will, Abel.'

'She's a good girl. Tom – too much of a hothead . . .' Pause. 'Thought he'd settle down wi' her, being steady . . . ' Breath. 'But I'm feared he never will.' Breath. 'Sometimes life's a bit of a puzzle,' he ended.

'Abel, you're a weaver,' Mr Redmond said. 'You weave one row red, one row black, and it looks a jumble. But when you see the whole pattern, you understand. Leave it to God.'

'Aye,' Abel answered. And now there was nothing but coughing.

Towards morning Mr Redmond sensed a change and roused Martha. She threw a cloak over her nightwear and went into the bedroom. 'Father,' she whispered, taking his hand.

Abel smiled, and now his face seemed quite peaceful.

'Susan,' he said, clearly.

Martha stroked his hand. But he was looking through her, towards the window, where the first streak of light appeared in the blackness. And as the cold dawn crept over the sky, Abel's racked body gave up the struggle, and he died.

Mr Redmond would dearly have liked to officiate at the funeral of his old friend, but this was against the law. He was among the mourners, walking behind Martha, Tom, and their relatives. It was snowing heavily as the coffin was lowered into the grave in the little churchyard where Abel's wife, Susan, lay, together with their dead children. The mourners returned to Martha's house for the small repast she could offer. Mrs Walters, crying loudly, handed round slices of ham given by a friendly neighbour who had killed a pig, and bread made by Martha. There was a little home-made wine to warm them, and they sat, talking soberly.

'Will you bring the Jacquard here now?' Tacy asked Tom.

He shook his head. 'No, Martha is going to carry on with this loom. Mine stays where it is.' He paused. 'We must get more Jacquards, Tacy.'

'I know.' But there was no way she could buy any looms now. She wondered if Tom ever pondered as to how he'd escaped prison, if so he never said, and she never told him. Probably he didn't. Tom accepted life as it came; if the gods were kind to him he arrogantly took it as his right. She wondered, now she had time to reflect on it, what Sir William had thought when she didn't turn up to meet him, and shivered a little. Then shrugged it off. What could he do, anyway? Tell people that he wanted to seduce her? Why, it would be horrible, he was so old . . . he was Francis' *father* for heaven's sake . . . He must be over fifty.

No doubt he'd forget it, as he had forgotten the loan. Or at least hadn't mentioned it. She was paying it off, but it was still a struggle, especially as she had to pay the weavers at the old List price. And George Healey still did not . . . We must get rid of him somehow, she brooded; it was an ever-present thought at the back of her mind. I'll go to London after Christmas. See if I can find some work from somewhere . . .

It was not until after the funeral that Martha could begin to think about Mr Redmond's words. She had known he liked her – was like then too soft a word? But she had never delved deeply into her own feelings.

Yet now she was troubled. She had married Tom, loving him, knowing the type of man he was . . . had she expected him to change? Had she not realised that as time went by she would require someone to sit and talk to by the fire . . . someone like Mr Redmond – she never, even in her thoughts, called him John, it would be getting too close. Tom was a good lover, but not a good husband.

Should she not have known? His father had always been a roistering, carousing rogue, who drank, and had been known to beat both his wife and sons. Ross, the eldest, was pretty much the same, though Mark was somewhat quieter.

But she'd loved Tom. Or – had there been perhaps a feeling of triumph over Tacy? Tacy, who ran to Abel's cottage with her talk, her triumphs, never knowing that Martha was envious of her. Marrying Tom was Martha's triumph.

But now . . .

How often did Tom come home? Thursdays, Fridays he worked late, so had to stop at his mother's. Saturdays he always went out. Mondays too he'd be at the races or at one of the many prize fights in the area. Or he was busy setting up the loom, or he'd been to the Weavers' Arms and didn't want to disturb her. So again he stayed at his mother's.

And he came to her just when he felt like it.

She knew there were other girls, little light affairs, for Tom was never the man to refuse what was offered. And she did not mind this too much. A man got drunk and was led astray . . . But she did mind Tacy. She was going to miss her father, that was for sure. It was good she had Mr Redmond to talk to . . .

John Redmond walked along the High Street. A waggon passed on its way to the mill, the driver walking holding the horse's head, lest it slip on the frozen cobbles. Farther along a donkey stood patiently, while its master loaded its back with sacks. Two boys slid along, shouting with glee.

He stopped outside George Healey's house, and looked to the side, to what had formerly been a wide entrance to the garden and was now an entry to a yard at the back. He walked up the entry, looked round.

Half a dozen tiny cottages clustered round the yard, poorly constructed of cheap discoloured bricks. Even in the cold most of the doors were open, and dirty children played in the doorways. Equally dirty women could be seen in the small rooms, and Mr Redmond took in the one pump in the yard, next to the privy. How could these unfortunate people keep clean in such surroundings? At the side of the privy was a mound of refuse, around which thin dogs sniffed, searching for food.

Mr Redmond went to the first door and introduced himself to the woman inside. 'Would you be interested in coming to the chapel?' he asked.

'Eh, I'd like to, but we daren't,' the woman told him.

'Why? What are you afraid of?' Mr Redmond asked gently.

'Lordy, it's the gaffer. He won't let us go to no chapel, he told us.'

'Is your husband a weaver?'

'He is now. Used to work on the land till he got the sack.'

'I see. How are you getting on here, in the house?'

The woman shrugged. 'It's all we got. It's this or nothin'.'

'Yes, of course.' And they couldn't afford to be turned out of this wretched hovel. 'Well,' he said. 'Anytime you need me you know where to find me . . . Good day.' And he walked away from Healey's Yard, heavy hearted.

He hadn't gone far when he heard a shout, and, turning, saw George Healey himself coming towards him, well-dressed in a new brown nearly ankle-length great coat, with a fine astrakhan collar, and on his head a black top hat. 'I want to speak to you,' he said as he drew near.

'Yes?' Mr Redmond waited, a few flurries of snow whitening his shabby coat.

'You're behind all this, ain't you?' the man asked. 'No, don't ask what, you know full well what I mean. Puttin' weavers out on strike, encouraging my weavers to do the same. Oh, I've heard about your goings-on, having meetings in chapel, rousin' em up to ask for more pay –'

'I believe the labourer is worthy of his hire,' said Mr Redmond equably.

'Oh, don't quote the Bible to me. And just you keep away from my workers. I've forbidden 'em to go to chapel.'

'Can you do that?'

'Oh aye. If they go they lose their jobs.' He sniggered. 'You don't have to worry about their souls – if they've got any, which I doubt. They can go to church, church don't meddle in workmen's affairs. Parson knows which side his bread's buttered.' He sniggered again, and the donkey in the road looked at him in mild surprise. 'I've enlarged my loom-shop, you know, that'll mean more workers comin' in.'

'And where will they live?'

'Oh, we keep on building houses.'

'In little courts at the backs of other houses,' said Mr Redmond, angrily. 'They're not fit for pigs.'

'Good enough for them,' said George Healey. 'Anyway, you just leave 'em alone. No meetings, no unions for my workers, else I'll have the law on you.'

A stout man returned to the donkey. 'Gee-up,' he

cried. 'Come on, my old beauty, let's get you home.'

Two more boys slid by, red mufflers a spot of colour in the whiteness. And John Redmond walked on, reflecting that nowadays humans seemed to be treated worse than animals.

Tacy boarded the London coach on the last day of December, and was glad to go. Chilverton was no longer the happy place it had been. Children still ran in the fields in the summer, building snowmen in winter, but women no longer gossiped in doorways, nor in their homes were such big fires glowing. No longer did the weavers advertise for help, now they needed help themselves. The death of Abel had upset her, it seemed all the old ones were going – and there would be more with the bitter weather, more children being carried into the churchyard.

The coach started early in the frozen morning, and as it jolted and bumped along the icy roads, she curled her toes in her boots and clenched her fingers in her fur muff. There were no other ladies in the coach, just two fat men, one of whom slept all the way, the other repeatedly taking snuff.

She had written to Mr Fotheringay to say she was coming, and as the coach drew in the Swan with Two Necks, and the steaming horses were pulled to a halt, she saw, among the crowds of shouting, gesticulating people, one who could only be he, standing aloof, waiting. No-one but he would be wearing blue tight pantaloons with hessian boots, a black velvet waistcoat studded with gold stars, and a green frock coat. His face was painted, and he reeked of perfume.

'My, quite the Dandy,' Tacy remarked as he greeted her.

'We like to appear in the glass of fashion,' answered Mr

Fotheringay. 'Come, my dear, I have a hackney coach waiting, here it is, let us board. I have a surprise for you.'

It seemed warmer in London, Tacy noted. It had been snowing, but the roads were now a mass of slush mixed with horse manure, which, here and there, a few crossing sweepers were endeavouring to clean up. 'Well,' beamed Mr Fotheringay, as they sat inside. 'There's no possibility of going to Vauxhall today, what?'

'No,' said Tacy, with a little shiver.

'No trip along the river today – though it is passable. But no, I thought what can I do for my fair visitor? And I decided to take you to my chambers. Wait!' and he held up his hand, though she had not spoken. 'Today, all is prepared, I have a dear buxom old lady as chaperone, and she will have a splendid meal waiting. Won't that be fine?'

'It will indeed,' Tacy agreed sincerely, having no desire to spend much time in Mrs Robinson's plain guest house, though she would have to spend the night there.

'You really should not travel through London on your own,' admonished Mr Fotheringay, as though he'd read her thoughts.

'What can harm me?' Tacy asked. 'I just take a hackney coach to see Mr Jarvis, then another to Mrs Robinson's establishment –'

'It's not safe,' Mr Fotheringay fussed. 'Why, not so long ago people were picked up on the streets and sold into bondage in America. The streets of London were full of kidnappers.'

Tacy giggled. But it was good to drive through the crowded streets, a flurry of snow falling and the drivers shouting words she pretended not to hear as the horses slipped and slithered along the icy roads, while ladies in fur hoods poked their heads out of coach windows and gentlemen added their shouts to those of the drivers, and hawkers shrilled their monotonous whining cries. They passed the Westminster rat-pit where one celebrated dog could kill a hundred rats in an evening, saw condemned prisoners being carted off to execution, children shouting and women screaming around them. Then to the quiet of Mr Fotheringay's rooms, in a quiet avenue off Park Lane, where plump Mrs Benson took Tacy's cloak and brought in hot soup, followed by roast chicken.

Then they adjourned to the drawing-room, small, but with a thick carpet and upholstered chairs in green and gold. A gold framed mirror hung on the wall.

'Now my dear,' said Mr Fotheringay. 'Sit by the fire and tell me your news.'

'It's your news I want to hear,' Tacy replied. 'What of the ribbon sales? What of the Court?'

'The Court! Oh, my dear. After the tragic death of the Princess Charlotte, the Queen called her sons and ordered them all to marry. Imagine, my dear, all those men, four of them. All unmarried, but with families of bastards by the dozen. I declare!'

'Yes, yes,' said Tacy, impatiently. 'But will it mean more celebrations?'

'Ah, that I doubt. I fear the marriages will be quiet little affairs, just to get an heir to the throne, you know. Of course, we cannot expect the old King to live much longer.'

'But that won't help us if the Court is in mourning –'

'There will have to be a coronation,' Mr Fotheringay said.

'And what about Princess Caroline? Will she be Queen?'

'Not if the Regent can help it. He sends her abroad, poor duck, tries to divorce her. He won't succeed, you know. But, my dear, I do have some good news for you.'

'More orders?'

'Not exactly. But fashion is changing. The classic line is on the way out, gowns are becoming more romantic. Look at these sketches, see the tiny waist, the fuller skirt . . . there'll be yards and yards more ribbons needed.'

'Oh, I do hope so,' Tacy said, looking at the sketch and nodding approval. Morning wear, full skirt, full sleeves, trimmed with ribbons. And evening wear frills and furbelows. 'Yes, indeed,' she said.

'And corsets will be worn again,' added Mr Fotheringay, touching his own pinched in waist. 'And silk drawers.'

'Really?' Tacy smiled. 'With ribbons?'

'I devoutely hope so,' replied Mr Fotheringay. 'I do, indeed.'

'I need more orders,' Tacy said, bluntly. 'I lost money after Princess Charlotte's death. You know I had ribbons made especially for a royal baby – '

'I remember,' agreed Mr Fotheringay. 'And I have the slightest hope of good news on that score.'

'You couldn't sell them?' Tacy asked eagerly. 'Not when they have crowns woven in – '

'One of the German princesses might be presenting her husband with a son,' replied Mr Fotheringay. 'It might be a daughter, true, but there are not many of these German princelings . . . one will be bound to have a son sooner or later.'

'Oh, Mr Fotheringay, that would be marvellous.'

'And there is more. I was at a social gathering recently, at the home of Lady Stafford. She is, as you know, a famous hostess, and Lady Eldred was there, looking so elegant in a most fashionable dress with a wide skirt edged with ribbons at hem and sleeve. Low cut . . . delightful. Well, she is to speak at her dress establishment, asking ladies to buy English ribbons. Already I have an order for fine gauze and sarsenets.'

Tacy was overjoyed. And before she left she was taken by Mrs Benson to the 'Necessary room', which was indoors, quite an innovation, and she saw a water closet for the first time, which she hardly knew how to use. We must install one at the Red House, she thought. When we can afford it . . .

But she went to Mrs Robinson's lighter of heart, and when the following day Mr Jarvis also placed a large order for summer fashions, she drove to Lad's Lane for the return coach in a much happier frame of mind, even though it was early morning and very cold.

The Swan with Two Necks was busy as always, and the mail-coach started on time. The journey was hazardous, with yesterday's slush frozen now into hard furrows, and the horses slid along, as best they could. But then they ran into a blizzard, and the driver and guard had to alight and lead the horses. Tacy and the other occupants shivered as they were jolted along.

At last the snow stopped, and they reached the welcome warmth of an inn, where they changed the horses and the passengers were able to sit by the big fire and eat and drink. When Tacy returned to the coach she carried a hot brick which she placed at her feet, and the journey continued.

It was dark at four o'clock, but the snow lit the fields in a white mask. Tacy's brick grew cold and she shivered anew. She thought longingly of the Red House and a warm fire, and bed.

It was nearly ten o'clock when they reached the Red Lion, and, stiff and cramped, Tacy alighted and looked round for Francis who always brought the chaise to meet her.

But tonight there was no sign of him.

Had he come and gone home, she wondered? But why

would he do that? Why not wait in the warmth of the inn? The other passengers dispersed, the coach started off. The road was deserted, the empty snow-bound fields stretched to the horizon. There was nothing to do but wait.

She went inside the inn, and Toby Bell, the landlord, as round and chubby as his name, came towards her. 'My dear Mrs Barratt,' he said. 'Come to the fire, do.'

'Has my husband not arrived?' she asked, holding out her hands to the welcome blaze.

'Not yet, no. Of course, the roads are bad – '

'But I have to get home,' she said. 'You do have a post-chaise for hire?'

'I do, yes. One and sixpence a mile with one horse and the boy.'

'Can you fetch him? I must get home.'

'Gladly.' And the landlord went through to the back.

Another wait, then at last Tacy was in the post-chaise. Tired, aching in every limb, she was bowled home. There were still a few stragglers abroad, some had obviously been to one of the beer-houses, other younger men were throwing snowballs. Two men on horseback. But no Francis.

She heard the church clock strike eleven as she entered. The house was in darkness. What could have happened to Francis? Damaris would be in bed, Bess and Sarah Jane too. Was he ill?

She went into the parlour and saw, by the light of the fire, the figure sitting near to it. 'Why, Francis!' she cried. 'Sitting in the dark?'

She went to the lamp and lit it, and from the first flickering light she could see Francis on a low chair, bending forward, almost crouching. He said, in a cold, hissing tone, 'You told him. You told Sir William.'

'What?' Tacy faced him. 'Told him what?' But she

knew, of course. Knew that Sir William had broken his promise not to tell.

'You told him that I was his natural son.'

'I – well – I couldn't help it. How do you – ?'

'He's been here. Laughing at me, at my mother, smirking – ' Francis was still sitting in this strange position, and Tacy felt a spark of fear.

She decided to put a bold face on it. 'I had to tell him,' she said. 'I had to ask a favour. It won't matter, Francis.'

'Won't matter? When I tried to forget it myself, forget the heritage he passed on to me – '

If only Francis would sit up normally. If only she wasn't so tired. 'Whatever do you mean?' she asked.

'I never told you, I never told anyone. How I let a boy die. How I nearly killed a man – ' he broke off.

'Why, Francis – ' But she backed away a step. 'What boy?'

He shrugged impatiently. 'It was in the Navy.'

'Well, men do die in the Navy. And the Army,' she ended bitterly. 'You make too much fuss, Francis. What did Sir William want anyway?'

'It seems you asked him a favour, so now he wants his – return – ' She flinched. 'He wants to build more cottages – in the garden of the Red House!'

She thought of the return he'd asked, and she'd refused. She shivered. She'd asked one favour too many. No, Sir William wasn't a man to be trifled with. And in that instant she knew she would never swing him to her way of thinking and away from George Healey. She'd have to manage on her own.

'But why did he ask you?' she stammered.

'Why? Because I am your husband, and as such I own the Red House. And the weaving business. Oh, I know you treat me as being of no account, but in law I am the owner.'

'Oh, Francis . . . what did you tell him? You didn't . . . agree?'

He laughed, a strange laugh that strangled as it came out. 'Wouldn't you like to know?' he taunted. 'Wouldn't you like to know what I am going to do, my little wife?'

'Francis.' She was really frightened now. 'Why are you so strange? Look, I'm sorry if I upset you, but it seemed the only way – '

'You didn't think to ask me, did you? Your husband? Oh no, not Tacy.' And she was silent, knowing it was true. But what was the point, when he didn't know – when he showed no initiative? Was that what angered him, that he wasn't good enough?

She said, cuttingly, 'You might be the owner, but I have to do all the managing. Because you cannot – ' she broke off. Francis was standing now, still in that strange position, watching her in the dim light of the one lamp. She took a step backwards.

'That's not all,' Francis continued, as if he hadn't heard. 'You didn't tell me what favour you asked of Sir William.'

'Why, it was just to be lenient with the prisoners – '

'Don't lie to me. *He* told me. You wanted Tom Jacques released. Not the others. Just him. Why, Tacy? Why Tom Jacques?'

'He's one of my best workers,' she stammered.

'I've been putting two and two together,' he said. 'All the things I never noticed before because I thought you married me for love. I trusted you to right the wrong that had been done to me by Sir William. To help me overcome the darkness that I know is there – '

'Francis!' Tacy was really alarmed now. 'What is it? What are you talking about?'

'You deceived me.' His voice had risen now and held a shrill, hysterical note. He took a step forward. 'You lied.

I've been helping you, saying nothing, thinking you were busy, and all the time you were in love with another man. You flaunted him before me when he came to London and took us to the theatre. It was all prearranged – '

'No!' she cried, appalled that he'd been nursing this grievance for so long.

He didn't seem to hear. 'How dare you?' he shouted. 'How dare you love another man. For you do love him, don't you?'

He was before her now, and she screamed in anger and fear, 'Yes! Yes, I do!'

Then his hands were round her throat and she could not breathe. He forced her backwards, back . . . they staggered against the table, which overturned, the lamp shattering into a thousand fragments. Tacy fell, and lay still.

Francis straightened up, his face a mask of horror. Then he was running into the street, shouting to the shuttered houses and the several passers-by. 'I've killed her! Take me to the justices! I've killed her!'

Chapter nine

Tacy opened her eyes slowly, painfully, dragging herself from the mists of unconsciousness. She saw Sarah Jane, Bess and Martha, bending over her, and was bewildered. Martha was bathing her head which was bleeding copiously. She tried to sit up.

'What – ?' she began, then, as she felt the painful bruising on her neck, memory returned. 'Francis,' she murmured, and sank back.

'Come now,' said Sarah Jane. 'Up to bed with you.'

They half carried her to the bedroom, undressed her, laid her on the bed. 'Shall we fetch the doctor?' asked Sarah Jane.

'No,' said Tacy.

She struggled to understand. 'How did you get here?' she asked Martha. 'How did you know?'

'Why, Francis went shouting down the street that he'd killed you. Everyone knows,' said Sarah Jane.

'Someone came to fetch me,' said Martha soothingly.

'Who?'

Martha paused. 'Why – Louie Healey,' she murmured.

'Oh no!' Tacy lay back. She could imagine it all. Louie smirking around, telling Martha, telling everyone that Francis had beaten his wife, enjoying herself . . . Of course, some men did beat their wives, but not the Barratts . . .

Her head throbbed. 'Where – where is he?' she asked.

No one answered for a moment, then it was Bess who spoke. 'We don't know. He was shouting that he was going to the justices 'cos he'd killed you – '

'Be quiet, Bess,' ordered Martha, sharply for her.

'Of course he won't go to the justices,' Sarah Jane scoffed. 'There's no penalty for beating your wife. Though there should be,' she amended, at a look from Martha.

Tacy closed her eyes. The shame of it. And that Louie Healey should be the one to know, to fetch help . . . Her head was throbbing again, and she touched it gingerly.

'You banged it when you fell,' Martha told her. 'There's a cut, but I've bathed it with comfrey. But I'll have to go home, Tacy, the boys are on their own, though I asked Mrs Walters to keep an eye on them.'

'I'll be all right now, with Bess and Sarah Jane,' Tacy murmured. 'Thank you for coming.'

'She misses her father now, he always helped her,' said Sarah Jane, as Martha left the bedroom. She went to the door. 'Such goings on I never did see,' she grumbled. 'Your poor father would turn in his grave. The Barratts were allis respectable.'

Bess blew out the candle and left too, but Tacy did not sleep. That Francis, the quiet, the meek, should have turned on her like that! She hoped he would never come back. She dreaded meeting people, wondering what they'd be saying behind her back. The only thing to do was to pretend that nothing had happened.

So she got up the next morning, stiff and sore, and went into breakfast where Damaris eyed her wonderingly but, primed by Bess, said nothing. She wanted to stay at home, but had planned to visit Mrs Bradley's millinery store, and did not see why she should hide so out she went, bonnet covering her head and the brim shadowing her face. The worst part was passing the Healeys, who of course, had to be around at the same time, pretending not to see the malicious smiles they gave. She held her head high and walked on.

But inside she was afraid. She had never been beaten before in her life.

The weather relented at the weekend, the ice melted, and on Saturday she was in the warehouse to give the work out as usual, and none of the weavers said a word, although her face was still bruised, and she wore a little scarf to hide the other bruises on her neck. Tom was last, as always, and when they were alone he asked, 'So what happened, Tacy?'

'I – ' she hesitated. If she told Tom the truth, what then? He'd likely seek out Francis and, knowing Tom's temper, there would be another fight, when, if it were serious, the justices might be called in. And she didn't want that, for Tom's sake. She had saved him from prison once, but he must not know.

She said, looking down, 'We quarrelled.'

He leaned over the counter. 'What about?'

'Sir William came to see him when I was in London. He wants to build houses at the back of our house.'

'But he can't. It's your land.'

'Francis' land,' she said, bleakly.

'But he wouldn't let him, would he? He seemed such a quiet fellow, Francis. And to do this – '

She said, honestly, 'I suppose I haven't treated him very well.'

'You shouldn't have married him, Tacy. You should have married me, we're two of a sort, you and me.' He grinned. 'Both out for ourselves, for what we can get.'

'You married Martha,' she reminded him.

'Because your father wouldn't have had me as a son-in-law. Oh, I knew, that time I went to see him. I think I knew before then. If he had I wouldn't have – ' He broke off and she tried to finish it for him. *Wouldn't have made love to Martha.* Was that what he meant? In seconds he'd walked round the counter, took her in his arms. 'My love,' he whispered.

He kissed her, and she rested in his arms, knowing that this was what she'd always wanted. Tom.

He said, 'When can we be together, Tacy?'

'We can't,' she replied, dully. 'There's nowhere.'

'I'll think of something,' he said, and again she rested in his arms.

On 2 January the Duke of York died, and there was no worry that this would affect the weaving very much. But when on 30 January, George III died, Tacy was pleased. There would be a coronation. There would be rejoicings, balls, all the ladies would require new gowns. And new gowns meant more ribbon sales.

She had heard nothing from Francis, and she began to think that he had left for good, and felt guiltily pleased, though she had no-one to work in the counting-house. She had to reckon the accounts herself, and this meant more long hours in the evenings. Damaris had asked where her Papa was, and had been told that he was away on business. And as both parents did go to London on business, Tacy staying for days at a time, Damaris saw no reason to question this.

Tacy encouraged Bess to take Damaris out as much as possible, and Bess was nothing loath. They were in the Market Square on 5 February when the constables, accompanied by a band, proclaimed George IV king. The band played 'God Save the King', but there were no crowds, the people took little notice.

But a week later there was a large procession. Bess called for Martha's boys and together with Damaris they walked to the Market Square. There the Under Sheriff, following the ancient custom of the county, proclaimed the new king, and then the procession started, Damaris clapping her hands with glee.

First came the peace officers on foot, with halberts, black bows of ribbon tied at the top, and a flag with blue ground bordered with orange ribbon and on one side a crown with a motto underneath, 'Our Religion and Laws'. Next came the Yeomanry Cavalry on horseback, more bands with flags, the Under Sheriff himself on horseback, the two clergymen of the area, Mr Hewitt and Mr Redmond, followed by most of the important people of the town.

The Under Sheriff read the proclamation in the Market Square and in the High Street as the clock struck twelve. The church bells pealed, and carried on ringing all through the day.

Martha heard the bells clamouring as she sat at the loom. She was glad the boys were out, it was good to be quiet for once. When she heard the knock at the door she called, 'Come in,' and sighed a little as she walked into the kitchen.

A man stood there. Francis!

'Can I talk to you, Martha?' he asked. 'Please.'

'Well – ' she pointed to a chair by the table. 'Have you been home?'

'Not yet. I've been so afraid. I thought I'd killed her.'

'No, you didn't. But you did hurt her.'

'I know. That's what I've always been afraid of.'

'Of hurting her?' Martha asked, amazed.

'Her or anyone. Oh, Martha, it's me, my heritage, I know. I nearly killed a man – I did kill a boy – and then I found out that my father was Sir William Fargate, a bad man.'

'I'll make us some tea,' Martha said. 'So calm yourself, then you can tell me all about it.'

The bells pealed louder than ever, Martha hoped Bess would not bring the boys back just yet, how could she explain Francis' presence, especially if Damaris came too? The pot boiled and she made the tea, handed a cup to Francis. He drank eagerly, and seemed to calm down. Then, as she sat opposite, in the chair her father used to use, he told her his story.

'It's what I feared,' he ended. 'That his bad blood would come out in me. And it has.'

Martha sat pondering, wishing her father were here to advise. Or Mr Redmond. She said at length, 'It's true Sir William is a rogue, but he's not all bad. He has courage. He was fighting in the wars, I believe, for a time. And besides – rumour has it that he has bastards all over the place, not just you.'

She offered him a piece of home-made cake but he shook his head.

'You see,' Martha went on. 'From what you tell me, your Mamma brought you up in a prissy sort of manner to be ashamed of being a bastard. Round here we don't bother so much. In fact, there's a woman lives at Borley Common who used to be a maid at the Manor, her lad boasts about being Sir William's son. And he's a decent enough fellow. So is the son he had with his wife, the one who ran away because he didn't get on with his father.'

'You mean it's nothing to be ashamed of?' asked Francis.

'Well, you can't help your parents, can you? I don't see any reason for wishing badness onto yourself, as we say round here. You can wish yourself into trouble.'

'Oh, Martha, you make me feel better.'

'So what are you going to do?'

'I don't know,' miserably. 'I ran away, went to Coventry, I even found a job helping in a store. But I knew that wasn't the answer. You see, I love Tacy, though I know now she doesn't love me. She loves –' he broke off.

'Well,' Martha said, a little sharply. 'That's all very well, but I think you should go back. It's put her in a muddle not having anyone to do the books. Did you not think of that?'

'N-no.'

'Perhaps you should, instead of worrying about whether your blood is bad or not.'

Francis thanked Martha and left, pondering. He didn't want to be here when Tom arrived. Nor did he feel ready yet to go back home.

Martha was not to know how her words would change Francis. He had, at the start, been desperate for Tacy to love him, her love would help him regain his self-respect. When he learned there was no love his crutch was wrenched away, leaving him more vulnerable than ever. Now, once his feeling of shame at being a bastard was gone, he gained confidence immediately. But the shame had also kept down the tendency to violence he suspected and feared was in him, and this he did not fully realise.

He walked through the Patch, which was nearly deserted, those who were not working were in the Market Square along with all the children. The bells still rang out as he walked along a muddy lane, and came to a row of cottages on the edge of the Common, poor cottages with thatched roofs. And here, as it began to rain, a woman came from one of the doorways and called to him.

'What ya standing there for? Come on in.'

He blinked. She was a buxom woman with brassy blonde hair and a painted face. He knew what she was even before she told him her name. Lottie Glover! But the rain was falling heavier, and he took his new confidence and vulnerability inside.

'I just want a bed for a couple of nights,' he told her.

'Oh, you can have a bed and all that goes in it.' She laughed loudly. 'Come on.' And she led him into an adjoining room with a bed in the corner.

He looked at it distastefuly. It wasn't particularly clean and the room was untidy, with dirty clothes piled on a chair, and a strong sour smell, with no herbs to sweeten the atmosphere. Francis had been through the dirt and smells of the Navy, had spent the last few nights in a dingy lodging house in Coventry. But his mother had been clean, and he'd been living in the Red House far too long to enjoy discomfort. But he placed himself by the bed and Lottie stood, facing him.

'So why aren't you going home?' she asked him.

'You know me?'

''Course I know you, I live here, don't I? Sit down.'

There seemed nowhere to sit but on the bed, so he sat. 'I just want to think,' he mumbled.

'What? About Tacy Barratt? What you gotta think about?'

'Oh – whether I dare go back or not.'

'Dare go back? What sort of fool are you? It's your house, ain't it? And your business. Oh, I know Tacy Barratt goes round as if she owns the whole town, but she don't. You're her husband and the house is yourn. She don't own nothing.'

Francis gazed at her thoughtfully as she drew the curtains, and took a bottle and two mugs from the cluttered chest near the window. 'Here,' she said, 'have a drink.'

He hesitated. He did not drink.

'Come on,' she urged. 'Them hymn singin' chapelgoers might not like a drop of brandy, but why should they stop you from enjoyin' yourself?'

She was right. Tacy and her father hadn't agreed with drunkenness, said there was too much of it around, but why should they stop him just having a little sip? He wasn't going to get drunk. He took the brandy. 'I hurt her,' he said.

'An' she deserves it an' all, the way she treated you. Little bitch. Spoilt by her father, she was, thought herself everybody. Didn't want to know the likes of me and Louie.'

'You're not weavers.' It was a statement.

'Nay. Our father was Irish, came to work as a navigator on them canals. Drunken old fool, he got hisself killed. No, we would have liked to be weavers, but they didn't want us. They're like that, you know, uppity. Louie done all right for herself marrying George Healey.' She nudged him. 'We know how to please a man, her and me.'

'So you took to this life?' He gazed round the room.

'Ah. I had to mek money somehow, and, as I said, the weavers didn't want us. Serves them right, an' all, them weavers, thought such a lot of theirselves, getting watchmakers to shell peas for 'em, now they've got nothing. Anyway, I like men. Come on, let me show you.'

Francis strove to remember his mother's teaching. 'A husband should care for his wife – ' he began. 'Not hurt her.'

'What? When she's bin' runnin' after Tom Jacques all her life? Fast little bitch, she is. An' treated you like you was dirt, while she runs round her fancy man. She deserves a good whipping.'

Francis didn't know why the remembrance of his hurting Tacy should suddenly make him *want* Lottie Glover. He drained his brandy, pushed her down on to the bed and forgot the past few days as he made violent love to her.

And when he lay back, he knew she had satisfied him in a way Tacy never could.

George III was buried a week later, and this time a Minute Bell was tolled throughout the day, most of the shops were closed, and there were services in both church and chapel. Tacy did not attend these services though Bess took Damaris, suitably attired with black armbands. Tacy was thinking about the coronation to come. Would the estranged Queen be crowned? Dare she make extra ribbons, after the fiasco of Princess Charlotte's baby? If she did, and it paid off, she could write off her debts. She sent a letter to Mr Fotheringay and awaited an answer.

It was nine o'clock in the evening when she returned to the parlour after struggling with the accounts. Damaris was in bed, Bess out somewhere, Sarah Jane in the kitchen. And Francis walked in.

Tacy knew he was in the area, Martha had warned her. She noticed that there was a new confidence in his bearing as he stood in the doorway and said, 'I'm sorry, Tacy.'

She did not answer.

'Tacy. I want to come home.'

Her eyes widened, and a jumble of feelings swirled within her. Disappointment that he was back; the knowledge that it was inevitable – and fear, which she successfully hid.

'Well,' she said, pretending coolness. 'I suppose I cannot stop you.'

'No.' He looked around the parlour, its velvet curtains, the polished table holding the lamp, Samuel's chair. And Tacy herself in her blue muslin workaday gown, for she had not bothered to change, the black slippers peeping beneath. 'This is my home, after all,' he said.

Now she was angry that he wasn't begging her pardon, and said, 'You should not have hurt me, Francis. I don't know that I can live with you again.'

'This is my home,' Francis repeated. 'And the business is mine too, since I married you.'

Tacy was silent with shock.

He went on, 'I am truly sorry I hurt you, Tacy. But I have been thinking things over. You were wrong to marry me when you did not love me —'

'Oh, Francis.' She rallied. 'Do you think everyone marries for love?'

'You should not have led me to believe you loved me,' he carried on in the same level voice which disturbed her, though she did not understand why. 'Now, as your husband, I own this house, the business. You cannot turn me away.'

She sat, trembling hands on her lap, clenched to hide their shaking, staring at this new Francis.

'You should not have told Sir William I was his son when I was emphatic that I did not wish it,' he resumed. 'That was the trouble. I wanted to hide it, did not want to remember I had bad blood in me. But now I think I've come to terms with it, I am no longer ashamed. So — I shall try not to hurt you again, but you must be honest with me. No more running after Tom Jacques.'

'Why, I never — ' she began. 'Tom is married to Martha.'

'Exactly. He doesn't want you. So keep away or you will have me to reckon with. Remember that I am the master.'

Her head jerked up.

'You never ask my opinion, you treat me like one of the servants, just to do your bidding, and I want no more of it.'

'But, Francis — you don't know about silk.'

'Pooh!' he said. 'All this talk by the weavers of not letting strangers into their guilds and not marrying out of the weaving is just a ploy to keep things in their hands. That's what you are doing. I am master here,' he repeated.

The clock in the corner whirred, and struck the half-hour. In the street a dog barked. 'I don't know if I want you in my bed again,' she said, sulkily.

'You are my wife,' he returned. 'And cannot refuse. But I'm not sure how often I want to lie with a girl who loves someone else. There are other women, women who do things I shall tell you about later.' He gave a cold smile. 'But if I do want you, then I shall have you. But don't worry – ' he held up his hand '– I shall not move back into your room, your chaste little room. I am quite content in James' old chamber. I like to be alone.'

She watched him walk away, and realised she had not asked if he had eaten. She shrugged. Her thoughts were still in turmoil. Part of her was surprised at this new Francis who was laying down the law. But a greater part was still afraid.

As the weeks passed Francis seemed to settle in without too much trouble. But there were differences. He was more watchful. Every Saturday he would follow her to the warehouse as she gave out the silk and took in the finished ribbons, standing behind her like a damned supervisor, Tacy muttered to herself. But none of the weavers spoke or smiled at him, they passed the time of day with Tacy, but reserved surly looks for Francis. She knew why. She might be sharp-tongued and occasionally lose her temper with them, but she was one of them, and they did not like a stranger hurting her. So, after a few weeks he stopped coming, but instead, would peep in from time to time, so that she felt she could not talk to

Tom as she had been doing. And ironically, except for that last time when Tom had comforted her when Francis had hit her, they had only talked about work. She missed this, discussing work with someone knowledgeable.

With Francis she was polite, no more. She was glad that she had kept to her father's rule of silence at mealtimes, which saved the effort of trying to make conversation. And though she answered his questions about the weaving when he asked she resolved that in no way would she give in to any changes that she felt were wrong. Never, she vowed. I'd sell the business first.

And realised that she could not sell the business, not without asking Francis. But *he* could. And now fear was with her all the time, and she strove to hide it, as always, with a toss of the head and a firm step.

But she did not smile so often.

Spring was cold, then suddenly blossomed into a warm summer. Work had been plentiful and the weavers, with no coal to buy for their fires, were happy. Bess took Damaris to see the visiting menagerie of wild beasts, and the Company of Players in the Haddon Rooms. And Tacy heard from Mr Fotheringay.

My dear, such excitement, he wrote. The Queen came back to England, painted face, a great hat on her head. Dressed in purple — mourning, don't you know? The people cheered her — and laughed because of the fun to come. But will she be crowned? Not if the King can help it. He is putting her on trial for adultery.

And now the whole country talked of nothing else.

The weavers discussed it as they stood in the warehouse.

'How can he divorce her for adultery?' asked Harry Pettit. 'You don't divorce queens.'

'Why not?' asked Joe Bates, robustly. 'She's got this Italian fancy man, she's had an illegitimate son, she carouses around Europe an' goes to balls naked from the waist up—'

'But what about him? How many women has he had?' asked Jim Bailey. 'Apart from the little matter of marrying one on 'em before this Caroline. Why don't she put 'im on trial for bigamy?'

'His marriage was invalid cos he didn't ask the King's consent,' said Luke Lakin.

'What do they mean, put her on trial?' asked Enoch Walters.

'Well,' pontificated Luke Lakin, tall and thin as a maypole, a man who read all the penny tracts that were issued and fancied himself as an intellectual. 'The government is preparing a Bill of Pains and Penalties to—' here he surreptitiously glanced at a paper in his hand — 'deprive Her Majesty Caroline Amelia Elizabeth of the title of queen, and declare her marriage to the king wholly dissolved.'

'You can't divorce queens,' repeated Harry Pettit, stubbornly.

'Yes, you can, what about Henry VIII?' asked Joe Bates, belligerently.

Then Francis appeared, and the talk stopped as if by magic.

Tacy waited to hear the result of the trial. It would affect the ribbons trade, and for this reason she hoped Caroline would win and be crowned.

The weeks went by, and the King was determined to have his divorce, the Queen was determined he should not. She rode out before the people, waving and smiling, her ugly face painted. 'The Queen's Trial' was the talk of the world. And as she drove through the streets she was hailed as 'The Queen' by the crowds, and graffiti were chalked on Carlton House where the King lived.

But the Bill received only a majority of nine in the Lords, and it was withdrawn, for the Prime Minister knew this was tantamount to a defeat, and it would have been rejected in the Commons. Parliament was suspended for a fortnight.

There was widespread rejoicing in London. The capital was illuminated for three nights and the Queen enjoyed a fortnight of popularity, while the King, vexed, considered a change of government.

In Chilverton there was rejoicing too. Bells were rung and some people wore white ribbons in her honour. And after Christmas the King acknowledged defeat.

The coronation was now fixed for 19 July 1821, but Tacy's problem was not solved. Would the Queen be crowned? Mr Jarvis ordered more fine gauze and sarsenets, but in December 1820 Tacy knew she had to make the decision. More ribbons for the Queen's coronation? Or not? She wanted to discuss the matter with Tom, but it was difficult now to even talk to him with Francis peering round the bales of silk and stepping in unexpectedly, it put her on edge the whole time.

Francis had said no more about Tom, yet, as they sat in the parlour, she found she was really afraid of this new Francis. He seemed somehow to have a watchful air. He also seemed to eye Bess in a way he never had before, and encouraged her to bring Damaris into the parlour – and Bess was nothing loath.

He had never, since his return, been to Tacy's bedroom, and, although she was thankful, she wondered why. She did not know, of course, of Francis' dilemma, a dilemma caused by the warring emotions inside him. His enjoyment with Lottie Glover made him wonder if he dare see her again. He remembered at times how he had wanted nothing but to be married to Tacy to protect him from his own violent feelings. But Tacy did not love him, so what was he to do? Be free to see other women, have other desires? With Lottie? Things a man would not ask his wife to do?

A little shamefaced at first – for he was sensitive to the talk of others, and had noted the weavers' sullenness at his approach – he had crept down to Lottie's house, then, bolder, had visited more regularly. And she always had a little drink waiting for him, and would gladly sell him a small bottle of brandy which he could conceal in his pocket and drink in the privacy of his room. And the whole time Lottie talked against Tacy, and this Francis also welcomed, it strengthened his belief in himself as a wronged husband. He was in the right. Then he realised that freedom also meant being able to desire other women.

As he sat in the parlour on a cold January evening, with the fire burning brightly to keep out the chill, he said to Tacy, 'It is time Damaris went to school.'

'What?' Tacy had been poring over a fashion book. The romantic look really was coming back, puffed-out sleeves, which necessitated the widening of the skirt, and of course, the narrowing of the waist. But it would mean more ribbons.

'Damaris is nearly five years old,' Francis pointed out. 'She should start school soon,.'

'Yes, I suppose so. I used to go to Miss Barrymore in Coventry. It is a Quaker school, the Quakers believe in education for women the same as for men. Papa used to drive me there.' Tacy dropped her book as she remembered. The trotting through country lanes between fields starred with flowers in summer; lazy days in schoolroom, then Papa waiting outside. The carriage in winter, unless the roads were too miry or icy to travel at all, when she would sit by the parlour fire with her books. She sighed for the happy days now gone for ever, and regretted that Damaris could not have such a happy childhood, not realising that each generation of children finds its own happiness. 'Damaris will have to attend a local school,' she said. 'There is Miss Anson.'

'I thought I might teach Bess how to drive the chaise, then she could take Damaris to school.'

'Well – yes,' said Tacy, surprised. 'But Miss Anson is not far away, she can walk easily.' In some matters Tacy was as unworldly as her father had been.

'But there might come a time when we decide to send her to a Coventry school.'

'I doubt it,' replied Tacy. 'We cannot afford it.' She returned to her fashions. 'If only I knew whether the Queen would be crowned.'

'Why not? She is the King's wife. How can she not be crowned?' asked Francis.

'I'll have a word with Tom,' said Tacy, without thinking.

'Why Tom?' asked Francis, stiffening.

'Because he is my right-hand man,' returned Tacy. 'He knows as much as anyone in Chilverton about silk.'

'And about coronations and the ways of kings and queens?' asked Francis, acidly, and Tacy said no more.

Francis started teaching Bess to drive the chaise, ready for when Damaris began school, and this seemed to take a long time, but it did mean he no longer walked into the warehouse when Tom was there. No more peeping from behind bales, for which she was thankful.

The weavers argued as always. 'She won't be crowned,' said Joe Bates.

''Course she will,' retorted Harry Pettit. 'Whoever heard of a queen not being crowned? She's got to be.'

'The Regent, I mean the King, don't want it,' said Joe.

'How can he stop it?' asked Jim Bailey. 'I'm wearing my white ribbons for the Queen anyway.'

'George Healey's making extra ribbons for her coronation,' said Luke Lakin.

'What do you think, Tom?' Tacy asked when the others had gone. 'Should we make more ribbons for the Queen?'

'No,' Tom replied, vehemently.

'You think she won't be crowned?'

'I think not. But anyway, the King is having a wonderful coronation, and he's ordering all the velvets and satins for the Royal mantles from Spitalfields – we'll get some ribbon orders.'

'I hope you're right,' Tacy said, doubtfully. 'If we are wrong, won't George Healey crow?'

'And if we are right, he can afford to lose money, we can't,' said Tom.

Tacy gave in. But as the coronation drew near, she said to him, 'I can't wait to hear. I shall go to London to see what happens.'

'I might come with you,' said Tom.

'Oh Tom, no. We couldn't travel on the coach together, Francis might think – ' She broke off.

'Might think what?' Tom asked. 'That I was going to see the coronation? Anyway, I wouldn't go on the coach.'

'Then how would you get there?'

'I can walk.'

She snorted. 'And take a week.'

'Well, there's the carrier's cart. And waggons.'

'But Martha – ' Tacy said, weakly. She knew that Martha was again with child.

'It won't happen for some weeks after,' said Tom.

He said no more on the subject, and Tacy wondered if

he had forgotten. Yet she knew a little thrill every time she thought about it. Tom and she – together. Oh, it was wrong, of course, or was it? If she just bumped into him accidentally . . .

She told Francis she would be going to the coronation. 'I must know whether she will be crowned or not,' she said.

'Will you take Damaris?' he asked.

'I think not. It would be too tiring for a child.'

'You'll stay overnight?'

'Of course. I can hardly come back in one day.'

The nineteenth of July 1821 saw London *en fête*. Flags and banners hung from windows, church bells pealed. Tacy had arrived the day before and now looked out of the window of her room in Mrs Robinson's establishment. There were crowds of people milling everywhere. Well-dressed people, drunks, beggars, gipsies with drays pushing through, butchers' carts, fine carriages . . . It was early, but she could not wait. She ran down to breakfast, and hurried through the bread and kippers.

'Mrs Robinson, will you call me a hackney coach?' she asked, as she finished her cup of tea.

'Lord, you won't get a hackney coach today,' said that lady. 'It'ud take hours for one to get here.'

'How about the river? There'll be boats?'

'I suppose so. But there'll be crowds there as well.'

'Then I'll have to walk,' retorted Tacy who thought Mrs Robinson at times a trifle overcautious.

'Well, do be careful,' she fussed. 'Hold tight to your reticule, watch out for pickpockets . . .'

'I will,' Tacy called, as she set off. Dressed in a blue pelisse over her grey walking dress, beribboned bonnet on her head, she stepped into the street and walked to the corner.

And a voice said, 'May I escort you, Madam?'

She stopped. 'Tom!' And was filled with gladness, just to see him, to be alone with him in the crowd. The throngs took on the air of princes and princesses, the very beggars were altered into lords. The sun shone, ignoring the refuse in the streets, showing only her own prince, dressed in brown double breasted coat, marcella waist-coat over grey pantaloons, dusty from the waggon he had ridden in. Tom.

'You came,' she whispered.

'I came to see you,' he said, and she put her hand in his.

It was not far to Westminster Abbey, but she would cheerfully have walked miles. She forgot Francis, forgot Martha, forgot the worries of the weaving; she was a girl again, savouring those pleasures she had had to forgo, the delights of a girl in love, walking with her lover and no-one to heed. Already crowds were gathering outside the Abbey as they reached it. And at half past ten a grand procession set out from Westminster Hall, along a covered walk three feet high, so the spectators might see the King. Tacy craned her head and stood on tiptoe.

First came the Royal Herbwomen and maids, scatter-ing nosegays along the route. Then the Household Band and the Corporation of the City of London. Peers in full robes, Privy Councillors, the Foreign Secretary in white and blue satin. Dignitaries of State carried crown, orb, sceptre and sword, dignitaries of the Church a pattern, a chalice and a Bible. And then the King, beneath a canopy of cloth-of-gold, his train of crimson velvet twenty-seven feet long, his hat decorated with ostrich feathers.

'The Queen isn't there,' said Tom.

But wait. Who was that woman driving in a carriage to the doors of the Abbey? Painted, huge hat on a beribboned wig, dressed in finery that seemed a little gaudy, waving to the crowds? 'It's the Queen,' breathed

Tacy. 'She said she was determined to be crowned.'

There was a sudden hush as the Queen drove to the Abbey door but was refused entrance. The carriage wheeled, drove to another door, where she was refused again. And all the time in a dreadful silence, all cheering stopped.

Then someone shouted, 'Go home,' and the cry was taken up. 'Go home. Go away!'

She was driven away. A pathetic figure now. The Queen who could not be crowned.

'How fickle people are,' said Tom. 'You won't need extra ribbons now, Tacy.'

He put his arm around her and she nestled close to him. 'There'll be fireworks later in Hyde Park,' he told her. 'Shall we go to see them?'

'Oh yes, Tom. Yes.'

The coronation service was to last for five hours, and the crowds were thinning. And suddenly Tacy grasped Tom's arm. 'Tom,' she whispered. 'I've just seen Francis.'

'Francis? You couldn't have. He didn't say he was coming, did he?'

'No, but he watches me, Tom . . .'

'Oh come on, you're imagining it. Where did you see him?'

'There,' she said, uncertainly.

He peered over the crowds. 'No, you're mistaken. He's not there. Come, let's get something to eat, then we'll go to Hyde Park.'

It was a wonderful day. A little meal in a coffee house, where ladies didn't usually go, but today was different, today all rules were waived, even those of marriage. They walked to Hyde Park and sat on the grass, his arm around her, waiting for the dark. And then the fireworks, the glitter, the coloured stars and whirling lights.

'It's lovely,' breathed Tacy.

'You're lovely,' said Tom. And when at last the display was ended, and darkness fell over the park, with straggling revellers still shouting, he whispered, 'Shall I come back with you?'

'Oh Tom.' She was filled with longing. To have Tom to herself all night, to make love to him, to be lost in his kisses. Just one night out of all eternity . . .

She said, 'I'm afraid.'

'Why, Tacy, what of?'

'I'm sure I saw Francis.'

'Well, then, let's find another lodging.'

'You know we can't, not tonight, everywhere's too crowded. And besides – he might find out.'

A group of youths ran past, shouting and yelling. Tacy and Tom stood up. 'You're afraid of him,' Tom said. 'Let me –'

'No, Tom . . . Tom – there's something else. He doesn't sleep with me now. If I had a baby . . . he'd kill me, I think.'

Lamps were lit in the streets, the park was dark. 'Oh, Tacy –' Tom muttered.

'Take me back to the hotel,' she said, miserably. 'It's been such a lovely day . . .'

They walked back in silence, revellers still shouting around them, Tacy wouldn't let Tom enter the road where the little guest house was. She kissed him yearningly, and walked inside.

Into the square lobby with its potted plants. And sitting on the cane chair a man. Francis.

Tacy's heart beat so that she felt faint. She had been right. He had been spying on her . . . had he seen her?

He rose as she entered and bowed. 'My dear,' he said. 'I had almost given you up.'

She found it difficult to speak, her heart was still pounding. 'What are you doing here?' she whispered.

'Why, I came to see the coronation as you did.'

'Then why didn't you tell me you were coming.' She was recovering now from the shock.

'I only decided at the last minute. Besides, I had a visit after you left. From Sir William.'

'*What?*'

'He wanted an answer about building the houses.'

She caught her breath. 'And you said?'

'I said no. Not to please you, my dear, but to displease that man. But there is a condition.'

'Yes?'

'I am your husband. You must never see any other man. You must love me, Tacy. Only me. Or I'll ruin Barratts.'

She looked at him and thought how he'd changed in the short time she'd known him. He stood up, tall, urbane, well-groomed, yet with a cruel twist to his mouth that never used to be there. She said, cuttingly, 'Do you know, you are like your father.' And then she pushed past him and walked upstairs.

But she was shaking at her narrow escape.

Martha sat in her kitchen smoothing her side where the pain had started. The baby wasn't due for another three weeks, but babies had a habit of coming in their own time as well she knew. Even so, she had been annoyed when Tom had announced that he was going to London.

'What for?' she'd asked.

'To see the coronation. What else?'

What else indeed? She hadn't really minded till yesterday morning when she went to Mrs Bailey's little shop and saw young Jobey there buying bread.

'What, going away?' fat Mrs Bailey asked.

'Not me, the missus. Goin' to London to see the coronation.'

'Oh, is she? With you?'

'Nay, on the coach.'

Mrs Bailey passed him the bread. 'And is Mr Barratt going?'

'Nay, he stops at home wi' Damaris.'

As Martha walked home she felt a sudden urge of – what – the old jealousy? It was more like anger that swept over her and left her trembling.

She reached the house, passing Martin and Mossy playing cricket with an old piece of wood, and a pig's bladder. William held two-year-old Joey's hand. Why hadn't she sent Martin to the shop? Why?

She knew Tom had gone to see Tacy.

So what was left for her?

She was angry with Tom. He came to her bed when he fancied, leaving her with babies . . . And she was resentful.

She wanted no more children, not born like this, carelessly, whenever Tom decided to stay with his wife. Yet how could she prevent them? Babies were sent by the Lord, it would be wrong to try to stop their coming, even if she knew how.

But this was too much.

She went to see Mrs Walters and told her her pains had started.

'Oh me dear, and Tom's away. Not that he could do much. He's done his share. Where's the kids?' She went to the doorway. 'Now you lads, run down to your Grandma Jacques, she'll give you your dinner. Tell her your mam's not well. Go on now. Take Joey, William. Yes, Mam'll be better tomorrow.'

'Until the next time,' muttered Mrs Walters. 'Look how many I've had, nothing but childbearing all the time.' She bustled back to Martha. 'Come on, me duck, up to bed wi' you. P'raps it'll be a little girl this time. Ay well, you'll remember this day, won't you, the coronation?'

Tom arrived home the next day, as the sun was staining the sky red, tired and dusty from the waggons he'd ridden in. Mrs Walters met him at the door.

'Another lad,' she said.

'What – now? But it wasn't due till next month.'

'Well, it's here now. You'd better go up and see her.'

Tom tiptoed in the bedroom, shamefaced. 'I'm sorry, Martha. I wouldn't have gone if I'd known. How are you?'

Martha's black hair was spread over the pillow, her face looked sallow in the sunlight. In the crook of her arm was another black-haired baby, another little Jacques. 'I'm all right,' she said, and sounded weary.

Tom peeked at the baby. 'What are you going to name him?'

'Charles.'

'Charles?'

'Charles Wesley.'

'I see.'

'And Tom.' Martha rallied. 'When I get up we'll move this bed into the landing room. The boys can have this bedroom. It's bigger.'

He knew what she meant. He wouldn't be able to share the landing bed, not in full view of anyone passing through, of anyone at the foot of the stairs.

He did not argue . . .

PART TWO

When trade was good the weavers would spend their extra earnings on lamb out of season, fowls and dress . . .

It was impossible for respectable families to procure domestic servants, young women looked down with scorn upon it, and preferred the liberty of Monday to Saturday, the exemption from confinement, and the little finery, with the liberty to wear it, which the loom procures them.

Revd Mr King, local curate

In many cases the young woman is *enceinte* before marriage and there is little disgrace attached to it. Nor is there any disgrace in bastardy.

Relieving Officer, Nuneaton

If the labour of the man can be made a sufficient source of income to the family, and that of the wife and children rendered quite subordinate to it, the former left chiefly to the due performance of domestic duties, which are her proper office in civilised life, and the latter trained in order, religion and intelligence, the philanthropist will have good reason to congratulate humanity.

J. Fletcher
from *The Report from the Assistant Hand-loom Weavers Commissioners*

Chapter ten

In 1828 Nonconformists were admitted to Parliament, and a year later Damaris Barratt, at thirteen, was fast developing into a young lady. She did not have her mother's beauty; her face was rounder, her hair darker. Her lips were soft, yet firm when closed, and her grey eyes clear and untroubled.

Daily she went to Miss Anson's school in Chilverton, dressed demurely. Not in a uniform, that was for the children at charity schools; Damaris wore a blue dress with a white cap on her head. Daily she came home, changed, and ran down to Aunt Martha's, where she stayed for as long as she was not missed. She grew up with the Jacques boys: Martin, who teased her and with whom she tried to keep up when he ran in the fields and climbed trees; quiet William, and the younger ones, Mossy, Joey and little Charley, now seven.

Together they would crowd into the little kitchen when work was over, William worked with his mother on the loom, the younger boys helped and wound the pirns. Martin, now fifteen, was apprenticed to his father on the Jacquard, and it was here Damaris liked to be.

She remembered the first time she'd seen the Jacquard when a small girl, how she'd gazed at the huge loom in amazement, with its separate bands of silk threads streaming down from a great height. Only when she approached did she see that the rows of marching silk was woven by the shuttle — holding several coloured quills — into beautiful lengths of wide ribbons, each with patterns of leaves in autumn colours of brown and old gold. She remembered how she'd asked if the brown cards were Black Magic when Uncle Tom told her they made the pattern, and how she'd thought the silk shop a wonderland; some of the sense of wonder remained to this day.

She'd been eleven on the day two more Jacquards were installed at Uncle Tom's shop, in the enlarged building in the garden, and she was still curious. She had stared at the brown cards that somehow made the pattern come on the ribbon and asked, 'How do they get there?' And he explained again that the pattern was transferred onto the brown cards. And she asked, 'Who makes the patterns, Uncle Tom?' and he'd explained, as he always did when she asked questions, that they were done in Coventry.

'How?' she'd asked.

'Well, first there's the drawing. Then it's transferred to a big sheet of squared paper, each square representing one thread of silk. Then it's put onto the cards. You see?'

'But who makes the drawings, Uncle? Does someone make them up?'

'Yes, of course. I'll take you to see them one day.'

True to his promise he had taken her, and she saw it all happen. First the design, then the sheet of squared paper, and she listened eagerly as Uncle Tom explained that each warp thread was represented by a vertical row of squares and the weft by a horizontal one. She listened as he told her that each small square meant that either the warp thread lay over the weft or vice versa, and this had to be shown. 'Do you understand?' he asked.

'Yes, of course,' she replied, and he laughed.

'That's my little weaver,' he said. 'Weaving's an old trade, Damaris, and silk is older still. It's something to be proud of, weaving. And it's an inherited skill, it's in your blood.'

'But Papa isn't a weaver,' she said, frowning.

'No, but your Mamma is, and her parents were, so you see it comes to you.'

And she knew it was true, and would sometimes spend time in the warehouse, watching how Mamma gave out the silk and who worked what. Plain satins or sarsenets to the Pettits, who had Dutch engine-looms; or lustring, which was stouter than sarsenet. The 'fancies', gauzes and tartans, which had the greatest number of different coloured shoots, went to the hand-looms, such as Luke Lakin's. And finally, the Jacquards.

She did not dislike her mother, but she regarded her as she would a distant aunt, while Aunt Martha was her true mother, though she never put any of this into words. Nor had she any great love for her father, he was always kind to her and to most people, though not to her mother, and there were times when he was a little odd in his manner, when his eyes seemed to stare.

It had been a cold spring, followed by a hot summer, and now the farmers would be haymaking, and she wished she could be out watching them, seeing the great horses pulling the waggons, flocks of starlings wheeling above. She was restless, but both her parents were in the parlour, so she followed them, and sat quietly.

'The weaving is down again,' said Tacy.

'And won't get any better,' Francis answered.

Damaris stared through the window at the garden, untidy these days. Sometimes Jobey tidied it up if he had time, more often than not it was left. Damaris herself had planted hollyhocks and pinks, given to her by William; honeysuckle twined round the posts, and clematis clung to the wall, while the daffodils came up year after year, nodding their yellow heads triumphantly. They would not be put down. Damaris thought they were like the weavers.

She wondered why her father so often contradicted her mother. She knew there had been a fearsome quarrel some years ago when she was much younger, and Papa had left home for a few days, indeed she vaguely remembered it. But it was her mother's fault, he told her. Tacy said nothing about it either then or later. Papa seemed determined to please since then, he started taking Damaris for walks, and he would stop and chat to people in the street, raise his hat and talk pleasantly. He'd talk to Damaris too, about how her mother was unkind to him, so he had to leave home, but he came back because he loved Damaris so much. And outside, he'd sigh if Tacy's name was mentioned. 'Yes,' he'd say. 'I like to take Damaris for little outings, her mother has so little time.' And he'd sigh again. And people would think he was such a pleasant man, if there had been trouble, well, it must have been Tacy's fault. After all, she was a bossy piece, running the business herself instead of letting her man take over. All right if you were a widow and had to, but when you had a husband, well . . .

Only Uncle Tom wouldn't hear a word against her mother. She remembered the day when Papa had been talking to Aunt Martha, repeating how he liked to take Damaris out because her mother was so busy. Aunt Martha said nothing, and neither saw Uncle Tom come in.

'If Tacy's busy it's because she's working for the whole town,' he'd said.

Papa had stood up, his face had gone quite white. Aunt Martha looked alarmed, but she did not speak. And Papa said, 'I think we'll go, Damaris.'

And when they reached home he'd been in quite a temper and had been cross with Mamma.

But this day he was quiet, and it was Mamma who

said, 'Damaris, I've been thinking. Next year you should leave school.'

'Oh?' asked Papa. 'Should she? First I've heard about it.'

Tacy sighed, she had forgotten for the moment that Francis liked to make the decisions, so she said, hurriedly, 'Well, she will be fourteen next year, I think it will be time she began to learn the business.'

Now Damaris perked up. 'What do you mean, Mamma?' she asked.

'Well, the business will be yours one day, there's no-one else to inherit. I thought you might start now, come with me to London and meet the buyers and brokers, study the accounts with Papa, and so on.'

'No,' said Damaris.

Now both parents stared their surprise. Damaris didn't usually argue; if she were told to do something, she did it – or so they thought. Neither really knew how often she appeared to agree with them, then went her own way. Bess could have enlightened them.

'What do you mean, no?' asked Tacy.

'There's something else I want to do first. I want to design for the Jacquards.'

'Well,' Tacy began. 'That's a nice thing to want to do, and I am sure we can fit it in. But – '

'No, Mamma, you don't understand. I don't want to fit it in, I want to work at it full time, learn how to draw, learn how to transfer to the squared paper, then onto the cards.'

'But that's done at Coventry. We buy them – ' Tacy began.

'Yes, now. But we're getting more Jacquard looms, and we shall need more in future. We need good designs now. It would save money for us to make our own. I should go to the Mechanics' Institute.'

Tacy stared at her daughter as if she had said she wanted to take up chimney-sweeping. 'The Mechanics' Institute?' she asked. 'You cannot do that.'

'Why not?' asked Damaris.

'Because the Mechanics' Institute is not for young ladies. It is for those who have not had much schooling. You had your education at Miss Anson's. And you learned drawing there, surely?'

'Not the kind of drawing I want to do. Not how to transfer to the cards. Not draughtsmanship.'

'I cannot hear of it,' said Tacy, dismissively.

'But, Mamma, it is what I want to do.'

'A child's whim,' Tacy disagreed.

'No, not a child's whim, it is what I've always wanted to do since the new Jacquards came. We shall have more in the future, Mamma, we shall need a designer. Oh, I will study the other aspects of the business too, of course I will, but without a good designer we cannot compete. Had you not thought?'

'There is nothing wrong with the designs we have,' objected Tacy.

'The ones Coventry doesn't want, but with more French ribbons coming in all the time – and the French are good at designing – '

'She's right,' said Francis.

Damaris stared at her Papa. She might have known that he would agree if her mother was against it. But she was too honest a girl to play one parent off against the other. She just wished Mamma would see it her way.

'We'll talk about it another day,' said Tacy, shortly.

Francis left the room. He said no more, but his displeasure was in the set of his thin shoulders, the tightness of his mouth. Damaris sighed, and went out too, wondering if she could slip down to the meadows, it wasn't too late.

Tacy sat deep in thought.

The weaving had fluctuated over the years. There had been worry when, in 1824, it was proposed to take off the banning of French silks as a step towards free trade, and the weavers had sent a petition to the House of Lords. The Minister made some alterations, and, heartened, the weavers were in full employ, and on the fine gauze ribbons were back to earning £1 a week again, more than twice as much as the agricultural labourers. But in 1826 the bill was passed, a tariff replaced prohibition, and there was an immediate reduction in the prices paid in London. So again Tacy had a hard time. And always George Healey undercut her. If only he would go away . . . If only work would improve permanently . . . they said the King was dying, that he never left Windsor Castle now. That he'd deteriorated both physically and mentally, that he slopped around in a dressing-gown, taking laudanum to ease his pain. He suffered from gout and from dropsy, his bulk was enormous. When he died there would be yet another funeral, but there'd also be a coronation to follow.

The clock struck nine and she moved into the garden. A red and apricot afterglow was still in the western sky; these summer nights seeemed hardly to get dark at all. Swifts flew overhead, screaming and crying, and she watched them, thinking they'd soon be gone to Africa. She sat on the wooden bench and thought over Damaris' strange request. She wanted Damaris with her in the warehouse, for though Tom still gave her a hand, Francis was liable to stalk through at any moment, watching. With Damaris there she could talk to Tom without Francis glowering in the background. She needed Tom's help and advice.

Francis had never mentioned seeing her in London all those years ago – and if he did, Tacy thought rebelliously, we weren't doing anything. Why should I have to live in fear all the time? Francis had not changed with the years, if anything he seemed more odd, saying little, except to criticise and remind her that the business belonged to him. She had tried to talk to him, ask him what was wrong. 'You're so different from when we married,' she'd said.

'If so, it's your fault,' he replied.

'How is it my fault?'

'Because you told Sir William he is my father.'

'But what difference does that make? He hasn't said any more. He doesn't see you.'

'But he knows. I did not wish him to know.'

'Well, I'm sorry, I wish I hadn't told him. But can't you forget?'

Francis just stared at her broodingly. He did not mention Tom.

She never went to the church socials now, for this might mean inviting people back to the Red House, and this she did not want to do, not with Francis. She knew, from the odd occasion when someone did call, that he would be pleasant and charming, only to relapse into sullen silence the moment they had left. Tacy herself could not act that way, could not pretend to be happy and content when all the time they were hardly on speaking terms. So she would say little and this simply added to the general assumption that she was to blame for any marital difficulties.

So she led a lonely life. Francis always retired to his room immediately after supper at nine o'clock, and for this Tacy was thankful. She had absolutely no idea that he spent his time there drinking. To Tacy, drink meant noise. If Tom drank too much he became merry and would sing. She saw drunken men outside the beer-houses, shouting and fighting, and had seen the gin-sodden women lying in the gutters in London. That some people might drink in solitude would have amazed her, and she would not have recognised the smell of brandy had it been flung in her face. From the beerhouses came the stale odour of ale, from the gin-shops the sweeter smell of gin. That was all she knew.

The sky was darkening now except in the west where the glow had faded to a paler pink edged with light blue. A little breeze sprang up, though it was still warm. She went back indoors, deciding to see Sarah Jane in the kitchen before she went to bed. She left the arranging of meals to Sarah Jane, just checking with her from time to time.

She liked the kitchen. The copper pans glowed in the half-light, a small fire burned in the grate. All the dishes were put away, the scrubbed table was covered with a blue chenille cloth. There was no sign of Bess, but Sarah Jane sat in her old rocking chair, sipping a mug of warm milk.

'Everything all right?' Tacy asked.

'Some things are,' Sarah Jane said, lugubriously.

'Plenty of butter and cheese in the markets? The butcher's sending the meat you ordered?'

'Aye.'

'Then what's amiss?'

Sarah Jane's long face grew even longer. 'Have you seen her?'

'Her?'

'That one. Bess.'

'No. Why?' Tacy sat down with a little sigh.

'Then you should. Did you not know she was expectin'?'

Sarah Jane was, to use her own expression, a 'poor crittur' these days. Her hands shook with a palsy, her legs were so swollen that she could only shuffle around in old slippers. Tacy had called in the apothecary, who sniffed and gave her some lotions, but said carelessly that she was afflicted with age. Tacy told her to rest, and she did occasionally, but she preferred to shuffle around keeping an eye on Bess.

The bulk of the work now fell on Bess, and she did not complain. She ran the house, seeming to grow in stature too, and this Sarah Jane could not abide. She was jealous of the young woman, her usurper.

'Who does she think she is, the missus?' she'd ask. And, to Tacy, 'You want to keep an eye on her, you know, what she gets up to.'

Tacy neither knew nor cared what Bess did in her spare time. At least, not until now. Now she faced Sarah Jane and asked, 'Are you sure?'

''Course I'm sure, I've guessed it long since.'

'Where is she now?'

'Talking to the master.'

'Oh well, I'm going to bed, I'm a little tired. I'll see her in the morning. Is Damaris in bed?'

'Aye.'

Tacy did not call in her daughter's room, she went straight to her own and drew the curtains. A thin sliver of moon was rising, candles began to shine from the houses. She began to undress. She would deal with Bess in the morning.

At seven o'clock another fine day was heralded. Horses clopped by, some children ran past, shouting. Bess brought in the breakfast and Tacy studied her. Yes, it was obvious, there was a thickening of the waist beneath the apron, though, as Bess had a buxom figure with ample breasts, her pregnancy was not so noticeable as it might otherwise have been. Tacy wondered if Francis had detected anything. He was especially sullen and withdrawn in the mornings, but his hawk eyes never missed a thing.

Damaris went to school, Francis to the counting-house, and Tacy went to the kitchen where Bess was alone, washing the plates in the big yellow stone sink. She did not turn as Tacy entered, until she said her name.

'Yes?' Bess asked.

'Are you with child?' Tacy asked, without preamble.

'Yes.' There was no shame in her voice, nor manner, and this irritated Tacy a little.

'And who is the father?'

'I dunna want to say.'

Bess had lit the fire and the heat further irritated Tacy, though she knew it had to be done. 'Then what are you going to do?' she asked, sharply.

'Nothin'. I shall have the child, then carry on as normal.'

And though Tacy was quite willing for her to do this, she was annoyed at the assumption that it was taken for granted. 'Shouldn't you ask first?' she wanted to know.

'Oh, I did.'

'I don't recall.'

Now Bess did turn and faced her mistress, wiping her hands on her apron. 'I asked Mr Barratt. He said it's all right.'

'You asked Mr Barratt?' Tacy was incensed. 'Shouldn't you have come to me first?'

'Well, he is the master.' Now her tone was insolent. Without another word Tacy went in search of Francis.

He was sitting at the high desk with one of his ledgers, and he looked up at Tacy's entrance, and saw her obvious anger. He waited, calmly.

'Francis,' Tacy burst out. 'Bess tells me she is with child.'

'Is she?' His quill hovered over the ledger as if waiting to write.

'And that you told her she could stay here.'

'I did.'

'Surely it is for the mistress to say who stays and goes in her kitchen.'

'No, it is for the master. And I am the master.'

'Yes, thanks to marrying me.'

Now he put down his pen. 'What did you say?'

'Nothing. Let it go.'

But he was angry, and as always when angry, he wanted to hurt her. 'I am the master,' he said. 'And the child is mine. So she stays.'

Tacy swung round in utter amazement. Oh, men did father children on to servants, she knew, though she hadn't expected to find such a happening in her father's house. And wherever it happened, the men seldom boasted of it so brazenly, and never to their wives. She said, 'I don't understand you.'

'What don't you understand?' He had that cruel look on his face, the look she dreaded, which meant he would carry on insulting her for hours if she couldn't get away.

She said, wearily, 'I don't understand why you are like you are. What have I done to you that you should treat me so?'

'You do nothing for me,' he taunted. 'Nothing at all. Bess cooks my meals and warms my bed while you gallivant around pretending to see to the business.'

'We all work at the business — after all, it is our livelihood, yours as well as mine.'

'I shall go with whom I please.'

She was both shocked and angry. She had had no idea that this went on under their roof. Mentally she thought of the bedrooms, hers at the end, then Damaris', then Francis'. On the opposite side of the passageway was the large bedroom that had been her parents', now unoccupied, and another small room, also empty. Sarah Jane slept upstairs in one of the attics, but Bess had a room round a corner over the warehouse, given to her when Damaris was a baby, for the two to share. Now it was hers alone.

She said, 'What would you do if I went with another man?'

'I'd kill you,' he said in a calm voice that was even more frightening than bluster.

She turned on her heel, and he watched her go, broodingly, heard the tap tap of her shoes on the stone floor of the warehouse. She didn't understand.

She didn't understand that a man needed two women. More than two. His wife, a good woman, and the others, with whom he could do those things he could not with his wife for, if he tried she turned away in disgust, and yet he understood this, she was pure underneath. Bess excited him. Tacy didn't excite him. And it was Tacy he loved. Tacy was a good woman, like his mother had been, and once she realised she loved him it would be as when he was a boy – heaven.

That was the happiest time of his life, when he had been with his mother. He wished she hadn't died. But of course, they had taken him away from her, press-ganged into the Navy. He didn't remember much about the Navy now, didn't try to remember. It made his head ache.

His mother had loved him, hadn't wanted anyone else. That's how it should be. That's how Tacy should be. He must guard her carefully lest that no good Tom Jacques led her astray, he feared for her sometimes, mixing with all those men in the weaving. Perhaps she'd be better if she did not do any work, just stayed at home looking after him. It was a recurring idea now, and he took pleasure in the thought. Somehow she must be made to see that her place was in the home, and he must persuade her of it, even if it meant giving up the business completely.

He returned to his ledger, to the item, from Mr Hood, spirit and wine merchant: To seven bottles of brandy . . . He marked it paid, then went to the next item.

Martin Jacques, Senior, had led a full and turbulent life, hard drinking, hard working.

As a young man he'd travelled around the country, coming back with enough money to buy a piece of waste land at the side and rear of his house. No one knew exactly how he'd made the money; some said horse-racing, others by prize-fighting. But once home, he married and went back to his old trade of weaving. As his sons grew he set them to build a loom-shop where they all worked, and as they grew up he built on bedrooms over the loom-shop and here Mark and Ross and their wives lived. The sisters married and went away, as Nancy had. Tom stayed there more often than not, though he always called to see Martha on Saturdays, giving her housekeeping money.

It was still hot when Damaris came from school, though several small white clouds like little puffballs drifted by. She entered the loom-shop, but no one stopped working as she went in. There were three Jacquard looms being worked by Ross, Tom, and their father. The other brother, Mark, was at the hand-loom. Hester, Mark's wife, was picking up, Sally was winding, and Martin worked with Tom. Damaris went to inspect the ribbons: Ross's white with a blue cornflower in the middle; Tom's an all over pattern of lilac and green; Mark's were wide swathes of blue and gold. The looms whirred and clacked, the Jacques family worked fero-ciously, and Damaris, used to this, went to stand by Tom.

'Can I talk to you, Uncle Tom? It's about the designing.'

'Yes, when I've finished work,' he said. 'Won't be too long today, it's Wednesday. Go to Aunt Martha's, I'll be round in about an hour.'

Martin moved from the back of the loom and he looked at her. He was a tall youth now with black hair and eyes like his father, and black down on his upper lip. And there was something in his eyes that made Damaris shiver inside, and she knew things had changed between them. He was no longer her childhood playmate, not now, not now he looked at her as if she was a woman. Not now her figure was changing into a woman's, not now she had the knowledge inside her, and had for some months, that she was no longer a child, and childish things had gone for good. And she wished with all her heart that she had gone home first and taken off this silly school dress, put on something more womanly. She must ask Mamma for a new dress, one like she'd seen in the fashion magazines, a beautiful tight waist, long ankle-length skirt, wide, trimmed with gorgeous ribbons. And perhaps a hat with a big brim trimmed with more ribbons and lace. And she'd need corsets too, women wore them again now, and really she was too childish in this silly dress, she wanted to look more like Bess, full bosomed, bowling along like a ship in full sail. Then she could return Martin's looks and . . .

She retraced her steps to Aunt Martha's, who was preparing the evening meal while William worked on the loom in the front room, Mossy and Joey helping. Charley was out on the Common picking up firewood. When William came in he didn't give her saucy looks, maybe he didn't realise she was a woman now. Still, William was only fifteen, a child, really, compared with Martin.

Damaris took off her hat and helped Aunt Martha put out the plates. Charley ran in with the wood, and then

Martin followed his father in, and Damaris' heart began its bumping again as he looked at her. He did not speak, he did not need to, it was as if they were communicating with each other and no-one else could understand, there was no-one else in the world but Martin and Damaris.

Tom washed his hands in the bowl on the wooden bench outside the door and came in wiping them on a towel. 'Well, Damaris, you wanted to talk to me?' he asked.

'Yes, it's about the designing. Mamma doesn't want me to do it.'

'Oh?' Tom sat at the table, Martin followed, and soon all the boys were crowding round, talking, laughing, Charley pinched Mossy, and had his ear cuffed for his pains. 'Why not?' Tom asked.

'She wants me to learn the business first.'

'Well,' Tom said, judiciously. 'She is your mother, Damaris. It is for her to decide.'

'No,' Damaris contradicted. 'I want to do this because I think it is important. You said it was important, Uncle Tom, that we get our own designs.'

'Your uncle is set on his Jacquards,' said Aunt Martha, ladling out the stew, and handing a plate to Damaris.

'And I'm right,' Tom said. 'We must improve, expand, it's the only way. Get more speed.'

'Yes,' agreed Damaris.

Tom took a spoonful of the stew and crumbled a piece of bread in his fingers. Charley dropped his spoon on the table making a clatter, and Tom absent-mindedly slapped his ear. 'Well,' he said at length. 'What do you want me to do?'

'Could you not speak to Mamma? Oh, please – ' as he hesitated. 'Please, Uncle Tom. I want to do this so much. I can learn all about it at the Mechanics' Institute.'

'I'll have a word with her,' Tom said. 'I can't guarantee

that she'll take any notice. Your Mamma goes her own way.' He grinned down at the girl. 'Like others I could mention.'

Tom strode down to the warehouse, top hat set rakishly on his head, green coat over pantaloons in hessian boots. Tom always looked smart.

Tacy was packing ribbons into boxes and she did not stop as he approached. 'Tacy,' he called. 'I want to talk to you.'

'Just a minute, Tom, I must get these away, we are late now.' She tied up the box, went to the door and called Jobey. He shambled in, and she ordered him to take the box down to the canal.

'It won't go tonight,' he said, sullenly.

'Yes, it will, Dick Barlow's fly-boat is waiting. Go on now, Jobey.'

'You heard your mistress,' ordered Tom. 'Get a move on.'

Jobey departed, box in his arms, and Tacy called, 'You can take the horse.' She turned to Tom.

'I want to talk to you,' he repeated.

'All right. Only don't be too long.'

'Don't be too long or Francis will come in,' Tom said, impatiently. 'Peeping round the door, wondering if we are making love on the bobbins.'

She did not smile. Only she knew what happened if she displeased Francis, especially if he thought Tom was involved. Only she knew of the night to follow when he would enter her bedroom and talk about things she hardly liked to remember. She said, 'Well, tell me quickly, Tom.'

'No, I won't tell you quickly,' he said, his temper flaring. 'It's business I want to discuss, not to take advantage of you. Surely there is somewhere we can meet.'

'You know there isn't,' she said. 'We've talked of this before. If we both go out of town he'd get to know, and if we're together when he's out of town, someone would tell him.'

'Have you ever stopped to wonder who?' Tom asked.

'Oh yes, he told me. Lottie Glover.'

'He *told* you?' Tom was taken aback.

She smiled thinly. 'And I don't doubt there's others.' Her eyes darkened as she remembered the things he told her about Lottie Glover, taking pleasure in her humiliation, till she learned to hide her feelings behind a mask, trying not to listen.

'The man should be horsewhipped,' Tom burst out. 'Oh, Tacy, if I had known –'

'But you didn't,' she said, quickly. 'Neither did I when I married him. Though he's changed, I think. Unless it was inside all the time. I don't know.'

'Listen,' he said quickly. 'I will not be treated this way by that madman. Martha is gone to her club meeting tonight. Come down, and I'll get the boys out of the way.'

She thought of what she'd learned this morning – was it only this morning? – about Francis. Tom was right. Why should they be treated so? 'All right,' she said, recklessly. 'I'll come. But what of the neighbours?'

'Oh, when you go I'll come to the door and shout, "Sorry you missed Martha, Mrs Barratt." Anyway, I don't think Mrs Walters is one of Francis' doxies.'

She did smile then as she thought of fat, middle-aged Mrs Walters. 'All right,' she agreed. 'I'll come.'

Tom retraced his steps to the Patch. Martin, he knew, was out, William was indoors, the younger boys played in the road. He called them inside.

'There's a prize-fight tonight between Ed Cross and Jupiter Payne in the Windmill Fields,' he told them.

'Here's the money, you can all go and see it. You too, William. I want to be quiet tonight, get my accounts done.'

The younger boys took the money with whoops of joy, and ran down the road, shouting happily. William went too, more quietly. Then Tom waited.

It was eight o'clock when he heard her step. The sun was sinking, but a cooler breeze was springing up; in the distance a dark cloud waited. Tacy came into the kitchen and he closed the door.

It was warm and cosy in the little kitchen. They could hear children shouting outside, hear a dog barking. Tacy loosened her hat ribbons and sat at the table, Tom opposite. He said, 'It's about Damaris. She wants to design for the Jacquards.'

'Yes, she told me.'

'Why are you against it, Tacy?'

She shrugged. 'I'm not exactly against it. But she has to learn the business properly. And she's only a child.'

'And how old are most children when they start working? We can't afford to wait, Tacy. Damaris is a bright girl, and it's important that we have a good designer now.'

'How do you know she is good?'

'She's shown me a couple of her designs.' And Tacy was silent, wondering why Damaris had never shown them to her. It was the old story, she knew, at bottom, it was the old jealousy reasserting itself, jealousy of Martha, that she had everything, Tom, now Damaris.

'We must move forward,' Tom was saying. 'Jacquards will take over the hand-looms in time –'

'You know the finest work is done on the hand-looms,' she objected.

'Yes, there'll always be a place for them. But for quickness, to earn money, no. Don't shake your head,

Tacy, you must earn money and you know it.' He paused, the boys in the street seemed to be playing football, from time to time came a thump as the ball hit the wall. 'There's talk in Coventry about steam power. In a factory.'

'Tom,' she said, wearily. 'They've been trying steam power for silk for *eighteen years*, and it won't take it, silk's too delicate. The threads break –'

'They think they've found how to conquer it,' Tom said. 'I was over in Coventry last week, talking to a man from Macclesfield. The silk is stretched on frames and picked by hand before being mounted in the loom – in some cases every thread is passed between small cylinders or steel rollers, and fine needle eyes, which stop the knots and level all the inequalities. That's broad silk, of course, but it won't be long before it's ribbons too.'

The ball crashed against the wall, and Tom went to the door, ordered the boys away. Tacy was shaken at his news. They sat in silence for a time, then Tom stood up and lit the candle on the mantelpiece. 'Did I ever tell you about my Uncle Ned?' he asked. 'The one who went to America?'

'No.' She roused a little. 'Was he sent as a convict?'

'Oh no. He was another wild one, and he got in a bit of trouble so he thought he'd skip. He went out on one of these schemes where the farmer at the other end pays his passage then he has to work for him for some years. He worked his time, then he was free.'

'So what did he do?'

'He was a silkman, a weaver originally, so he moved around. And he wrote to me last week that they're thinking of trying silk out there.' He paused. 'Sometimes I think I'd like to join him. He always asks. Says there's plenty of work there, plenty of land, and you don't have squires breathing down your necks.'

And she was filled with panic that Tom might just do that, he was reckless enough. What would she do without him?

'I never heard of any silk weaving in America,' she said.

'Not weaving, no. They tried with raw silk. Way back in 1608 James I wanted to raise silkworms in Virginia, as the climate was warmer than here. 'Course, an English law prohibited colonists from producing finished goods from raw materials, so that would have meant we had the supply of raw materials, while they had to depend on us for the products.'

'Typical,' Tacy murmured. 'So what happened?'

'Producing raw silk was abandoned. But Uncle thinks they could import the raw material and start manufacturing. There is some interest.'

The boys had gone from the road, it was quite quiet. The dark clouds had lengthened, the one candle hardly lit the room. Tom's low voice was like a lullaby in the twilight, and she sat, almost mesmerised. This was the first time they'd been alone for years, and she could think of nothing but his nearness. If Damaris wanted to design, what did it matter? She couldn't think clearly.

He was looking at her now, noting her confusion, He asked, 'Did Francis really tell you that he'd been with Lottie?'

'Yes.'

'But why?'

She shrugged. 'Just to be cruel, he tells me what he does.' And as he stared she knew he'd hardly understand. Tom was wild, went with women, he had a violent temper . . . but he was not sadistic, he would never be deliberately, coldly cruel to a woman.

She tried to shrug it off. 'Some men are funny, I suppose. He never really forgave me for telling Sir William he was his son.'

'His *son*?'

'Yes.' She was babbling now, as always when she was nervous, realising what she'd told him. 'I thought it would help me, you see, when I went to ask –' She broke off.

'Ask what?' he persisted.

'Oh, I forget.'

'But what did Sir William say to upset Francis?'

'Oh, he told him . . . that I'd been to see him.'

'Tacy. Why did you go to see him? What did you want to ask Sir William?'

She said, wildly, 'Nothing. I forget.'

'Tacy!'

'I asked him to set you free.'

'I see. So that's behind it all. Sir William told Francis. That's why you're afraid to be with me.'

She looked down. Why had her stupid tongue run away with her like that?

'Oh, Tacy,' he muttered. 'All this was because of me.'

Now her heart beat more wildly than ever. 'I love you, Tom,' she cried, recklessly. 'I always have.'

She never knew afterwards who made the first move; they seemed to move together, standing, touching. And then their arms were entwined, and he was kissing her. Not in Francis' cold, calculating way; not in Sir William's insulting manner, but warmly, passionately. She took off her hat, laid it on the table, and without a word they went up to the bedroom.

And it was all that she had dreamed, she and Tom together, making love, kissing, stroking, moving together, gently, then passionately, his arms holding her tight, she, running her hand through his black curls so close to her own. And when it was over and his head drooped on to her neck she lay back, still holding him close.

He whispered, 'I didn't mean this to happen.'

'I know.'

'What can you do?'

'Nothing,' she answered. 'You know there's nothing I can do. I can't leave him or he'd just take everything I own.'

Neither mentioned Martha.

Outside, in the road, William walked along, whistling. He had left early, for prize-fights weren't to his taste. He knew his father would be busy, he'd told them so, getting his accounts ready, he'd said, and Tom liked to be quiet when he was reckoning. But a chill wind had sprung up, he'd just call in for his coat, then go for a walk.

He opened the door, was about to call 'Father', when he saw by the light of the flickering candle the hat on the table. It wasn't his mother's hat, but he knew whose it was. Mrs Barratt's. He heard the murmur of voices upstairs.

He went out quietly, but he was angry. He knew his father philandered, but Mrs Barratt! Supposing his mother had come in!

He walked towards the Weavers' Arms and stood outside, moodily, waiting for Martha when the meeting was over, hoping to put her off, if she decided to leave early.

But he'd never forgive his father for hurting his mother.

Tacy walked back to the Red House in a glow of euphoria mixed with guilt, which her strict upbringing ensured she felt. She had committed adultery, she was wicked. What would Papa have said? He would turn in his grave if he knew. But, she told herself philosophically, the things I do he's likely spinning round and round by now . . .

It was quite dark when she reached the Red House, the

candles in the hall were lit. She went straight upstairs and stood before the mirror. She had a lover. Tom was her lover. She gazed at her reflection. Tumbled hair, glowing cheeks, sparkling eyes. Did Tom think she was pretty? She was thirty-three, still slim, but thirty-three, a great age. But pretty or not, she was his, she would follow him to the ends of the earth; they belonged together, cut out of the same piece of cloth – or silk. She was a part of Tom.

Slowly she took off her clothes, put on her nightdress, got into bed. She hoped and prayed Francis wouldn't come to her room tonight, she wanted to be alone, to think, to dream, of Tom . . .

She did not draw the curtains but lay watching the moon rise in the deep blue of the sky. If only she were free. But then . . . and now she allowed the thought that she had been suppressing, to enter. There was Martha. Martha, who *slept in his bed*, who had his children.

But tonight she had taken him away . . .

Tom went to his mother's after Tacy left, but William caught up with him the next day as he was leaving for the warehouse. 'Father,' he said, 'I have something to say to you.'

'Don't be long then, I'm in a hurry.'

William said in a low voice that no-one else might hear, 'What is it with you and Mrs Barratt?' And as Tom turned, amazed, 'I saw you last night. How can you treat my mother so?'

Tom looked angrily at his son. 'None of your business,' he said.

'It is my business if my mother gets hurt,' William said, his young face stern.

'Your mother – ' Tom began, then broke off. 'Leave it,' he said. 'You mind your business and I'll mind mine.' And he walked away.

Chapter eleven

In the spring the road in the Market Square was Macadamised, watched by groups of weavers who had little work. And in May Bess was brought to bed. Damaris had gone to school willingly now that her mother had surprisingly changed her mind about her going to the Mechanics' Institute later the previous year. Damaris had noted Bess's condition but said nothing; she knew, more than anyone, of her fondness for the men, and no-one told her who was the father. Only Sarah Jane went around, muttering.

Tacy was leaving for the warehouse when Sarah Jane said that Bess was in labour. 'Well, I suppose you'll have to fetch a midwife,' Tacy answered. 'Has she arranged anything?'

'How do I know?' Sarah Jane sniffed.

Tacy left, and when she returned it was to see Francis standing in the hall removing his top hat. 'I have a son,' he announced, a malicious glint in his eye, a glint that had been there ever since her visit to Tom. That he knew about the visit she learned in the following nights, when he came to her room after she had retired to bed and sat, first talking about Bess and what they did together and then, when Tacy tried to shut her ears, continuing viciously, 'So you went to see Tom Jacques on Wednesday night?'

'I went on business,' she replied, wondering how he knew.

Yet know he did, though not about their love-making,

that was surely impossible. But he had taunted her ever since that night, had thrown his relationship with Bess at her every moment when they were alone, and, worse, had restarted his visits to the warehouse when she was giving the work out, and when she talked to Tom. Now Francis would stand at the side, waiting till he had gone.

That Tom was angry about it she knew too, but managed to caution him to silence. If Tom started a row it would only make things worse for her.

Now, this announcement that he had a son was the culmination of his taunting, and she tried to stay cool. 'Oh?' she asked, removing her bonnet, more in vogue these days than hats, and put on her indoor cap. She walked into the dining-room, Francis following, and they saw the table was not laid. Francis looked round with displeasure, then pulled the bell-rope. After a wait of some ten minutes Sarah Jane shuffled in.

'And where is dinner?' asked Francis.

'There ain't no dinner. Bess is in bed and I've bin having to wait on her.'

'You mean nothing is prepared?'

'I've only got two hands and one pair of feet.'

'Well, prepare something immediately, if you please.'

Sarah Jane shuffled out again, and Francis said, 'We shall have to get another serving maid.'

'What for? To wait on Bess? I doubt we can afford it.'

'I shall decide what we can afford,' Francis replied grandly, and Tacy thought, he sees himself as some lord of the manor, and felt disquieted. Did Francis imagine things these days? Did he not see things as they were? Sarah Jane had told her quite bluntly that he wasn't sane.

'I've seen the like of it before. He's not normal nowadays. And remember the time he attacked you? He's likely to do the same thing again if he's crossed.'

Tacy didn't quite believe that, either. Mad people, like

drunks, shouted and screamed and tore their hair, and were locked up. Some poor creatures were put in cages at travelling fairs and all the people came to mock them and throw garbage. But it was all a little disturbing.

Bess was up and about again in three days, and resumed her chores, with baby Simon, a fretful, wailing infant, ensconced in the kitchen, and she entered the dining-room a little shamefaced.

Bess Harvey had been born on a small farm, with a mother worn down by too much work, she early found respite from her own labours in the arms of any farm worker who took her fancy. But when at the age of sixteen she became pregant, her tyrannical father turned her out and she was thrown on the mercy of the Parish.

She had been happy enough at the Red House, happy to take up with any weaver she fancied, and when Francis Barratt showed his preference for her she took him to her bed more as a matter of course than for any liking for him. She had been more than a little surprised – and not too pleased – at his peculiar practices, but could not see how to stop him. He was, as he reminded her, the master. Though her enjoyment at driving the chaise and the occasional sums of money he gave her, was some compensation.

She knew he drank, and knew he came to her when drunk. He hid this well, Francis could always hide his feelings, and drinking did not make him loud or obstreperous, just the reverse, he sat brooding – then went to Bess.

She hadn't wanted the baby, nor did she particularly want to hurt her mistress in any way. But she had no choice. She knew that, in one sense, she was protecting her, for if she were not there . . .

She did not like Sarah Jane pottering around after her, finding fault, it got on her nerves. She hoped the old woman would decide to take to her bed and leave her alone.

And her wish was granted sooner than she expected. Sarah Jane, so long ailing, collapsed, and though Tacy sent hurriedly for the apothecary, she was dead within two days.

A new maid was brought in, another orphan from the poorhouse. Annie looked scraggy and bedraggled, and never lost that look however much she ate or however many new clothes she had. Her lank hair was dragged back from her thin face, her bones showed through her muslin frock. She was not humble in any way, and though she had not Bess' ample charms and fondness for the men, she held her own.

Tacy missed Sarah Jane more than she would have believed possible, she had been there ever since she could remember. Cantankerous of late she may have been, yet she had always been on Tacy's side, being, in one sense, a confidante, her only confidante. The funeral was paid for by Tacy, for Sarah Jane had no living relatives, and she would not hear of her going to a pauper's grave. Now Tacy had no-one. She wished more than ever she had some friend in whom to confide. Her worries about the business, her fears about Francis, his watchfulness which was getting on her nerves. She prayed for something to change.

And her prayers were answered. Walking back from a visit to the milliners' she saw a figure in the distance and stopped. Then: 'Nancy!' she cried. 'Nancy Jacques – is it really you?' She saw her black cloak and dress. 'Is someone . . . ? Oh yes, I heard, old Mrs Pettit's dead.'

'Fred's mother,' Nancy replied. 'That's why we're here.'

'Oh, Nancy, it's so good to see you. When is the funeral?'

'Tomorrow morning.'

'I'll try to come. When are you going back?'

'The day after, I expect.'

'I'd love to talk to you again. It's been so long – '

'Well, come to the house. You do look a mite peaky,' Nancy said with the candour of an old friend.

'Your house?' Tacy drew back. 'Oh no.'

'Whyever not?'

'I – never go there.'

'Well, you're coming now and explaining why. Come on, it's starting to rain, and there won't be anybody in the kitchen, the men'll be in the shop.'

So Tacy allowed herself to be taken to the Jacques' kitchen, untidy as ever, its furniture worn, though an air of prosperity still lingered, as an old castle holds its former glories. A spatter of rain beat against the window-panes, and Tacy poured out all her worries about Francis. 'He pretends to be such a good husband, a good father,' she said. 'People think I'm the bad one. I wouldn't mind, Nancy, but I've no-one to talk to, not even about the work, and he spies on me. And with Sarah Jane gone . . . Bess tells him everything, of course.'

'Can't you talk to Damaris?'

'Not really. She doesn't know anything about how he really is, and it isn't fair to turn her against him. I don't know how he can be so hypocritical, I don't know how he can *pretend* so.'

'She doesn't know Bess's child is his?'

'No. I can't tell her.'

'And what of Tom?' asked Nancy.

'Tom?'

'Come on, it's me, Nancy, you're talking to. I know you loved him.'

Tacy stood up and walked to the window. The rain was coming down heavily now, it seemed to have settled in for the day. The sky was dark, the daffodils bowed before the storm. 'I still do,' she said, in a muffled voice. 'But there's Martha.'

'Tom's seldom at home from what I gather,' Nancy said. 'And Martha no longer has him in her bed.'

'What?' Tacy turned away from the rain.

'I don't think there's been a falling out. It's just that they have realised they were never in love at all.'

'But how long?' Tacy gasped. 'Was it when I – oh, Nancy, I went to see Tom last autumn and we – made love. It was the only time,' she ended, hurriedly.

'No, it was when Charley was born,' Nancy told her.

'But doesn't Martha still love him?'

Nancy shrugged. 'She seems taken up with Mr Redmond.'

'Mr *Redmond*?' Tacy was astounded. Once before, long ago, she had been amazed that Martha, the plain, had advanced along the road of love, while she, Tacy, was still thinking about it, but now, 'Mr Redmond is the minister,' she gasped.

'And a man,' said Nancy. 'Are they not all the same?'

Tacy swung round. 'You don't mean that they are having an affair?'

'Oh no, at least, I don't think so. I mean that he is smitten with her, he's always at the house.'

Tacy turned back to the window, thinking how her own jealousy had kept her from seeing Martha. Had she visited, she might have learned about this – might, for Martha was notoriously quiet about her own doings. Nancy, of course, would know that Tom lived at his mother's most of the time.

But Martha. How was it that such a plain person could catch, first of all, Tom, the most eligible bachelor in Chilverton, and now Mr Redmond . . . ?

But whatever the reason, it meant that she need not

feel any compunction about seeing Tom again. And at the thought she was filled with such delight that she hardly knew how to contain herself, she could not sit still, she jumped to her feet and looked out at the garden, newly dug over by one of the brothers. Nancy eyed her.

'You seem pleased,' she said. 'Sit down, do, you're like a Jack-in-the-box.'

'Oh, Nancy, if only you knew. Oh, if only I could see more of Tom . . .' Remembrance came, of why she could not even talk to Tom these days. She said, 'If only I could see him to talk to again, just discuss the work as we used to.'

'Well, why can't you?'

'Francis,' said Tacy, dully. 'He knows somehow I went to see Tom that night and he's taunted me about it ever since, though he doesn't know what really happened. I don't understand him, it's as though he hates me, he's so awful to me, he has these other women and tells me about them, yet he won't let me look at anyone else.'

'He won't let you talk to Tom in the warehouse? Not about the work?'

'No. He comes in, stands watching. And if he can't come he sends Bess. I'd like Tom to help me. He knows about the silk, and of course I'd pay him extra.'

'The cheek of the man,' Nancy exploded. 'Treating our Tom so.' She pursed her lips. 'I'd like to see him,' she said. 'Invite us to dinner or supper or whatever you eat at the Red House. They keep changing the times of dinner till it's supper anyway. Then we'll catch the late coach back.'

'You aren't afraid of Francis?' asked Tacy, dubiously.

'Afraid? Tacy, I've seen my father beat the living daylights out of all my brothers, and when they were fighting among themselves, he'd pick one up and throw him at the other.' She grinned, and Tacy smiled too.

She went back thinking Nancy had grown even more sharp with the years. Yet she'd always had a touch of the Jacques temper. But she told Francis she'd invited them to dinner and she asked Bess to make a special meal, perhaps a chicken, with fruit pie, made from the last of the stored apples.

Fred looked quite prosperous, she thought, as they entered the following day. She wished the weaving was doing as well as the watchmaking so obviously was.

Nancy was introduced to Damaris. 'My, I haven't seen you since you were small,' she marvelled.

Talk was desultory at first but, of course, the subject of the weaving was broached. 'I hear the weaving is having a troubled spell,' commented Nancy.

'Indeed,' Francis said. 'Sometimes I think we should get rid of it altogether.'

'And what would we live on then?' Tacy asked, wishing she could speak in Francis' hypocritical tone. Did nothing discomfit him?

'Surely Tacy needs a helper in the warehouse,' suggested Nancy, as smooth as Francis. She turned to Damaris. 'Well, miss, and why don't you help your mother?'

Damaris looked her surprise. 'I'm going to learn designing.'

'But your poor mother is worn to a shadow. Look at her, trying to do two people's work. When Mr Barratt was alive, he did the buying and selling and had an undertaker to give out the work. Tacy does it all.'

'I know – ' Damaris began, but Francis interrupted smoothly, so smooth that only Tacy could sense his anger that anyone dare criticise his household.

'Damaris will help later on,' he said.

'And in the meantime, why can't she have an assistant

in the warehouse? Someone reliable, who knows the work thoroughly, someone like my brother Tom. He'd be glad of the extra pay.'

'I – well –' Francis began.

'Tom seems to think that you don't want him there,' pursued Nancy inexorably. 'My father wouldn't like to hear that, or that you were doing him out of extra work and pay.' She paused, while they all waited, and Francis moved his lips soundlessly. 'You know my father, Francis?' she carried on. 'He's a big man, used to be a prizefighter. It doesn't do to upset him or my brothers.'

She paused, and Francis asked, 'Upset them?'

'They have funny tempers. They get mad if they think anyone doesn't treat our family right. They beat up a man once simply 'cos he looked at me. They have funny ideas. They don't like to think anyone is spying on them for instance, they wouldn't stand for it at work. Well, of course, Tom himself nearly went to jail because of some trouble, didn't he? It's not nice being sent to jail, people talk so. But they *will* do it.' She sighed.

Francis stared straight ahead, saying nothing. Nancy changed the subject. But when she left he barely said goodbye and Tacy shivered, wondering what humiliations he had in store for her now.

But she had forgotten Francis' desire that all men should think well of him, and he said nothing. Nor did he come to the warehouse so much, so Tom was able to come in one or two nights a week after he'd finished his weaving, and on Saturdays, when she gave out the work. Nancy's blackmail had paid off.

In July George IV died, and the accession of William IV was proclaimed in different parts of the town by the sheriff's deputy, and there was a procession with a band. Damaris did not watch any of this, she was busy saying

253

goodbye to her schoolfellows. The term was ending, and she would not return.

Another funeral, Tacy thought, dismayed, and already work is mighty depressed. She wondered how the new king would turn out and regretted that the Princess Charlotte had died. Now they had another of the brothers, William, Duke of Clarence, bluff and hearty, who'd been in the Navy, who was nicknamed Silly Billy, and who was the father of the ten bastards by actress Dorothy Jordan. With the death of the Princess, his mother had hurriedly married him off to Adelaide of Saxe-Meiningen, after several ladies had refused him. But folks said she was a nice lady, Adelaide, quiet and kind, not given to outrageous behaviour and wild parties like poor Caroline, who had died a few weeks after the late King had refused to let her be crowned.

But without parties and balls ladies would not need so many ribbons. Their position was becoming precarious. Tacy admitted now that Damaris was right, they did need a good designer. They needed something desperately.

The Mechanics' Institute was a plain brick building, standing where the Market Square met Borley Road, the winding road that led to the mining village of Borley Common. Damaris walked up the steps to the heavy oak door, open now, went inside and waited. She could hear a buzz of voices from one of the adjoining rooms, and soon a man came towards her.

'Did you want something?' he asked.

'I want to take lessons,' she said firmly.

'Er – ' He was plainly puzzled. 'We haven't had many women – young ladies – ' he began.

'But there's no reason why you shouldn't, is there?' Damaris asked.

'Well, er, no. Just a minute, I'll fetch Mr Thorne.'

Damaris looked down at her dress, showing beneath her pelisse. She looked quite old, really. Mama had agreed that she needed new clothes, she was growing both upwards and outwards, and Mrs Bradley had been summoned to sew for her. So her new green muslin dress had a small waist, helped by the corsets so necessary these days, and the skirt flared out just to the tips of her black shoes, whilst her hat was fashionably large and be-ribboned.

Mr Thorne, it appeared, was the headmaster. A tall, spare man, he too seemed puzzled as he saw Damaris. 'You'd better come into my office,' he said, and she followed him into a small room, with desk and wooden chairs. 'Now,' he pointed her to one of the chairs. 'What was it you wished to study?'

'Design,' said Damaris, firmly.

'Design? Oh, I'm afraid we don't do any fancy work here.' *No fripperies for young ladies*, his tone suggested. 'Arithmetic, reading and writing, geometry –'

Damaris sighed. She knew what she wanted, she always knew what she wanted, and she could never understand why other people always seemed to make difficulties. 'Design,' she repeated. 'For the Jacquards,' and she showed him her designs. 'I am Damaris Barratt,' she ended.

Mr Thorne pondered as he studied this self-possessed young lady who so obviously knew her mind. 'I see,' he said. 'Well, we have no school of design as such here, though they are going to build one at Coventry, I believe, in the future. So how can we help, hmm? There's Mr Vernon,' he tendered. 'He teaches geometry now, but he has drawing and draughtsmanship skills. He could teach you, but you would have to sit with the others –'

'Of course,' said Damaris. Where had he thought she

would sit? Outside?

She was taken to a room full of weavers, many of whom she knew, and Mr Vernon endeavoured to help her in between teaching the men. So it was that Damaris not only began to learn design, but a smattering of geometry too, though she discarded it almost immediately as being of no use to her. Damaris never wasted time on things useless to her. She was told to bring one of the big cards the next day, together with a sheet of the squared paper, and they would see about enlarging her designs to transfer them to the squared paper.

And Damaris left, not quite satisfied, but thinking this was better than nothing. She moved out of the room, down the steps, the weavers, mostly young, around her. Luke Lakin's young brother, Jem, Dick Roberts, Harry Pickard, one of Martha's cousins. William Jacques. And – almost last – Martin Jacques.

He came towards her, black-haired, black-eyed, arrogant. 'Cock o' the walk' his uncles called him, teasing. She saw the admiration in his eyes as he stood before her and was again glad she was wearing her new dress. 'You came then?' he asked.

'I told you I would. What are you learning, Martin?'

'Everything. Grammar, algebra, geography.'

'Why do you want to learn all that?' she asked.

'I want to know all I can. I want to be educated. What do these Sunday schools teach us except to read the Bible and be good, and the charity schools the same. Teach us to be good little workmen and not ask for more. I want more.'

'Do you, Martin?'

He looked down at her. 'You look very pretty,' he said, softly. 'Shall we go for a walk?'

She had walked with Martin before, but not as a young lady in a new dress. She nodded, and they walked into

Borley Road and on until the houses ended and there was only the odd cottage here and there. William stood and watched them till they were out of sight.

She said, as they walked, 'You won't give up the weaving, will you, Martin? You have served your apprenticeship.'

'Yes, and when it's finished what will I do? There are no spare looms, we can't afford to buy another.'

'But you won't leave the weaving?' she persisted.

He pulled a piece of hawthorne from the hedge and began to chew the leaves. Then he turned to look down at her, quizzically. 'You don't want me to?'

'Oh – ' she moved impatiently. 'Uncle Tom's so dedicated. To him silk's the very breath of life.' She paused. 'And to me.'

'And would I not be the same, being a Jacques?' he asked. 'I know how my father feels, that's why he makes trouble, he's apprehensive about the future, he fears that our whole way of life might change. I can understand that, but I think some changes must come.'

'Me too. Though I'm not sure that steam power is the answer. It's all right for Derby, with their plain black ribbons, it wouldn't do for us.'

'There's a Coventry man talking about a factory. Though the weavers don't want it,' he said.

'I understand their feelings.' She looked down at her dress, dragging a little on the ground. 'We'll do something, Martin, we must.'

They came to a stile and halted. Farmer Bates' fields lay to the left, to the right was the Common, with its blackberry bushes filled now with luscious berries for the children to pick and their mothers to bake in pies. The sun had set and the sky was darkening, though over to the west there was still a golden glow, with streaks of red.

'Fine day tomorrow,' said Martin.

In the fields they could hear a horse cropping the grass, and Martin suddenly bent his head and kissed Damaris. In the distance children shouted, a few late rooks flew to their nests. He said, 'Why don't you come to the chapel social gathering, Damaris? With me.'

'All right.'

'Will your Mamma agree – for you to go out with me?'

Damaris shrugged. 'If I want to go, I shall go.'

So began the courtship of Martin and Damaris. But she did not tell her mother.

Since the ending of the war, the whole country had been in a state of unrest. There were riots and disturbances, and this was put down to the high food prices and to lack of work. But it was more than that. Their way of life, the way that their fathers and grandfathers had known, that had, it seemed, been there since the beginning of time, was being taken away from them, the way of life where each man had worked in his home, had carved chairs and tables, grown his vegetables, and his wife had spun and woven their clothes. Now they were making factories, big brick buildings, ten times the size of their homes, where they were to be herded together and work at someone else's bidding. The only places they knew like this were prisons and workhouses, and the people hated both. They were afraid. And nowhere was this felt more than in Chilverton.

Trade had been depressed for months, and a number of weavers had to apply to the parish. These were, mainly, George Healey's workers, for he had no compunction in cutting their pay and, when he had little work, in closing his doors to them. But, in work or out, they still had rent to pay, or they would be thrown out in the streets, and, as many of them were not local people, they could claim no parish relief. More than one young man had been seen sleeping in the streets, more than one young girl was found soliciting outside the Bull and Butcher, while thieving increased. Trade was hit, and John Baxter, auctioneer, went bankrupt and fled to America owing a thousand pounds. Mrs Payne's little sweet shop closed. Miners in Borley Common were also hit by the general depression, for if weavers had no money, they could not buy coal, and a gang of them were seen pulling a waggon of coal through the streets of Chilverton on the way to London, where the government refused to see them. Farmer Bates, whose chickens were in demand when the weavers had money, also had to cut back.

The weavers were standing outside the chapel, gloomily discussing the situation. 'Things are gettin' wuss,' said Joe Bates. 'They say that man in Coventry is wantin' women for his factory, an' payin' less wages. So what are the men supposed to do?'

'Healey's payin' less wages now,' said Bob Pettit. 'He's dropped the price of sarsanets again, they tell me.'

It was Wednesday, but none of them had much work. Tacy had been apologetic on Saturday. 'I just haven't any more to give you,' she said.

The day was fine, though cloudy, with gusts of wind blowing the leaves from the trees. They saw a figure approaching and turned, hopefully, thinking it was Mr Redmond. It was not, it was the Reverend Hewitt. He stopped before them, his thin features disapproving. 'You know it is illegal to hold meetings,' he said, peremptorily.

'We ain't holding a meeting, we're waiting for the minister,' said Joe Bates.

'It looks like a meeting to me. And be so good as to touch your forelock when you speak to your betters, my good man.'

'I ain't your good man, and I ain't touching my forelock, not to you nor nobody,' said Joe Bates, the most belligerent of all the weavers. 'You ain't my parson, thank God.'

Mr Hewitt drew himself up angrily. 'I shall have a word with the constable about you,' he told them, and walked on, indignation in every line of his departing figure.

'Old goat,' said Joe Bates to his retreating back.

'Shut up, Joe, no use upsetting him,' said Bob Pettit. 'Don't want to land in jail again.'

'I thought they repealed them Combination Laws that wouldn't let us hold meetings,' said Joe Bates, aggrieved.

'They did, but there was such a rapid increase in trade union activity and strikes they brought it in again,' Luke Lakin told him. 'Now we can't meet, nor picket, nor strike else we'll get three months' jail. Come on, better get inside.'

They filed into the little chapel and sat on the wooden pews.

'Reckon I'll go to Americy,' said Joe Bates. 'Where the auctioneer's gone. Where everybody's goin'.'

'Don't know what sort of country that'll turn out to be, wi' so many convicts and bankrupts,' said Bob Pettit.

'And plenty of honest men who just want to work to make a decent living,' said Mr Redmond, who had just walked in. 'I'm sorry I'm late, I went to see old Mrs Caswell.'

'Good evening, minister,' they chorused. And, 'At least in Americy you don't have to touch your forelock, so they tell me,' said Joe Bates.

'We've just bin told off by Parson Hewitt,' explained Jim Bailey. '"God bless the squire and his relations and keep us in our proper station." That's all they learn us here.'

'Meks you wonder about this socialism they're talking about,' said Bob Pettit. 'There'd be none of this then.'

'You want to borrow books from the Institute library,' said Tom Jacques, who, with his brothers, had arrived just after the minister. 'They tell you all about these things.'

'It'll never happen here,' said Matt Walters. 'You've got to go to a new country, start all over. You won't get squire saying you're his equal, Bob Pettit, else he might have t'give you a bit of his land. What do you think, Mr Redmond?'

'You know the chapel teaching. We are all equal before God.'

'Then somebody should tell Parson Hewitt.'

'They say the vicar's a nice old feller, even if he only comes once every three months,' commented Mark Jacques. 'He reads out a sermon so clever nobody can understand it so they all go to sleep. Then when it's over Vicar goes back to vicarage, drinks his port and goes to sleep an' all. Reckon that's what upsets Mr Hewitt, he does all the work and Vicar takes the money.'

'Yes, well, the Church is very lax these days, and abuses crept in, that's why Dissent was begun,' said Mr Redmond.

'What are these books you was on about?' Jim Bailey asked Tom.

'Well, there's Tom Paine's *Rights of Man*, for a start. He thinks there should be votes for all, to get a democratic Parliament, and all old people should get a pension from the State.'

'Oh, ha ha,' laughed Matt Walters. 'That day won't ever come.'

'Let's leave pensions for the time being,' said Ross Jacques. 'Let's talk about our livelihood. George Healey is cutting prices again. What do we do?'

'Strike,' said Joe Bates.

'Striking is still illegal,' said Mr Redmond.

'Every damn thing is illegal,' shouted Joe Bates. 'It's just to keep us down, that's what. What do they care in London if we starve?'

'Hush, Joe,' said Mr Redmond. 'Yes, I agree with all you say, but there is no point in putting yourselves in jail. Why don't you talk to Healey's men first, ask them if they are willing to stand with you, to ask for more pay? If it's all done quietly it won't be against the law.'

The weavers agreed, somewhat unwillingly, and they said they would send a deputation on the following day to meet Healey's men when they left the loom-shop. Tom and Mark Jacques, the Pettits and Jim Bailey were to go.

But Mr Redmond had underestimated the weavers' anger, or perhaps the visit just got out of hand. The four men waited outside Healey's for the weavers to come out at eight o'clock, when they were free to go to their little hovels in Healey's yard, and as they came they were asked if they would agree to withhold their labour for more money.

'It's starvation wages he's paying you,' Tom Jacques said. 'An' you bring us all down to your level.'

Healey's men were strangers to them. As a matter of principle the local men never made friends outside their own weaving. Healey's men, knowing this, never frequented the Weavers' Arms, but went to the Bull and Butcher, where, in the low, raftered taproom the noise and smoke were heavy, and drunks lay on the sawdusted floor. Now they were hesitant, knowing the truth of Tom's words, but frightened of what George Healey might do.

'He'd just get rid of us,' said one pallid youth.

'He can't get rid of all of you, he's got nobody else,' said Mark Jacques. 'If we all stick together we shall win.'

Still they hesitated, and Jim Bailey shouted, 'Come in wi' us or we'll donkey you, you rotten lot of scabs.'

Then suddenly the road was filled with weavers. Joe Bates ran up with his aunt's donkey; someone else had obtained another. Mr Redmond came running, but before he could reach the men, two of them were on the donkeys' backs, and were being driven through the street, to shouts and catcalls. And the whole area was filled with milling, shouting crowds, women as well as men. Some were fighting.

Tacy had heard the commotion from the quiet of the warehouse, and she went out to see what was amiss. Now she heard the shouting, but nothing prepared her for the scene of tumult. Donkeys were being pulled into the street, George Healey's workers were being placed on their backs. Men were shouting, 'Strike. General strike.' Stones were thrown. A shout went up: 'The constables. Get away. The constables.' And the weavers began to run. Joe Bates, his donkey, and the man upon it, disappeared towards the Common. Only a few men remained, Tom Jacques among them.

'Tom! Get away,' shouted Mr Redmond. 'Tom!'

Tacy was here now, and her heart sank as she saw that Tom was in the thick of it, and sank even further as the constables moved in. The ones on foot moved in with truncheons, but the weavers had scattered. Not so Tom, and the constables moved towards him. But Mr Redmond was quicker. He punched Tom on the nose, felling him to the floor, and was himself grabbed by a burly constable.

It all happened so quickly that Tacy was amazed, she stood, mouth open. And when she recovered the constables had marched two of the weavers away – and Mr Redmond.

Damaris had joined her. 'Who's been taken?' she asked. 'Not Martin?'

'No, nor Tom.' And she went to him, sitting up now, dazedly, wiping the blood from his streaming nose.

The Reverend Mr Hewitt was gratified. 'What did I tell you?' he asked anyone who would listen. 'Didn't I say that man was a trouble-maker? But a minister in jail. Tch. Tch.'

'I should think he'll be dismissed,' said Mr Peabody.

'He should be horsewhipped,' snapped his wife.

The chapel discussed it too, with the deacons. 'He did it deliberately,' said Tom. 'To save me.'

'Why should he want to save you?' asked Mr Green, of Green's grocery store in Half-Moon Lane.

'Because he knows I've been in trouble before, and this time might have meant transportation. But I shall go to court and tell them what happened.'

'Do you think it would have meant transportation?' Tacy asked, when they were alone.

'Probably. And I couldn't have borne that. Not working away from silk. Oh, I wouldn't mind the hard work, the hot slog, I wouldn't mind leaving England. I sometimes wish I were away from all this. It's all so different from when I was apprenticed. I don't know what's happening to the country. And the more we let it go on the worse it'll get. We've got to get rid of George Healey.'

The men were held in jail to appear before the magistrates on Saturday. Tacy approached the court in some trepidation. She was alone, Damaris had agreed to give out the work, should any weavers turn up in the warehouse before she returned. She sat in the public gallery and watched as the magistrates, one of whom was

Sir William, entered. The prisoners were brought in, the two weavers, Bill Masters and Henry Cotterill first, and they were committed to trial at the Assizes. Then it was Mr Redmond's turn. He was charged with assault.

'Assault? On whom?'

'On a man named Thomas Jacques, your worship.'

The chief magistrate, Sir Edward Graves, known to be fairly lenient unless the prisoner had been poaching his game, when it meant prison for sure, peered over his spectacles. 'The weavers were causing an affray and you struck a weaver. Why?'

Mr Redmond opened his mouth to answer, but before he could speak Tom shouted out, 'He was protecting me, that's why.'

'Who are you?' asked the magistrate.

'Tom Jacques. He knew I'd get in trouble if the constables took me, so he knocked me out of the way. That's all.'

The magistrate, who wanted to get home for a day's hunting, as did Sir William, looked at Mr Redmond. 'Is this true?'

'Yes, your worship.'

The magistrate turned to the constable. 'The man Jacques does not seem to be harmed, and he did not bring the charge. Surely the accused was merely doing his duty.'

'He is known to be on the side of the rebels, your worship.'

'But he was not – er – donkeying the men.'

'No, your worship.'

'He was trying to stop them,' shouted Tom.

'If you don't keep quiet I shall have you charged for contempt,' said the magistrate. 'But I do not see why we should waste any more time on this charge. Case dismissed.'

★

Sunday was a calm October day, the nights were drawing in fast, and as Tacy and Francis walked to church in the evening, she saw groups of weavers standing around. They did not seem to be talking, just staring silently, and she was filled with apprehension, for she knew their anger was still there.

The service began. Psalms, prayers. Tacy hardly listened, she had never known the weavers so angry. She wished with all her heart she had more work to give them.

It was time for the sermon, and Mr Hewitt walked to the pulpit, Tacy settled down for one of the learned discourses which he read to them and which bored everyone to tears. But today he stood for a moment before he spoke.

'Friends,' he said, stentorously. 'There is a spirit of lawlessness abroad in the town, and I am sorry to say that a supposed minister of religion is at the head of it, and was taken to jail. I know the people involved, I knew something of this sort would happen, I passed by last week when they were holding an unlawful meeting. But the Dissenters have always been troublemakers right from the start, those who stoned them did well. A hundred years ago we had the misguided Quakers, who used to throw themselves around and *quake* and were put in jail for their pains, which did them good, they are much quieter now.'

'Rubbish,' muttered Tacy under her breath, though Mrs Peabody, sitting in front, wearing a huge hat trimmed with green ribbons and flowers, nodded so vigorously that the flowers almost fell off.

'Now,' Mr Hewitt continued. 'They override the authority of the Anglican Church, and bow to a doctrine they call *socialism*, and this misguided minister is at the forefront of this movement. I happen to know that he belongs to a revolutionary sect of Radicals, who say that all men are equal.'

'Equal before God,' muttered Tacy, and Mrs Peabody's enormous hat turned, its flowers jumping vigorously. Mr Hewitt drew a breath and his face turned purple with anger.

'Socialism is a sin,' he declaimed. 'What does the catechism teach us? "To submit myself to all my governors, teachers, spiritual pastors and masters. And to do my duty in that state of life to which it shall please God to call me." The poor you have always with you, Christ himself said. Those who are poor must learn to suffer in silence and not take part in unlawful acts such as striking against their employers. They must – '

He broke off as a stone was thrown through the window.

The congregation, who were mostly of the employing classes and thus enjoying the peroration, jumped to their feet as one, and made for the door. And the labouring poor at the back, this time were the first out. 'We shall all be murdered,' cried Mrs Peabody.

'Wait,' cried Mr Hewitt. 'Don't push. There is no cause for alarm.'

'They must be punished,' blazed Mrs Peabody, brandishing her umbrella as she fought her way to the door.

Tacy left more slowly, afraid of what she might find outside. There was no one there. The culprits had fled.

But she was filled with apprehension. Trouble was coming. And she did not know how to stop it.

William Jacques had always admired Mr Redmond. He listened eagerly to his speeches, and always welcomed him to their home, though he had no idea that it was his mother Mr Redmond came to see. Mr Redmond said little about his early life; they knew he had been very poor, but had later been helped by a family who saw to his education. He was a quiet man, except when preaching the Word of God; a peaceful man except when he was provoked and his anger would erupt. It erupted now as he sat in the little kitchen on the day following Mr Hewitt's attack. Martha was sewing at the table and the younger boys were out in the street as ever.

Martha said, 'There was no call for his attack.'

'We have always been at loggerheads,' replied Mr Redmond. 'But next Sunday I shall reply to him.'

'What will you do?' asked William.

'I shall hold a meeting. No, not in chapel, this is for everyone to hear. I shall hold it in the marketplace.'

Martha stopped sewing. William stared.

'I sat up most of the night writing leaflets which I shall distribute round the town,' said Mr Redmond, and now they could see his anger.

'He should not have said you are a member of a revolutionary sect!' said William.

'Oh, but I am,' replied Mr Redmond. 'Or no, we are in no way revolutionary. But I shall tell about it on Sunday. Now, I must be on my way to give out these leaflets.'

'Let me take some,' offered William.

'Thank you, William, that's very kind. Here, take these. Fasten them onto gates; word will soon get round.'

William took the leaflets and departed. Mr Redmond was on his feet, but Martha stopped him.

'It was most kind of you to save Tom,' she said. 'But I fear it has got you into a lot of aggravation.'

He paused in the doorway. 'I didn't do it for Tom, but for you,' he said. 'You have enough trouble.'

Martha stood up and went to the fireplace where a small fire smouldered. 'Mr Redmond –'

'No, don't tell me I shouldn't. Maybe I shouldn't, but I fear you are wasted on Tom Jacques.'

Martha picked up the poker and tended the fire, keeping her face hidden. 'Too late for that,' she said in a muffled voice. She turned. 'I have the boys.'

'Yes, and I hope they're good to you.'

'They are. William especially. Martin—' she sighed. 'He seems taken with Damaris Barratt and I don't know how that will turn out.'

He took a step towards her. 'You look tired, Martha.'

She sighed again. 'It's hard when there's so little work. It encourages wildness when the boys have nothing to do.'

Mr Redmond patted her arm, all he dare allow himself. Then he turned to go, sighing in his turn. It wasn't often he saw Martha with her defences down.

Mrs Peabody was so proud of her new hat which, she thought, went well with her green mantle with its fur tippet, that she walked to church instead of taking the carriage, together with her husband, fine in his greatcoat, close-fitting over his ample stomach, with their children bringing up the rear. It was a quiet walk usually, but this Sunday, she saw, to her surprise, a crowd in the Market Square around a man on a box, a tall man with fair hair. Mr Redmond. And the crowd were not all weaver, either, some were well-to-do people who should have known better. Others were serving wenches and men, who should not be allowed to listen to this man. Mrs Peabody stopped in indignation.

'Last Sunday,' Mr Redmond was saying, 'a charge was laid against me by the curate of the church, and I am here to refute this, and to put the matter straight.'

He drew a breath. 'He said I belong to the Radical Dissenters. So I do, in a group that meets in Birmingham and London. But I would like to explain what we stand for. Freedom, Liberty, Reason, Rights. We do not aim to bring down the government, but to reform it. We wish to have more control on what Parliament does, and to make MPs subservient to their constituencies. We believe in the rights of the individual.'

Mrs Peabody bristled. How dare this whippersnapper talk so? And the people were listening too . . . Monstrous. She knew she ought to go away, but felt she had to stay in case some of the watchers were misguided enough to take heed of what was said.

'Since the French Revolution,' Mr Redmond went on, 'people of high rank here have been scared out of their wits. They fear that the poor in this country might revolt too, and they fear anyone who tries to reform. So what do we believe in, we of the Dissenting faith? In education. We have built many fine schools since the normal grammar schools and universities are closed to us, fine, modern schools, not dreaming of the classical past in Latin and Greek, but teaching science and modern languages. We know the world is changing, though whether it will be for the better I cannot say. All I do say is – let us be careful. Let us not throw people onto the streets without hope, without any future. If we have to build factories, let us think carefully how they will be done, not let small children work long hours away from their mothers in soul-destroying work.'

'Tosh,' muttered Mrs Peabody. 'We don't want to featherbed the poor.'

Mr Redmond paused, noting who spoke. 'Perhaps,' he said, 'those who criticise the poor have no knowledge of poverty.'

'Bah!' called Mrs Peabody. 'What do you know of poverty, sir?'

'Oh, I know!' replied Mr Redmond. 'I was brought up in poverty. Not born into it, for my father had work on a farm – until he was turned off when the enclosures came. He went to London to find work, together with my mother and my five younger brothers and sisters. But we did not find work. Instead my father found drink.'

He saw William in the crowd, listening eagerly, and went on. 'Gin-shops, where you can get drunk for a penny, dead drunk for tuppence, isn't that what they say? We moved from a decent room to a slum, next door to a gin-shop, and there my father spent what little money he had. There, in the end, he died of it, and all my brothers and sisters one by one. My mother died from lack of food. And I was turned into the streets.' He paused. 'Oh yes, Mrs Peabody, I know about poverty.'

Someone shouted, 'So what happened to you?' and the voice was not antagonistic, merely curious. After all, his story was not unusual.

'I was befriended by a good couple,' replied Mr Redmond. 'They saved my life. And what more natural that I join those who are against drink, who want to care for the poor –'

'But we care for the poor too,' cried Mrs Peabody. 'Those of us who have money have opened a subscription for the suffering poor, we are to have a ball next month to help them. You are not the only ones to help the poor.'

'No, but can't you see? We don't want the poor to have to live on charity, but by their own efforts, by good living and honest work –'

But now shouts were coming from the church people. 'You want to overthrow the authority of the Church and the nation.'

'You've no respect for your superiors.'

'You want revolution. To bring us all down to the gutter.'

And counter-shouts from the Dissenters. 'We believe in the love of our Saviour. Salvation through Christ.'

Soon there was just a struggling mass as the long feud between church and chapel erupted anew. Mr Redmond stepped down, defeated.

Chapter twelve

The autumn sun shone on a festive town. The coronation of William IV and Adelaide was being celebrated
by a grand procession. A band of music led the various
societies, followed by the carrying of twenty-five
sheep, all of which were to be roasted in the streets and
given to the poor, together with a small portion of ale.
For work had not picked up, a soup kitchen had been
opened six months ago selling soup at one penny a
quart, though the bread was free. Today, the weavers
looked forward to the welcome treat of roast
mutton.

Joey and Charley Jacques could be seen dancing along
at the side of the band, Mossy walked more quietly, as
befitted a young man of fifteen, while somewhere at the
back Damaris was talking to Martin.

'Are you going to the ball at the Assembly Rooms?' he
was asking.

'I don't know, I hadn't thought. Why, are you?'

'I'd like to. It's a bit expensive, five shillings a ticket,
but the proceedings will go to the soup shop.'

'I'll ask Mamma,' Damaris said.

She had still not told her mother that she was seeing
Martin for she knew Tacy did not particularly like him;
she had never said so, but Damaris had seen her
expression when he came into view. Not that he met
Tacy very often, for that was another strange thing,
Mamma never seemed to want to visit Aunt Martha. So
Damaris went her walks with Martin when she left the

Mechanics' Institute, and if she was a little late, no-one seemed to notice.

She caught her mother alone when they went into the parlour after dinner, for no-one was working today. Papa disappeared, as he always did, and Tacy sank into one of the easy chairs. Damaris sat too, and asked, 'Can I go to the ball next week, Mamma?'

'What did you say?' Tacy had been studying the damask curtains, thinking how shabby they looked. They were clean, Bess did her work well enough, but constant washing, plus sunlight, had faded them over the years. Yet she knew she could not afford any new ones.

Damaris repeated her question. 'We should go, Mamma, the money is to go to the poor of the town.'

'Yes. But you are not really old enough for balls, Damaris.'

'I'm fifteen, Mamma.'

'So you are,' said Tacy with a sigh.

'And we're not planning a coming-out ball for me, are we? And I shall need a new dress when I come to London with you.'

'You're coming with me? Why, have you decided you've finished at the Mechanics' Institute?'

'Well, I've been going for a year. I don't think they can teach me any more.'

'You know how to design for the cards then?'

'Yes. Of course, we shall need one of those little machines to make the holes in the cards before we can do them ourselves. And I shall still try to improve my designs, of course.'

Tacy looked at her daughter, shrewdly. 'You're not altogether satisfied with your work?'

'I still feel I can improve. But I did say I'd learn the business, and so I will.'

'Good. Well, you can come with me next time I go to London.'

'And I can have a new dress?'

Tacy smiled. 'I suppose Mrs Bradley can run you up something quickly.'

'Thank you, Mamma.'

Damaris went to her room and took out her fashion magazines. She must dress well for Martin. She looked at the picture of an evening gown, round, low décolletée, puffed shoulder sleeves, tight waist, full skirt, a little shorter than day dresses, trimmed round the hem. It would look good in blue silk – if Mamma would allow it. She was glad the loose fashions of the early part of the century were completely out now, it was waists and corsets again. Though she wasn't sure that she went along with all the changes that seemed to be taking place. The old robust speech was becoming more refined, it was indelicate to say 'with child' or 'bowels' now. Stuff and nonsense, thought Damaris, what did you say in place of with child?

Bess had been with child, and little Simon was over a year old now, though kept mostly to the kitchen. Damaris wondered who the father was. Still, Bess was always fond of the men, she had known that since childhood . . . But she liked this gown, if Mama would let her have it . . .

Alone, Tacy too thought of the ball. She hadn't been to a ball for so long. Even now, she didn't feel she should. So many of the weavers were short of work, and yet – if the ball was to help them . . . Their anger had not disappeared, it was submerged, Tacy could feel it when she walked through the town, when the weavers would stand, saying nothing, doing little. But there was, underneath, this seething anger, it was like a pot coming to the boil, and if it should boil over . . . ? Yes, she must go to

London again, try to persuade Mr Jarvis to order more, see Mr Fotheringay again . . .

She wondered if Tom were going to the ball, she must ask him. How wonderful it would be to dance a waltz with him, to be held in his arms. They had not been together alone since the time they made love at his house, he had warned her against it, saying William suspected. Tacy frowned. Was there nowhere for them to be together? Every time they talked in the warehouse she wanted to kiss him, sometimes she would stare at him, thinking *if only I could* . . . and he would look up and his eyes would darken, and she knew he was thinking the same thing.

Francis was still morose and sarcastic, luckily he left her alone these days. Whether he still went with Bess she neither knew nor cared very much. But she did wonder why it was all right for the husband to commit adultery, while the woman was scorned. Life did seem unfair.

The clock struck eight, Annie came in to light more candles and the lamp. 'I don't think you need bother with them,' Tacy said. 'I shall be going to bed.'

'So soon, mam?' asked Annie.

Tacy shrugged. 'I've nothing else to do these days.'

The Assembly Rooms were already quite full when Tacy, Francis and Damaris arrived. It was a clear October night with a touch of frost, but their gowns were long, it would be impracticable to walk even such a short distance, so there was nothing for it but to take the chaise. Brownie ambled along, he was getting old, Tacy thought; sometime in the future they'd have to look for another horse.

Damaris' eyes sparkled as she entered and saw the chandeliers with their many candles brilliant in the glass lustres. The gentlemen were smart in tail-coats, fancy waistcoats and white pantaloons, or, in the case of the stouter figures, such as Mr Peabody, in tight trousers. The ladies' gowns were of the very latest fashion, with bouffant sleeves, and much trimming. Damaris looked quickly to note if they were wider than her own new blue silk. Mrs Peabody's short, stout figure was encased in a tight-waisted gown of pink satin, and she seemed to have difficulty in walking. Mrs Broadbent, always over-dressed, had rows of ribbon fancies round and up and down her skirt. There was much waving of fans and tapping of shoes, and at one end of the room the musicians were already tuning up. Damaris' eyes sparkled anew.

Then she saw Martin walking towards her, splendid in evening dress – how could he afford it? Though she knew Martin always got what he wanted. And she felt her mother stiffen beside her and wondered why.

In truth, when Tacy saw him approaching she thought at first it was Tom, he was so like his father. And it was this, coupled with the fact that he was Martha's firstborn son, and not hers, that was the cause of her dislike. She could never forget that, but for this boy, Tom would not have married Martha.

So she nodded coolly when he stood before them, saying, 'Good evening, Mrs Barratt, Mr Barratt, Damaris.' And, 'May I have this dance, Damaris?'

Damaris did not ask her mother's permission, but went on to the floor. Francis asked Tacy to dance, and they followed.

Tacy looked round the room. Where was Tom? He had said he was coming. Did she look well enough in this gown that was not new, that had been trimmed yet again by Mrs Bradley? Mrs Peabody saw her and pointedly looked away; she hadn't forgotten the altercation with Mr Redmond, though Tacy failed to see how it was her fault. Mrs Warren, handsome in rose organdy over a white slip, nodded and smiled, one of the young Peabody girls stood at the side smiling hopefully, Mrs Jennings fanned her face vigorously. But no Tom.

The dance ended and, as the next one started, Tacy too, sat back, then roused as the man before her asked her to dance. It was Sir William, resplendent in dark blue coat with velvet collar, white satin waistcoat and white breeches, his florid face unsmiling.

Francis turned his head away as she stood up and followed Sir William on to the floor. She was thankful it was not a waltz, at least he would not hold her close.

Neither spoke. It had been so long since she had seen him, she had deliberately kept away from the meetings, mainly to avoid him. She could not forget that she still owed the bank money, though thankfully, it was almost paid off now. Of the arrangement to meet him when he released Tom she thought nothing, indeed, she hardly remembered it. After all, one did make arrangements with men and did not go – at least when one was young.

He said, 'You have not been to any balls recently.'

'No.' Tacy twirled round. 'The weaving is so depressed I haven't had the money – or the heart – to dance.'

'No point in worrying about the weaving,' he said. 'Time to move on to something else. That's what I do. I was into canals, now I'm letting that go for railways, that's the coming thing.'

'But the weaving will not go,' Tacy said.

'The hand-looms will.'

'But you – ' She broke off. 'You have interests in George Healey's loom-shop,' she continued.

'Not any more,' he said. 'I'm pulling out.'

She was startled. Was this good news or bad?

The dance ended, to her relief, and she returned to Francis, noting that Damaris had danced with Martin yet again.

And then she saw Tom.

He came straight over to her and he too looked smart in fancy waistcoat and white pantaloons. He neither nodded nor spoke to Francis, but bowed to Tacy, and as the musicians struck up a waltz, took her in his arms.

And this was heaven, this being so near to him; the trembling candlelight, the rustle of silk gowns, the murmur of voices, occasional laughter, scents and pomades, all blended into a heady brew. They did not speak, they had no need. They swung around, the touch of their bodies raising each to a rapturous content.

Dr Warren asked her for the next dance, and then — suprisingly — Constable Jennings. Francis, she noted, was maintaining his nice pleasant image by dancing with the elder Miss Peabody — quite a handsome girl — and then Mrs Warren. And this gave Julia the excuse to talk to Tacy when the dance ended, and they all crowded into the supper room.

'I have not seen you for such a long time,' said Julia.

Tacy repeated the excuse she had made to Sir William. She had neither the time nor the heart.

'Oh, but surely with less work you have more time to spare,' Julia said. 'I was hoping so as I intended to ask if you would help out at the soup kitchen.'

'Why yes, I could certainly help Mondays,' Tacy answered, guilty that she hadn't offered before.

'Monday it is,' Julia said, happily. 'And we still have the committee meetings, you know, we need to help the poor more than ever.'

'Yes, I must try and come,' Tacy replied, thinking that it was more than soup kitchens that was needed, it was a wholesale restructuring of industry.

She dare not go to talk to Tom in the supper room, not with so many watching, with Francis watching. But back in the ballroom, a waltz was begun and he immediately asked her to dance.

'I shall be helping at the soup kitchen on Monday,' she told him, when she really wanted to say *Let us go outside, let us find a quiet spot to be alone.*

Tom said, 'Will you, indeed?' meaning *I want to kiss you, I want to make love to you.*

The dancers swirled by and he whispered, 'You are lovely,' and she flushed, radiant.

She came down to earth when Sir William, with his paunchy figure and his heavily pomaded hair that failed to cover his bad breath, claimed her for the next dance. He said, 'Who is the young girl with you – your daughter?'

And she was suddenly filled with guilt that she had been so busy watching and dancing with Tom that she had not noted what Damaris was doing. A fine chaperone she was turning out to be!

'I must dance with her,' Sir William pursued, and now Tacy, for the first time, realised that her daughter was indeed growing up. She had ignored the signs of maturity, the developing figure, the interest in fashions, even the dancing with Martin had been dismissed as the longings of a little girl wanting to be older. Now she realised that her daughter was becoming attractive to men, and was horrified, as she remembered her own past struggles with Sir William. She was concerned, and as he led her back to her seat, she looked for Damaris and saw she was with Martin.

Sir William did ask Damaris to dance, but she seemed to Tacy, watching, quite composed and in no way nervous or shy. But then, Damaris wasn't shy, she reflected.

It was past twelve o'clock and the numbers were dwindling. Some went into the next room to play cards, and Tacy saw to her delight that Francis was among them. So now she was able to dance with Tom, and free to let him guide her into a small ante-room on the pretext of getting more wine, where they were alone, and where he took her in his arms. And then they saw stairs leading to rooms above, and they went up – and there, in the bare little attic, with lumber around them, and hearing the strains of music below, they made love.

They returned separately to the ballroom, and Tacy sat, her face flushed, her eyes lit with a glow that outshone the candles. And when Francis came back and suggested they go home she agreed. 'It gets a mite boring,' she said, and they prised Damaris away from Martin.

They drove home in silence, each with their own thoughts, and both Tacy and Damaris went to bed dreaming of the night. Only Francis was gloomy.

And he made the reason clear to Tacy the next morning after breakfast, when Damaris had left for the Institute. Francis said to Tacy, 'I would like a word with you, if you please.'

She saw his forbidding expression and immediately thought, 'He knows.' But she said, calmly, 'Yes?'

'It's Damaris,' he said. 'She was with that young Jacques all the night. I don't approve.'

'Oh?' She stared.

'Damaris will marry eventually, and marry well,' Francis went on. 'And I do not wish her to get entangled with that no-good Jacques family. Why, he's just after the business.' Tacy thought rapidly. She guessed that Francis' reason was not quite what he told her. He did not want them to get too friendly with Tom.

Yet – did not she want the same thing for Damaris? Did she really want her to marry – should it come to that? – the young Martin whom she disliked so, the young Tom?

She knew that she did not. For once she was in agreement with Francis.

'You must tell her,' Francis said. 'It will come better from you.'

'Very well,' Tacy nodded. 'I will tell her.'

Francis watched her broodingly, his eyes hooded, knowing he had startled her, knowing why. He hadn't seen her go upstairs at the ball, but he had noted her glowing face, seen her dance with Tom. And when he went to play cards it was because he saw Healey there, and when Healey took a turn to sit out a game he did too, and talked to him. It was an interesting conversation, one he intended to repeat as soon as possible. As the nights drew in and November fogs covered the town, who would see if he chose to visit Lottie Glover, and what more natural than George Healey visiting his sister-in-law too?

I am doing it for Tacy's good, Francis told himself, self-righteously. She must stay at home, she is in danger from Tom Jacques.

The soup kitchen was situated in the Parish Rooms attached to the church, as both church and chapel united in this effort. There was one large room where the soup was ladled out, with a small kitchen at the back containing a huge fire to heat the soup. Tacy took her turn willingly at the table, watching the long queue shuffle in, a queue that stretched outside and quite a way down Gate Street. They came in, pallid women, some holding babies or with small children clinging to their skirts, shawls pulled round their shoulders, and men wearing top hats and greatcoats, if they possessed them, for the weather had turned colder. Some of the children were coughing, some had runny noses, most looked unhealthy.

In the back room, coals were heaped on the fire as the great pots were heated, though Tacy wished they could have put more than one pound of meat to every gallon of soup. But she wished even more that she had work to offer these people, and she resolved, when she went to London, she would try her utmost to get more orders.

There was a mutter of conversation, especially among the men, and as they neared the table Tacy overheard some of the topics discussed. And she was a little alarmed. The word factory seemed to crop up time and time again, and she wondered what was going on. Enoch Walters approached, he with the five children, and Tacy asked, 'Have you heard anything about factories, Enoch?'

'I don't know,' Enoch replied.

'Except we don't want 'em.' Enoch's wife, Prue, stood behind him, a sharp-nosed, sharp-tongued woman of around thirty, with a baby in her arms, her other children standing behind her looking avidly at the hot soup. 'That man in Coventry is putting women in his factory, they say, at less pay than the men have. So what do the men do then? What does Enoch do if I go to work and he stops at home?'

'He'll have to go to the pit,' put in a voice behind her.

'Oh aye? And walk five miles to the pit and five miles back? And what happens to the kids all day? Leave 'em in home on their own? To mebbe set theirselves on fire or cut their legs open wi' knives or summat? Live on the streets like they do in London? We don't want London ways here, nor folks from London telling us what to do. So they can put that in their pipes and smoke it.'

'Hush, Prue,' cautioned the man behind her, and Prue walked on, leaving Tacy more concerned than ever. She knew trouble was brewing, what would it be? She wanted to ask Tom, but, as work was short, he hadn't been needed to help in the warehouse this week.

She soon found out what the trouble was. It was her soup day and as she walked through Market Square into Gate Street she heard shouting, 'They're coming. They're coming,' and a crowd of men and women swept by her.

Caught up in the maelstrom, she went with them. And there, along the Coventry Turnpike, were men with donkeys, and both men and women on their backs, followed by crowds shouting, 'Turn 'em out o' town. Donkey 'em all the way.'

Tacy turned to her neighbour. 'What is it?' she asked. 'What goes on?'

She saw the man was one of the Baileys, and he seemed exhilarated. 'It's the Coventry factory,' he explained. 'They've donkeyed 'em for working in it. An' they'll burn it down to the ground.'

And then all was chaos. People were shouting. Stones were thrown at Healey's warehouse. Windows were broken. Children were yelling. The High Constable appeared with a group of special constables, and between them they calmed the people down. Peace was restored but at a price. Tacy heard later that Beck's factory in Coventry had been burned. A furious mob had invaded the factory, cut the silk from the looms and broken the looms to pieces before setting the place on fire. The old parish hand-engine was quite unable to put out the flames and the factory burned to the ground. The ringleaders were sentenced to hang, but after an appeal by the local Member of Parliament, this was commuted to transportation.

'It was bound to happen,' Tom said to Tacy as they sat in the warehouse some days later. 'The weavers are so angry. And they don't want factories.'

Tacy sighed. 'Neither do I. But does George Healey?'

'If he does he knows what to expect,' said Tom.

Notice was taken in high places of the riot. And it was decided to hold a Royal Commission into the state of weaving, which would, they hoped, answer questions put by the Society of Distressed Manufacturers – as all weavers were known – by orders of the government.

'When are we going to London?' Damaris asked her mother. 'If we wait much longer we might be snowed up. Frances Peabody said they fell in a snowdrift once, and they had to dig the horses out. They nearly froze to death. And they were terrified a highwayman might come along –'

'I've never seen a highwayman yet,' Tacy answered shortly. 'But I shall go the first week in December.' And she wondered fleetingly if the railways Sir William had mentioned would really run round here. True, they said this steam engine was already starting in the north . . . would it be better to send the ribbons by steam? She doubted it, they went now by canal, on fly-boats, non-stop on galloping horses, they got to London in a day. But steam trains would put Tamarisk Calder's packet boats out of business, and that would be a pity.

Damaris turned to go, but Tacy halted her. 'One moment, young lady, I want a word with you.'

'Yes, Mamma?'

'You seemed to be dancing a lot with young Martin Jacques at the ball.'

'Well, why not?'

'I would rather you did not see so much of him, that's all.'

'Not see him? Why, Mamma, I've been seeing him since I was born.'

'You know what I mean,' Tacy said. 'You are young, I would not want you to be carried away with some silly idea of a romance.'

Damaris bent down to smooth the hem of her dress. 'What would be silly about it?' she asked.

'It would be very silly. You know what a family they are, always into trouble.'

'Martin hasn't been in any trouble,' Damaris retorted. 'It's Uncle Tom who was nearly sent to jail.'

'Nevertheless, we don't want you to have any sort of relationship with Martin.' Tacy was firm.

'We?'

'Your father and I.'

Damaris straightened up and faced her mother. 'Supposing I said I wanted to marry him?'

'Damaris, you are not yet sixteen. You must not think about marrying yet.'

'But you have not answered my question, Mamma.'

'We would never agree to it,' Tacy answered, still shortly. 'We would never give our permission.'

Damaris said no more. She was a little surprised to hear her father objected, he usually gave her what she wanted. But she had no intention of giving Martin up. He was the one she wanted to marry, and that was that.

They set out for London on the first of December. It was cold, though not frosty, the roads should be passable. Jobey drove them to the Red Lion, where they caught the coach, filled now with a lady and her maid, with two gentlemen on the outside. And it was an uneventful journey, except that the lady felt faint for much of the way, and had to be revived with smelling salts. There were no highwaymen, the coach ran smoothly, and they arrived safely in Lad's Lane, at the Swan with Two Necks, where Mr Fotheringay was waiting.

Damaris stared at him, an Exquisite, from his violet frock-coat, with its tight pinched-in waist and short, full skirt, his brilliant green shot-silk waistcoat, his nankin pantaloons, buttoned at the ankle with two gold buttons, to his shoes with buckles of polished cut steel.

'My dear ladies,' he intoned, raising his hat and bowing low over their hands. 'So delightful to see you both. Such a charming girl, your daughter, Mrs Barratt. I thought today, as time presses, it would have to be a quick meal at Mrs Robinson's – if you have no objection? No? Let me call a hackney coach.'

Damaris had never been to London before, and she enjoyed every moment of the journey, from seeing the little crossing sweepers to the milk maids with their pails on yokes over their shoulders, a herd of bullocks being driven to Smithfield market, brewers' drays, bow-windowed shops. And everywhere rackety noise, from the great iron-shod wheels, to the shouting of the vendors, the bells from dust-carts, clattering hooves, and shrill cries of ragged urchins. And once in a wide street of big shops she glimpsed a narrow opening with a few dirty ragged people hurrying away to slink in the shadows of its fetid alleys. 'What place is that?' asked Damaris, and Mr Fotheringay held his embroidered handkerchief to his nose as he said that was a bad place, the Seven Dials, home of thieves and murderers, where the constables dare not enter. Then they were back with fine houses and roads and it was as if the narrow alleys had never existed.

Mrs Robinson, whose dull brown dress beneath her greying hair made her seem like a plump sparrow beside Mr Fotheringay's popinjay splendour, welcomed them and showed the ladies to their room while she prepared dinner. Down again into the dining-room as brown as its owner. But the meal was good, even though Mr Fotheringay did seem to look down his nose at the fare.

'I expect you take your pleasure at much grander edifices,' said Damaris, who noted.

'One does,' said Mr Fotheringay, waving his handkerchief drenched in eau-de-cologne.

'Do tell me,' urged Damaris. 'Where do you go?'

'Well, there are the clubs, of course. Crockford's and the Roxborough – princely food and service there.'

'And gambling,' added Damaris.

'Of course. What else can a gentleman do? It is one of the pleasures of our age. Sometimes the play carries on for several days.'

'Winning or losing?' asked Damaris.

'We-ell. Both, of course. Lord Sefton lost a small fortune at Brooks. Sir John Bland squandered his vast estates, which included the whole city of Manchester. Why, even Charles James Fox lost £140,000 before he was twenty-five – he'd often play for twenty-four hours at a sitting. It's part of the fun.'

'And where I come from people are starving,' said Damaris, disapprovingly.

'Is that so?' Mr Fotheringay sounded bored.

Tacy said, hurriedly, 'What news of fashions, Mr Fotheringay?'

'Little good news, I fear. This court is somewhat dull after the splendours of the late King's. But the Queen is a worthy woman – ' he sounded as if this were a shameful thing to be, thought Damaris.

'Yet the *ton* still hold balls, ladies still buy gowns?' put in Tacy.

'Of course. But also they are buying French ribbons now. They say they are finer, though they're not, of course.'

'Oh dear,' said Tacy.

'That is competition,' said Mr Fotheringay. 'It will be the making of our country.'

Mr Fotheringay soon departed, leaving Damaris and Tacy to talk for a little while before retiring.

'Mr Fotheringay!' snorted Damaris. 'He's nothing but an old tart, his compliments as empty as his head – ' and Tacy smiled to herself. 'And surely that was a wig he was wearing?'

Tacy pondered. Gentlemen no longer wore powdered periwigs, but there was something a little unnatural about the copper colour of Mr Fotheringay's curls. They seemed to emphasise the lines on his face which could not be covered completely by powder. She sighed. Mr Fotheringay, that familiar figure of her childhood, was getting old, and she hadn't realised until seen through the clearer eyes of youth.

'Do we really need him now?' Damaris pursued. 'You pay him, don't you? And for what? He's just an old hanger-on.'

'He does keep me informed,' Tacy replied. She supposed Damaris was right – she so often was – but she did not want to stop seeing Mr Fotheringay, he brought a lighthearted touch to her life, a whiff of other days, of high life and ease, of the comfort of the time with Papa, a change from the grimness of life with Francis.

'Come, we're both tired,' she said. 'Let's go to bed. We see Mr Jarvis tomorrow.'

The next day dawned bright with just a touch of frost in the air. They breakfasted early and, prompted by Damaris, went to the docks by boat, ferried by a cheerful waterman. Damaris gazed in awe at the grey river, flowing seawards; the great heart of the city, and source of its wealth; gazed at the white walls, the wherries, the barges, seeming to cover its surface.

And then the reaches below, lined with wharves, warehouses, timber-yards, where the river was dark with masts, and great ships lay at anchor like birds at rest. The tide was on the turn, one was preparing to sail, and as they watched her move slowly away, Tacy murmured, 'I wish I were on her.'

'Why, Mamma,' said Damaris, surprised. 'Where would you like to go?'

'Anywhere. To the ends of the earth.'

Damaris looked at her mother. She seemed different today, away from Chilverton, softer, more approachable. Tacy too, felt closer to her daughter, and wished this state of affairs could continue.

'You wouldn't leave the weaving?' Damaris asked.

Tacy sighed. 'I don't know.' How explain that the life she had entered so eagerly had somehow become a burden?

'I never would,' Damaris said, positively. 'Never.'

And as they went to the warehouse and visited the broker, Tacy was impressed by her daughter's business sense. She asked intelligent questions, and knew what she was talking about.

Their last visit, after a meal in an inn, was to Mr Jarvis, in his office overlooking the river. Damaris liked Mr Jarvis immediately. Dressed almost Quaker-like in plain brown coat and trousers, he was a businessman after her own heart.

But his news was no better. 'I'm afraid I have no more orders for you,' he said. 'I'm sorry. I do my best.'

'I know you do,' Tacy replied. 'Mr Fotheringay tells me it's because of the French competition.'

'He's right,' Mr Jarvis agreed.

'But are they really better?' Tacy asked. 'The ribbons our hand-looms weave are second to none. That's why I feel there will always be a place for hand-looms. Factory work could never improve on them.'

'I agree. But some of the French designs are very good. And ladies are buying them.'

'I am learning design,' put in Damaris. 'Or at least, I was. There is no proper school of design in Chilverton.'

'That's a pity,' Mr Jarvis commented. 'We do have an excellent school of design here in London.'

'I wish I could go to that,' Damaris said eagerly. 'It's what we need, I've said so all along.'

There was a little silence, and they could hear the sirens of ships on the river, hear the cries of the watermen, the banging of hammers. Mr Jarvis said, 'Can you not come to London?'

He was looking at Tacy. 'How could she?' Tacy asked, practically. 'Where would she live? I would not like to think of her in some common lodging house, at the mercy of thieves and pickpockets and worse.'

Again the silence, broken only by the sounds from the river. Mr Jarvis picked up his pen, studied it, put it down again. 'She could stay with us,' he said, at length. 'My wife would make her most welcome. I have two daughters about the same age . . .'

'Oh yes,' Damaris breathed. 'Oh *yes*!'

'I don't know.' Tacy hesitated. 'Would Mrs Jarvis really be willing to take her?'

'You have met my wife,' Mr Jarvis replied. 'We have known each other for a long time, Mrs Barratt, I knew your father. I regret that the ribbon trade is failing, and I would sincerely like to help. Damaris would come to no harm with us and we attend chapel as you do. So if it would help – and I think it might if Miss Barratt is keen –'

'She is keen *and* talented,' said Tacy. 'But I don't know. It would mean a considerable outlay –'

'I agree. But if you are to meet French competition.'

Tacy thought rapidly. It would be a help. And it would also take Damaris away from Martin Jacques for a year. She was young and would forget – and more important, so would he – or find another girl.

'I shall have to ask her father, of course,' she said, at

last. 'But if he agrees – and I think he will – then yes. Damaris can come to London.'

In Chilverton the weeks before Christmas were far from merry. The soup kitchen was still in operation, and there was still an undercurrent of anger beneath the weavers' silence. On Saturdays, those who had work took it back to the warehouse, but as always now, there were more weavers than there was work for them. Damaris and Martin walked together from the Patch, through Half-Moon Lane, towards the canal, where they climbed down to the tow-path.

Damaris wore a warm cloak over her woollen dress and thick boots on her feet. There had been a heavy frost and the fields were still white; the canal ran dark, though was still navigable, and they watched the gaily coloured boats glide along, pulled by willing horses, eager to get back to their stables.

Damaris said, abruptly, 'I shall be going to London for a year.'

'What?' Martin turned to face her. 'A year? When?'

'In January. To study design.'

'But you never told me.'

'I didn't know till we went to London last week and Mr Jarvis suggested it. It will be good for trade, Martin, we need good designs. Good designs mean we can sell more.'

'But a year,' he said, sulkily.

'It will soon pass, Martin.'

He turned away moodily. Walking on the tow-path was frowned upon by the Canal Company, and as a packet boat came towards them, horses galloping, the postillion sounding his horn, the driver shouted to them to get out of the way. They moved back, watching the seventy foot of gleaming hull pass by, its cabins worked with colourful roses and castles, its merrily smoking chimneys, the passengers waving as they passed.

Martin said, 'I love you, Damaris.'

'I know. I love you, Martin.'

'I want to marry you.'

'Oh Martin.' She snuggled close to him. 'I do, too. And we will. But – we can't marry yet. Mamma wouldn't allow it. And I'm only fifteen.'

The packet boat was out of sight now, the canal was quiet. He put his arm round her and led her under the little hump-backed bridge. He kissed her.

'Damaris,' he said, feverishly. 'I can't let you go. Not without – ' his hands fumbled with her skirts, but she pushed him away.

'No, Martin.'

'We can go over the fields.'

'No.'

'But why? We love each other. I shall know then that you really will marry me.'

'I will marry you. I do love you. But I won't do that.'

'You don't love me,' he accused.

'Yes, I do love you. But I'm not getting in the family way. Not yet. I want to go to London first.'

'You'll forget me.'

'No, I shan't, Martin. I intend to marry you. But you know Mamma is against it. And I must go to London to help the business.'

'Suppose I find another girl?' he asked.

'Please yourself.' And she turned on her heel and walked away.

She was not angry, simply sure of herself. She had no intention of getting in the family way. She had seen enough of that with Bess. Her Mother didn't approve of Bess, and that was understandable, what wasn't so easy to understand was that her father seemed to like her; he had taught her how to drive the chaise, let her take it out for shopping and so on . . . She would not let her thoughts go any farther, telling herself that all the men liked Bess. But it was not for her. She knew her Martin. Oh, he loved her, but he was mercurial, intense, moody. She was calm, controlled. In any battle of wills she always won simply by sitting waiting.

He caught up with her. 'I'm sorry, Damaris, I didn't mean it, you know I didn't.'

'Well, don't threaten me, or I'll take you at your word.'

'Damaris.' He took her arm, turned her towards him. 'I do love you. Really I do. But –' he stopped, another boat came by, a slow boat, with a woman at the tiller, face brown as a nut, who smiled knowingly at the couple as she steered. 'What's the point of it all? My studying grammar and arithmetic, when I can't even get my own loom.'

She said quickly, 'We'll work together, Martin. Me designing, you –'

'Yes, me what?' he asked.

'We'd be ideal helping Mamma,' she said, thoughtfully. 'You could see to all the things in London, the buying, the selling. You'd do well, for you have more time than she has.'

He moved impatiently. 'But your Mamma doesn't like me, you know that. I don't know why – and I'm not planning to wait for dead men's shoes. Oh –' he broke off abruptly. 'I'm sorry, I didn't mean –'

'It's all right.' She understood how he felt. Frustrated at not being able to work as he should. He was clever, Martin, he had a better brain than she had. 'We'll work something out,' she said optimistically.

They walked on, as another boat came by, and now she let him put his arm right round her. 'We can run the business together,' she said. 'Somehow, some day . . .'

Chapter thirteen

Damaris liked her life in London. The Jarvis family lived in a tall house overlooking the river, and from the windows they could see the ships sailing up and down. They were at the edge of Whitechapel, where there were still fields to the rear. Nearby was Spitalfields, once a village of large, well-kept houses built by the Huguenot silk weavers, now becoming overcrowded, its gardens obliterated by mean dwellings. The Jarvis family was quite well-to-do. Mrs Jarvis was a neat, quiet lady, who ran her house, her four servants, and two daughters and one son, competently.

Daughter Lucy was Damaris' age, Joan a year older, while Edmund, nineteen, was learning the business. They were all friendly, though they all smiled when Damaris assumed, when they suggested a walk, that it meant through the streets instead of round the garden.

'Can't we go round the shops? Explore?' she asked.

'Oh heavens, no. Not in London,' laughed Lucy.

'Not unchaperoned,' said Joan, the serious sister. 'If you run around here on your own, you'd likely never be seen again.' Seeing Damaris' face fall, Lucy said, 'We'll get Edmund to take us out in the carriage, Damaris. May we, Mamma?'

'If you wish. And I will take you to the shops.'

So between them, the family showed Damaris London, which too often had a pall of smoke hanging over it. She went with Mr Jarvis to the warehouses on the docks, with the forests of masts, the captains shouting orders, ships loading and unloading, empty casks rolling along the stones, dark-skinned sailors from India, lascars, and the smell of rum and spices.

And one unforgettable night they all took her to the market in the Whitechapel Road where everything was sold from beds to boots and flowers, and which went on till midnight. It was lit by candles and naphtha flares. There were hot pies and pea soup, quack medicines, musicians, acrobats.

But best of all was the fact that she was actually attending the School of Design. Not too far from his home, Mr Jarvis drove her there in his gig every morning on his way to his office, and called for her in the afternoon. And here Damaris could, at last, learn the true art of design.

'I think you're so clever, being able to draw,' Lucy sighed one evening. 'I could only manage a few simple flowers at school.'

They had just dined, and were now in the parlour, a fine room with its heavy brocade curtains, moulded ceiling, and gilt mirror over the fireplace. Lucy, who liked to dress well, wore a striped silk gown, and she looked down at it in wonderment. 'Fancy having to sketch a dress,' she added.

'Oh no, I just do the designs for the ribbons,' Damaris explained. 'I'm so glad to be able to do it, it will be such a help when I get home.'

'You still have hand-looms in Chilverton, do you not?' asked Edmund.

'Yes, of course. A man in Coventry built a factory but the weavers destroyed it.'

'But won't he build another?' asked Joan. 'I mean, steam power will come, won't it, Papa?'

Mr Jarvis leaned back in his chair. 'I'm afraid it will,' he said.

'Why afraid?' asked Edmund.

'Because it means the end of a way of life. Of people working for themselves.'

'Of course,' agreed Damaris, eagerly. 'That's why our weavers will never go into factories. They are much against it.'

'But if everyone else uses steam power, what then?' asked Edmund.

Damaris hesitated. She didn't know. But the very next day she had a letter from Martin.

My dearest Damaris.

How are the designs going? I must tell you about the new ideas here. You know how my grandfather built his loom-shop with bedrooms over the top? Well, I went to Coventry last week and there is talk about this new idea of building a row of houses with the loom-shop running along the top. I mean, since Beck's factory was burned down, they've never dared build another, so maybe this is the way forward. They call them Topshops, or cottage factories. Hand-looms, of course.

I do miss you, Damaris. Please write soon. I send you a thousand kisses, and cannot wait to hold you again in my arms.

All my love, Martin

Damaris wrote back:

My dearest Martin,

I know my designs are improving. But I miss you so and there's no freedom here as there is at home, I cannot go out. So I spend all my spare time reading books about silk from Mr Jarvis's library.

Did you know that one of the earliest records of silk

is mentioned in the Saxon Chronicles: 'Offa, King of Mercia, received a present of two silken vests from the Emperor Charlemagne in 790. Though it is doubtful if silk weaving was practised in England before the fourteenth century, and that only plain work. Rich velvets and figured silks were imported from Italy, where the weaving of it spread to France and then it came to England . . .'

Oh, Martin, I wish you were here with me. The Jarvises are so nice, Lucy and Joan, and there is a son, but don't get jealous, it is you I love. What do I care that in the early days only the Knights of the Garter and their wives were allowed to wear satin and ermine as my book tells me? Or that after the Wars of the Roses great prosperity dawned for all classes, and rich silks and satins were more generally worn? I just want us to be together.

I must close now, it is time for bed. And I shall wish you were with me, holding me in your arms, kissing me, and I will show you that I love you just as much as you love me.

Then she carefully crossed out the last lines and ended, primly, 'All my love, Damaris.'

And sometimes now, the noise and bustle of London seemed just too much, and she thought sadly of Chilverton, its quiet lanes, the slow flowing canal, the boats with their horses, the setting sun hanging like a great red ball in a sky all aflame. And when she had a letter from her mother about the happenings in Chilverton she felt she was missing all the fun.

1832 was a momentous year. The Reform Bill was passed. More men would get votes, though not all, and for the first time Chilverton would be represented in

Parliament. There were many celebrations. In June an aeronaut descended with his balloon into the grounds of the Manor. Subscriptions were asked for a great festival to be held in July, with beef and ale given to the poor. It was a warm summer's day, the church bells rang, there was a great procession, with bands and people carrying lighted candles. And it was made known that there would be two candidates, Sir William Fargate and the young Charles Waring, who was married to one of the Calders.

Tacy did not go to see the procession. She had been up most of the night with Jobey and the old horse, who, it seemed, had come to the end of his life. And when she sent for the horse-doctor, he agreed. 'I'll take him away for you,' he offered.

'No, you won't,' Tacy retorted. 'I want him shot here where I can see. No selling him off to some charlatan who'll work him till he literally drops. I've seen poor old nags being forced to drag heavy loads when they can hardly walk.'

The horse disposed of, Tacy returned wearily for breakfast. Francis was in the dining-room, his eyes bleary and unfocused, and Tacy wondered fleetingly why he always looked so peculiar in the early mornings. But she had no time to wonder.

'We must get another horse,' she told him. 'I'll send Jobey over to Jem Weston, the blacksmith, he'll likely know of one.'

'You'll send Jobey nowhere,' said Francis, grandly. 'I'll buy a horse.'

'But you don't know anything about horses – ' Tacy broke off. Telling Francis he didn't know something was the worst thing she could have done.

'I'll go to the fair in Shropshire,' said Francis. 'It's on this week.'

'Oh, Francis, it will be full of horse traders and – '
Dealers and cheapjacks . . . dyed horses and doctored up
old nags . . . didn't he know that he would quite literally
be taken for a ride?

But no use protesting. Francis had the money. He was
the master. 'How will you go?' she asked.

'I'll hire a horse from Farmer Bates. No, two horses.
I'll take Bess with me.'

Tacy turned on her heel and left.

Bess wasn't too willing to go to the fair. She was
beginning to be afraid of Francis. She hated the way he
would take off her clothes and gloat over her, but when
she once refused he had picked up a stick and threatened
to beat her senseless. Remembering what he'd done to
Tacy, she'd known he meant it.

'Hey you,' she said to Annie. 'Don't ever let the master
touch you – not that he's ever likely to, plain scarecrow
that you are.'

'I don't want 'im,' retorted Annie. 'Why, don't you
enjoy it then? Don't he pay you enough?'

'He pays me little enough,' Bess said, darkly. 'And he
gets his money's worth I can tell you.' She sighed. 'I wish
I was married and out of it.'

'Well, you want to hurry up then,' Annie said, cheek-
ily. 'You're gettin' on, ain't you?'

So Bess had gone to the Bull and Butcher one evening,
where the men congregated. And when she came home
Francis was waiting in her room. He cut her face with the
whip.

'Cor,' said Annie. 'What'll the missus say?'

'She won't see me,' said Bess. 'You take the meals in.'

Now she wanted to leave. But how? She could hardly
apply for work in Chilverton where she was known.
Who would take a woman with a child? The mistresses
would think she was after their men.

The other way was to go to the Statutes – the hiring fair. But she still had the child. The only people likely to hire her would be farmers, thinking the boy could be used to scare crows in a year or two. But remembering her own life on the farm she hesitated. She knew her father had taken any girl who worked for him, so if she were stuck out on some lonely place, worked to death and with a man perhaps as bad as Francis . . . better maybe the devil you know . . . She was trapped.

They returned from the fair with a young mare trotting at the back of their mounts. Tacy took one look at its rolling eye and her heart sank. Jobey put one hand on its back and it reared up and nearly kicked him.

'It'll calm down,' Francis said. 'It was a bargain. Only twenty pounds.'

'I'm sure,' said Tacy, sarcastically.

The mare, surprisingly, did let Jobey put her between the shafts of the chaise. But she did not like anyone riding her, and especially without a saddle.

'That is nonsense,' Francis said. 'You just don't know how to ride.' But he took care not to ride her himself, Tacy noted.

It was a clear fine evening. William could see through the window of his little office that the sun was setting. It would soon be time to go home.

When His Majesty's Commissioners started their inquiry into the condition of the hand-loom weavers in the United Kingdom, a Mr Joseph Fletcher was sent to the Coventry area, and while there he asked at the Mechanics' Institute for several of their best scholars who could write well and clearly to help him copy his reports, and William was one of the chosen, to his gratification. It was only temporary work, soon there would be an army of clerks in London writing it. But in the meantime he helped, and this meant payment. Mossy could work the loom, with Joey to pick-up if there was any weaving to do.

The report was of massive proportions, dealing with trade, industrial, political and moral conditions, and it was this last that William was copying.

Unfortunately for Mr Fletcher and the commissioners, the weavers did not take kindly to people looking into their moral conditions, and William began his copying with Mr Fletcher saying, 'I must lament that this investigation should be merely supplemental to hasty inquiries . . . To make a "report" from such data is impossible, I can only throw together the memoranda as hastily collected.'

So what use would that be? William asked himself, and looked down at the letter received that morning from the Reverend Coker Adams, of Anstey, near Coventry. 'Our schools are entirely supported by private charity, and have nothing to do with your enquiry. This is also the case with the national schools at Coventry, the master of which has transmitted your enquiries to me. I should inform you that he and the master of the schools here have general instructions not to answer any questions without due authority from their employers. I was not aware of the inquisitorial nature of your enquiries.'

William chuckled to himself. So much for the report.

The church clock struck eight, and William put down his pen, stood up, nodded to his fellow copiers and left the building. Once at the Patch, he saw Mossy, Joey and Charley playing cricket on the green, and he noted their shabby clothes.

Not that the two younger ones bothered overmuch about clothes, especially Charley, who always looked – said his brothers – as if he'd been dragged through a hedge backwards. Mossy did like to look neat, now he was sixteen, he, too, had an eye for the girls.

William walked into the kitchen, where Mr Redmond was sitting talking to Martha. William thought nothing of this. Mr Redmond was the minister and Martha was his mother. To neither of them did he ascribe any sexual feelings whatsoever, especially his mother. His father yes, he knew of his peccadilloes, but his mother was like Caesar's wife, above reproach.

'How's the copying going?' asked Mr Redmond, as William joined them.

'Has he been to see you about the weavers' moral conditions?' asked William, smiling. 'Because he says "The livings of the Church are held by non-resident clergy. With one exception I found these gentlemen from home when I called. This neglect has led to the erection of many Dissenting places of worship."'

'True,' said Mr Redmond. 'And no, he has not been to see me. I presume he thinks only the church ministers matter.'

'He did find someone to talk to him,' said William. 'Mr Hewitt.'

'Of course,' said Mr Redmond. 'And did he have a good word to say about the weavers' morals?'

'Oh no. He said the women spend their money on dress when they have money. This he puts down to the feebleness of their morality.'

'Is it feebleness of morality when rich women spend money on dress?' asked Martha tartly. 'I can't see what morals have got to do with weaving anyway.'

'Mr Fletcher says the farm labourers envy the weavers their working hours, and respectable families cannot get servants.'

'I don't like the sound of all that,' said Mr Redmond. 'To what is he leading?'

'Well, his own feelings are that factories would be a

good thing; he wrote . . . "The engine trade, by rendering the woman's earnings more subordinate to the man's, and by thus throwing her exertions more towards the domestic duty and his towards providing solely the means of subsistence, afford an important step towards emerging from this state of affairs."'

There was a little silence. 'It's as I feared,' said Mr Redmond. 'I read a similar report, which goes even further. We are being pushed into believing that factory work for men is the best policy, while women stay at home. Yet the truth is, it is women who are going into the factories.'

'The weavers won't like it,' said William.

'Will you tell them?' asked Martha.

'Of course. It is a public report and will be published. It's no secret.'

Martha stood up. 'I must prepare supper,' she said. 'You will stay for a bite, Mr Redmond?'

'Gladly. But I have some important news for you, Martha. I think I've found a customer for your hat trimmings. A good one.'

'Oh?' Martha paused by the cupboard in the corner.

'Squire Mountford of Basford has two sisters living with him, Lady Susan and Lady Grace. When their father died, the estate was entailed, and the elder son – their brother – did not wish them to continue living at Marley Towers, so the younger brother – the Squire, gave them a home.'

Martha pondered the strange ways of the aristocracy. The weavers would never turn two women out to fend for themselves. 'And they need *my* help?' she asked.

'They don't like to spend too much,' Mr Redmond said with a smile. 'Young Lady Grace will soon be coming out and she badly needs her gowns and bonnets refashioned, or so I gathered.'

Charley ran in, throwing his cap on a chair, his hair standing on end. 'But how do you know them?' he asked.

'Don't be rude,' Martha admonished him.

'Oh, it's of no matter,' Mr Redmond said, easily. 'My knowing them goes back a long way, to my boyhood in fact.'

'Tell us, Mr Redmond,' said Charley.

'Well.' He sat back. 'You remember I told you about my father.'

'How he drank, and died,' said William. 'I remember. And you were put on the streets. How did you live?'

'Oh, I earned a copper here and there, holding horses and the like. If I had no money I stole. We all did.'

Mossy and Joey had come in, and all listened in surprise at this from the minister.

'Didn't you go to chapel?' asked Joey.

'No, nor to church, either. I had started when I was a child, in happier days. But when things got so bad in London I'm afraid church was the last thing on my mind.'

'So what happened?' asked Joey. 'Did the Bow Street Runners get you?'

Mr Redmond smiled. 'No. Something much better. A man and his wife, Mr and Mrs Redmond – yes, I took their name – used to come round the streets looking for just such as I. They gave me a home, sent me to school . . . I could never repay their goodness, never.'

'And they went to chapel,' said William.

All the boys were sitting now in a half circle, listening, absorbed.

'They went to chapel, and they sent me also,' he told them.

'And they found you work?' asked Joey.

'As a boy in the home of – yes, you've guessed it –

Lady Susan at Marley Towers. She is a little older than me, though Lady Grace was not yet born. Their father married twice, you see. But yes, I worked for them and in time it was made clear to me that I would be promoted to footman and even higher. They sent me to church with all the servants and family, but I somehow couldn't forget the chapel I'd been brought up in. And then one day I knew I had to make a decision.'

He paused, and Martha quietly put the plates on the table.

'I had talked with the Redmonds about my father. As a child I had hated him, I thought he was wicked. Now I came to see that the thing I feared, his drinking, was not evil, but was more like an illness. I decided I wanted to help the other unfortunates like him who still lived in the wretched alleys in London. I looked round at the lovely countryside where every little flower is so perfect, and could not believe that God wished men to live like pigs — no, not pigs, pigs are clean animals. So — I became a minister in time.'

'And did you work with those people?' William asked.

'I did, for many years, till I came here.'

'But how can you help them when they spend all their money on drink?'

'By letting them know there is someone they can lean on, a friend, always ready to help.'

'You mean yourself?' asked Charley.

'No, Charley, though I am there. But I mean our Saviour.'

There was a silence, and outside the shouts of children died in the distance. William said, moved, 'I think I would like to work like that.'

'Oh, William,' Martha cried. 'What would I do without you to help me?'

'Yes, of course,' William said.

And when Mr Redmond had gone, it was William who sat in his chair. He kept the younger boys in order and acted in his father's place, for Tom was seldom home these days, and Martin, too, would often sleep at the Jacques', saying there was more room there. William had bought a straw mattress which he placed in the front room with the loom, saying he liked to be private to read and study. Of all her sons, William was Martha's favourite.

She was darning one of Charley's socks and she said, carefully, 'William, is the reason you want to go to work in London because of Damaris?'

William pursed his lips. 'No. Not altogether,' he replied. 'I have always been interested in Mr Redmond's work, you know that, Mother.'

'But you do like her?'

'Yes. But I know it's hopeless, it's Martin she cares for.'

'She might change her mind. Martin still goes out and enjoys himself.'

'Yes, but we won't tell her that, Mother.'

Martha broke off a thread. 'I'd be sorry to lose you, William.'

'Well, we'll see.' And William said no more.

Basford Hall was a plain grey stone building of no particular architectural significance. Martha had ridden on the carrier's cart as far as the road would take her, then walked the rest of the way. She was expected, and was led to a large room where two ladies were sitting. The elder, a thin figure with iron grey hair and dressed in black alpaca which made her look like a housekeeper, was obviously Lady Susan. The other was a young girl with a pretty face, fair hair, and dreamy blue eyes. Lady Grace.

'So you're the seamstress,' said Lady Susan. 'Good morning.'

'Good morning,' returned Martha.

'My sister needs a little work doing to her bonnets and dresses, or so she says,' Lady Susan continued. 'I don't hold with such fripperies myself. Well, better take her to your room, Grace, if you have to change your gown.'

Grace smiled shyly, and led Martha up some stairs into a bedroom, which, Martha noted, was also quite plain, though the curtains and bed hangings were of rich damask, the one bedroom chair was of a soft velvet, while the brushes on the dressing-table were backed with gold.

The girl closed the door, and said, 'You see, I am asked to parties now, and I need to look – well, at least something like the other girls do. They have such lovely gowns.' She was taking off her own plain grey dress as she spoke and slipping on another. Martha stared. This was her party dress? It looked no different from the first one. Plain and grey, and not so much old-fashioned as being of no fashion at all. The sleeves were long, there was little or no waistline, its only redeeming feature was that the skirt was quite full. In fashions now the emphasis was on breadth; exaggerated shoulder lines, ballooned sleeves, a full skirt and a tiny waist. Lady Grace saw her stare and said, apologetically, 'My sister won't let me buy many new dresses.'

Mr Fletcher would approve of that, Martha thought with an inward smile, then said, 'Well, for a party I would suggest trimming the skirt with swirls of ribbon. I have a beautiful blue and silver which would be ideal. See, I have brought a sample. I could take in the waist and sew more ribbon round it, then cut the sleeves short, and try to give them more fullness.' *It's the best I can do* she thought, wryly. 'Do you have any others?'

'Oh, they're mostly the same.' The girl looked crest-fallen, and Martha thought, *Poor child. Why won't that old dragon buy her more gowns?*

They went through more grey dresses until Martha's ingenuity was all but exhausted. She said, 'Forgive me, your ladyship, but all these alterations will cost as much as buying a couple of new gowns.'

'I know,' sighed Lady Grace. 'But my sister will have it so. At least I shan't be ashamed to go out now. Perhaps you could look at my bonnets? I don't have a maid, you see, who could sew for me.'

They returned to Lady Susan, who seemed quite impressed with the work. 'We shall want it as soon as possible,' she commanded.

Martha was given a sewing room. Every day she took the carrier's cart and walked the rest of the way to the Hall. As she worked she learned from the other servants the story of the family. They were children of the Earl of Morley who had never cared for his eldest daughter, Susan, and had refused to let her marry. His home, Morley Towers, was twenty miles from the Hall, and he owned all the land in between. And, as Mr Redmond said, when he died, his son no longer wanted his sisters, nor his younger brother, at the Towers. So he gave the latter Basford Hall, on condition he took the sisters to live with him. He did so, and proceeded to ignore them henceforward. Lady Susan became an embittered old maid, and only the neighbouring families were preventing Lady Grace from being forced into the same mould.

As the weeks passed and summer turned to autumn, Lady Susan began to take an interest in the actual ribbon weaving. 'You have worked well,' she told Martha. 'When Grace meets her friends she shall tell them about you.'

And indeed, the grateful Lady Grace did so, and

Martha found herself with more work, and was thankful that Mr Redmond had suggested her in the first place.

The weavers had heard about William's copying of the report, and wanted to hear all about it. They were standing in the warehouse on the last Saturday in September, a warm day, but with signs of autumn on the trees.

William was quite willing to tell them. 'He talks two roads,' he said. 'He says on the one hand that we have a book society, a library, and the hand–loom is frequently called the "weaver's study" where he prepares speeches and so on – "the intelligence and dexterity of the leaders of the men is very remarkable". But on the other hand he says factories would be better, although "the factory system is the great propagator of socialism" and the influence of the factory is generally bad. Mr Redmond thinks we're being pushed into factories.'

'What is this socialism?' asked Enoch Walters.

'Mr Fletcher says it is a community of property and exchange of women,' said William, with a smile.

'Hey, I like the sound of that,' said Joe Bates. 'I allis wanted a change from my old woman.'

'And if she hears that you'll have a pot broke over your head,' laughed Bob Pettit.

Tom Jacques said, 'Forget this report. Nobody will take any notice. I have more important news.'

'What's that, Tom?'

The weavers crowded round him, and Tacy left the work and went to stand beside him.

'George Healey is going to build a factory,' Tom said, heavily.

Tacy's heart sank. 'Are you sure?' she asked.

'He's making no secret of it. He was boasting about it in the Bull and Butcher,' Tom replied.

But Tom didn't tell Tacy all he'd heard George Healey say, that this time he would put Tacy Barratt out of business for sure. And when someone asked him how, Healey had winked knowingly and said, 'Ho! I've got plans. Big plans.'

'What worries me is that now Sir William is no longer backing Healey, he'll be desperate to make money somehow, anyhow,' Tom said aloud.

'What can we do, Tom?' Tacy asked, worriedly.

'The same as they did in Coventry,' cried Joe Bates. 'They ain't built another there yet.'

'I don't know,' Tom said, heavily. 'We'll have to think about it.'

The weavers took their work and dispersed. Tacy put away her books and money box and walked to the outer door with Tom. They stood silently, each knowing what was in the other's mind. They had not been alone together since the night of the ball, they had no opportunity; all they had were the talks in the warehouse, which, to Tacy, were both a comfort and a heartache: comfort that she could be near him for a time, heartache that she had so soon to leave him.

He pressed her hand and she caught her breath in a half-sob. 'Oh, Tom – ' she murmured.

'I know,' he said. 'I know.'

Dusk was enveloping them. A bat flew by. She leaned towards him. And from the house they heard Francis' voice calling Jobey.

She drew back. 'I'm worried, Tom,' she said. 'Francis keeps trying to persuade me to sell to Healey.'

The voice came again. 'You'll have to go,' she said.

'Yes.' And as they heard steps in the warehouse, 'Don't worry, Tacy,' he murmured. 'We'll work something out.'

Chapter fourteen

Martin and William Jacques were as chalk and cheese. Martin scorned William as a chapel-going goody-goody, and hadn't been too pleased when he was chosen as a copyist for the report. He himself had passed all his exams at the Institute with flying colours, but it was steady, dependable William who was picked. And, of course, William was his mother's favourite, so Martin, once he was established as his father's apprentice, followed his example and stayed more and more often overnight at the Jacques' house. It was, after all, so much easier to sleep where you worked.

And he liked the company of his father and uncles. Since Grandma Jacques died some years previously, Aunts Hester and Sally cooked the meals. Then, in the evenings, Sally would visit her married daughter, or she would visit them and there would be teasing and laughter, Sally and her daughter giving as good as they got. There was always plenty of laughter at the Jacques', and sometimes quarrelling too; Mark's son had displeased his grandfather some time ago and been turned out of the house, living now in lodgings at the other end of the town, which didn't please Hester.

But most evenings the men would go to the Weavers' Arms or to one of the many prize-fights, and Martin would accompany them. Martin was his father's son, impatient, impetuous – and handsome. He was sincerely in love with Damaris, but he fretted at her being away, and being no nearer to marriage. And when yesterday he had received a letter from her saying her return would be put off for another six months he was unhappy.

'It will help to have another few months at the school,' she wrote. 'And besides that, Lucy will be having her coming-out party in June, and they want me to be here. It will be so exciting, I don't want to miss it. The only trouble is that you cannot join me. But I do love you, Martin, and soon we'll be together for always . . . Your loving Damaris.'

But would they, Martin asked himself. Didn't the Jarvises have a son, and how did he know that Edmund would not want to marry Damaris, with a much better chance, for he had better prospects. He, Martin, had nothing. When he finished his apprenticeship, he would still no loom of his own, nor did they know when they could buy another. Work was still slack, the soup shop was opened intermittently; some weavers, tired of the poverty, had gone by canal boat to Derby to take up work there on power looms. He had seen them go, a pathetic little crowd, with their children and their bundles, waving goodbye as they boarded the gaily coloured packet boat.

He smoothed down his cord pantaloons, brushed his coat — Martin always liked to look smart — before entering the loom-shop. His uncles were not yet here, but his grandfather was working, and Tom was on his loom, so he moved to the back and started picking up.

'Hey, Martin,' Tom said. 'What are you looking so miserable about?'

'What have I got to feel glad about?' Martin asked. 'No work, no loom, just helping you as I did when I was twelve.'

'I know, and I'm sorry. We'll get another loom when we can. Maybe when Damaris starts giving us better designs work'll improve.'

Martin said nothing and Tom stopped work to look at him. 'That's it, isn't it? Damaris?'

'I want to marry her, and her mother won't allow it. I suppose it's 'cos I've got no money.'

'No, I don't think so.'

'Then what is it?' And as Tom didn't answer, but moved back to his loom, Martin left the picking up and followed his father. 'Can't you have a word with Mrs Barratt?'

'No,' Tom replied. 'I can't go begging her to let her daughter marry my son.'

'I don't see why not.'

'No,' Tom said. 'Maybe you don't. Just accept that I cannot.'

'Well, we shall marry, whatever Mrs Barratt says.'

'When you're both twenty-one you can marry without permission.'

'There's another way,' Martin said.

'You mean get her with child? Oh no, Martin. Not that.'

'You're a fine one to talk. How many women have you had?'

Tom turned to face his son. 'And have you ever asked yourself why?'

'What do you mean?'

'Never mind.'

'Anyway, Damaris won't,' Martin said.

'Then she is sensible,' Tom said. 'Look, I'm sorry, really I am. Do you think I don't want more work? What do you think I'm agitating for? We're going to start a trade union. Come and join us.'

'Who's we? Not George Healey's men.'

Tom shrugged. 'It's up to them. All the country's starting unions. We've got to fight the masters somehow.'

'It isn't up to them if he won't let them join.'

'We've got to get rid of Healey.'

'So you keep saying. And when he builds his factory he says that in time he'll only need a few young girls to mind all the machines – at low pay.'

'I know. That's why we want a union.'

So Martin, being at a loose end, threw himself into the proceedings with gusto. All the Jacques joined, Mark, Ross and Martin senior, who was always ready for a fight.

In April 1833, the newly formed trade union had a procession through the streets of the town, with flags and bands. Indeed, widespread turn-outs of workmen all over the country were leading to moves for general unions. There was industrial unrest in South Wales, Merthyr was occupied by miners. The churches joined the fray. In Chilverton a Church Party movement sent a petition to the House of Lords against the claim of Dissenters to be admitted to universities on equal terms with members of the established Church, and the bill was thrown out of the Lords. Three weeks later the church bell ringers went on strike, saying they would not work unless paid, or the profits of the Belfry – now given to the clerk – were given to them. On Sundays the bells were silent, and the King's birthday passed without a single peal. The Reverend Mr Hewitt ordered the choir to stop singing Psalm 134, 'Come bless the Lord', because it was part of the Dissenters Service Songs and Hymns.

Tacy said, 'What's happening to the country, Tom? It never used to be like this.'

'What's happening? Too many people are getting too greedy. And so the rich get richer and the poor get poorer. We never used to have soup shops and men taking to thieving because they can't work.'

In June cholera broke out in George Healey's cottages,

and three people died. The Board of Health ordered interment to take place within twelve hours of death, and as few people as possible were to attend the funerals. And Tacy wrote to Damaris telling her not to come home until they were clear of infection.

There were gales in August, the leaves blew from the trees in a frenzy. Tacy, driving the chaise with Dolly in the shafts, tried to get home before the mare became too startled. Dolly was all right provided she heard no loud bangs, when she was likely to bolt, and she still would not let anyone ride her. Tacy sighed for the patient old Brownie.

But when she saw the two young girls outside the Bull and Butcher beerhouse she jerked on the reins. 'Whoa,' she cried, and the mare skidded to a halt.

She fastened the reins to the post, and went to the girls. They looked barely thirteen, and wore transparent dresses with nothing underneath, showing their stick-like limbs. They had put rouge on their cheeks and lips and it shone garishly under the lamp. Tacy was filled with pity.

'What are you doing?' she asked.

'Nothin',' the first girl said, defiantly.

'I saw you approaching men. If the constable sees you you'll be put in the House of Correction.'

'Well, what's to do?' asked the first girl. 'We ain't got no food, no money, nothin' since Healey put us off.'

'Where were you from?'

'Borley Common.'

'Can't you go back home?'

'Nay, our mams don't want us, they hev enough to feed, an' me dad's out of work an' all.'

'Is he a collier?'

'Yes.'

Tacy pondered. 'Do you go to chapel?' she asked.

'Nay, Healey wouldn't let us go.'

'Come with me,' said Tacy.

She bundled them into the chaise and wondered where Mr Redmond was likely to be. She tried his lodgings in the Patch and was told he would be at the chapel, taking a class. She turned the mare again, and went to the little chapel on the hill.

It was beginning to rain as she led the girls inside and told him they were homeless. 'We can't leave them out in this weather, and they were outside the Bull and Butcher, looking for men.'

'They can sleep here in the chapel tonight.' Mr Redmond looked careworn. 'I have some blankets, a society in London sent a bundle. And we'll have to start a collection for food until the soup shops open again.'

'I'll send some food down,' said Tacy. 'And I'll go to the next meeting of the Committee. It's time things were livened up.'

Tacy did not see much of the church crowd these days, she saw little point. She could not ask them to her home with Francis being so awkward, so she went occasionally to the evening service and left it at that. But since Sir William showed no animosity towards her she felt able to attend the committee meetings when there was something important to say. And now was such a time.

As she entered the committee room she saw there was a new member, the new doctor in the town. She had heard of Dr Phillips, that he was young and eager, and had lots of new-fangled ideas which didn't go down at all well with the Old Guard, especially Dr Warren. She said 'Good evening' to the assembled company and sat waiting until she could make her views known.

'Is there any other business?' droned Mr Peabody, in the chair.

'Yes. I must bring to your attention the fact that,

because of George Healey, people are starving,' Tacy said, loudly.

There was a little pause. 'It isn't altogether George Healey's fault, the whole country is changing,' said Mr Broadbent. 'Changing to industrialisation. Hand-looms are changing to factories – '

'But it is George Healey's fault the way its being done. Bringing people in from outside, paying them less, turning them into the streets when there's no work. That's never been done before,' Tacy interrupted hotly.

'You would have faced the same problems whenever it was done,' said Mrs Peabody.

'No, because we would have found a better way. My father would never have allowed this to happen. Nor would he have built those terrible cottages. That shouldn't be allowed.'

Now Dr Phillips spoke. 'Those cottages will cause illness,' he said. 'Because there is no clean water. I believe the recent cholera outbreak was due to that.'

'I have no patience with this new-fangled fad of cleanliness,' said the High Constable, testily. 'I think the late King started it when he was Regent, and it was all right for him, he was rich enough to afford baths, but the lower classes don't want to be clean.'

'Maybe they have no choice,' murmured Dr Phillips. And then, louder, 'What I mean is, the cesspool is too near the drinking water. The privies get full, overflow, water and excrement seep into the drinking water – '

'Really, Dr Phillips,' protested Mrs Peabody.

'A bit of dirt never hurt anyone,' said her husband. 'They say we all eat a peck of dirt before we die. We get hardened to it. In any case, we cannot stop a man building houses where he will. This is still a free country, thank God.'

'And we cannot stop a man bringing people in and

letting them starve,' retorted Tacy, angrily. 'So much so that girls of thirteen are turning to prostitution. We wouldn't treat cattle that way.'

There was a silence. 'It is true we don't want more prostitution in the area,' boomed the High Constable. 'Well, I will have a quiet word with George Healey, but there is nothing really in law that I can do.'

Tacy was driving the pony chaise two days later when George Healey stopped her. Dressed in a fine caped overcoat, and top hat which he did not remove, his face adorned with moustache and side-whiskers, he said, 'It was you! Getting me told about my workers. What right have you to tell me what to do? None at all.'

'Just the right of a decent citizen of the town,' Tacy replied, coolly. 'One who hates your methods.'

They were in the Market Square, and now Louie joined them, coming from a visit to Mrs Bradley, the milliner. She was wearing a voluminous mantle of green satin with a broad black collar edged with a red fringe, and with red ribbon bows down the front. Her straw bonnet was tied with wide green ribbons and had a bunch of imitation flowers standing up on the crown. If Tacy had not been so concerned she would have laughed.

George Healey saw her eyes widen and this only fuelled his anger. 'You're just envious that I'm making money,' he sneered. 'But I'll tell you one thing, Mistress Barratt. I shall go on making money, long after you've lost all your trade.'

'I shall not lose my business,' Tacy retorted.

'Oh yes, you will, and I'll put you out.' Healey's face was mottled now with anger. 'I offered to buy you out once, when your father died. And you refused. But I'll do it yet. You'll see.'

'You never will!' she cried. 'Never! Now get out of my

way. Gee up, Dolly.' And she drove away.

George Healey watched her, angrily. He hated Tacy Barratt and always had. *She* got herself into everything where he was denied, he, who worked so hard to make money.

And he *had* made money, he thought resentfully. And he'd thought that this would automatically put him in the same class as the old Master Weavers. But it hadn't. He went to church regularly, yet no-one asked him to their homes. But the minute Tacy Barratt went to a ball what happened, *she* was invited to visit. He went to the balls too, and was ignored. He had expected, when Sir William put money in his business, that this would make them partners. And what happened? When he approached Sir William at one of the balls to ask about being on the committee, Sir William all but cut him dead. Yet Tacy Barratt was on the committee, no problem.

'Who do they think they are, royalty?' he'd said to Louie. 'You can't speak to them until they speak to you?'

And now Sir William was not putting in any more money. Instead of being a partner, he'd just drawn the profits when they were there, now he was moving to more lucrative fields. He, Healey, had just been used.

He turned to his wife, pettishly. He hadn't missed Tacy's look at Louie's ensemble. Louie's clothes never looked *right*. 'Do you have to wear such loud colours?' he asked.

'What do you mean? Colours are fashionable.'

'Yes, but not so glaring – '

'What about Mrs Peabody? She always wears bright colours and big hats.'

'Yes, but – ' It wasn't the same somehow, though George could hardly explain the difference. He wished Louie had been a weaver, then she would have been used to matching colours. And Mrs Peabody, being the lawyer's wife, had already arrived in the society of Chilverton; when you were making your way you had to be circumspect. He supposed the ladies of Chilverton wouldn't want to mix with Louie, coming from the family she did. Yet he was fond of old Lou, and more important, she had a keen brain, even if her family were trollops.

But he hated Tacy Barratt. And he'd see her finished, somehow, if it were the last thing he did.

Martin Jacques, Senior, died at the age of 69, leaving people surprised that he'd lived so long. He'd quietened down somewhat as the years passed, but he'd never quite lost his rebellious streak, it was widely believed that he was the one who'd thrown the stone through the church window some years ago. And when the union was started he was one of the leaders.

He died suddenly, as he would have wished, and the funeral was arranged for the eighteenth of June. About sixty members attended, the six leaders wearing their union regalia, but when they reached the church yard a number of policemen appeared.

'What's going on?' Ross, the eldest son, asked.

'You can't go in. No trades unions. Order of the curate,' said the constable.

'You mean we can't bury my father?'

'That's our orders. Not wearing your gowns.'

'We will go in,' shouted Tom. 'Come on, lads.'

'No, steady, take off your gowns,' advised Bob Pettit, the peacemaker.

Furiously Tom threw the offending regalia into the cart that had carried the coffin, and then went to the grave, where they threw bunches of laurel onto the coffin.

Tom Jacques went home, still angry. He had loved his

father. It was just another tinder waiting for the spark to set it alight.

But with the death of his grandfather a loom was vacant, and young Martin, now nearly twenty-one, was given his chance. And at the end of August, Damaris returned. She alighted at the Red Lion, and stood a moment looking round. An elegant figure, her pelisse sleeveless to accommodate the huge gigot sleeves of her gown, both in pale green. Her hair escaping from her bonnet, a reticule in her hand. Then she saw Martin, waiting, and he hurried towards her.

'Damaris. I'll order the post chaise to take you home –'

He was about to kiss her when a voice said: 'I have the chaise waiting.'

She turned. 'Father,' she said, flatly. 'Well, Martin can come in the chaise with us.'

'I'm afraid there won't be room,' said Francis, smoothly. 'Come along, Damaris.'

She whispered to Martin, 'I'll see you later, at your house. This will be an opportunity to talk to Papa.'

Martin stood moodily watching her as she was helped in the chaise and drove away. 'It's so good to have you home,' Francis said.

'Papa. About Martin.'

'Yes?' Francis steered the chaise past a large wagon.

'We want to marry. He is nearly twenty-one, I am nearly eighteen.'

'Damaris.' Francis's face wore his pleasant expression. 'I love you dearly and I want only your happiness. But I think you would be better not to marry one of the Jacques family.'

'Oh, I know, they get in trouble, but that's all over now.'

'Oh no. Only recently the curate refused to let them in the church to bury the old man.'

Damaris was startled. 'For heaven's sake, why?'

'Because they were causing trouble as usual. But that's not the only reason for my wanting you to choose someone more suitable. Martin Jacques has nothing, no prospects.'

'He will have, Papa, when I start designing.'

'He won't, Damaris. Your mother is thinking of selling the business to George Healey.'

'Nonsense, Papa. She would never do that.'

'We talk about it often. There is no future for the hand-looms. George Healey's factory is built, he is installing the looms and he will prosper. We should get out while we have the chance.'

'Then why have I been studying design?'

'You can always work for him. But that's not all –' as she made to speak. 'Even if things stayed as they are you would be unhappy, he would be unhappy married to a woman who owns a business, reminded day after day that he is a nobody, as I have been. I feel my position acutely, and so would he.'

Damaris did not answer. She had no reason to doubt her father's word. That he and her mother were unhappy she knew. So was that the reason? Her mother made him unhappy because he was a nobody – or told he was? She alighted at the Red House, her pleasure in coming home considerably dampened.

She felt she could hardly ask her mother if she looked down on her father, but she did tackle her about selling to George Healey as they sat in the parlour after dinner, when Francis had retired to his room.

'Of course I won't sell to George Healey,' Tacy replied. 'I detest the man.'

'But Papa said you often talk about it.'

'We do. When he brings up the subject,' said Tacy, shortly. *When he tries to persuade me to sell, when he tells me that we shall just keep on losing money.* How could she tell Damaris the truth? Would it not sound like one parent contradicting the other? And Francis was so plausible as she knew, she couldn't beat him at that. 'We are hoping that your designs will save us,' she ended. 'I have prepared a room for you to work here, the one with the biggest window, with the most light. It is –' she swallowed, 'my father's old room.'

'Oh, Mamma. You did that for me?' Damaris knew that Samuel's room had never been touched since he died, had been kept as a sort of shrine. Now Tacy led her upstairs and she saw that the great four poster bed had been removed and the room redecorated with a light paper. By the window was a table with drawers at the side. 'You can get anything else you might require,' Tacy added.

'Oh, thank you, Mamma. Thank you.' Damaris had intended to ask her mother about Martin, but this was not the time. Not now.

Mr Jarvis had approved Damaris' designs in London and already obtained orders, so they were able to be put in production immediately on her return, ready for the spring sales. She would walk down to the Jacques' loom-shop and watch the pattern on the squared paper being transferred to the card-cutting machine worked by Mossy, where holes were punched in the Jacquard cards, ready for the loom. There were so many cards needed, so many different colours, meaning an involved and – to an untrained eye – inextricable confusion of threads in the harness of the loom. Damaris was impatient to see the results, but fitting up the loom took time. However, she was happy, work was going well, the weavers were busy, and she could see Martin, though in the first hectic days they had no time to be on their own, for once the actual weaving started, Damaris would rush back to the Red House and start on her designs for the next season.

So for the winter of 1834 the weavers were busy. But they were still wary. Healey was going ahead with his factory, and made it clear he would only employ young girls at even less pay. And if the locals wouldn't accept this, then he'd bring women in from outside.

Christmas passed happily for the weavers were able to buy presents for their children. But as the winter wore on, with cold and frost meaning more coal and warm clothes to buy, and as the first orders were completed, worries began again. Another report, the Hickson, was published praising the new factories, and was read with alarm. 'It is mistaken to believe that factory labour is unfavourable to health and morals of a community, or happiness of domestic life,' they read. 'In a factory he has the exercise of walking to and from the factory, but when there, lives and breathes in a large roomy apartment in which the air is constantly changed. Some factories are models of neatness, cleanliness and perfect ventilation. We are convinced that factory labour is more favourable to the moral state than piece-work at home. The reason—regularity of hours, therefore of habits and constant superintendence through the greater part of the day . . . One of the greatest advantages resulting from the progress of manufacturing industry is to raise the condition of women . . .'

The women discussed it with incredulous dismay as they sat in the cosy parlour of the Fleur de Lys at their weekly Benefit Club meeting.

'Where are these model factories?' asked Sally Pettit. 'He's not been round Healey's, that's for sure.'

'Hickson talks as if we were children, telling us what we should do, as if we don't know what we want,' stormed Sally Jacques. 'And we know what we *don't* want, and that's factories.'

'They say there've been dreadful accidents to children left alone in their homes in the north. The kids can set the house on fire, be burned to death,' put in Mary Pettit.

'Anyway, factory work debauches young people, deprives them of family discipline,' worried Betty Lakin.

'I don't want to go in no factory. It'd be like being in prison. Can't have no freedom to go out if you want.' It was well known that the Pettits always enjoyed a day at the races at Warwick when they fancied and had the money to spare.

'We can't afford to go out much now,' objected Sue Bailey.

'No, but that ain't the point. We could go if we wanted.'

And the men talked in the taproom, over their pipes and their ale. 'Constant superintendence, the report says. As if we were kids,' marvelled Jim Bailey. 'As if we hadn't been working all our lives on our own.'

'Oh, I've heard about them superintendents. They pay a man just to walk up and down to see the men or women are kept working all the time,' said Luke Lakin.

'That's a degrading system to a freeborn Englishman.'

'I'd like to see men refusing such slave masters. What do they think we are?'

'We've got to stop Healey,' said a voice from the back.

'How?' asked Mark Jacques.

'They stopped Beck in Coventry, didn't they? They haven't built another factory yet.'

'We must let them know we are against factories. Never mind what they do in the north, we won't have it here,' said Tom Jacques. 'We are free.'

And suddenly there was a chant. 'We are free . . . we shall remain free . . .'

Martin Jacques, who had been sitting quietly at the

back, suddenly rose and went out. And the next day he had a word with Damaris.

She had come to the loom-shop in the afternoon, as much to see Martin as the work, and he said, 'Wait till we've finished, I've an idea to put to you.'

So she waited, and when the looms were silent he took her into the yard. 'Look,' he said. 'What do you see?'

'The loom-shop,' she replied, puzzled.

'Exactly. Now come with me to my bedroom.'

'Martin!'

'Come on,' he said, impatiently. 'I want to show you something.'

So she followed him to the room he shared with Tom, and waited as he went to a chest of drawers and took out some drawings.

'We live in a loom-shop,' he said. 'Now, here's my idea, and I want to put it to your mother.'

She listened as he talked, and was infected with his enthusiasm. 'Come on,' she said. 'Let's go now. If we're lucky, we'll catch her before she leaves the warehouse.'

As excited as children, they ran down to the Red House. Tacy was there. She turned as they burst in, out of breath. 'Why, whatever is the matter?' she asked.

'Mamma!' Damaris cried. 'Listen to Martin. Please.'

Martin spread his papers on the desk. 'The weavers are still determined not to go in factories,' he began. 'And I've been thinking. About the loom-shop my grand-father built, the houses and the shop together. I heard that in Coventry they are thinking of doing this on a big scale, Cash's have a plan to build a hundred houses where the weavers could live comfortably. But with the loom-shop running along the top, holding the looms. Topshops they call them, or cottage factories. It's a new idea, unique to this area, unique in Europe, they tell me, perhaps in the world. So the weavers wouldn't have to go to factories, they could work as and when they pleased.'

'Yes,' said Tacy. 'But they do that now in their homes.'

But this has the advantage of giving them a whole house to live in. And in time perhaps, if necessary, the looms above could run on power, with a shaft running through the topshops, and an engine at the end in the yard. 'See?' He pointed to his drawing. 'But the weavers could still work when they pleased.'

'Yes, I see,' said Tacy. 'A good idea, certainly. But who will build these topshops?'

'Why —' Damaris stammered, a little taken aback at her mother's lack of enthusiasm. 'Why, I wondered if you would —'

Tacy gave a short laugh. 'Out of the question,' she said. 'We haven't the money.'

'But, Mamma —'

'Build a row of houses, buy more looms?' Tacy asked.

'We could adapt a present row of houses,' Martin said. 'Move the looms.'

'But we'd still have to build a top storey,' objected Tacy. 'Anyway, your father deals with the money, Damaris.'

'Yes, but he would agree, surely, he always does,' Damaris said. 'I mean, you are in charge, aren't you?'

'Am I?' Tacy asked, bitterly.

'Well, we'll ask Father,' said Damaris. 'Leave the papers, Martin, I'll ask him. He must see that this is the solution. No, wait, let's see him now, in the counting-house.'

But Francis' answer was the same. They could not afford the outlay.

'But we'd soon get the money back,' Damaris pointed out. 'My new designs have sold well. Healey can't compete with us now. If we only build topshops with steam power added later, nothing would stop us.'

Francis' eyes narrowed. But he still said no, and they left, dejected.

'It's Mamma's fault,' Damaris said, angrily. 'Father always gives in to her. Oh, how could she?'

And privately she remembered her father's warnings about her mother wanting to sell to Healey. Surely she wouldn't want to sell out now?

In truth Tacy was desperately worried about money and Martin's idea couldn't have come at a worse time. Francis kept the books and gave her the totals every month or so. She never queried the figures, and never checked or reckoned up herself. Yet she knew what was bought and sold and had a good idea of what profit – or loss – there should be. So she was a little concerned when, after good sales with the new designs, there showed little gain. She had mentioned it to Francis, who gave his cold smile.

'I did warn you,' he said. 'We shall never make money. We should sell out now while we can.'

She turned away. But she wasn't satisfied. 'Can I see the books?' she asked.

'Of course,' Francis replied, and she was shown the neat columns of figures. They added up.

Yet she still wasn't satisfied. That night she crept out of bed at about two in the morning and went silently to Francis' room. He was not there, which did not surprise her, but he had left his keys on the chest of drawers. She took them, and, feeling like a thief, walked down to the counting-house, unlocked the drawer where the books were kept.

It did not take her long to find out what was wrong. Francis kept two sets of books. One he showed to her, the other with more items of expenditure, and she studied these in amazement. To: Mr Hood, wine and spirit merchant. £10. Mr Hood, wine and spirit merchant; the list went back a long way.

She returned the keys, went back to her room. But not to sleep. Who had been drinking all the spirits? There was only one answer. Francis. Drinking alone in his room night after night. She was appalled.

She did not know what to do. There was little she could do. She could work herself to a frazzle to make money, Francis would spend it. And when there was none left he would sell to George Healey.

It was a long hot summer, sultry and humid, with a copper sun in a metallic sky. Tempers frayed, tension was high, people quarrelled for no reason. Work was spasmodic as they waited for the winter and the new orders, with everywhere Healey and his new factory in the background, and an air of impending trouble – though no-one quite knew what would happen. The Barratts and the Jacques were at odds with each other and the others' families. Damaris could not understand her mother's refusal to build topshops – unless she did mean to sell out. Martin, too, was angry at Tacy's refusal, and was annoyed with his father because he wouldn't intervene. Tacy worried about money, she did not know what to do. Should she confide in Tom? But supposing he made trouble with Francis? Francis would call the constable and Tom would be the one to blame. For Francis was not doing anything wrong. He was entitled to spend his wife's money if he chose. Or to sell the business . . . Tom himself would have liked to broach the subject of Martin and Damaris but did not quite dare. It would look as if he wanted to get his son into the business – and Tom was proud. So they circled round each other warily like puppets in a macabre dance – with

Francis pulling the strings.

Damaris did not see much of Martin during the summer. She was busy working on the designs for next year, for the samples had to be approved, orders taken before the winter, so that production could start ready for the spring fashions. She sat at her table, the heat beating down; the wide-open window only seemed to make the room hotter. And if she drew the curtains she could not see as well as she wished. But she was determined to make these designs the best she had ever done. These were to save the family fortunes. She was especially pleased with one showing red poppies on a yellow background – taken from her memory of Martha's comments, when she was a child, and called Poppies in the Cornfield. If they sold well – and they must – then her mother would have no excuse for not building the topshops. And with topshops and power looms, they could compete with George Healey's inferior designs.

So Damaris worked, and in August Tacy sent off the completed samples to Mr Jarvis and they waited confidently for his approval.

Martha was pleased Damaris had used her idea. Like all of Chilverton's weavers, Martha wanted them to succeed. For if George Healey won the battle, then it would mean Tacy losing out, and all the weavers working on George Healey's terms. Already he had installed his looms and started a few young girls to watch them, dismissing most of the men in his employ, and these were sullenly walking the streets, thrown on the parish – if they were local people and thus entitled – if not they had nothing, until the soup shop opened.

Martha had given the new designs to Lady Susan who was now in London with Lady Grace. But Martha still had work for the ladies in the area, who would either send down a servant to her house with instructions, or to ask her to call on them. And Lady Susan promised to do her best to obtain orders in London, both for herself, and more orders for the weaving. 'If we attend a Drawing-Room at the palace,' she said, 'I shall try to interest Her Majesty herself. For the Queen is a kind lady and would, I know, wish to help the weavers in any way she can.'

Martha, pleased, told Tacy, who wasn't quite so hopeful about the Queen sending orders, but nevertheless she arranged for Martha to have samples to take. She herself pinned her hopes on Mr Jarvis. When he placed a large order – as he must – she would have the matter out with Francis, once and for all, make him see that they, not Healey, had the key to the future.

The drought ended in September, when it rained. Everyone drew a breath of relief. Now they could get back to work; now the farmers could see crops growing again. The weavers, who had been mooching around the fields, waiting, now tidied their looms for the work that would be coming.

And Tacy received a letter from Mr Jarvis.

My dear Mrs Barratt,
    I am so sorry, but I cannot sell any of your designs. Those who usually buy gladly tell me they have already bought all these designs, exactly the same, at a lower price. Again, I am sorry. If there is anything I can do you have only to ask.
    Your sincere friend . . .

Tacy read this in growing bewilderment. How could this be? She showed it to Damaris, she called Tom. Together they stood in the warehouse, the rain dripping outside, and studied the letter in amazement.

'They are *my* designs,' wailed Damaris. 'How could anyone else have them? Unless Mr Jarvis sold them elsewhere.'

'Why would he do that? Tacy asked. 'Anyway, I would trust Mr Jarvis with my life.'

'Wait a minute,' Tom said. 'What's this? He says these designs are exactly the same. Not that they *are* the designs.'

'We'll go to London,' said Tacy. 'Damaris and I. Tomorrow.'

They took the coach in silence. Damaris was shattered. All her work gone for nothing. All her studying that had led up to this moment, all the hot summer's endeavour – for nothing? Who could have had exactly the same ideas? For without these sales the weavers would have no work, Martin would have no work, they'd never be able to marry . . . She slumped in her seat.

In London they went straight to Mr Jarvis' office, and he received them with pleasure mixed with the consternation he felt.

'Please sit down,' he said. 'I will order a little wine, and perhaps something to eat?'

Tacy brushed this aside. 'No food, thank you, Mr Jarvis. Yes, perhaps a little wine. But tell us . . . what about these designs?'

'How has anyone taken my ideas?' asked Damaris hotly.

'As to that, I don't, of course, know,' Mr Jarvis replied. 'All I know is that when I called on Mr Boston, one of my buyers, he told me that he had exactly the same designs, and had ordered some of those, so did not want more.'

'Did you not see them?'

'Did he not tell you from whom he ordered them?' Tacy and Damaris spoke together.

'No, to both questions. He had not then received the finished ribbons, and he would not tell me his supplier's name. The same thing happened wherever I went.' He paused. 'You do know that there are people who pirate designs?'

Tacy and Damaris looked at each other.

'Give me Mr Boston's address,' said Tacy. 'We will go and see him.' And without finishing the wine, mother and daughter called a hackney coach.

Bostons was a large drapers and haberdashers in the West End of London. There was already a display of ribbons in the window, and they stopped to look. 'There,' Damaris said. 'My poppy design. No-one else could have thought of that, it is mine. Mine and Aunt Martha's.' She peered more closely. 'It isn't woven so well,' she exclaimed. 'I can see faults from here.'

'Come,' ordered Tacy. 'Inside.'

Inside the store she asked to see the buyer, and when that gentleman approached she asked if he could give her the name of the supplier.

The buyer hesitated. 'It isn't usual – ' he began.

'I'd like to order some for myself,' Tacy lied. 'I have a shop, a small one in the provinces.'

The buyer's face cleared. A small provincial store wouldn't affect his sales. He said, 'I obtained them from Healey, in Chilverton. Do you want the address?'

'No, it isn't necessary,' Tacy said. And, as a parting shot, 'I noticed faults in the ribbons. Not the best quality, I fear.' And she swept out.

'Healey!' Damaris muttered. 'He's stolen my designs.'

'But how can we prove it?' Tacy asked, practically.

She asked the same question of Tom as they gathered in the warehouse on their return. Who had stolen Damaris' designs?

'And more important, how are we going to stop it

happening again?' asked Tacy.

'Someone either took them from our loom-shop, or from your house,' said Tom.

'From a bedroom in the Red House?' asked Damaris.

It would be easier to steal from the loom-shop, they agreed. Even before production the design was there, the big draft hanging on the wall. Though to take them then would be cutting things a little fine. But friends had always walked in the loom-shop as and when they pleased.

'We must keep watch,' said Tom.

'The damage is done now,' Damaris objected.

'We shall start new designs. Give out that you are planning more as your last ones didn't sell. Start another, good or bad, it won't matter, the thief won't know till he sees them.'

'And remember,' he added. 'Not a word to a soul.'

'So,' Damaris said to her mother. 'How do we watch the room at the Red House all the time? Would it not be simpler to lock the door?'

'No, we must catch whoever it is,' Tacy said. 'You must stay in throughout the day – as you already do. And we'll take it in turns to stay in all night. But don't let anyone see you.'

So Damaris let it be known that she was starting new designs. She talked about it when they were all together, and when Bess or Annie came in. She returned to the room and began a drawing, and at night they watched.

They watched for fourteen days, and Tom told them he watched too. But they saw no-one. And Damaris grew more downhearted.

On the fifteenth of September Damaris slid as usual into the room, just as the clock struck eleven. She hid behind a chest in the corner and waited, a little dis-heartened, wondering how long this was going on, wondering if it were all worthwhile. The new designs were in a folder on the table. The curtains were undrawn, and moonlight shone into the room.

At twelve o'clock she heard the door handle turn.

She tried to hold her breath. She could see nothing behind the chest, so she cautiously peeped round one side. And what she saw made her pause.

It was Bess' child, Simon, who went to the table and took the folder, then left the room.

Damaris followed. To Bess' room, where she flung open the door just in time to see the child handing the folder to his mother, and to see that her father was also in the room.

She called, 'Mamma!' Tacy came running. And then all was pandemonium.

'He's only a child,' said Bess. 'I didn't know he was going to take them.'

'Rubbish,' cried Tacy. 'You stole them, and the ones before, and gave them to George Healey.'

'We shall prosecute,' added Damaris, then she turned to her father. 'What are you doing here?'

He ignored her. 'You won't have a case if you do prosecute,' he said. 'As Bess told you, the child took them. A childish prank.'

'And did the child sell the first ones to Bostons?' asked Tacy. 'Did he take them to George Healey? No, it was you, Bess, and you're the one who'll go to jail.'

'No, I won't, it wasn't my idea,' shouted Bess, afraid now. 'It was him. Him! Your father who put me up to it. I didn't want to steal from you. And you can whip me all you want, Mr Barratt. I ain't going to jail for you nor nobody.'

'*Father!*' cried Damaris. 'You've sold my designs? *You?*'

'It was all a mistake,' Francis told her. 'George Healey is no friend of mine.'

'Then how – ?' began Damaris.

Tacy said, 'Leave it now, Damaris. We'll deal with it through the proper channels.'

She led her daughter back to the bedroom, and Damaris slumped on the bed. 'I can't believe that Father did this,' she said. 'How could he? My designs, my work?' She was crying, and her eyes were those of a child who had been slapped hard for something she didn't understand.

Tacy put an arm round her daughter as she looked at her with pity. 'I don't know,' she replied, truthfully. As she didn't. Even in her wildest dreams she hadn't suspected Francis of stooping so low. 'Try to sleep now,' she soothed. 'We'll talk about it in the morning. We're all exhausted.'

She helped Damaris undress and into bed. Then she returned to her own room, where she tossed and turned, and fell into a troubled doze until light began to seep through the curtains.

She went down to the dining-room as the clock struck seven. Damaris was already there, red-eyed, white-faced. And Francis came in.

He sat down, abject, almost cringing, his hands were trembling, his face grey, out of which his eyes stared wildly. Tacy almost felt sorry for him, then, remembering, hardened her heart.

He did not look at her, but spoke to Damaris. 'I'm sorry,' he said. 'I didn't think, I didn't realise how it would affect you.'

Damaris stared at him, bewildered. 'You didn't *think*?' she asked. 'After all my work?'

Francis hung his head. 'I let Healey persuade me,' he said.

'But why?'

'F-for the money he offered. We – we haven't too much money.'

Tacy pursed her lips and Damaris said, 'But my designs would have earned money.'

'I didn't think,' Francis repeated. And now he spoke to Tacy. 'You – won't prosecute?' he asked.

'I don't know,' Tacy replied.

Damaris said, 'No, we won't, Father.'

Nothing else was said. Annie brought in the breakfast, but no-one ate very much either.

Before Tacy went to the warehouse she sent Jobey down to Tom. 'Tell him I must see him,' she said. 'Ask him to come here as soon as he can.'

He arrived within half an hour, and she told him what had happened. 'My God!' he uttered.

'I threatened prosecution,' she said. 'But I doubt if it would do any good.'

'It wouldn't,' said Tom. 'They'd simply say the child took them as a prank. And we can't prove that they stole the first ones anyway.'

'But why?' Tacy asked. 'If Francis wants to sell to George Healey, why try to ruin me first?'

'Easy,' said Tom. 'Because if you are practically bankrupt then Healey will get it at a low price. Plus the fact that with those excellent designs of Damaris', they've got a foothold in good shops. No doubt he and Francis have worked out a deal. Francis will get his share – if he's lucky, knowing Healey.'

'I can't believe anyone would do this.'

'Healey's behind it all, of course. What goes on in Francis' mind I cannot guess.'

'He told Damaris that he didn't realise how he'd hurt her, and to be fair, I don't think he did. He is fond of her. Oh – ' she broke off. 'I must go and see where she is.'

'She's down the loom-shop, or was, talking to Martin,' said Tom. 'He's fond of her too, Tacy.'

'Yes, I know,' she said distractedly. She paused. Then, 'What do we do?'

'I don't know. But one thing I do know. Healey's desperate. He'll do it again. If Francis won't help him, and I assume he won't again, he'll find another way. He's evil, that man. We can't stop people seeing the designs and we can't barricade the weavers in their own homes, day and night.'

'He told me he'd ruin me,' she said. 'We'll have to do something.'

'Leave it with me,' said Tom.

He turned to go. 'One thing,' Tacy added. 'Don't let all the weavers know about Francis' involvement. It will only hurt Damaris.'

He nodded, and she placed a hand on his arm. 'And Tom, don't do anything violent, will you?'

'I won't.'

'Promise me.'

'I promise, Tacy.'

She leaned towards him, kissed him gently and he left the warehouse.

A fine drizzle of rain was falling as Martin ran into the loom-shop. 'Healey stole Damaris' designs,' he cried.

'We know.' He saw that, for once, his father and uncles were not working; the looms were silent, and they stood in a little bunch near the window. His aunts were not there.

'So what are we going to do?' Martin asked.

'It's over now, we've caught him,' said Mark.

'But it'll happen again, it's bound to. He'll find a way to steal again. And then Barratts will be put out of business.'

There was a pause. 'He's right,' Ross said.

'And it's not fair to Damaris,' Martin cried. 'She's been working for years to get this far, learning design, going to London. Have we got to let it all go?'

'All right, hothead,' said Tom. 'We're thinking about it.'

'We must teach him a lesson,' said Mark. 'No trouble, just a warning.'

'We should break his machines,' said Martin.

'No. There's still the death penalty for Luddites,' said Tom.

'That man who was the ringleader in Coventry didn't hang. His MP got him off.'

'I think,' Tom said, 'it would be enough to take the silk off his looms and throw it in the canal. That should be a warning to him that we know and won't tolerate it.'

'Is that all?' asked Martin of his father. 'Why, you've always been the one who wanted to burn him down –'

'Quiet, young rooster,' ordered Mark, and Martin subsided.

'Has it not occurred to you,' Tom asked his son, 'that Damaris' father is involved in all this? That if there is too much trouble, or if word of it gets out, then he might suffer too, and through him, Barratts?'

Martin stared at his father. 'You think the weavers might attack Barratts?'

'An angry mob will do anything,' said Tom, darkly. 'I know from experience. If we keep it between just a few of us, warn Healey . . .'

Martin grunted acquiescence. 'Just us then?' he asked.

'No, not just us,' replied Tom. 'We must get the weavers' approval, can't do it all off our own bat.'

'But not all of them,' Ross said. 'Select a few we know can be trusted not to talk, Jim Bailey, the Pettits, Luke Lakin. Not the Walters, not Joe Bates, he talks too much when he's been drinking.'

'And not Mr Redmond,' said Mark. 'And that means no telling Martha, Tom. Nor William.'

'How do we get in the factory? Does anyone sleep there now?'

'I don't think so. Those girls live about ten in a room in one of Healey's houses. We'll have to break the door.'

'And then cut the silk from the looms, throw it in the canal. He'll understand what we're trying to tell him.'

'When?' asked Mark.

Tom paused. 'Thursday. Martha is going to see Lady Susan, who'll be back from London, and Mr Redmond takes a Bible class in the evening, so he'll be out of the way while we get together. We'll all assemble here, then wait till midnight. Agreed?'

It was agreed.

There were no streetlights near George Healey's factory, and there was no moon as the seven dark figures crept silently through the night: the four Jacques, Harry Pettit, Luke Lakin and Jim Bailey. They carried crowbars to lever open the doors, and scissors to cut the silk. Martin had in his pocket a paper on which he had written, 'Be warned. Don't steal our designs again.'

It wasn't difficult to force the door as George Healey's buildings were not of the best quality. And once inside Tom produced a lantern which he lit and placed on the floor. Methodically they cut the silk from the looms, and put it in a pile. Martin placed his paper on one of the windows.

Tom and Mark picked up some bundles of cut silk, walked out to the canal, and threw it in, where it floated away in coloured ripples.

'That's it,' Tom breathed. 'Let's fetch the rest of it.'

'Wait!' cautioned Mark. 'I heard something.'

They stood stock still.

And suddenly the road was filled with figures, jostling, shouting. 'Get him. Get Healey. Come on, lads.'

Horrified, Mark and Tom raced back into the factory. 'Hush,' cried Tom. 'Go back. The work's finished.'

But he was too late. The room was filled with weavers, brandishing crowbars, hammers, blocks of wood, anything they could lay their hands on. 'Did you think you could come wi'out us?' yelled Joe Bates. 'We know all about the stolen designs, we all know. Healey won't get us for his factory.' And then they all started chanting, 'We will be free,' women as well as men.

Outside it was pandemonium, the crowd was completely out of hand. Stones were thrown, men were shouting. Both Mr Redmond and Mr Hewitt were there, trying to calm them down, in vain.

'Quiet, you fools, you'll have the constables here,' cried Tom.

Too late.

First on the scene was George Healey himself. The High Constable appeared, and disappeared.

'Out!' shouted a voice. 'Run!' But in the scramble to escape from the factory the lantern was knocked over. In seconds the piles of silk waiting to be thrown in the canal were ablaze, as everyone pushed for the door.

The High Constable returned with more than a hundred special constables. A magistrate read the Riot Act from the window of the Fleur de Lys.

Tom picked up the lantern, looked in vain for something to put out the fire. There was no water, nothing.

'Father!' shouted Martin at the door. 'Come on! Quick!' The constables were moving in with truncheons, and another cry went up, 'The military! Soldiers!'

They rode in, soldiers with drawn swords. And the crowds fled, huddling into entries, scattering into alley-ways, frightened, their hysteria over.

Tom was the last to leave the factory, and the soldiers and constables were waiting.

'Ha! It's you!' the Constable shouted. 'It's always you, ain't it, Tom Jacques? Always the trouble-maker.'

'Let me go, you fool, I wasn't doing anything –'

'Ha ha, you weren't. You've got the lantern in your hand. The lantern that set the place afire. I've got the ringleader,' he shouted to the soldiers, excitedly. And to

Tom, 'Come on, my beauty. Down to the cells.'

Tacy hadn't been asleep. Tom had told her what was going to happen, but he'd promised not to make trouble. She was dressed, she ran outside down towards the factory. A nameless dread surged through her, a dread that grew stronger as she neared the factory. She could hear shouts, see people running around the smoking ruins of Healey's factory. At the side was the old hand-operated fire engine, its leather pipes quite unable to deal with any big blaze.

It seemed the whole of Chilverton was there: Mr Peabody, swelling in anger, Mr Broadbent, Mr Hewitt, Mr Jennings and a whole row of constables. The military.

Mr Redmond came over to her. 'What happened?' she asked through parched lips.

'They – well, it seems there were only a few of them at first – in the night, but then others joined in. They cut the silk from the looms, threw it into the canal, broke the looms, then set the place on fire. George Healey will be ruined.'

'Where is Tom?' she asked with dread.

'Tacy, let me take you home.'

'Where is Tom?'

'The constables took him.'

She saw Damaris at her side, and Francis. Martha, still clasping in her hand the order paper Lady Susan had given her from London. William.

'What will it mean'?' she asked heavily, taking off her bonnet.

'This time, transportation at least,' said Mr Redmond. 'They might hang him.'

Martha turned away, led by William. But Tacy stood, appalled.

Chapter fifteen

The weeks that preceded the trial at Warwick Assizes were torture for Tacy. She went over it all again and again. Why had she not stopped Tom from doing it? Why hadn't she realised he'd be caught? Why had all those others joined in? Why? Why? Why? Useless to tell herself that he'd have gone ahead whether she approved or not, she *had* approved, and felt that she was to blame. She could not sit still, she wandered round the house, thinking, worrying. They wouldn't hang Tom, would they? Not Tom.

Damaris tried to console her, but she was worried too. Francis said nothing, but he wore an air of triumph that Tom was safely behind bars, but Tacy no longer cared what Francis thought. She was no longer afraid of him. He could do his worst. He had done his worst. If he had not conspired with George Healey none of this would have happened.

She found a little comfort talking to Mr Redmond. 'They won't hang him, will they?' she asked.

'We must pray not. They didn't hang the men in Coventry for the same thing. Just transportation.'

Tacy sighed.

'Of course, you know George Healey is ruined?' Mr Redmond asked. 'He is leaving the town.'

'I don't care,' Tacy said. 'He tried to ruin me, he's ruined lots of weavers. You could say he'd got his just deserts.'

She had no sympathy for George Healey. None at all.

If only Tom were free . . .

But he wasn't. And he wouldn't be set free, not this time.

She could only hope and pray that the worst would not happen. And in the meantime there were weeks of waiting . . . Anxious weeks.

She gave out the work as usual. The weavers were subdued yet triumphant underneath. They'd bested George Healey. They'd got rid of their hated rival. Things would be back to normal now. Why, that man in Coventry had been forced to abandon his plans, they said it would be years before he could think of starting again. Years! Anything could happen in the meantime.

But when they heard Tom was accused of being the ringleader, they were horrified. "Tweren't his fault,' they said. 'Not this time.' And Joe Bates, remorsefully, even went so far as to tell the constable that he had persuaded the weavers to join him that fateful night.

'We knew Healey had stolen our designs,' he said. 'We were in a rage. And it were me started it – '

But the constable wouldn't listen. 'I know you lot,' he said. 'All sticking together, trying to get him off. I saw him with my own eyes.'

Defeated, the weavers signed a petition stating Tom's innocence, and clubbed together to pay for a lawyer for his defence.

They engaged a Mr Godderidge, not a local man, and not a top-ranking lawyer, but all their money could produce. He was a small man with sparse hair and protruding teeth which gave him the look of an elderly rabbit. He talked to Tom, but was somewhat put out by his refusal to say very much.

'You say Healey stole Barratts' designs,' Mr Godderidge said. 'What proof have you of this?'

Tom did not answer. Francis had admitted to Tacy

344

that he took the designs, but he would not admit this in court. And anyway, this would mean dragging Tacy into it, and then she might be accused of helping him, Tom. So Tom said nothing. He was not afraid of what the weavers might do to Barratts, not now, their violence was over. He was afraid of what those steely men in wigs and black gowns might do to Tacy. Tom had little respect for the machinations of the law. So he kept silent, and not all the pleading of Mr Godderidge could move him.

Mr Redmond went to see him. He, like the weavers, knew the designs had been stolen, but did not know how they had found out.

'You know, Tom,' Mr Redmond said, 'Healey will accuse you. He will see this as a means of getting back at you for his loss – and it should not have happened.'

'The fire was an accident,' said Tom, doggedly. 'I went to cut the silk, that's all.'

Tacy too visited him, but all Tom would say was that everything was going all right. She had to wait for the trial.

Tacy drove with Damaris in the chaise, Jobey putting the restive mare between the shafts. But she carried them without mishap, and they entered the crowded court-room and found seats in the public gallery.

The trial commenced.

Tom was pale but defiant. He had been to cut the silk, no more. He had not known all the others were coming, he had not broken machines nor set the place on fire. Tacy wondered why he did not talk about Healey's pirating of the designs.

The chief witness for the prosecution was George Healey, smart in black broadcloth, the epitome of an exemplary businessman. 'That man,' he said, pointing to Tom, 'is guilty. I saw him there, he had a crowbar in his hand and was breaking my machines. Then he picked up a lantern and set fire to the factory. He had the lantern in his hand when he came out.' He paused, drew a breath. 'He's always been a troublemaker,' he declaimed. 'This isn't the first time he's been in court.'

'Did you not steal some of Barratts' designs?' asked Mr Godderidge. 'Was not that the cause of the trouble?'

'I did not, my Lord,' said Healey, emphatically.

In vain Tom's lawyer questioned Healey, but he stuck to his guns. Tom was guilty. In vain Tom said he intended only to cut the silk as a warning. He was not believed.

The constable too testified that he'd seen him with the lantern in his hand. But no one else from Chilverton spoke against Tom, not even Mrs Peabody, who disliked trades unionists, Radicals and Dissenters fervently. Nor even Mr Hewitt, to Tacy's surprise. She could only conclude that Chilverton, being a small, clannish town, might have a falling out between its own people, but this did not mean they would encourage outsiders to attack them. And of course, Healey himself was an outsider, as, for that matter, was Francis. Only the fact that he had been accepted by the respected Barratt family made Francis eligible to be received by the Chilverton society, and that not very willingly.

Mr Redmond spoke eloquently for the weavers. 'These men,' he said, 'have always regarded themselves as skilled artisans, and indeed, a complicated hand-loom requires a high degree of skill, delicacy of handling, patience and ingenuity on the part of the weaver, so is it any wonder that so many of them have been men of high ideals – '

'Yes, yes,' interrupted the Judge. 'Is all this necessary?'

'I think so, my lord,' replied Mr Redmond. 'If I may finish – '

'Oh, very well, if it doesn't take too long.'

'So many of them love nature, poetry, philosophy and science, and belong to literary societies and scientific clubs – some have distinguished themselves in these fields. My lord,' concluded Mr Redmond. 'Is it right to put these men to be slaves to machines in factories, when they have always been free?'

'I hardly think slaves is the correct term,' commented the Judge, drily. 'Some of these factories are pleasant places, they tell me.'

'What I mean is, the men do not destroy out of wickedness,' said Mr Redmond. 'They see steampower as a threat to their livelihood and their craft. They see their way of life threatened.'

The Judge raised his eyebrows, as one whose only sight of silk ribbons was at a London ball, and who cared little how they were made. There were upper classes and lower classes in his eyes – he hardly recognised a middle – and the lower orders had to work, it was as simple as that. It was not for them to question; they took orders from those who knew what they were talking about.

Mr Redmond resumed his seat. Another witness, surprisingly, was the Reverend Mr Rivers, Vicar of Chilverton, Basford and Borley Common, brought in from his country home. Yes, he said, he had always had a high regard for the weavers, and they had been good living men until the recent crises forced them into criminal acts.

Tacy wondered what Mr Hewitt thought of that, and how on earth the Vicar had been persuaded to come. And why Tom hadn't told the court about the pirating of the designs. But she could not stop to wonder now, she had to wait for the verdict.

It came. Guilty.

And the sentence? Transportation for life, said the judge.

Tacy collapsed.

The news was received quietly in Chilverton, but with relief that it was no worse. Transportation was one of the hazards of life. And though for the most part those transported were never heard of again, yet there was that man who was sent to Georgia in America, some years ago, and he did well . . . Pity they hadn't sent George Healey out to New South Wales . . . he was finished, anyway, he'd be leaving the town, and good shut to him.

Tacy talked to Mr Redmond. 'I must thank you for your help,' she said. 'It was you being a witness saved Tom from the gallows. You and the Vicar. I wonder how he was persuaded to come.'

'That's easy. It was Martha.'

'*Martha?*'

'You know she sews for the ladies at Basford? They know the vicar well, in fact, the living is in their gift. So it was a small matter to get him to come along.' Mr Redmond smiled wryly. 'So are things decided. The more influential people you know the better.'

When he'd gone Tacy sat thinking. She was in the warehouse, the June sun was glinting through the open door. Why hadn't Tom told all about the design stealing? Why hadn't he said that Francis had helped Healey? Was it – could it be to protect her? And Damaris? The more she thought about it, the more convinced she became. And if this was so, then it was up to her to help him . . . somehow . . . How? . . .

The more influential people you know the better . . . who did she know who could help Tom?

Sir William.

Oh, he was not a judge, but he knew all those people. He knew Members of Parliament, had hoped to be one himself; he knew the Lord Lieutenant of the county, another powerful man. He would know the Home Secretary. He was one of those whose word could – and did – control the lives of the poor.

Would he help again? She could but ask.

She'd go today. No, this time she would give the matter more careful thought. Tom couldn't be sent to New South Wales, away from his silk and all he held dear. Think carefully, Tacy. If you go to the Manor you must know what you are to say. And you must dress well, look like a lady. Impress him. And no foolish talk about Francis being his son – if he was. After all, that would make Damaris his grandchild, and this was not something she wished to dwell upon.

She decided to go the following evening, and she dressed with care, in her blue gown with the draped bodice and gored skirt trimmed with the blue and silver ribbon which had always been her favourite; it also trimmed her large hat. Throwing a light cloak around her shoulders, she called Jobey, and was driven to the Manor.

She left the chaise at the end of the drive, then passed the well-kept lawns, up the stone steps, and rang the bell. And to the maid who anwered, 'I would like to see Sir William, if you please.'

'And who is calling?'

Tacy handed her her card, and was led into the wide hall, her heart beating a tattoo as she waited.

She seemed to wait a long time, but at last she saw him descending the stairs.

'Mrs Barratt,' he said, coolly. 'What can I do for you?'

'I would like to talk to you for a moment.'

'Then we will go into the salon.' He led the way.

He did not ask her to sit, and she looked round wildly at the great heads of deer on the walls, the portraits of long-dead Fargates looking down at her superciliously –

were they sneering? Then she threw back her head and looked at him. She was Tacy Barratt. 'I – I have a favour to ask of you,' she said.

He motioned her to a seat, but he stood, saying nothing, and she was furious that he would not help her in any way, that she had to go on talking, pleading. She went on, 'Tom Jacques is to be transported.'

'I know. You begged for him once before if I remember. But this time I cannot set him free. His crime is too great.'

'But he didn't do it,' she said. 'Not break the machines, not set the place on fire.' She explained what had really happened. 'You don't know how people have suffered because of Healey, starving, girls thrown into prostitution.' She broke off, remembering that Sir William's money had been tied up with Healey too. 'Finally, he was pirating our designs,' she ended.

She watched him, for she understood his code. A gentleman might owe money to his tailor but always pay gambling debts. He might pay his workers a pittance but would not steal designs like a common thief.

She turned and looked through the great window, at the lawns, the flowerbeds, the pool, the setting sun dappling the water. He wouldn't set him free. Not this time . . .

But there was another way.

She moved away from the window, took a step towards him, as she chose her words carefully. 'He is a weaver,' she began. 'A silk weaver, it is what he loves . . . working on rough soil in burning sun would kill him. Oh, not the work, not the hardship, but the loss of his trade, his skill.'

'So?' he asked, a slight sneer curling his mouth, making her feel she detested him. 'You want me to start silk weaving in Australia?'

'No.' She drew a breath. 'No, but I want you to

change his destination from Australia to America.'

Now his impassivity left him, he was plainly astonished. 'But we don't send convicts to America, it is no longer our colony.'

'I know you couldn't do it officially. But you could arrange it, Sir William, you have the power. You are a justice, your word is law.'

He looked a little gratified. 'But why?' he asked.

'Because in a place called New Jersey they are thinking about silk weaving. He could work there.'

Now his face changed, he looked almost angry. 'He'd be a free man then,' he said. 'Is that what you suggest? That a man convicted of a serious crime should be freed?'

'How can he be free when he's forced into exile? He could never come back. But – working the land, he'd hate it so.'

She had murmured the last words to herself, but he overheard. 'He is being punished,' he told her. 'He is not meant to enjoy his work.'

'But he is so good, he could help the weavers in America.'

'And why should we help the weavers in America? They've broken free from us. Let them stand on their own feet.'

'Why shouldn't Tom help America?' she flashed, anger getting the better of her. 'His own country doesn't want him. They've taken his livelihood, they want to change him from a free artisan to a factory slave. Other men have had to go to America to find freedom, why shouldn't he?'

There was a glint in his eyes now and she wasn't sure what it meant. She half turned to go, but he said, 'Wait.' He laughed. 'You are a fiery little minx, aren't you? And I do like fire, it amuses me. At my time of life one gets bored with sameness.'

She stopped, but did not look at him again. He studied her. A woman in her thirties, still attractive to a man of jaded palate who looked for something different in his women. He said, 'Maybe we can come to some arrangement.'

Now she half turned, but did not speak.

He came towards her, touched her arm. 'Once before I did a favour for you for this same man,' he said. 'And you promised me a reward, but did not pay me.' He paused, and she was still, while he began stroking her arm. 'Maybe I will help Tom Jacques get to America – if you grant me the favour you denied me before.'

His meaning was clear and she stood frozen, not turning. She could see through the great window the sun sinking redly, see a bank of clouds above. 'When?' she asked.

He laughed. 'Oh, you won't run away from me this time. No, we'll settle the debt now.'

'*Now?*'

'It is a small price to pay, surely.'

She did turn then, but tried not to look at him. His mottled, blotched complexion, his decaying teeth, repelled her. She remembered how he'd kissed her years ago; she'd hated it then.

He was still stroking her arm, bare beneath her cloak. 'There was a time,' he said, 'when you tried to get me to help you with the weaving, was there not? You borrowed money from my bank endorsed by me. You seem to be always coming to me for favours. Is it not right that you should give something in return?'

'Power,' she muttered. 'Because you have all the power. If all men had votes, power would not be in the hands of the few – '

Now he laughed aloud. 'You read Tom Paine,' he mocked. 'Do you think the day will ever come when little labourers have votes? As well give them to women.'

She thought of Tom. Tom working beneath the burning sun of New South Wales, cut off from everything and everyone he loved – for ever. He would die, she knew that as surely as she knew anything. He would die, not of hard work, but of something deeper, a slow pining in an alien life. Could she let that happen?

It is a small price to pay . . .

A small price for a man's life and perhaps happiness.

She said, 'Very well.'

If he was surprised he did not show it, but led her out of the room, up the stairs, into a small well-furnished bedroom. He closed the door and locked it, then turned and sat on the bed.

'Well, mistress,' he said. 'Take off your clothes.'

'All of them?'

'All.'

Slowly, hesitantly, she began to disrobe, turning away from him, her face stony. And when she was naked he came to her and pulled her hair loose from its pins. She was glad, for it covered her, if only slightly.

He fondled her for what seemed a long time, before he said, 'Come to the bed.'

And she prayed. Please let it be quick.

But he wasn't quick. He fondled her breasts, he kissed them, he let his mouth swoop downwards. She shuddered in distaste. He looked up and gloated over her body. And when finally he lifted himself onto her, she asked, 'How do I know you will do this for Tom?'

'You have my word,' he answered.

He moved a little, she was still. 'Come,' he said. 'Show me a little passion, I thought you had fire.'

And slowly she lifted her arms and put them round his neck, wishing she had a knife to stab him in the back.

★

353

She left the Manor, let Jobey take her home, her face hidden even though it was dark. She was emotionally exhausted, shivering with disgust as she thought of what she had done, trying to think of Tom, Tom who would be able to go to America.

She reached the Red House almost in a state of collapse, thankful that Jobey was not acute enough to notice that something was wrong. Indoors, stumbling up the stairs, calling Annie to ask her to bring the bath upstairs with hot water. 'I feel dirty,' she told her. 'It was dusty on the roads.' And when the water was brought she wondered if anyone had seen her at the Manor. A servant . . . ? She hadn't noticed any, but they must be there, they'd see the horse and chaise . . .

Forget that. Tom was free. He could go to America and start a new life.

But what would she do without him?

Now she had to see him, find out if he really was going. Oddly, she believed Sir William. Rogue and grinder of the poor he may be, but he was a gentleman and gentlemen kept their word. She must see Tom before he left. Supposing there was a boat sailing immediately?

There was no excuse she could think of to make such a journey so she didn't try. She told Francis she had to see Tom before he was transported. 'To tell me about the work,' she said.

'You mean you want to see him,' Francis said. 'Well, go, then. It won't matter now. Soon he'll be *en route* for Australia and you'll never see him again.' He smiled cruelly. 'Then you'll be mine, all mine.'

And when she went out he muttered to himself, 'mine all mine. It will be as it used to be, just the two of us.' Only now he was thinking of his mother . . . funny how the two seemed to get mixed in his thoughts these days . . . Mine, all mine, he nodded, rocking himself to and fro. I can shut her up in her room if I like then she'll never see another Tom. He thought pleasurably of this, Tacy shut in her room, with no Tom Jacques to ask where she was. He could sell the business then to Healey.

It was afternoon when Tacy reached the prison, and she stood for a moment staring at its forbidding exterior. Then she went to the great door where a bell rope hung. She pulled, a tiny aperture was opened, and two eyes peered out. 'I have come to see one of your prisoners, Tom Jacques,' she said.

'Sorry, can't let you in.' He made to close the aperture.

'It is on the orders of Sir William Fargate,' she said, hurriedly, and, as he hesitated, 'Send a messenger to him if you don't believe me.' Then she took out several gold coins.

The man's eyes glistened, and he let her in. She followed him along the passage, into a large room, the walls dripping wet, the air thick and dank, crowded with ragged prisoners who regarded her curiously. Through, to a small cell, there several men huddled together – and one of them was Tom.

There was no sanitation in the cell and the stench was stomach-turning. No beds, no furniture, just a tiny barred window high up in one wall. And Tom, always so fastidious, here . . .

He came towards her, as if he couldn't believe his eyes, and the other men stood back. She glanced at them, none of them were weavers. She dismissed them from her mind. 'Tom,' she said, clasping his hands. 'You are to go to America.'

He stood back, surprised. 'What – you know?' and she realised her mistake.

'Ye-es, I heard. Are you glad, Tom?'

'Of course.'

'You'll be able to work out there, help with the weaving, oh Tom – ' and she flung her arms around him.

'Don't,' he said, moving away. 'My clothes stink. And I'm covered with lice.'

'What do I care? Oh, Tom, I'll miss you so.'

'Does Martha know?' he asked.

'Why – I didn't think to tell her – ' She broke off.

'Martha doesn't know? My wife? Then who told you, Tacy?'

'Oh, I – I forget.'

'Don't lie to me, Tacy, I always know when you're lying. Do you know what the turnkey said to me when he told me? You must have friends in high places, Jacques, to get your sentence changed like that. Who changed it, Tacy?'

'Sir William,' she said, glad now of the near darkness of the cell.

'He came and told you? Or did you ask him?'

She was silent.

'Tacy . . .'

'All right, then, I asked him. I knew you'd hate Australia.'

He paused, and from somewhere she could hear the drip-drip of water. A man was shouting in the distance, a long high-pitched cry. Tom said, tiredly, 'I remember you asked him once before, didn't you? And what did he ask in return?'

'Don't, Tom.' She shivered suddenly and turned away from him, but he swung her round to face him.

'What?' he asked. 'He wouldn't do this for nothing, it was a big thing. What repayment did he ask?'

'Oh Tom,' she said, brokenly. 'Oh Tom, don't – don't remind me.'

'He took you, didn't he? You paid for my release?' And, as she looked down and didn't answer, he said,

356

softly, with a break in his voice, 'Oh, Tacy, I know how you hated him. Tacy – you'd do that for me?'

And now she was sobbing in his arms, never minding his stinking clothes. Tom understood, he always understood, and they stayed together, Tom thoughtful.

'Tacy,' he said, at last. 'Come with me.'

She looked up, her sobbing ceased in sheer surprise. 'W-with you?'

'You'll have to. How can you go back now? Suppose someone finds out? Suppose Sir William tells, as he did before. Francis – what would he do?'

Now thoughts were milling round in her head, thoughts that had been there at the back of her mind all along, but she'd been afraid to bring out into the open. Supposing someone had seen her at the Manor? Suppose Jobey talked, Jobey who hadn't the wit to keep silent? Worst of all – suppose Sir William thought he had her now where he wanted her, suppose he asked her again to – to . . . suppose if she didn't he threatened to tell Francis, *as he had before* . . . She knew only too well what would happen. Francis would kill her. She would live in fear for the rest of her life . . .

She strove to think clearly. To go away with Tom, her love . . . put all this behind her . . . *what else could she do now?*

'What of Martha?' she asked.

'Martha wouldn't come to America. Not to leave the boys. And the boys wouldn't come. Not to leave – ' he broke off, and Tacy silently filed in the missing words. Mr Redmond.

'But – my business. It would go to Francis – '

'Damaris is there. She'll inherit. And that young lady has her head screwed on the right way, she won't let him do anything she doesn't want.'

She stepped away from him, seeing as though for the

357

first time the other men in the cell, they took no notice of her. She said, 'Oh –' and paused, and it seemed as though heaven itself was opening before her. To be with Tom . . . no more Francis . . .

'Oh,' she said, longingly. 'If only I could.'

'What's stopping you?' he asked.

If only she were like him, able to go where he pleased without a thought for – for what? Martha? Martha no longer cared for Tom. What people would say? She'd be gone. She then came to the most important point – her upbringing, her father's honourable code. What would he have said?

But, a little voice whispered, if he had let you marry Tom in the first place none of this would have happened . . .

'I couldn't come with you, Tom,' she tried to argue. 'When will you sail?'

'Not on the same ship, perhaps. Anyway, I'm not sure when I go, but I think quite soon. I'd let you know immediately I sail. You would have to get the first available ship. You wouldn't want to go with me, the conditions on board for convicts are terrible –'

'But you wouldn't be on a convict ship, Tom. Not to America.'

'No, you're right. Maybe we *could* go together –' he broke off.

'But would they let me land?'

He grinned, the old devil-may-care grin. 'If you bring money.'

Money, how would she get money? Oh, she'd think about that later. She'd find a way . . .

'Is it all arranged for you to go?' she asked.

'Yes. My uncle is to be responsible for me, and he will be for you too. We could start a business out there.'

Now she laughed too, almost lightheaded in her relief

that she wouldn't have to lose Tom. 'Trust you. You just want my money.'

'No, I don't.' He was serious. 'I want you. I always have.'

'All right, Tom. I'll come.'

She caught the coach and rode home in a state of euphoria. Then she started to make plans.

She needed money. How much? One hundred pounds, to get her there and give them a start. And how would she get the money when Francis did the accounts? How could she get one single penny when everything belonged to him? Money she'd worked for all her life, that her father had worked for – and it all belonged to Francis. What sort of law was that? Oh, Tom Paine was right, changes were needed. She could not get her own money. She should have asked Sir William for it when she was with him . . . and what would that make her? What else could women do, for heaven's sake? They had to marry for money, what was the difference . . . ?

Towards morning she knew there was only one way to do it. She would have to ask Bess.

She waited till she knew she was alone in the kitchen, when Annie had gone to the market. Francis was in the counting-house. She walked in. Simon was grizzling in a corner. 'Bess,' she began.

Bess looked up with a start.

'All right. I'm not going to attack you.' She drew a breath. 'But you do owe me a favour. However, I understand that you were forced into stealing the designs by Francis –'

'I was, Mrs Barratt. I only wish I could get away from him, the drunken pig.'

Tacy stared. 'Well, you can. And earn yourself five

guineas into the bargain. What would you do with five guineas?'

'I'd go away,' returned Bess, promptly. 'To London, mebbe. I don't like what I do, honest.'

'Well, listen carefully. And if you tell Mr Barratt I'll kill you myself.'

'I won't. Honest.'

'I shall give you a paper. Never mind what is on it, it's nothing to do with you. All I want you to do is get Francis to sign it – when he's – drunk. Could you do that? Without him seeing what is on it?'

'Oh yes, I'll do that. If it means I can get away. If I won't get in any trouble from him.'

'You won't. Because he won't remember the next day, will he?'

'No. Not he.'

'All right. I'll let you have it when it's time. In the meantime, not a word.'

She was thinking clearly now, planning carefully, all her instincts, her very being concentrated on this last gamble – for gamble it was. She wrote to Mr Jarvis, knowing she could trust him, and told him she had to go to America, and would write more fully later. Damaris would take her place. And would Mr Jarvis kindly let her know of the times of sailings?

And then, incredibly, the gamble paid off, and everything ran smoothly. Tom sent a letter telling her he was sailing on the sixth of July, Bess got the withdrawal form signed which Tacy took to the bank, asking for the money in cash. Only then did she speak to Damaris.

'I shall be going to London next week, and I'd like you to come with me.'

Damaris agreed.

There was one last thing to do. She packed as many clothes as she could into a travelling bag and, when it was dark, slipped out to the stable and put it at the side of the chaise, inside a sack.

She and Damaris ate breakfast at dawn, before Francis arose. She pretended calm, but was filled with trepidation underneath. This was the last lap. Nothing must go wrong now.

Down to the chaise, and, 'Oh, Jobey, that sack. Put it in the chaise, will you? It's something I want to take to London.'

And not till they arrived at the Red Lion and Jobey was gone did she take out her bag. 'Wait,' she said to Damaris. 'I'll explain later.'

She said little on the journey and was glad that they shared the coach with a lady who chattered all the way, keeping Damaris occupied. It was not until they arrrived at Mrs Robinson's, and were in the bedroom, that Tacy spoke.

'No, we aren't meeting Mr Jarvis. Sit down, Damaris, I have something to tell you. It will take quite a time.'

Mystified, Damaris sat on the cane chair before the window, where she could see, in the street below, passers-by hurrying about their business. 'What is it, Mamma?' she asked.

Tacy looked at her daughter, then away. Took off her hat. 'It's a long story,' she said. 'And you have never known the truth – not all of it.' She began to tell her – her love for Tom; Francis. 'I don't like to talk against your father,' she said. 'Though you know now that he is far from perfect. So I must tell you some of it –' and she sketched in his treatment of her over the years.

Damaris sat, quite still. 'How was it I never knew?' she asked.

'Because you were never at home very much, were you? It was easy to miss the signs. And Francis was very cunning.'

Damaris stood up and looked through the window, thinking over many things she hadn't understood – her father's continual putting down of her mother; Bess, Simon; the night she'd heard a noise and opened her beroom door to see him tiptoeing down the corridor. Why hadn't she guessed? Hadn't she wanted to know? 'Why didn't you tell me?' she asked.

'Oh, because – you and he got on well together, I didn't want to turn him against you. Or you against him.'

'But, Mother, that's what he's been doing all these years, trying to turn me against you.'

'I see. I didn't know that.'

There was the sound of people talking in the street below, someone shouting goodbye.

'I shouldn't have married him,' Tacy said with a sigh. 'It was always Tom for me. But now, if I go to Tom, will you be all right?'

'Of course I shall. I won't let Father bully me.' She paused. 'But what about Martin? Why are you so against my marrying him? Because we love each other.'

Now it was Tacy's turn to pause. 'I think your father was against it because of Tom. With him out of the way it won't matter so much.'

'But you were against it too?'

'Maybe I was envious,' said Tacy. 'Martin is so much like his father . . . But if I go –' she hesitated. '*Shall* I go?'

'Yes, Mother.' Now Damaris left the window and came to stand before Tacy. 'Oh, Mother, what a pity we didn't know all this earlier, we've wasted so many years . . . But I'll see you again, won't I? Tom can't come back, but you can.'

'Of course. Or you can come and visit us. We shall do well out there, you'll see. It's the land of opportunity.'

They talked far into the night, and the next morning

drove to the docks, where the *Lady Mary* rode at anchor. The sea was a calm grey blue, gulls screamed overhead. Men were hauling ropes, there was the smell of tar and the fumes of rum and tobacco, the fragrance of coffee and spice. Coopers hammered at the casks on the quay, chains rattled. They stared in silence at the ship that was to take her over one of the roughest oceans in the world to her promised land with Tom.

Goodbyes were said. 'Don't cry,' whispered Tacy. 'And don't come aboard, just stay here . . .'

She was numb now, knowing feeling would come later; now it meant nothing that she was leaving her own land, her daughter, her business to set forth into the unknown. Dry-eyed, she let the sailor help her on deck.

Damaris stood. Watched the *Lady Mary*'s sails unfold, watched as the tide turned and a light breeze sprang up. Slowly the ship moved . . .

Damaris watched until it was a speck on the horizon. Then she let her own tears fall. But she was crying for the years of loss, of misunderstandings. The wasted years.

She hoped her father would not see her come in, because she wanted to be alone for a time, to think about the day's amazing developments. Tacy had said she had written to the bank and to the silk brokers that Damaris would now be taking her place, so as she jolted home she thought of what it would mean. She could carry out her own wishes, she could build topshops, which she was convinced was the next step forward.

Jobey could not meet her for he had not known when she would be back, so she had to hire the post-chaise. She was home before it was dark, the western sky streaked with red. But as she let herself into the hall, Francis was there, almost as if he knew something was going on, as indeed he did. He had noticed the last few days' hectic movements on Tacy's part, her preoccupation, her seeming neglect of the warehouse. He was suspicious — of what he did not know.

'Damaris,' he greeted her. 'Where —'

'Father. I want to talk to you. Let us go into the parlour.'

'Yes.' He followed her restlessly. 'Where is your mother?'

'That is what I have to talk about.' Damaris took off her bonnet, loosened her pelisse. 'Sit down, Father.'

'What is it?' His voice was querulous, his hands were shaking. He had had to take a little more brandy than usual to keep himself from getting angry.

'I have some news about Mother.'

'What?'

Damaris looked at her father. His face was pinched in the half-light, his skin mottled. Had she ever loved him? She wasn't sure. If she had she no longer cared about him. The confessions she had heard coupled with the knowledge of his perfidy regarding the designs — *her* designs — meant that she could find no wish to soften the blow as she might otherwise have done. She said baldly, 'She isn't coming back.'

'What?'

'She isn't coming back. No, wait,' as he glared, 'you must know she isn't happy here.'

'What do you mean? I love her. Where is she?'

'She's gone to America.'

'America?' His voice was shrill. 'America? How could she?'

'She sailed yesterday.'

'But why? How dare she without telling me, her husband? How dare she?' His face was red, his hands shook as he stood up, gasping as though for air.

'Father, sit down. Let me explain.'

'No, I won't sit down. Why did you let her go? How could you do this to me? I'm her husband. She belongs to me. To me, I tell you. Why has she gone to America? Why? Are you telling me the truth? Has she gone with that no good Jacques?'

Almost apoplectic with rage he ran out of the house, Damaris following. He ran to the stables, pulled out the mare, and to Damaris' horrified eyes, mounted her.

'Father, don't – ' she called. 'Let Jobey get the chaise. You know she won't be ridden. Father!'

Francis didn't listen. He whacked the startled mare who reared and galloped away. Damaris ran to the road. Francis was clinging for dear life, people scattering as he passed.

Jobey had appeared. 'Quick!' Damaris called. 'Go to Martin, tell him what's happened. Ask him to follow him on his horse.'

She waited. Bess came in with Annie from the kitchen to see what was going on. Briefly Damaris told them.

'The mistress gone?' asked Bess. 'Good for her.'

They waited. In less than an hour the mare returned – alone. And Francis' body was picked up just outside the Red Lion on the Watling Street in the exact spot where he had almost fallen beneath the coach twenty years ago.

Chilverton rocked with talk. Tacy Barratt run off with Tom Jacques – the hussy! She always was after him! And poor Martha, left on her own. Though according to some, she wasn't so alone after all. Now the talk veered. That Mr Redmond always visiting her, stays there for hours they say . . . And Tom never seemed to sleep at his own house . . . Ah well, those quiet ones were always the worst . . .

The gossip reached Mr Hewitt via his pale yielding wife, who had been trained to tell her husband everything. 'They say that Mr Redmond visits Martha a lot.'

'What are you saying, Mrs Hewitt? That theirs is an improper relationship?'

'They say . . .'

Mr Hewitt's anger knew no bounds. Hadn't he always said these chapel people were knaves? Didn't the Duchess of Buckingham, no less, say that they were impertinent and disrespectful to their superiors? The man was a hypocrite, he should be hounded out of the town. Mouthing platitudes about the love of God, while all the time practising sinful living. And worse, mouthing seditious nonsense about equality. Well, now he was shown in his true colours!

Mr Hewitt's anger was taken to the magistrates, to Sir William who, being less than perfect himself, and no hypocrite, was amused by the whole affair. He applauded Tacy for her action, always knew the little woman had fire. And he didn't care tuppence about the doings of some unimportant minister. But others were not amused. There were meetings and reports and letters.

Mr Redmond was summoned to a meeting of the deacons of the chapel.

Martha sat at her kitchen table, stitching one of her bonnets. A low fire burned in the grate, although the day was warm, but it was heating the brick oven William had built, and the stew in the round earthenware pot. William was on the loom, she could hear its clack-clack as she worked. She cut a piece of ribbon and wished she had another room, she could start a shop. She had a number of customers now from Basford, well-to-do ladies, who were only too pleased to find someone to trim their gowns and bonnets, or make new ones. She wondered if she could afford to rent a shop in the Market Square.

Martha was nearly forty, her hair was still black, but her face had changed from the girl she had been. There were lines below her eyes, yet her expression was tranquil. She knew William had been worried about how she'd feel when they heard that Tacy had gone with Tom, but she told him she had had a letter from Tom, posted before he sailed.

'Oh?' William had looked up expectantly, but she did not tell him the contents of the letter, though she knew it off by heart.

Dear Martha.

When you get this you will have heard that Tacy has sailed with me. This wasn't arranged, but we had to do it. Tacy saved my life – but she put her own life at risk in doing so. Francis would kill her so she had to come. It was my idea.

I won't pretend I didn't want her. You know how it's always been – and you know that I've never been a good husband to you. I don't suppose I'll be any better with Tacy, but she will put up with me, I expect. You have the boys and your friends.

We shall not meet again, Martha. I send my love and ask your forgiveness. Tom.

No, that was not for William's eyes. Martha felt sometimes she had put too much on William, she had put him in Tom's place and it wasn't fair. But she had been puzzled at the reference to Francis.

And then Damaris and Martin had come in. Damaris had told her of the way Francis had treated Tacy over the years. And any rancour Martha might have felt had disappeared. It didn't matter now, the old envy had gone.

And Martin and Damaris were to marry. She was

pleased about that, she liked Damaris, though she suspected William did too.

Of the gossip about herself and Mr Redmond she heard little. No one quite dared approach her. She did glean snippets of talk from conversations that stopped when she went in the grocer's shop, but Martha never heeded gossip, and she thought that it would soon blow over. Mr Redmond had not visited them since Tacy had left, but that was not unusual.

She heard the clatter of feet, the sound of boys' voices, and the three young ones ran in the kitchen. Hearing them William stopped his loom and came in too.

Martha put away her sewing, draped a cloth over the table and went to the oven for the stew. 'Mam,' cried Charley. 'Have you heard about Mr Redmond?'

Her face froze. 'I've heard the gossip, yes.'

'He's been called to a meeting of the deacons at chapel tonight. Because he comes here. They want to send him away.'

Martha put down the stew-pot, and turned to William. 'Is this true?'

'Yes.'

'And you didn't tell me?'

'I didn't want to worry you.'

Martha stood motionless, and William turned away, his face strained. He hadn't dare face his mother with the gossip. When he'd first heard it he'd been angry, then doubts had crept in. Oh, he knew his mother hadn't *done* anything, not his *mother* . . . She didn't love Mr Redmond, did she? Not in that way. Not his mother.

Martha still stood, unmoving. 'He's been called to a meeting? Why?' she asked.

'Well, I suppose it's about – because, as Charley says, he comes here. Oh, I know it's stupid.' William's words were hurried now, trying to convince himself as much as anyone else. 'But they want him to go. Oh, it's Hewitt's doing, he stirred up all the trouble –'

'And this meeting is tonight?'

'Yes, but –' he broke off at the look on his mother's face.

'Trust Charley to tattle-tale,' said Joey. 'He's like an old woman.'

'No, he did right,' Martha said. 'I should know. Now, eat your stew.'

But she did not eat herself and, agitated, she went to her bedroom. Mr Redmond, being sent away? Oh no . . . And she did not know whether she was thinking of her own loss or of his.

She stood, deep in thought, then squared her shoulders, and took off her apron. When she went down she had put on her bonnet and shawl.

'Mam,' William said, uncertainly. 'Where are you going?'

'To the chapel. Where else?'

'But you can't. They won't allow you in –' protested William.

'No? Not when it concerns me? I'm going.'

'Then I'll come with you.' And he followed her outside.

The chapel stood on a hill just outside the Patch. Women were standing in doorways, chatting, and they stopped as she walked by. But she looked neither to right nor left as she marched on. She was appalled and angry. How could they do this? How dare they? William was talking to her but she did not answer, did not even hear.

A group of weavers waited outside the chapel but she did not heed them as she went to the door, and they took one look at her face, then fell back. The meeting was in progress as she entered, the weavers following, and now the room was full of men. She saw the deacons sitting at the front: Mr Green, Mr Forrest, Mr Jepson. And Mr Redmond standing before them. She marched down and faced them.

No-one spoke.

'Well, go on,' said Martha. 'Carry on with your meeting.'

Mr Green, the grocer from Half-Moon Lane, moistened his lips and rubbed his hand over his black broadcloth coat. 'Oh – I – er, I don't think – ' he began.

'You should not be here,' said Mr Forrest, the clerk from Basford, sternly.

'Not be here, when it concerns me?' asked Martha. 'Tell me what Mr Redmond is being accused of, if you please.'

Mr Forrest said, 'We feel that Mr Redmond does not act in a proper manner, and that he should leave.'

'Why?' asked Martha. 'What is not proper about his behaviour?'

'It is not proper to visit a married woman regularly as he has done,' said Mr Jepson, the saddler.

'You mean because he visits me? So he's a sinner.' She turned scornfully. 'You call *him* a sinner, he who has done more for the poor than any of you. And why? You think he has committed adultery with me. Because to you men that is the only sin that counts, who a woman goes to bed with. How can you be like this? Turn against a man when he's been so good? And you're all wrong. Mr Redmond is a dear friend of mine, and nothing more than a friend. Look at me,' Martha was almost shouting. 'I am forty. I have five sons. Do I look like a woman who entices men to her bed? He is my friend and he will stay my friend. He has no home of his own and he will always be welcome in mine. Mr Redmond shall not be hounded out of town by a pack of jackals.'

And a voice of one of the weavers from the back

shouted, 'If he goes from this chapel then we all go. We'll start another chapel. Is that what you want?'

Now all was pandemonium. A few voices were raised above the din. 'He sat wi' my old father all night when he was dying.' 'He walked all the way to Coventry to fetch a soothing balsam for my sick child!' 'Look how he helped the weavers when we had nowt.' 'We'll never find a better.' And Joe Bates' voice: 'If the man wants to go to bed wi' a woman why shouldn't he?'

Mr Forrest raised his hand. 'We are going to vote on it,' he said.

They voted. One of the three voted against.

'He can stay,' shouted the weavers. 'He can stay.'

And, not looking to right nor left, Martha walked out.

She turned to William. 'Wait for Mr Redmond, and ask him to supper,' she said.

He did not come to supper. She put food on the table, they ate, the younger boys staring at their mother in silence. She did not eat, she walked to the cupboard, returned, waited, and then washed the plates. William sent the boys to bed, and, subdued, they went without a murmur.

Martha sat down and poked the fire. William, still standing, said, 'I didn't know.'

She gave him a straight look. 'There's nothing to know.'

'You love him.'

'I love many people, my family, friends.' She paused. 'It is for me to give my love where I choose. That is what the chapel deacons must understand.'

William felt she was explaining a lot of things. That a woman has choices too. That she had chosen not to sleep with his father. To welcome Mr Redmond.

He gazed at her with respect.

Martha thought. Poor William. I should have let him go to London, not try to keep him in his father's place. Maybe he'll go now, when this blows over.

She said, gently, 'You should go away, William. Now Damaris is to marry –'

He nodded. 'Maybe I will.'

He went to bed and still Martha sat. But Mr Redmond did not come.

He came the next morning, Saturday, when William was at the warehouse. His face was strained, his fair hair, thinning now, was rumpled, his threadbare jacket creased.

Martha had been sewing, the fire gave a ruddy glow to the cosy room. She took in his shabby appearance and thought he needed a woman's care. But she did not speak.

He said, 'I didn't sleep last night. I was – on my knees.'

She drew a breath, was silent.

He went on, 'I should go away.'

Still she did not speak. It was his decision. His alone.

He came to her. 'I should. But I can't. I can't leave you.'

'Then why should you?' she asked, low.

He did not touch her. 'When I met you all those years ago – knowing you were married, I should have left then.' He turned a little away from her. 'At first it was torture, knowing I could never possess you, then gradually – I don't know. I think I found a sort of content.'

'Only sort of?' she asked, wryly.

'Knowing I could never possess you,' he repeated. And now he looked fully at her, and it was her turn to look away. But she was silent. That too, was his decision.

'Don't try yourself too hard,' she ventured.

'No. But I love you, Martha. It's in the open now, I can say it.'

There was no sound in the room but the ticking of the clock. Somewhere outside a woman shouted, a dog barked, but it seemed far away.

She said, 'Do you remember when my father was dying? He said life was a jumble and you told him we cannot see the full pattern when we're too close. When I met Tom I thought I loved him. Then I found I was mistaken – he should have married Tacy. They were right for each other. So I turned to the boys . . .'

She sighed painfully. 'I wondered what the pattern was. But now – Tacy's daughter is to marry my son, Tom's son – there'll be a new pattern woven for us, from us.'

He inclined his head.

'And you, Mr Redmond – John – will be able to marry them now that Nonconformists are allowed to marry in their chapels. I'm sure the law was passed just for us.'

He smiled, faintly. 'Yes,' he said. And, 'Come and sit by the fire, Martha. Let us talk about the wedding. We will leave the future to God.'

The wedding took place at the end of October on a bright day with the sun glinting on the brown and orange leaves dancing around the chapel. That morning Damaris received a letter from her mother.

She read it, blinked away a few tears, and put it down the front of her chemise.

When Aunt Martha and Annie came to help her dress, the letter was still there. Her wedding-gown had been made out of a length of white silk obtained from Macclesfield. It was low-cut, tight-waisted and full-skirted, but there was no ornament. On her head was a long lace veil that her great-grandmamma Barratt had worn. She carried a bouquet of roses from William's garden. Martin was handsome in black coat and white pantaloons, with a gold-trimmed cashmere waistcoat. William, in more sober black, was best man.

They walked to chapel, as was the custom, the road crowded with weavers all come to wish her well, and even the church people deigned to smile at her. Julia Warren stood in her doorway, Frances Peabody, who had been to school with her, stood openly at her gate, and waved, while Mrs Peabody unbent so far as to peer through the window.

So Damaris and Martin were married in the chapel on the hill, filled now with all the flowers the weavers' autumn gardens could furnish, michaelmas daisies, chrysanthemums, and the last roses of the season. Mr Redmond officiated. The weavers crowded into the chapel, and when it was over, as many as could be accommodated were invited to the wedding breakfast; for the rest there was cake and home-made wine in the yard.

And when they'd eaten Damaris and Martin went outside to them. Damaris stood on a little stool and said: 'I am so pleased to see you all, and I have a piece of news for you. This morning I received a letter from my mother,' she drew it out, 'and I would like to read it to you.' She cleared her throat and began:

'"My dear daughter, just a brief note to tell you I landed safely and am with Tom and his uncle. This seems a pleasant land. The trees in the country are so beautiful in autumn. But I will write more later. I hope this reaches you in time for your wedding, so you will know that I am with you in spirit" –' Damaris' voice wavered, but she continued, 'She ends by sending her love to you all.'

There was a cheer and she went on, 'I'm sad that my mother and Martin's father have had to leave this town they loved and where they worked so hard. They both worked for you as much as themselves. Uncle Tom was a rebel, yes, but only because he wanted to keep our way of life, this is what he fought for. Maybe it wasn't progress, but he knew that too many precious things can be lost in the name of progress. So he has been banished, but he has opened the way for our future.

'Now the good news. Martin and I are going to work together at Barratts. Martin will see to the buying and selling, I shall design, and for the time being we shall share giving out the work. We need an accountant, and I would like to offer the post to William, if he decides to stay here.'

She paused. 'Now, where do we go from here? You don't want the new ways and we cannot keep the old and compete. The rest of the country builds factories but we don't want factories. So what do we do? We shall go our own way, and find our own solution. We shall build topshops, a cottage factory, where you can live in your own houses and work your loom in the room above, when you please, as now. Perhaps in the future we shall add steam power, and thus we can rival factories.'

She stopped speaking, and again there was a cheer from the weavers. Now there came the sound of music as three fiddlers came to the door playing a lively tune, and soon everyone was dancing. The sun shone on the merry scene and Bob Pettit cried, 'Here's to Barratts in the future.'

And Joe Bates shouted, 'And if I know Tacy and Tom, there'll be a new Barratts in America.'

Damaris smiled and put her hand in Martin's. Confidently, they stepped towards the Victorian age.

All Orion/Phoenix titles are available at your local bookshop or from the following address:

Littlehampton Book Services
Cash Sales Department L
14 Eldon Way, Lineside Industrial Estate
Littlehampton
West Sussex BN17 7HE
telephone 01903 721596, *facsimile* 01903 730914

Payment can either be made by credit card (Visa and Mastercard accepted) or by sending a cheque or postal order made payable to *Littlehampton Book Services*.
DO NOT SEND CASH OR CURRENCY.

Please add the following to cover postage and packing

UK and BFPO:
£1.50 for the first book, and 50P for each additional book to a maximum of £3.50

Overseas and Eire:
£2.50 for the first book plus £1.00 for the second book and 50p for each additional book ordered

---

BLOCK CAPITALS PLEASE

name of cardholder .... *delivery address*
.... *(if different from cardholder)*
address of cardholder ....
....
....
....
postcode .... *postcode* ....

☐ I enclose my remittance for £.............................

☐ please debit my Mastercard/Visa (delete as appropriate)

card number ☐☐☐☐☐☐☐☐☐☐☐☐☐☐☐☐☐☐

expiry date ☐☐☐☐

signature ....

prices and availability are subject to change without notice